The Hungry Ghosts

ANNE BERRY

The Hungry Ghosts

blue door

Blue Door
An imprint of HarperCollins*Publishers*
77–85 Fulham Palace Road
Hammersmith, London W6 8JB
www.harpercollins.co.uk

Visit our authors' blog: www.fifthestate.co.uk
First published in the UK by Blue Door in 2009

1

A catalogue record for this book is available from the British Library

This novel is entirely a work of fiction.
The names, characters and incidents portrayed in it are the work of
the author's imagination. Any resemblance to actual persons,
living or dead, events or localities is entirely coincidental.

HB ISBN 978-0-00-730340-3
TPB ISBN 978-0-00-730339-7

Typeset in Bembo by
Palimpsest Book Production Limited, Grangemouth, Stirlingshire

Printed and bound in Great Britain by
Clays Ltd, St Ives plc

Mixed Sources
Product group from well-managed
forests and other controlled sources
www.fsc.org Cert no. SW-COC-1806
© 1996 Forest Stewardship Council
FSC

FSC is a non-profit international organisation established to promote the
responsible management of the world's forests. Products carrying the FSC
label are independently certified to assure consumers that they come
from forests that are managed to meet the social, economic and
ecological needs of present or future generations.

Find out more about HarperCollins and the environment at
www.harpercollins.co.uk/green

*For my matchless husband Anthony, and my amazing
children, Andrea, Antonia, Ivan and Ruth.
The value of their unflagging support continues
to be of inestimable worth to me.*

ACKNOWLEDGEMENTS

My special thanks to my exceptional agent, Judith Murdoch, and my inimitable publisher and editor, Patrick Janson-Smith, also to my editors Patricia Parkin and Laura Deacon.

Be thou a spirit of health or goblin damn'd,
Bring with thee airs from heaven or blasts from hell,
Be thy intents wicked or charitable,
Thou com'st in such a questionable shape
That I will speak to thee.

WILLIAM SHAKESPEARE, Hamlet, Act 1, scene 4

PROLOGUE
Ghost

I am dead. No, strictly speaking that is not the truth. I am neither fully alive nor fully dead. I am 'undead'. I am unable to relinquish my present and consign it to the past. I am unable to accept I have no future. Thus I am static, earthbound, my feet anchored in mud, while my essence, my Chi, is being pulled, tugged, drawn towards the ghosts of my ancestors, towards the dominion of death. Sometimes I feel like a bone being worried at by a dog. This is an appropriate image because that is exactly what happened to me. This 'half-death' does not make for a peaceful spirit. I am troubled and I am trouble. You see I just have to stir things up, play with the laws of physics to prove . . . to prove what? That I may still be the cause and have an effect. When the ancestors clamour I tell them to be patient. I am not prepared for death I say.

My name was Lin Shui. I was the daughter of a fisherman. I lived on the island of Hong Kong and I was not ready to die. But nor were thousands of others, dying all around me every day. This is not what keeps me here. It is my gnawing hunger that fixes me to the earth.

I was murdered on a perfect summer's morning. It was early June, the year 1942. We had seen a black Christmas come and go. Our tiny island was infested with Japanese soldiers. They had invaded our shores. They held us in their vice-like grip. Father told me that the British could not withstand their venom, that, though they fought with courage, a time had come when they buckled and fell. He explained to me in his customary soft voice that our Governor, Sir Mark Young, had gone in person to the Japanese headquarters in the Peninsula Hotel, and surrendered on Christmas Day. I thought that was odd, to hand over our island home in a place where people had once come to dine and dance, and wear fine clothes and sparkling jewels, and talk of nothing in particular. But Father told me that everything in the time that was coming would be odd, and often not just odd but terrible as well. He told me the devils of war were unleashed, that we must bear their madness with fortitude. I listened like a child, and feared like the woman rising up within me. Father told me the worst that could happen had happened, that we were an occupied island now, that they could take no more from us. But in this he deceived me, for one day a Japanese soldier was occupying me, and what he took from me was my life.

My death is like a tune that plays over and over in my thoughts. I cannot rid myself of the melody.

I am alone. My father and our junk have been taken. My mother, who paved my way into this world with her own life, is no more than a shadow to me. For months now hunger has been my constant companion. With each passing day it consumes more of me. I know that soon there will be nothing left. When you are stripped of everything, I reason, it is good to climb a mountain, for then you will see the way ahead. So I slip through the busy streets of Aberdeen dodging the soldiers, ducking out of the way of jeeps, and diving into the maze of alleys. I find the narrow path that winds its way up to the Peak. I will climb this path, I resolve. When I am high up, I will look down on Aberdeen harbour and I will know what to do. Perhaps my spirit mother tries to warn me, but I am headstrong and do not listen. Perhaps the ancestors barrel into me, a wave of consciousness holding me back. But I am stubborn and plough on. Perhaps he has been watching me for days, my murderer, has seen that I am alone, vulnerable, an easy target? Like the hunter he stalks me as I ascend.

It is already warm when I set out. A June day when the sky is clear as glass, and when the sun, as it swells to its zenith, exudes a smouldering heat that makes your skin prickle, and your head throb. The blood drums in my ears. I can feel the sweat pool in the dip between my shoulderblades, and trickle down my back. I can hear birdsong and the sounds of distant traffic. Sometimes a gunshot rings out, and then the birds, startled, fly up from their perches in the thick green canopy that surrounds me. From time to time I stand at the edge of the path and gaze down the slope, judging how far I have come, how high I am, how much further I have to go before I gain the summit. I look across a tangle of trees and vines and grasses. I am cocooned in confusion. But I am climbing the mountain that will spin lucid strands from all that is dense and opaque, I whisper.

I hear him then, his boot on the dusty ground behind me, and a stone slipping away, falling into the untidy green expanse. I turn but see nothing. Three times I spin round and the third time he is there. Neither of us speaks. We both freeze for a moment, statues on the rutted path. Even then I realise I am on the cusp, on the brink of stepping out of time, of sinking in the bottomless well. He glances over his shoulder, and when he is certain we are alone he walks purposefully towards me.

'Run,' cries my mother, wrapping around me. 'Run and together we will shun him.'

There are only a few yards between us now. I can hear his short breaths, and smell his stale sweat. If I face him he will not harm me, I tell my ancestors. They mock softly, but my mother keens. He pauses feet from me, and there is a space between us where our breaths mingle. I can see wet patches on his khaki uniform, under his arms, across his chest, around his groin. He is wearing a cap and his face is partly shaded. He has a rifle slung over his shoulder. He mutters something in Japanese, his voice harsh and dissonant, specks of cloudy spit fires from his mouth. His eyes narrow to thin wet lines. His mouth splits in a yellow-toothed sneer.

Someone will come by and by, and all will be well, I tell myself.

This is in my head as he swings the rifle off his shoulder and rams me in the chest with the butt of it. I feel a shock of pain, a sickening thud, a splintering crack. I reel backwards, lose my footing, and fall against a hard bed of dirt and stones. He has knocked the air out of me. I am gagging, trying to bite in breath. The soldier does not wait for my lungs to fill. He throws the rifle aside along with his cap, leans over me, seizes the top of my blue cotton tunic, and rips it from my body. A slither of oxygen filters into me. Looking down I see my small breasts, the nipples raised, tight and hard against the cedar brown of my flesh. I am going to crawl away, but the pain in my chest blossoms now like a flower. Again the soldier lurches forwards. This time he grasps my trousers. As he wrenches them away my slippers tumble off. My bare feet scrabble in the dirt. I try to draw my knees up to hide my shame, but he lays hold of my legs and thrusts them apart. He thrusts them so wide I think I might split in two. Here, hunched between my open legs, with one hand he frees his penis, with the other he jams fingers inside me, tearing at my soft virgin centre. My scream dies in my throat, paralysed with terror.

He waits a single interminable beat before he drives into me. In that beat his immutable eyes lock with mine, and he brings his fingers up to his mouth. I see they are coated with flecks of blood and matter. While I watch, he sucks at them ravenously. I have found my voice but he smites it with this same hand. My cry is suffocated and becomes no more than a gurgle. I taste myself in the blow, the sea-musk at the core of me, and my own blood, the metallic sweetness of it on the fingers that are clamped across my mouth. As he slams into me I feel rivers scorch and become runnels of ash. With his free hand roughly he kneads a breast, bruising and crushing it, pinching it so hard I am sure his fingers will meet, claw through my soft flesh.

But when the moment comes and he shudders out his power, I cheat him of victory, for I have left my body and am looking down from a great height. My eyes, which have been stretched wide, aflame with fear, are smothered. They set in a dead fish stare. The stare enrages him. He lets go breast and mouth, and sits back heavily. He is gasping, his penis still ramrod straight between his sweat-slicked loins. He clenches a fist and then slams it into my face. The force of the blow breaks two teeth and cuts into my cheek. A trickle of blood courses down it like a single red tear. From above I snigger at him, and the face of that other girl below breaks into a toothless grin, as she joins me, coughing and hacking with laughter. His manhood shrivels then. It becomes a poor thing at the peal of our contempt, and we can see it is no better than a worm. In the same moment he glimpses it too, and his sallow skin is empurpled with fury as he grapples at his belt.

'What have you got for me now?' I taunt him, my voice as light as the breeze at his back. 'You have occupied me and I am still whole. How will you plant your filthy flag with its rising sun now?'

It is then that I see the glint of the knife, the bayonet he has freed from its leather sheath, and I know how he will plant his flag. The red of his sun will be stained with my blood when it flutters in the wind. He thrusts forwards with all his might, up beneath my broken ribs where he hits his mark. My heart gives a mighty shudder, unreels in a final leap and freezes, the blood curdling within it. I watch him come back to himself, caging his demon deep within, hefting out the knife, and springing back before the rush of red that fountains up to meet him. He drags my body to the edge of the path and rolls it roughly into the deep green cavern. But the ragged tear in my chest snags on a branch and my body hangs there. My blood spills onto the bark, cloaking it thickly, dripping darkly, and even now drying to a crisp beneath the unforgiving sun. The soldier cleans his bayonet blade in the earth, slicing the wetness off it, slipping it back in its sheath. He adjusts his uniform, stoops to retrieve his cap, slips it on, takes up his rifle and slings it back over his shoulder. He gathers up my garments and slippers, wipes his hands on them, balls them in his fists and hurls them after my body. They do not snag on the branch but unfold as they spin, performing mid-air acrobatics as they shake off their creases, before landing, hidden in the undergrowth below. He scuffs the pool of blood over with earth, kicking at it, as if the merest sight of his sin is now abhorrent to him. Then he is gone, the beat of his boots ebbing away on the dusty tide.

I watch from my perch in the tree where I rest now, beside Lin Shui's body. Soon all is still once more, but for the 'drip, drip' of my blood against a waxy leaf, scalding red, striking cool virgin green. How easy is it then, this business of dying, the ancestors trumpet, preparing to welcome me into their starry fold. That is when the fury unfurls inside me. I shrink from them.

'I am not ready to go with you,' I say, clinging to my body, smelling the black hair with just a trace of the mineral sea, and the skin, cotton fresh, and blood that oozes still, salt and copper and cloying with sweetness. And when their rhapsody swells and they pluck at me in their impatience, I hiss and lash the air up into a wind. Then they are frightened and disperse.

The flies come first, bent on blood, crazed with the rancid whiff of decay. And while they swarm over Lin Shui, I consider the shame I might bring on my family if I am found like this. If my father returns and discovers me with the blood bubbling between my thighs, it might prove too great a disgrace for him. I reflect over the buzzing of the flies that it would be better if I was never found. I summon all my strength, pushing the flesh that had once been mine, trying to dislodge it, but it is heavy as lead. When the chorus of cicadas start, I implode, gathering up all the spidery range of me. I slip into the branch, where the limb that bears Lin Shui's body angles from the tree. I seep into the taut, woody fibres there, already stretched with the weight of their load. I saw at them, fuelled with anguish, and at last there is a great crack. The branch breaks, and Lin Shui's bloody corpse, *my* corpse, pitches downwards, the green opening up to her like water, and closing over her when she is gone. Now you can no longer see her from the path. She is hidden, a covert child. I slither down to her. She has landed with a twist. She lies on her belly, her head corkscrewing round, her face still wreathed in its broken-toothed smile, crowning her back.

That night the dogs come. At first there is only one, a sad creature, all ribcage and weeping sores, that skulks nervously around my body, snarling and baring his dripping fangs for several minutes before tucking in. He laps and licks the blood thirstily. He tears at sinew and muscle and flesh. He crushes and crunches bones. His teeth grind and grate. The cacophony of his feeding frenzy appals me. He is joined by another. First they scrap, hackles up, wearing what fur they have on their mangy carcasses like ruffs, gnashing their teeth, growling and snapping over their prize. In the end they realise there is enough for both of them, and they settle down together to feast on Lin Shui. I cannot stay here, I think. If I stay here I shall be reminded that I am dead. So I rise up and shiver on the thermals, and see days come and days go. I soar with the birds. But even here there is buzzing, silver planes somersaulting and diving and chattering, and far below me a seething sea, carved up with sail-less pewter ships, all hard lines against the scrolls of the sea. I want somewhere I can repose and gather my wits, some refuge that I can lose myself in.

I know it is ironic for someone cheating death, but I settle at last on a morgue, the morgue of a British army hospital. Perhaps I have more in common with the dead than I realise. It is a gigantic red-brick building, three storeys high, with tiled floors and wide stair-cases. The patients' wards, the operating theatres, the laboratories and the offices, which nestle within it, are bordered by long corridors, open to the elements but for the arched colonnades that line them. There are smaller barrack blocks standing on the terraced slopes above it. The edifice is reassuringly solid, rooted comfortably, as I still am, to the earth. It rises grandly from its site in Bowen Road. My morgue lies in a roomy basement at one far end of the hospital. It is quenched of light.

This then is how I come to stave off death, with nothing but my will for weaponry. And it is how, paradoxically, I find myself housed in a sepulchre of death. Above me a battle rages, but I choose to reside below with the defeated. They lie stiffly in the tenebrous ward that all mankind must come to, with their shattered bones and gory stumps. Some have empty red sockets where the jelly of an eye once swivelled, some ragged flesh where once an ear thrilled to the music of life, some scorched bloody caves, where tongues wagged and lips were bellows, pumping the body's elixir of oxygen. Beneath their shrouds I trace the puncture patterns of bullets, reliving the impact of each one, the flesh yielding with a judder to their sting.

These then are my playmates, my companions, these cold rigid cadavers. Sometimes I concentrate very hard and jerk their waxy limbs. I make their petrified, pale eyelids twitch. As I move over their ruined bodies like a lover, my presence soft as gentle rain on their ugly wounds, they tell me their sad tales of death. They speak of lovers left behind, of mothers longed for, and of filth and gore and carnage. They tell me how they grew fluent in the language of horror, of shrieks torn from bodies racked with pain, of groans dredged up from a Hades of everlasting torture, of grief that had not the luxury to linger. Theirs was a lottery of limbs yielded up to blade and bomb and bullet, their drama, the inestimable tragedy of war. And in turn I croon them to sleep with memories of breath, and the urgency of it, and the beat of blood, and the flood of sensation, and the tick of life. I tell them stories of our junk, *Heavenly Sea*, bucking and pitching across a bowl of liquid gold. I recount how my father, a simple fisherman, was taken by the Japanese, a suspected informer for the Gangjiu Dadui, one of the Chinese resistance forces. I confide my yearning for the inconstant ocean, the salt smack of her rough embrace. I impart that it was the South China Sea that bore me up, when my child's body grew weary with its chores.

So we share our burden of loss, the dead and I, robbed of our lives and of our loves. Once, one of my soldier playmates is brought to the morgue, like me hovering in the half-light between life and death. Before he slips away, he makes a gift to me of his ethereal British army jacket.

'To shield your modesty,' he says, insisting as he departs that he no longer has a need for it.

Then a dawn breaks, that is marked by a ringing silence. Gone is the clattering, booming, jarring disharmony of war. The staccato guns have stopped firing. The crescendo of marching feet is stilled. The medley of horses' hooves is muffled. The dreadful ululation is spent. My dead companions no longer come to see me, and the building above my head grows thick with quietude. I am thinning with lone-

8

liness, for dust motes and dried blood make for poor company. Curious, I creep out of obscurity. It is dusk. I alight on a curve of railing. I am aware that time has rolled by and all is changed. I stare down the skirt of the mountain at the harbour, Victoria harbour. I see it transformed, the dimpled sea freckled with crafts of every imaginable shape and size. Ribbons of road packed with cars and lorries and buses wind about the slopes. There are more buildings beaded with lights than I could ever have dreamt of – buildings so tall they seem to brush the clouds. I am blinded too by the shimmering pictures facing some of the tall towers, pictures that bounce out across the water, luminous sea snakes, electric colours that crackle and spit into the night. Lin Shui's life is faded now, like an old book left in the sun and rain too long. Some days I allow myself to drift towards death. When I do, I think I see a small boy crouching in the shadows, an urchin with hair of spun gold, and skin that shines like varnished teak. He is barefoot and clad in black rags. I start to sink into the soporific infinite blackness at the centre of his eyes. And he stands and smiles, and opens his arms to me in greeting. Like a moth drawn to a flame, I am drawn to him. But always just before he enfolds me, I rouse myself and kick out.

My voice might be weaker but still it cries, 'I am not ready yet. Not yet.'

Then one day the children come. Among them is Alice.

Ingrid – 2003

The one person you can reliably guarantee will be missing from a funeral is the deceased. Then why, at the funeral of Ralph Safford, did I have the distinct impression that two people were missing? I suppose that my charge, Lucy Holiday, the deceased's sister, was largely responsible. I had been employed as a carer for Lucy for several years now. Childless, widowed, in her eightieth year and in fragile health, Lucy defied expectations, clinging tenaciously onto life. On the day of her brother's funeral, Lucy, with her wisp of wild, white hair, and bright, periwinkle-blue eyes, was enjoying a rare moment of lucidity. She sat in her wheelchair alongside the pew-end, humming tunelessly to all the hymns, her eyes darting around the congregation, and alighting first on one face then another.

At length, she gestured for me to lean closer, and closer still, then whispered in my ear in her scratchy-record voice, 'Ingrid, where is Alice?'

To which I naturally replied, 'Who is Alice?'

She fidgeted with the fabric of her black polyester dress, and rubbed her matchstick legs before answering, and so long was she that I couldn't help wondering if I'd lost her again. 'Alice is my niece,' she said at last, on a rising note of triumph.

'The daughter of your brother Ralph?' I sought confirmation.

Lucy nodded her affirmation. I was puzzled. As far as I knew, Ralph Safford only had three children. I had met the family a few times since they settled in England four years ago. I recalled the first occasion being held at the Saffords' home, Orchard House, at a party to celebrate their return from abroad. Besides this, Lucy had spoken of them, if not often, certainly enough for me to be well acquainted with their names. Jillian was the eldest, and Nicola the middle child, while Harry was the baby of the family. But of this 'Alice', up to now I had heard nothing. With Lucy's customary fits and starts, I had also gleaned a little of the deceased's life, certainly enough to whet my appetite for more. Here, it seemed, was no ordinary man. Apparently Lucy's brother and his family had lived overseas, in the then British Crown Colony of Hong Kong, where he had been employed by the government. 'A high-ranking official,' Lucy had confided to me with a knowing wink, on more than one occasion, often adding enigmatically, 'In the land of the blind, the one-eyed man is king.' Quite what this meant I did not know. However, it only seemed to enhance the impression that Lucy's brother had been out of the ordinary. Apparently too, the Saffords lived at one of the most enviable addresses at the summit of Victoria Peak. This, Lucy had explained, was the highest mountain on the island, and was known locally simply as 'The Peak'. I had also discovered that Ralph and his wife Myrtle only returned to England a year or so after Hong Kong was handed back to China in 1997, though it seemed the children departed some time earlier. But of Alice, until today, there had been no mention. I was intrigued. However, the middle of a funeral service was neither the time nor the place to probe family history, unearthing who knew what skeletons. So when Lucy asked me yet again where Alice was, I did my best to bring the matter to a close for the present.

'I expect she's up at the front with Myrtle, your sister-in-law,' I whispered. Then, without thinking, I added, 'All three children are sitting alongside their mother.' But to my relief Lucy gave another nod, and seemed satisfied.

The priest was offering up prayers now, and a bald patch on the crown of his head loomed somewhat indecently into sight. I could not help noticing that it was a surprising shade of mustard yellow, and gleamed dully with beads of perspiration.

I straightened up, and tried to concentrate on the proceedings once more. Though this was easier said than done, I thought, as the vicar's nasal voice see-sawed on monotonously. But again Lucy beckoned me down to her, frantically flapping her crêpe-paper hand, freckled with age-spots, and roped with prominent, deep-blue veins.

'Four,' she said, and for a moment I was nonplussed.

'Four?' I repeated at a loss.

This time Lucy raised her cracked voice to its very limit. 'Four,' she huffed. And then, when I still looked blank, 'Four children. Ralph had four children.' This last, she said so loudly that several heads turned to glare in our direction.

'I'll find out where she is later,' I hissed, enunciating each word as clearly as I could, without causing further disturbance. Luckily at that moment the organ struck up, and though I could see Lucy was speaking again, her words were drowned out by a thunderous rendition of 'Onward Christian Soldiers'.

And to be honest as the service went on, and, it seemed, Lucy quietened down, I let her supposed concerns slip to the back of my mind. Naturally, with a job like mine, funerals have a way of cropping up regularly. But for the most part these occasions have the sting taken out of them. The death of an elderly person who has lived their life to the full is both inevitable and, in a way, a cause for gratitude. They have managed to reach the end of the game despite the many hazards life would have thrown in their path. Bearing this in mind, my primary concern as a carer for those of advanced years is that my patients make a good end. And yet . . . and yet, the more times I witness death, no matter how peaceful it is, the less comfortable I am with it. These days, I can't help wondering if behind that pallid face, those fluttering breaths, that seemingly limp body, a tussle with death is playing out, fuelled by regrets, opportunities missed, words left unspoken, and last but not least, the indignity of it all.

But for now I abandoned this unsettling train of thought, and cast my eyes around the beautiful old Sussex church. I took in the small sober congregation, clad in their suitably melancholy outfits. These faces were, I noted, no different from the many others I had seen at past services, obviously more unsettled by this grim reminder of their own mortality than distraught with grief at the passing of another. The prickle on the back of the neck, the leaden sensation in the stomach, the feet squirming in their shoes, the longing to be outside filling your lungs with fresh air, the sudden shadow subduing the chirpiest of characters, these were not signs of sorrow, oh no, but of their own disquiet. Nor could I claim that I was exempt from such reflections. Sooner or later, the service, you knew, would be yours. And at sixty-two the 'sooner' undoubtedly applied to me.

Despite this, I let my eyes linger on Ralph Safford's coffin, set to one side of the altar. There was no denying it made a fine spectacle, fashioned in a rosy mahogany, or at least the veneer of it, with flowers draped luxuriously over the lid. I picked out some of my favourites – fragrant lilies, golden roses with tight corollas of whorled petals, fluffy cream carnations, lacy lilac delphiniums, and strident white and yellow gerberas, all arranged in glorious sprays. The soft colours were echoed in the arrangements that were decked throughout the church. The magnificent stained-glass windows drew me too, weathered by time and changing seasons. The summer light, as it poured through them, was transmuted into magical colours, iridescent beams moving over the patina of old wood, transforming the wan faces of the mourners into something unearthly. For a while I became wholly absorbed in a particularly lovely pair of arched windows, depicting two cloaked women in lucent blues and purples and silvery greys.

Then my attention was drawn back to the service again. Nicola Safford was addressing the congregation, delivering a eulogy to her father. Impeccably dressed, she had shown no sign whatever of nerves, or indeed heartache, as she strode confidently up to the lectern. Then, like a consummate actress, she had paused, her eyes sweeping over the pews to ensure she had the full attention of her audience. Now, unsurprisingly, her delivery was flawless – word-perfect, in fact one might almost have said a little too well rehearsed. She spoke of the years of sublime happiness the family spent together in Hong Kong, of her father's absolute devotion to his wife and his children, and of the invaluable contribution he had made on the island.

'He was at the helm in good times and bad, serving his Queen and country without flinching. He faced the challenges of keeping the colony on an even keel throughout the period of unrest that culminated in the riots of 1967. With immense bravery he stood proud, in the front line. He defended the citizens of Hong Kong from the bloodthirsty insurgents who threatened the stability of the island. Under my father's auspices order was restored. And for his exceptional contribution to his monarch, Queen Elizabeth the Second, and to the British government of the time, he was awarded the OBE, and made an Officer of the British Empire.'

I listened, rapt, as Nicola Safford's clear, well-modulated voice, echoed off the stone walls of the thirteenth-century church, revealing yet more admirable facets to her father's character. Finally softening her tone, lowering her gaze, and blinking back tears that very nearly convinced me, she spoke of the love she had for her father.

'I was so grateful . . . grateful for the opportunity to demonstrate the veneration in which I held my father, grateful to be close to such a fine man, doing what little I could to ease his passage through those final years.' Her last words, delivered at a slower pace, the volume swelling, the pitch deeper, resonated like the closing chord of a great symphony. Nor do I think I imagined the slightly awkward moment that followed, in which the impulse to applaud had to be quelled by the mourners.

Nicola Safford's address had certainly pushed Lucy's perturbation to the back of my mind. But if I thought I had heard the end of Alice, I was mistaken. In fact it was just the beginning. Later, when the service had finished, and my charge and I joined the little queue, to pay our condolences to Myrtle Safford and the children, Lucy took up the same refrain. Where, she wanted to know, was Alice? She could see Harry, Jillian and Nicola, but surely Alice should be with them. It would have mattered to Ralph that his youngest daughter was here. Alice would have wanted to attend too. Even, more ominously, what had they done with her? There was no doubt about it, I had a Miss Marple kind of curiosity awakening inside me.

I soothed Lucy as best I could, easing her forwards in her chair

14

and plumping up the cushions behind her, checking that she was comfortable. Then, as we neared Harry Safford, I promised her that I would make inquiries about Alice. I shook her nephew's clammy hand, reminded him of my name, told him how sorry I was for his loss, how beautiful the flowers were, and how moved I had been by the service. This over, I had the distinct impression that Harry had already dismissed me from his mind. But once set in motion I am like an ocean liner: it takes considerable effort to stop me. I leaned in towards Harry, resolved not to move on until I had questioned him on behalf of my charge. I took a deep breath. Suddenly I felt nervous. How ridiculous, I told myself, as I sent out the first scout in search of Alice.

'Your Aunt Lucy is feeling a bit anxious,' I told him, pushing my rimless spectacles more firmly up my nose with a fingertip. 'She wants to know where your sister Alice is?' Did I imagine it or was there a flicker of something in his cold, bluish-grey eyes. Recognition? Anger? Or perhaps even fear?

'Alice?' he queried with a dry little laugh. 'Really? Who is Alice?' He placed crossed hands over his rotund belly, almost defensively.

'Forgive me. I thought that Alice might be your sister,' I explained. 'Your Aunt Lucy seems convinced you have another sister. Alice?'

'Well, my aunt is mistaken,' Harry said curtly, looking at my charge with undisguised displeasure. He bent over the fragile form of Lucy and bellowed, 'What rubbish are you talking now, Aunty, getting Ingrid all upset? Ralph would be ashamed of you making up such silly things.' I detected, though subtle, a slightly lazy 'r' in his speech.

'I'm not upset,' I assured Harry Safford. 'It's just that your aunt seems so certain. She keeps saying that Alice should be here. She seems concerned that something may have happened to her.' Harry arranged his features in an expression of extreme bafflement. But I was not to be so easily thwarted. I pointed my next words. 'To Alice I mean. That something may have prevented Alice from coming.'

'What is all this nonsense, Aunt Lucy?' Harry blustered, his face reddening, more with annoyance, I guessed, than embarrassment.

'Why is Harry shouting at me?' Lucy wanted to know, hunching further down in her chair. 'I'm not deaf. But then he always was a bully.'

Now it was my turn to colour. The old, like the very young, do not screen their words, parcelling them up and sending them out in acceptable packages for this world to receive, as most of us do.

'I'm sorry,' I apologised on behalf of Lucy. 'She's a bit tired, and probably a touch overwrought with the emotion of the day.'

'It's quite understandable,' Harry said shortly, eyes unblinking, giving me a perfunctory smile. He turned away from us then towards his mother and sisters, ruffling back his short ash-grey hair in an impatient gesture.

'It's just that Lucy appears to be quite fractious about . . . well . . . about Alice you see,' I persisted.

Reluctantly Harry turned back. But this time he recruited his sisters to add weight to his own voice.

'Aunt Lucy has been bothering Ingrid with foolish stories about someone called Alice,' he said, with the air of a parent whose toler- ance is being pushed to its absolute limits. Again, I thought I saw a furtive glance pass between Nicola and Jillian.

Jillian, a large lady, whose considerable height was diminished by her width, gave a slight shiver before speaking. She tossed back her startling, shoulder-length red hair, greying at the roots. 'Poor Aunt Lucy,' she said at last. 'She gets very muddled.' She reached out a hand tentatively and touched her aunt's bony shoulder. It was hard for me to read the expression in her flint-grey eyes, with her large, square-framed glasses reflecting back the bright sunshine at me. She did not, I observed, have her sister's dress sense. The variation in shade, however slight, from the black tailored trousers, to the dark navy jacket, was disconcerting. Added to this, the jacket appeared rather snug and the trousers at least one size too large.

'That's right,' Nicola chimed in, her tone liberally soaked in pity, 'poor Aunt Lucy hardly knows what day it is, bless her.' She shot me a swift appraising look, critically taking in my own cheap black suit, practical flat shoes, and hurried attempt to pin up my straight salt and pepper bob.

She was a little shorter than her sister, and slimmer in build. From a distance her outfit had looked smart, but close up it was stunning. The knee-length black dress with matching jacket, delicate gold flowers stitched into the fabric, had the unmistakable sheen of heavy silk. The outfit was finished off with inky stilettos, a designer's golden tag glinting at their heel backs. Her hairstyle was eye-catching too. The overall shade was altogether more natural than her sister's, a deep mocha-brown, aflame with red and gold highlights. It was cut into irregular bangs that suited the fine bone structure of her face. But bizarrely her hands, I noticed, were those of a nineteenth-century scullery maid, rubbed red and raw. Now she fixed me with her own inscrutable eyes, just the colour of the slab of liver I had purchased for Lucy from the butcher's that week.

'You really shouldn't be concerning yourself with Aunt Lucy's ramblings, Ingrid. Surely you're experienced in caring for the elderly? You should know what to expect.' And I could have sworn there was a warning edge to a voice that had an unsettling, forced bright-ness in it.

'Of course,' I said, understanding that the conversation had been brought to a close.

I pushed Lucy onwards, briefly shaking Myrtle Safford's hand. The matriarch of this family was a tall woman with a proud but guarded face, gimlet eyes, glittering jewels, and outdated clothes which never-theless screamed quality. However, I barely had time to express my sympathy, before her children whisked her away to speak to a less troublesome mourner. My thoughts in turmoil now, I steered my charge to a quiet spot in the churchyard, beneath the shade of an oak tree encircled with a wooden seat. I tucked a cheerful tartan rug I had brought with me about Lucy's knees, and told her gently that she must be mistaken about Alice. Was she perhaps thinking of someone else, from her husband's side of the family? Another niece or perhaps the child of a friend? When she said nothing, I crouched before her, my hands resting on the arms of her wheelchair, levelling my gaze with hers. For a moment her sharp blue eyes had a promising intensity about them. She opened her mouth and took a shaky but deliberate breath.

'You see, Ingrid, Alice is . . . is . . .'

'Is what?' I urged her eagerly. But the elusive thought had wriggled away, and Lucy's eyes suddenly shut tremulously. 'You're tired. I'll take you home now,' I told her, unable to keep the disappointment from my voice.

But just before I helped her into my car she grasped my bare arm. I had peeled off my jacket by then and was only wearing a short-sleeved cream blouse. Now Lucy's fingers scrabbled against the flesh of my forearm, splayed and light as birds' feet.

'Where is Alice? Alice should have been here. Ralph would be most upset, Ingrid, you know,' she croaked. Shortly after this I bundled her into the car, and she immediately fell into a deep sleep, snoring lightly.

I was staying overnight with Lucy in her small terraced house in Hailsham. After her tea, cottage pie and raspberry jelly, I decided a warm bath might settle her for the night. I never quite got used to the shrivelled bodies I handled daily, with their spun-glass bones and their tracing paper flesh. As I sponged the curve of Lucy's back, knotted and wrinkled as the bark of some ancient tree, my mind played over the events of the day. No matter which thread of thought I plucked at, they all seemed to lead back to Alice, as if by merely uttering her name Lucy had conjured up her ghost. Later, when my charge was tucked up in bed, just before I slipped out her false teeth, I tried once more.

'Are you sure your brother Ralph had a fourth child, a child called Alice?' I asked softly.

The last thing I wanted to do was to distress Lucy just before she fell asleep. But I needn't have worried. She looked at me blankly, and then the coquettish smile of a flirtatious young woman wreathed her wizened face.

'Who . . . is Alice?' she said.

For the remainder of the evening I watched a bit of television, and then settled to a crossword puzzle. I like doing crosswords, everything fitting into its correct space, all the words connected, interdependent. Just before turning in, I drew back the green velour curtains, and stared out into the tiny garden. The pane had misted lightly with the cool of the night. I wrote the name 'Alice' very carefully on it with my index finger.

'Alice who?' I whispered and climbed the stairs to bed.

Myrtle – 2003

I am sitting in the back room of Orchard House. I am always sitting in the back room waiting for something to happen. And when you sit, as I do, for hour after hour, you find yourself reminiscing. You cannot help it. You begin to wonder about how it all came to pass. The young look forward. The old look backward.

I remember the child I once was, the child who visited Kew Gardens with Mother and brother Albert. I craned my small neck, looking at the red pagoda that rocked upwards, diminishing into the unremitting drabness of an oyster-grey sky. And I dreamed my dreams. All the way home, as the bus rumbled and coughed, and juddered and spluttered, through London traffic, I watched a fly fling itself against a sooty pane of glass. Turning my head, I could see Albert, beautiful Albert, with his piercing ice-blue eyes, sensuous red mouth, and dark curls. And I could see my mother, her brown hair neatly crimped, her own prim mouth, bright with deep pink lipstick, her round cinnamon eyes, dancing with obvious delight. Their heads were touching, mother and son, their voices low and intimate, washed into one another. Close as conspirators they were, oblivious of me, gazing at them from across the aisle. So I turned away, back to the fly buzzing and battering itself against the glass, its frenzy futile. I imagined smashing that pane of glass with a closed fist, hearing it shatter. I pictured the fly bursting out into the infinite space, and whirring away, hardly daring to believe its luck.

I recall how years later, shortly after the war, my gentle giant of a father died. His disease-ridden heart, the organ that had prevented him fighting for his country and earned him a coward's feather, finally gave out in peacetime. It seized up and froze before a plate of pink blancmange. As the breath trickled out of him he keeled over, right into the cold, gelatinous pinkness of it, a single bubble of breath breaking the surface seconds after. I remember my dismay looking on, knowing I had lost my only ally in the gloomy red-brick house in Ealing.

And I recollect my first sight of you, Ralph – dark, tall and dashing, with alert steely-blue eyes, clasping a camera before you. You were covering an amateur show for the local rag, and had come to photograph its parochial stars. I was numbered among them. Gwendolen in Oscar Wilde's *The Importance of Being Earnest*. At best, my performance could be described as lacklustre; at worst, wooden. But you, it appeared, had seen a different play altogether, as you posed me for your photographs, your face so animated, those beguiling eyes of yours sparkling. Next to your striking looks, it was the enthusiasm that captured and held me. It was as if there was nothing you couldn't do with it. Take a shabby little amateur production in a village hall, with threadbare costumes and tatty scenery, and transform it into a glittering spectacle, showcasing the astonishing talent that lay at the heart of a thriving community. Or, perhaps, take a dull British girl destined for banal suburbia and transform her into a shimmering princess?

'What a superb show! I don't know when I've laughed so much. And you, well, you were wonderful Miss Lambert, entrancing. I brought Lucy, my sister, along too. And she loved your performance.'

That's what you said to me, as you pushed a strand of hair back from my face and, with a finger under my chin, adjusted the angle of my profile. You were wonderful. I knew I wasn't. Hadn't the director, Ron Fowler, spent eight weeks informing me of the fact? And all the while his invective boomed out, those expressive fingers of his would spear back his leonine mane, and his fleshy cheeks would colour plum-red.

'Do lighten your delivery, Myrtle. This is Wilde at his finest, witty, effervescent repartee. It's a comedy, darling, not a wake. Must you keep clinging onto the furniture, lovey? Anyone would think you were on the *Titanic*, hanging on for dear life, seconds before the bloody thing went down. Sweetheart, do pick up your cues a bit more promptly, you're slowing down the pace to a deathly crawl. Must you keep folding your arms, darling? You look like the genie from Aladdin, not the alluring Gwendolen Fairfax.'

They just kept coming, and the worst of it was knowing the comments were completely justified. I had no talent: my foray into amateur theatre only served to confirm what I had always suspected. I did not have the fascination of the sea about me, no glittering treasure lying undiscovered many fathoms down. It was disheartening to realise the truth. Oh Ralph, I just wanted to shine for a time, the way Albert did, for Mother to be just a little in awe of me . . . as if . . . as if I really was an interesting person. Is that too much to ask?

You did that. Looking back, I think something in your exuberance answered to my reticence. I was self-contained, you were abandoned. Opposites attract, isn't that what they say? But I knew, almost immediately I knew. As I sat there wishing I was not quite so tall, that my hair would not fall so stubbornly straight, that I could instil some mysterious depths into my eyes, like Rita Hayworth or Bette Davis, and your camera clicked and flashed, I knew. You were my ticket out of there, away from Mother and the ever-present reprobation in those grim button eyes of hers, away from Albert, the brother, the boy, the son and heir, who had been given so many gifts that there were none left over for me. And away from the gloomy corners of the red-brick house, and the grey that I felt my soul was steeped in.

I sensed you were attracted to me that first meeting. It was quite enough to be going on with. Had director Ron only known it, I followed my dismal debut as Gwendolen Fairfax with a breathtaking improvisation of Myrtle Lambert, the woman every man wants by his side, his perfect helpmeet, the accomplished hostess, the contented housewife, the adoring lover. I gave it everything I had, because, you see – and here, believe me I am not exaggerating – my future relied upon it. And when you didn't ask for your money back, but seemed entirely swept away by the illusion, indeed, just kept following curtain-call with curtain-call, I knew I had a triumph on my hands. Maybe not worthy of the Oscar which all Hollywood actresses hanker after, but then who wanted some old statue gathering dust on their shelf when instead they could have handsome, dynamic Ralph Safford for their very own. And more, a life as far away from dreary Britain as it was possible to get, thrown in with the bargain.

So we were married – you for love, and me for . . . ah Ralph, for a force much stronger than that: the longing for freedom. I was entirely satisfied with the arrangement, and be honest, so were you, to start with anyway. When you were posted to Africa, Kenya, as a government photographer, I was by your side. You whisked me away, leaving Mother seething far behind in the red-brick house, claiming she had been abandoned by the pair of us.

I used to love sitting on the veranda of our bungalow in Kenya, sipping scotch. I close my eyes and I am there. It is very hot. The air pulses with the heat. The chill of England seems so distant. I open my eyes sleepily, just a fraction, smile and take another sip of scotch. Having a drink together in the evenings was all part of the ritual. Do you recall, Ralph? The servant bringing the bottle of scotch on a tray, together with the ice tub and two glass tumblers, each already filled with chunks of ice. I loved the way the ice cubes chimed as I rolled them round the glass. I loved the whisper of the cold, golden liquid going down, a thread of flame tightening inside me. I was enthralled by the extremes, the last rays of the dying sun scalding through me, the cold of the frosted glass against my cheek. Sunsets were very different in Africa, weren't they, Ralph? The sun was a fireball that sank very slowly into the parched red clay. The skies were almost obscenely brilliant – topaz, coral, mauve, malachite, banks of radiance shifting from second to second. Actually, I found the evening displays a trifle vulgar, wasteful, the squandering of so much colour.

It's raining now, an insistent drumming on the rooftop, runnels of rain coursing down the sash windows, the sound of spattering droplets closing in on me. It always seems to be raining here in England. It wasn't like that in Hong Kong, was it Ralph? Except of course during the typhoon season, or when the mists settled on the Peak, and the mizzle closed in.

God alone knows what possessed Nicola to choose that dreadful wallpaper for this draughty room. White flowers plastered over a red background. It calls to mind the new regional flag they've chosen for Hong Kong. An uninspiring design if you ask me. It looks like one of those handheld windmills you buy at a fair, or at the seaside. Hardly something you can take seriously. It can't be compared to the Union Jack. Now there's a flag you can be proud of, a flag that means something.

The roof of this wretched building leaks. Why Nicola persuaded us to buy it I will never know.

'Orchard House. The two of you will love it.' That's what she said, as if we didn't have any choice in the matter. And, quite honestly, looking back, I'm not sure we did.

There are buckets placed at strategic points to catch the drips. I can hear them plinking now. It is a bit like a form of Japanese water torture, waiting for the next plink, watching the buckets and pails slowly fill, wondering when the silvery skins will rupture, and the collected rain will trickle down the sides and soak into the Persian rugs. I think I can say that the state of the roof is the most weighty problem here, but there are others. Damp in general, peeling wall-paper, rotting window-frames and cracked panes, missing floortiles, banging pipes and a faulty central-heating system, to name but a few. I think we may even have a bit of woodworm on the first floor that needs treating. Oh, we have mice too. Larry, my son-in-law, claims he's dealing with them. But I doubt it. He says a great deal, and as far as I can see does very little. And Jillian's not much better. What I wouldn't give for a couple of amahs to set the place to rights. I thought Nicola said that having Jillian and Larry living with us was going to make life much easier, that it would alleviate all our diffi-culties. What's more, I could have done without the boy being foisted on us. Amos. What a ridiculous name for a child! It's not even as if we're great ones for religion. Besides, I have never been maternal. I can't think why Jillian and Larry spent all that money trying to have a baby. When the doctor told her they had problems (something odd about Larry's sperm, not that I pressed them for any details you understand), in my opinion she should have just accepted it. I would have. Gladly, as it happens!

I'm sorry, Ralph, but you know I never really wanted children. Not all women hanker after a family you know. We aren't all programmed for reproduction. Some of us don't need miniature replicas of ourselves to make our lives complete. Conversely, in Alice's case, far from completing me, she very nearly destroyed me. I had her for your sake you know, so you can't blame me entirely for what happened, what happened to our daughter, Alice. You were determined to have your son, weren't you? Oh, you never put it into so many words, but the understanding was implicit. I did my best, Ralph. You must give me that. I tried my hardest to produce your boy, your heir. And if it did take me four goes, I managed it in the end. Don't judge me, Ralph, wherever you are now. You have no idea what it was like for me producing girl after girl, producing Alice at that hospital in Ealing. I had to feel Mother's scorn at my inability to get a son for my husband – not once, not twice, but thrice. After all, she had managed the feat first time, hadn't she?

We didn't put Alice's name on your gravestone. The children wanted to make a dedication to you, a personal thank-you to their father. We talked about adding her name after theirs, but in the end we decided it wasn't appropriate. We felt she hadn't earned her place there. And Ralph, this once you weren't around to make a fuss. So there it is, Jillian, Nicola and Harry, but . . . no Alice. If you want my opinion, and you never really did when it came to Alice, this is as it should be.

'Is it a boy?' I asked the midwife repeatedly. She was quite terse with me in the end.

'It's a girl,' she snapped. 'I've told you it's a girl, a lovely girl.'

That was an oxymoron to me by then, Ralph. Can you understand that? I'd had Jillian and Nicola, and each of those pregnancies cost me dearly. But as a man you could never appreciate that. Besides, delivering Alice was meant to be my last messy natal performance. I deserved to have a boy. I deserved a son by then. You know what they say, Ralph, third time lucky. Well, it wasn't for me. Having Alice was the most unpropitious thing that ever happened to me. Our daughter, our third daughter filled me with dread. But not you, oh no. You adored her, didn't you?

The midwife was a big, hearty woman, with apple-red cheeks, and large pink hands, butcher's hands I recall. She reached towards my chest and started fumbling with the tie of my nightie.

'No! No, no!' My voice was pitched too high. It reeked of panic.

'Put her to your breast,' she urged, still pulling at the lacing. She had a slight burr to her voice, though what the accent was I couldn't tell you.

I thrust her hand away. 'I am not feeding it myself. I need a bottle,' I told her succinctly. I had an image of a stray dog then, a dog I had seen on the streets of Nairobi, its dugs heavy with milk, puppies suckling frantically at them. Its eyes were rolled upwards to heaven, you could see their whites, but it lay in the gutter, and was coated with filth.

I suppressed a shudder. She stopped scrabbling at my painfully engorged breasts and nudged the baby forwards instead. I took it awkwardly, as if I thought it might bite me at any moment. I looked into the face. The wispy hair was lighter than Nicola's. The mouth that rooted hopefully towards me was pretty enough. But the eyes unsettled me. They were the rich brown of tobacco, and preternaturally alert. They were needy too. I have been told a newborn cannot focus immediately, but as this child stared steadily up at me I had my doubts. Returning her gaze, what I felt was not a trickle of love, but a wave of cold dislike. 'She' meant that I would have to do it all once more. She was unnecessary, surplus to requirements. She did not even have the decency to look abashed, as Nicola had done. And quite suddenly, with the smell of disinfectant and warm sweet blood, and the distant muted sounds coming to me from far corridors of rolling trolleys and muffled voices and footsteps, I felt afraid.

26

'Shall I show your husband in?' asked the determined midwife, her tone brisk, business-like. And when there was no response, she added with unnecessary emphasis, 'To see his beautiful baby daughter?'

For a second I wondered who she meant. Then Ralph, in you came. You took the bundle carefully in your arms, studied it for a moment, and then your face lit up. You looked so delighted.

'It is a girl,' I explained, thinking you had not grasped this. It was the year 1956 and I had given birth to yet another baby girl.

'I know,' you said. 'She's beautiful.' To my amazement, your shining eyes proved the sincerity of your words. The baby seemed to sense this, following the sound of her father's voice. Father and daughter's eyes locked. Ralph, you looked smitten, mesmerised. I felt a pang just under my ribcage and had to turn away.

'I think the name Alice suits her,' you said. 'Oh . . . yes, definitely. Alice. What do you think?'

I shrugged indifferently. 'If you like,' I said. I wasn't really bothered one way or another. Alice would do as well as the next name.

There was black magic involved in the coming of my son though. Oh, scientists would say that I was just being fanciful, but I know. I was in my sixth month. We had since moved to the British Crown Colony of Aden. Having developed extreme eczema, blistering and bleeding over your hands and lower arms – a reaction to the chemicals you used in photography – you had been persuaded by George Walbrook, your friend in the Foreign Office, to apply for a posting in government information services in Honduras. Failing to secure this, you were offered instead an administrative post in Aden. And it was here, in the merciless heat and chaos of this busy port, with its shark-infested harbour, that we settled with our growing family. This time, I had decided not to return to England for the birth. I did not think I could bear Mother's disapproval if yet again I failed to produce the necessary male. Besides, I had been assured that they had the very best of facilities and doctors here in Aden.

We were having a party when it happened. Do you remember, Ralph? We had many friends there, British and Arab. I was wearing a voluminous midnight-blue affair. Quite suddenly a tall Arab gentleman, with sable skin and very white teeth – dressed, I couldn't help thinking, with his turban and glittering tunic, a bit like a fairground magician – seized hold of the hem of my dress, folded himself in half, and with his other hand flung some white powder up under the bell of my skirt. It coated my mound. The gentleman's name was A . . . A . . . Akil, that's right, and he worked with you.

He fixed me with his black hawk eyes, Akil, and straightened up. As I moved away the remaining powder fell softly about my ankles, like a dusting of snow. I was taken aback. I had not been prepared for someone shoving handfuls of unknown substances up my maternity dress, and did not know quite how to react. He bowed to me graciously.

'The baby you are carrying, it shall be a boy now,' he said in a deep, sonorous voice.

I was so delighted with his prediction that I forgot to be annoyed. At least he understood the turmoil inside me. The thought of another girl growing there, another Alice . . . dear God! Later that night as you and I tried in vain to slumber in the heat, you mentioned the encounter. I didn't think you had seen it. Even in my tangle of sheets, hot and bothered, with the child stirring restlessly inside me, as if it too was finding the intense heat unbearable, I was surprised.

'That Akil has a cheek,' you mumbled through a yawn. 'Throwing talcum powder up your dress, and coming up with that mumbo-jumbo about our baby.' You thrust the sheet back from your body, and I saw that your skin was slick with sweat.

We were sleeping beneath mosquito nets, and I found the effect of that claustrophobic haze disturbing.

'He took me unawares,' I responded primly, pushing down my own portion of our sheet, sitting up, and resting back against the pillows. 'He told me that now we will have a son.'

You laughed. 'What, as if it was down to him!'

Outside the netting, the high-pitched whine of a mosquito could be heard, fading and then coming back, as it attempted re-entry.

'It might be true. It might be a boy,' I commented casually, as if I couldn't have cared less.

'And it might be a girl,' you said equably.

After that you fell asleep. But I remained awake for some time, my hands exploring my bump, glossy with moonlight. I could not bear to go through this again. There was no choice in the matter, and the child should know this. It had to be male. Our son was born three months later. Clearly he had been paying attention to our Arab friend. But he had obviously been a touch overwrought at the prospect of his much longed-for arrival, and had wound the umbilical cord around his neck like a noose. He emerged not a healthy shade of pink, flushed with his first breaths of life, but milky-blue, his lips an even deeper hue, kissed with death. The doctors were uncertain if he would make it through the night. They took him away to wrestle with the black prince, promising to do their best to snatch my son from his grip. I lay alone in bed that night, in a white nondescript room, in a hospital in Aden. I felt bleak. I had produced a son. Finally I had produced a son, and now he might die. I thought about our three *healthy* children – my firstborn, Jillian, a girl, but welcome for all that, and my second, Nicola, impossible not to like, with her indomitable charm and her discretion. She understood the boundaries so well and never overstepped the mark. And then our third daughter, Alice. Alice had already made it apparent that she did not understand about boundaries. She was colouring outside the lines. I felt annoyed just thinking about her. If I could . . . if . . . I could . . . swap her life for his, then . . . At first the thought was so terrible that it floored me. It had all the menace of dark fairy tales. I will give her up if you will . . .

But gradually in the dullness of that room my wicked thought glowed like a hot coal. You may take Alice but leave me my son. I will never renege on the contract. Take her. Take Alice. Take Alice. Take Alice, was my incantation. She's yours. I shall never want her back, only leave me my son. It seemed the demons were not listening, or perhaps they didn't want Alice either because as it was they both survived. The next day you brought our daughters to see their new brother. You stood, Ralph, and the girls sat on the low wall that surrounded the hospital. They squinted up through the fierce sunlight

29

as I stepped onto the balcony from my second-floor room, my fragile son in my arms. The doctors felt it would be better to keep my sickly babe away from any possible source of infection for the time being, until he grew stronger. They recommended no direct contact with our other children during those first crucial days.

The girls were wearing matching pinafore dresses, with white blouses, Jillian in French navy, her blonde hair in pigtails, Nicola in bottle-green, her dark silky locks cropped short, and Alice in red, blood-red, her mousy-brown bob with a side parting, held back from her face with a grip. The green and blue blended in with the flashing gold of the sun and the cooler acid green of the young palm trees. The girls waved. You waved, Ralph. I looked down at my son and felt pride wash over me.

'Here in my arms are all my hopes and dreams,' I thought.

But the red of Alice's dress hooked me back again. Even then she was a jealous child.

You were reassigned after that, this time to the British Colony of Hong Kong. When you first mentioned it to me, the new posting, I was intrigued.

'How would you like it if I spirited you away to a beautiful island in the Orient?' you asked, jumping up suddenly from the wicker chair you had been sitting in. We were in the bedroom of our bungalow home in Aden. Above our heads a fan rotated noisily, doing its best to hold the heat at bay.

'I should like that very much,' I said, only half listening, concentrating on our blue-eyed, golden-haired boy, wriggling in my arms.

'Then your wish is my command. I shall transport you to Hong Kong,' you shot back, unable to hide your delight.

'Hong Kong?' I said, trying out the name and finding it both familiar and unknown.

You elaborated. 'It's a small island in the South China Sea, not much more than 400 square miles I believe. But then there is the Kowloon Peninsula and the New Territories too, just across the harbour.'

'Oh,' I said, trying to sound enlightened. 'It seems odd that we should own an island so far away.' You smiled knowingly and continued.

'It was leased to Britain after some skulduggery which involved the shipping of a great deal of opium grown by us in India into China. Very lucrative apparently. When China, unsurprisingly, protested and asked that we desist in the trade, we were so outraged we went to war with them.' Here you paused mid-stride and chuckled.

'Ah,' I said, switching my son from one shoulder to the other, and patting his back gently. In a while I would call for his nanny, but just for now it was nice playing mother. You packed tobacco into the bowl of a wooden pipe, then paced thoughtfully around our bed. You used to smoke a pipe back then, though you gave it up when we got to Hong Kong. I rather liked the smell of it and missed it later. 'And we won?' I asked.

'We did, and among the spoils we acquired Hong Kong Island in 1842, and a bit later on, Kowloon and the New Territories, leasehold for 99 years.'

You perched on the side of the bed, Ralph, leant forwards and gently stroked your son's golden curls. Then you placed the stem of the pipe in your mouth, struck a match, and held the flame to the bowl, sucking hard until the fragrant strands of tobacco caught. For a while you puffed contentedly, your expression dreamy. After a bit you removed your pipe, those engaging eyes of yours searching my face. 'So how do you fancy a spell residing on Queen Victoria's ill-gotten gains?' you asked, your eyes alight with mischief.

I thought about it for a moment – only a moment, mind. I recalled a red pagoda towering up into the sky, the roof of each diminishing segment looking like an oriental hat, the brim curving upwards into delicate points. I recalled a fly beating its wings against the grubby window of a bus, longing for liberation, and I remembered too the dull greyness that seemed to encroach on everything back then.

'I think I should like that very much,' I said. So we packed our trunks and set off again. In the late spring of 1962 I had my first sighting of Hong Kong, as we sailed into busy Victoria harbour. We would come to know that bridge of water between the island and Kowloon as if it was an extension of our own bodies. The dull, green face of the sea was dotted with sampans and junks and ferries. From here, my gaze strayed past the mass of buildings that crowded the waterfront, and on up the verdant slopes looped with winding roads. We had docked off a bustling, mountainous island, the summits veiled mysteriously in dense powder-grey clouds. And it was a short while later up these mountains we wound in a shiny, black chauffeur-driven car.

'Our flat is set almost on the highest point of The Peak,' you told me, Ralph. 'Fabulous views.' We threaded our way higher and higher, into what seemed to me an impenetrable fog. 'That is of course, unless we are temporarily lost in the mist. I understand it can be a real problem here,' came your wry observation.

But any qualms I may have had about our mountain home were soon quelled. Here was a grand, airy, top-floor flat, situated right at the summit of The Peak, with the views you had boasted of to be enjoyed from every window. The white, flat-roofed building was only six floors high, double-sided, the central column housing the stair-well and the lift. Our front door opened onto a hall that would have graced any stately home back in England, while doors to either side of it led on the left to a lounge, this in turn giving onto a long, open veranda, and on the right to a dining room, and thence into a spacious kitchen. Beyond the kitchen was a communal sheltered area for drying washing. It led through to the servants' accommo-dation, six tiny bedrooms in all, with a shared rudimentary bathroom and toilet, and for their use a separate stairwell leading down to the ground floor. Returning to our hall I explored further, the children running ahead excitedly. My high heels clicked smartly on the wooden floors of the long corridor that ran the length of the flat. Light flooded through tall wide windows to my right, while on my left doors led off it into large bedrooms, the first of which had a luxurious en suite bathroom. A second bathroom lay at the end of the corridor from which, on fine days, you assured me, you could look out over Pokfulam and the sea.

There was room aplenty for the Safford family and we had soon settled in. I told you that, for the time being, I could make do with just two servants. So Ah Dang, with her glossy jet-black hair drawn back into a tight bun, her wide girth attesting to her own passion for food, and her glittering gold front teeth, became our housekeeper and cook. And Ah Lee, with her bouncy, dark curls and her constant nervous giggling, juggled the tasks of washing, ironing, cleaning and shopping and, it seemed, found plenty to amuse herself in each. We provided them both with the standard uniform − drawstring black trousers, and plain three-quarter-length white tunics. The children were dispatched to English-speaking Little Peak School and Big Peak School respectively, both within walking distance, Alice attending the former, and Jillian and Nicola the latter. Four-year-old Harry, our son, soon followed, so to a large extent I had my freedom. Quite what we would do when Jillian finished at Big Peak School I did not know, for exclusively English-speaking secondary schools were in very short supply.

Life on The Peak in Hong Kong was punctuated by regular letters from Mother. I had come to dread these epistles. I had forsaken her. I was on the other side of the world, living a life of opulence and indulgence. I never spared a thought for her. In these aspersions, Mother was wrong. I thought about her a great deal. After careful consideration, I decided to make a sacrifice to appease her. I would give her Jillian and Nicola. They would be dutiful in my place. It would soon be time for Jillian to go to secondary school. It made perfect sense to send first Jillian and then Nicola to a boarding school in England − and not just any boarding school, but the convent at which my mother was now employed part time teaching English and Drama. Of course, she had no qualifications for the job, but apparently rearing Albert, now a professional musical actor, was pedigree enough.'

'I'll miss Jillian,' you admitted, as we sat sipping scotch on the veranda one evening, watching dusk deepen and the lights of Aberdeen start slowly to glimmer, appearing one by one, as if by magic. You looked shattered. These days your only escape from work was on our boat, *White Jade*, and even then we had been tracked down by the marine police a couple of times with urgent messages.

I freshened up my own drink, and ran the frosted tumbler between my hands before taking a hefty swallow. Cars purred by on the road below. I waited a moment then took another gulp. The whisky seemed very watery tonight; the bite was slow in coming, and the accompanying numbness even slower.

'I'm sure Saint Mary's Convent is a wonderful school, and that the children will relish a bit of time with their grandmother,' I persuaded you.

You sat forward in your chair and sighed. 'I'm just not certain—' you began, but smoothly I interrupted you.

'These insects can be a real problem in the evenings,' I said, swatting away a flying ant. Even paradise has its drawbacks. 'Let's go inside. I'd better check that everything's all right with the amahs in the kitchen. Take your eyes off them for a second and they start doing all kinds of silly things.' I picked up the bottle of scotch and stood up. When you did not move, Ralph, but just sat brooding and staring into your glass, I told you dinner was almost ready and took the lead.

I had thought that sending Jillian and Nicola to boarding school would free me up to devote more time to you and my social duties as wife of an important government servant. I had even looked forward to seeing more of my friend and next-door neighbour, Beth Fielding, and enjoying a leisurely lunchtime drink with her once or twice a week. But this presumption was flawed. Alice, a demanding, insecure child from the outset, was becoming steadily more and more difficult. My mind teemed with a growing tally of unnerving incidents, where her behaviour was both unpredictable and extreme, incidents which no matter how much scotch I drank often refused to melt away.

The part of a king in the school nativity play became a nightmare when I tried to apply shoe polish to her face, in an attempt simply to make her look authentic.

'What are you doing, Mummy? You are making me all brown! It's horrid of you,' she wailed, plucking the crown from her head, and letting it fall to the ground.

My entreaties that it was just for the role she was acting were ignored. 'I don't want always to have a brown face!' she had screamed, so loudly that several other mothers in the school changing rooms looked round and grinned. 'Why have you done this to me, Mummy?'

Painstakingly I explained that with the help of soap and water, the shoe-polish would quickly wash away, but Alice only shot me a disbelieving look and abandoned herself to racking sobs. Finally she tottered onto the stage, her blotchy complexion attesting to hurried attempts at scouring her face of its autumnal hue. But even this did not assuage her histrionics, and she broke down before a baffled Mary, and had to be coaxed from the stage. This scene marked the first of several involving the parents of other children, teachers, and even on one occasion the headmistress. No matter how much I implored, cajoled and pleaded, there was no reasoning with Alice once her mind was made up.

In addition to this, you and I, Ralph, were called upon to attend many performances celebrating Chinese festivals. I had come to loathe these very public outings. Inevitably you would insist that the children attend, though goodness knew why. I felt they would do very well with the amahs at home watching a bit of Chinese opera. Certainly Alice would. But you were immovable on this, as you were on many issues involving our youngest daughter. So there we would be, in VIP seats at the front row for all to gawp at. Harry, of course, would always sit placidly, entranced by the colourful spectacle, Nicola on her best behaviour at his side. But Alice would fidget incessantly. Never content simply to be near me, she would have to keep tugging on my sleeve, stroking me, resting her head on me, reaching for my hand, tickling it, patting the necklace I was wearing, or the bracelet that adorned my wrist, or twisting the rings on my fingers. On one such occasion, a dragon dance by the harbour side, my patience snapped. Oblivious to the massive, bobbing, brilliant, red head of the dragon, with its swivelling, bulbous eyes, only feet from us, I suddenly sprang up, thrusting Alice from my lap where she had been settling herself.

'Oh do stop touching me, Alice, for goodness sake!' my voice rang out over the clanging Chinese music, as Alice tumbled to the floor. 'Leave me alone. For the love of God, get away from me!'

I must have shouted. Faces turned to look at me. Alice righted herself, and gingerly sat once more in her assigned seat between you, Ralph, and me. Locking eyes with you for a second, the look you gave me would have frozen blood. The dragon head bounced and shook, its gaudy finery a blur before me. Its striped body writhed and twisted. Then it froze for an instant, the great head seemingly suspended in the air right before my eye-line. Slowly it blinked its white, fur-trimmed eyelids. And in that moment, I would have liked to dash forwards and gouge its impertinent eyes from their teacup sockets. Like Alice's, their gaze was far too astute. Then the wretched little man who jigged by the serpent's side put his hands on his hips and shook with pantomime laughter. Not satisfied with this, he went on to clasp both hands over the mouth that was slashed into his enormous, lobster-pink, papier-mâché globe of a head. He wagged this monstrous mask from side to side, the focus of his slit eyes on me, the butt of the joke. Briefly I glanced down at Alice. Always she was thinking, the wide, solemn eyes seeing everything. Thinking, thinking, thinking! Then the beast shivered and burst once more into life. My daughter had shown me up yet again, in front of all the important guests in the audience. Even the Governor was there, enjoying the jest I presume. It was a high price to pay for losing my control, for letting my guard slip. Alice had humiliated me publicly, before the most important British official on the island.

Our daughter was making life intolerable, Ralph, whether you were prepared to acknowledge it or not. She went for sleepovers with friends, vowing that she wanted to go more than anything she could think of, only to be returned home, sobbing and distraught in the middle of the night. The cause of these upsets remained a mystery both to you and to me. She was beset with night terrors, where she roamed the flat in strange trances, sometimes dragging her mattress great distances to find rest. And being Alice, she was not content to suffer her insomnia alone. Stricken with fear, and knowing very well that she would get no sympathy from me, she would turn instead to you, her beleaguered father, and make you sit up the night with her. She would beg you to tell her that she was not alone, for she felt, she said, as if she was the only person living in the blackness, and that all the world was dead. As a result, struggling with the demands of your high-profile job and little sleep, you were jaded and consequently short-tempered with me. Her selfishness was astounding. But if you tackled her about these episodes, the resulting dialogue simply revealed Alice to be an irrational child, deaf to reason and common sense. Often in the evenings she would scream for me, and when I came running I would find her peering out of a bathroom window at the corridor's end, mesmerised. She would insist that I look at the sunset, exclaiming that she had never before seen anything so beautiful. She would gasp, and tell me that she could barely breathe at the wonder of it, that it made her want to cry and laugh all at once. After a time, like the villagers charging up the mountain in response to the shrieks of the boy who cried wolf, I would dismiss her summons, or just give her a cursory nod in passing.

I even spoke to you and arranged for Alice to have a dog. Of course at the time I said it would be a family pet and lovely for all of us. It was really for Alice though, to occupy Alice, to absorb her, and perhaps give the rest of us a little peace. We fetched the wretched creature from the Hong Kong SPCA. Alice chose him. If I'm honest I thought him a disagreeable mongrel, quite absurd in appearance – a motley assortment of colours, brown, black, white, grey and even a bit of yellow. He had a feathered tail far too long for the compact body, huge paws, a ragged ear, a long thin snout, and a black tongue which, when it hung out, very nearly trailed to the ground.

'Really Alice! Why him?' I asked her, running my eyes over the scrappy mutt. 'There are others that are so much prettier.'

But true to form, never taking her eyes from the dog she had selected, Alice seemed not to hear me.

'I shall call him Bear,' she had announced, as I filled out the paperwork. I resisted the temptation to state the obvious. It was a dog not a bear! I thought it an absurd name. Why not call the thing Rover or Sparky or Rusty? But Alice was adamant. And to be fair, 'Bear' did fulfil his allotted task of providing a preoccupation for Alice. It was not unknown for the two of them to disappear for several hours at a time. Though Alice, when present, remained just as challenging.

Why, I asked myself countless times, couldn't she just take things at face value? Why was she was forever digging under the skin, probing things best left alone. Yet despite this you seemed to relish her company, Ralph. And for her part, Alice would happily have followed her beloved father anywhere. As Alice began her final year at Big Peak School, my relief was palpable. Soon, very soon, she would join her sisters at the convent in England, and then it would just be you, Ralph, and me, and our son of course. I broached this subject one weekend after a particularly good meal, when I knew you were relaxed and mellow and would be most receptive. We were sitting at the dining-room table and enjoying a small cognac with our coffees.

'It's probably time for us to make arrangements for Alice to join her sisters,' I ventured. I waited. There was no response. I took a mouthful of brandy for courage and soldiered on. 'I can hardly believe it, but Alice is in her last year at Big Peak School, and with the problem of finding suitable secondary education here I—'

'I've been thinking about that,' you said, uncharacteristically cutting me off mid-flow.

Had you indeed, I ruminated. You continued.

'I've heard they're opening up a new school on Bowen Road. They're setting it up in the old British Army Hospital while they make a start building new premises on the terraced slopes above. In time they plan to demolish the hospital entirely, making way for further expansion. I want Alice to go there.'

I drew in a breath sharply. You gave me a quick glance. 'Is there a problem?' you asked, a dangerous note sounding in your voice.

I felt stunned, as if I had been slugged over the head and temporarily my eyesight was blurred. I tried to hold onto the salient facts. You had been thinking, you had been thinking about Alice, thinking about keeping Alice here with us, despite the chaos she was causing, Ralph, you wanted to send her to a new school they were building, a school I had heard nothing about.

'But darling,' I said, reaching for the cognac bottle, 'we don't know anything about this school.'

'I do,' you fired back. 'I've been to see the site. Nigel has been telling me all about it. They're considering sending Christopher and Anita there. Actually, I'm surprised Beth hasn't mentioned it to you.'

And so was I. Although this could not quite be classed as deception, my friend and neighbour Beth Fielding's omission to acquaint me with this startling news came a pretty close second in my book. I tipped up the bottle and refilled my glass. 'I see. Well. Well, well, well.'

'Myrtle, be honest with yourself,' you went on as I stiffened in my seat, 'it would be a disaster sending Alice to boarding school.' Under your breath you added, 'I'm not at all sure it's been a success for Jillian or Nicola either.'

I sipped my cognac, then cradled my glass, slowly swilling round the amber liquid.

'I feel we should at least discuss it,' was my face-saving remark.

'We have,' you said brusquely, rising from the table.

Tonight Alice is worse than ever. Sometimes you can almost believe she alters with the rising of the moon, a kind of moon-madness. She is like a lone wolf howling and prowling all through the night. Ralph is dealing with her. With Alice his patience is inexhaustible. Harry seeks refuge in my bed. We close our eyes and block our ears. Finally I drift off to sleep. I dream we are on our junk, *White Jade*, which we have moored in a pretty bay. We are floating on a cobalt-blue sea. I feel the gentle rise and fall of the boat like breath coming in and going out, the rhythmic lift and fall of the thing. The sun is shining. We are fanned by a light breeze. And we are fishing, Ralph and Alice and I. We have cast out nylon lines with hooks knotted at the end of them. We have speared wiggling maggots for bait. Time passes. Ralph catches nothing. I catch nothing. Then Alice reels in a fish. It is several inches long, and it flaps dripping over the wooden deck, the silver scales brilliant as coruscating diamonds kissed by the sun. We all point at the fish as it gulps in air, and slaps and slips about. Our faces are masks of delight. Then quite suddenly the fish starts to inflate, like a silver balloon spiked with prickles. It swells up obscenely until it no longer flaps over the deck. It is a motionless bubble. Its prickles become barbs, hooking into the soft flesh of the damp wood.

'It is a puffer fish!' cries Alice in dismay. 'It's poisonous!' She is standing now over the gasping, hideous thing, hypnotised. Then she looks up at me. 'If you eat my fish you will die, Mother,' she says, and I wake.

My hands itch all day. When Alice returns from school we have a row. I do not like rowing. Some people can shrug off rows like a dog shaking water from its coat. I cannot. Brutal words stay with me . . . well . . . sometimes for a lifetime. I keep count of them. I notch them into the bark of my life, so deeply that they will never grow out. I tell Alice she cannot carry on with her deranged nights. My voice is quite calm, quite steady. I tell her they are taking a dreadful toll on her father. I tell her how hard he works, and that she is making him very ill. And when none of this seems to have any effect, I tell her that she is coming between us, that she is forcing us apart, her mother and her father. Alice's voice rises up like a snake with its egoistic jingle-jangle, as if she really is the only person alive in the world, and not just through the long, dark nights but through the long bright days as well. My voice shifts key. I feel the 'demon rasp' tolling in me then, purifying, abrasive, because Alice smiles a foolish smile. The demon is full of wrath, and he spits words out at the smiling, loon-faced child.

We are in the bathroom, the same bathroom where Alice has summoned me so many times with her games. The window is open and the sky is red. I feel it bleed into me. I am dimly aware that my mouth is still working, and that my voice has grown deep and masculine, a war cry, and that my limbs are flaying. Alice is bold and stands her ground. And still she is smiling, smiling! I want to wipe that smile off her face. I draw back my hand and deal her such a blow

40

across her grinning visage, that she is sent reeling backwards, covering the distance of several feet to the window, sliding down the wall, crumpling on the floor, while incongruously, above her head, Alice's wondrous sunset is framed. I am transfixed by the white face looming through the long brown hair. The eye is already puffing up. The cheek is split with a deep gash. Her blood is such a vivid shade of red. It dribbles from the wound and down her chin. It drips onto her summer school uniform, flowering on the white cotton.

I think: I am wearing my wedding and engagement rings and they must have cut into her cheek, a marital knuckleduster. I think, I have committed a mortal sin, somehow or other the Mother Superior at the convent back in England will know of it. I am envious of Alice. I am envious of my daughter. Alice, who has roared through so many nights, is silent now. I cannot even hear her breathing. I watch the blood spill and grow more copious. It pools in a crease at her neck. This creates the impression, reminiscent of a horror movie, that her head has been severed from her body, and that, if you push it, it will tumble off and roll over the green, marble-effect rubber tiles of the bathroom floor. I wonder what time Ralph will be home. I have an idea he is out tonight and will not be back until late. By tomorrow it will not look so bad. Besides, a story can be told. I feel sure a story will come that fits my purpose. Alice, I know, will never tell. She will hold it all in, keep it contained. Like Iwazaru, one of the three wise monkeys, she will speak no evil. She will gag herself. I gaze unmoved at the sunset, then my eyes slide downwards and hold Alice's.

'At last,' I say, 'when I come, there is something to see.' My voice scrapes the silence. My hands have stopped itching. They are trembling now. I need something to steady my nerves.

Nicola – 1965

I never really grasped why Jillian made such a fuss about boarding
school. True, it was a bit of a blow the parents choosing Gran's school,
it being Roman Catholic and we being . . . well, heathens. But it
didn't really worry me. I knew we would have a laugh. I told Jillian
so, as she sat on her bed, in the flat on The Peak. The Easter holidays were drawing to a close, and she was red-cheeked and wretched.
She was flying back to England the next day and I was helping her
to pack.

'In September I'll be joining you,' I told her with a grin. 'We'll
shake things up, Jilly.' She managed a weak smile.

'I hate it there,' she said brokenly. 'I'm miserable.' She took off her
glasses and I saw her eyes were swimming with tears. 'The nuns are
bitches!'

I tossed in a T-shirt with a picture of kittens on it, shunted the
case along the bed, and sat down next to my sister. I put an arm
over her shoulder. This was an awkward gesture for me. I am not a
touchy-feely person. It is nothing personal but I experience a kind
of revulsion when things get sloppy. That day there had been a scene
at lunch, a spectacular scene. It was a roast dinner. We generally have
a roast on the weekends. Jillian, already feeling as if she was fading
away, as if she was only half visible, with her return to England imminent, was upset even before we sat down. Alice kept asking her silly
questions. What was it like at boarding school? Did she have a
boyfriend? Was she excited about the flight tomorrow? That sort of

thing. Jillian loathed Alice. She had told me late one night that she would like to slap her, that she could not bear her enthusiasm, her eagerness, her desire to please.

'She can afford to behave like that,' Jillian had said bitterly, screwing up her eyes behind their lenses, as she watched Alice chatting to one of the amahs.

I sympathised with Jillian. From time to time Alice got on my nerves too. But it was plain to me that my elder sister hadn't thought this through. Anyone could see that Jillian's vendetta against Alice did not work in her favour. For a start it maddened Father, who seemed to feel he had to keep riding to Alice's rescue, like some paternal knight in shining armour.

'Why not make a friend of Alice, then make that friendship work for you,' I suggested reasonably to Jillian.

But to no avail I'm afraid. Jillian's revulsion for our little sister knew no bounds. She gave long-suffering sighs when Alice walked into a room. On car journeys she insisted on winding up the window, claiming the draft was blowing her hair out of shape, knowing full well that Alice was prone to travel sickness. And she would stoically ignore our little sister when she bounded up to her full of adoring compliments. How lovely Jillian was looking, Alice would say. How she wished her brown hair was fair like Jillian's, and would Jillian help her pick out some new clothes because she had no idea what was fashionable in London at present. It astonished me that Alice did not seem to realise she was antagonising Jilly. But then she can be a little obtuse sometimes.

So when we all trooped into lunch that day, I had an idea that something was going to happen. Father carved the meat. It was roast beef. Jillian wanted an outside cut and so did Alice. Neither of them liked bloody meat, whereas I liked mine nearly raw. I was happiest with a middle slice, all pink and oozing blood. Father served Alice before her older sister, and Jillian clearly felt the snub. She made up her mind that all the best bits had gone to Alice, and that the cut she was dished up was undercooked. She took Father to task over this, complaining that Alice always got the choicest pieces of meat.

Mother piled in. As a matter of course, Harry, son and heir, had been taken care of first. Now he looked perturbed by the delay. Catching his mother's eye, he was given the go-ahead to start his meal. So while hostilities were breaking out, Harry was slowly masticating a mouthful, like a cud-chewing cow. All the while, his eyes focused hypnotically on two black and silver angelfish, gliding about in a tank, set up on the dresser behind the dining-room table. Then Alice made matters much worse by offering Jillian her meat. Typical. Why couldn't she just shut up?

'Here Jillian, we can swap plates if you like,' Alice suggested, lifting her plate and offering it to her sister.

'I don't want it now you've touched it,' Jillian cried, shoving the plate back towards Alice, so hard that the piece of crispy outside meat was launched off it, orbited briefly in the air, before landing with a 'plop', quite fortuitously as it happened, on Harry's plate. Harry's eyes rolled from living fish to dead meat, and stayed glued to the unexpected arrival, his jaws temporarily locked.

'That was uncalled for,' Father said angrily, hurriedly flipping over the joint, carving a slice from the other end, and delivering it to Alice's plate.

'No,' pleaded Alice. 'I don't mind really. Jillian can have it.'

'Didn't you hear me the first time?' Jillian shrieked, shooting a slaughterous look in Alice's direction. 'I don't want anything of yours.'

Alice began protesting that she hadn't touched it, so it couldn't be called *hers* yet. Then Mother, who kept running a thumb up and down along the blade of her own knife, where it lay at the side of her plate, told Alice to be quiet and to get on with her dinner. The colour was draining from Alice's face now, and she began clearing her throat as if she had something stuck there. Father wanted to know if she was okay and would she like some water.

'Oh for goodness sake, if you're feeling sick, Alice, leave the table,' Mother snapped. 'You're ruining everyone's dinner. You are making us all lose our appetites.'

As Mother spoke, I saw she had taken up her own knife and fork.

She was grasping them about their middles as if they were weapons, and then suddenly she threw them tetchily a little way from her, across the table. Her fork struck a serving dish full of vegetables, and her knife clanged against the metal gravy boat. Alice rose slowly from her chair. She looked bewildered, unsure if she should go or stay. Father smiled kindly at her and told her to stay put. Mother looked livid. Jillian slid malevolent eyes towards her sister, but her head remained motionless. Staying calm amidst the storm, Harry was moving his fork imperceptibly to snag Alice's slice of meat, all his concentration focused then on edging it towards the centre of his plate. At last Alice moved away from her chair and backed out of the room, bumping into the dining-room door once, before turning, opening it and disappearing through it.

'Come back as soon as you feel better,' Father called after her.

Alice closed the door with infinite care, as if terrified she would disturb a sleeping baby. After Alice's departure, I had thought things would improve, and was just tucking into a succulent morsel of red meat when father placed two fat roast onions on Jillian's plate. Now, if it was a fact known to one and all in our family that Jillian and Alice preferred outside cuts of meat, it was also virtually printed on Jillian's birth certificate that she hated onions, that no earthly force could induce her to swallow what she described as a single slimy mouthful of them, that even God would have his work cut out if he wished Jillian to polish one off, let alone two. Jillian eyes were riveted on the onions. Mother made a squeaking noise. Harry jumped, and then started mashing up a roast potato with admirable intensity. Father sat back in his chair, and with immense care loaded tiny portions of meat, potato, vegetables and onion onto his fork, patting the whole into a small, sausage shape with his knife, inspecting it for a second, popping it into his mouth, and chewing energetically before washing it down with a glug of red wine. Mother had more than a glug, polishing off nearly her entire glassful. The appearance and following inquiry from one of the amahs as to whether she should clear away, and were we ready for dessert, was met with sour faces, and she quickly scurried off again.

'I will not eat an onion,' announced Jillian in a voice of reinforced steel.

This was ignored by Father who made a great drama of having forgotten to say grace, something he hardly ever remembered anyway. He bowed his head piously.

'Dear God, we thank you for your bounty, for the food on our plates, for the meat, the roast potatoes, the gravy, the vegetables and the onions—' Father broke off.

He opened one eye. It rotated, taking in Jillian's raised head, her own eyes held wide open, flashing with defiance, and her folded arms. I ensured Father observed my willing participation in the rare ritual by making quite a drama of unclasping and re-clasping my hands. The fingers of Harry's hands were plaited together as well. His eyelids fluttered as he snatched sneaky peeks at his food, clearly distressed that the serious business of eating was being held in abeyance for the present. Mother's head drooped, but I had my doubts that she was lost in prayer.

'Why were you not praying, Jillian?' Father demanded, when at last grace was over.

'I am not thankful,' Jillian retorted. 'I don't want to be a hypocrite.'

Mother refilled her glass, and took several gulps in quick succession.

'I am just going to have a quick word with them in the kitchen,' she said gaily, her eyes a little too bright, her cheeks inflamed. She rose unsteadily to her feet. 'These servants need their hands held if they are going to produce a meal that is half decent you know.' She gave a shout of raucous laughter. No one seemed to share her hilarity. 'You will sit there until you eat those onions,' Father decreed to Jillian.

Mother scratched the palm of one hand with the fingers of the other, a nervous habit of hers I'd observed countless times, then made a dive for the kitchen door and was gone. To her credit Jillian slowly ate up everything on her plate . . . except the onions. Mother reappeared carrying another bottle of wine, hugging it to her under one arm. The remainder of the meal played out in silence, but for the 'pop' of the cork. One by one we were excused from the table, all but Jillian. At four o' clock Jillian was still sitting at the dining-room table, together with her two onions. By now I thought they looked a little dried out. Hovering in the hall, I shot her a sympathetic look through the open dining-room door, which she acknowledged with a flicker of her eyes. Father strode up and down the long corridor seething. Why, he demanded, couldn't Jillian just eat her onions? They were good onions. They had cost money, money that he worked very hard to make. Perhaps Jillian would like to go out, work hard and make money, so that other people could waste the onions she had bought, he thundered.

Alice was nowhere to be seen. Harry was out on his bike. Mother had passed out on her bed, snoring intermittently. And I was watching the *Flintstones* in the lounge, and feeling levels of anxiety uncommon to me, occasionally dashing out to check on Jillian. I would have scoffed the onions up myself if I could have reached them, but sadly Father was still patrolling the No Man's Land of the corridor, beady eyes scanning the hall. Finally, when the tension had reached a pitch that was unbearable, Father marched Jillian and her plate of onions to her bedroom, and said she was to stay there until she had eaten them. He slammed the door and stood vigil outside. At this point something must have exploded in Jillian, because she chose to take the two onions and fling them out of her window. Although I didn't actually see her do it, I certainly witnessed the aftermath. The onions must have gathered momentum as they fell. Beneath Jillian's bedroom window was the much-prized garden of the Everard family, attached to their ground-floor flat. Mr Everard was gardening that afternoon when the onions came hurtling down from above, he told Father later, decapitating several of his prize orchids in the process. He stood on our doorstep, the crushed pink flowers in one hand, the beige mess of onion pulp in the other. I had heard the front door and was peeping out of the lounge.

'Really, Ralph, this is too bad.' Mr Everard looked deeply offended. 'This is not what you expect from your neighbours when you settle down for a pleasant afternoon of gardening.' Mr Everard very nearly wiped his perspiring brow, but then he caught sight of the squashed onions nestled on his open palm. Mr Everard had a bald patch over which he arranged his nut-brown hair, disguising it carefully. Now his hair was all mussed up and a shiny pink patch of scalp exposed. 'Luckily I just happened to look upwards and I saw them. I saw them come flying out of a window from your flat, Ralph. I leapt out of the way just in time. Imagine that! You simply do not expect onions to start raining on your head on a fine afternoon. I could have been hurt, Ralph, seriously hurt, not to mention the damage done to my orchids.'

I nearly burst out laughing when Mr Everard said this. I imagined Mrs Everard wailing to Mother that her husband had been minding his own business, when he had been flattened by two onions and rushed to Queen Mary's Hospital.

'I'm sorry, Peter,' Father said, wisely in my opinion opting for brevity.

Mr Everard looked down dejectedly, first at his flowers, then at the onion mush. Mother appeared, walking blearily up to the front door.

'Hello, Peter,' she greeted our neighbour, her words just a touch thick and sticky. 'To what do we owe this unexpected pleasure?' She smiled graciously, dipping her head. Her bun had come undone and her plait was beginning to unravel. Her hands went automatically to her hair and deftly she pinned it up again.

'I was gardening, Myrtle, when two onions landed in my garden, just inches from my head,' Mr Everard said without preamble, his tone piqued. A drip of sweat made its way slowly down the side of his face. It trembled on his lower jaw before falling.

'Really!' exclaimed Mother, not batting an eyelid. 'How dreadful for you, Peter. You must have been very shocked.' Father looked as if he had been winded. He caved in slightly, and I saw that his cheeks were suddenly glowing. 'I do hope you weren't hurt?' Mother asked solicitously.

'Luckily no, Myrtle. But I might well have been,' Mr Everard reported peevishly, while Mother gave her appearance a quick once-over in the hallway mirror.

'Well, thank goodness for that,' Mother declared fervently, her expression one of immense relief. She snatched a little look heavenwards, as if touching base with God, and expressing her personal thanks to him for looking after her people. As her gaze left the celestial sphere, and returned to the tarnished world of mortals, she became aware of Mr Everard's hands, held aloft and brimming with onion paste and petals.

'Peter, won't you join us for a drink?' she invited smoothly. 'It's a wee bit early I know, but after all it is a weekend, and you've had a terrible scare.' She gave her most beguiling smile and winked at Mr Everard. Mr Everard hesitated. 'Ralph, tell Peter I shall be desolate if he doesn't join us.'

My father, lost for a moment in Mother's consummate performance, roused himself and reiterated her invitation. Mr Everard wavered a second longer and then gave in. The day was won.

'Do let me show you to the bathroom, Peter, to wash your hands,' Mother said, leading the way, Mr Everard, now fully tamed, trotting after her. 'Ralph, be a dear, and fix the drinks.' She paused and waited for Mr Everard to come alongside. 'Don't tell me, Peter . . . let me see, if my memory serves me right your poison is G and T, ice no lemon.' Mr Everard was duly flattered. 'When friends are important to me, I make a point of remembering these things, Peter,' she breathed. Then, as I watched, she tucked her arm through Mr Everard's, careful to avoid contact with the squashed onion, and they ambled down the corridor towards the bathroom. Pausing outside the door Mother leant in to him, and whispered in achingly manicured tones, 'This is such an unlooked for pleasure, Peter.' She was magnificent.

Father never spoke of the matter again. And the next time Jillian returned to England, I went with her.

Harry – 1966

Mr Beecham carried me in his arms, holding me like a baby. Although I felt woozy and my eyes kept closing, there were little flashes that I recall, like going to see a play and not watching it all the way through. That's it, each time they opened I found myself in different scenes.

In the beginning there were his curls, the grey of the clouds moments before the rain comes, and the tips of his upper teeth, tinged with a yellowy-brown, digging into his lower lip, and the specks of sweat breaking out on his large nose. I could feel him panting as well, with the effort, feel his lungs pushing against the weight of me. And the jolt, jolt, jolt, of my body held in his arms as he went down the steps, the several flights of them that ran from the playing field to the school building. But mostly I remember his eyes flicking down at me and what was in them. You see, it was fear, I'd recognise it anywhere. We were old friends. Then, in the middle, there were the blocks of blue sky that seemed to go on and on, and the glitter of the sun making my head throb and my skin prickle. And lastly there was the medical room, and me being laid down so carefully on the bed, how firm it was, how solid. You knew, just knew, that bed wasn't going to let you down. It was cool in there after the scalding sun, and quiet too. Like walking into the St John's Cathedral on a hot morning.

'Harry? Harry? It's Mr Beecham. You're going to be fine, Harry. You've had an accident but you're going to be fine.' Mr Beecham's the deputy head. He takes me for English. He's kind, doesn't make me feel stupid when I can't answer the questions, the way some of the teachers do. He smoothed my brow as he talked. I could feel his fingers tickling back my damp hair, smell the faint trace of tobacco that clung to them.

And the way he said it, I knew it was true. I was going to be fine. Then he said the doctor was coming and that was alright too. He said the doctor would make it all better, make me well again. I wanted to believe him, that someone, anyone, really had the power to do that. To make it all better. Only when he told me my mother would be here soon, I laughed. Of course it was in my head. I couldn't let it out. It would have hurt too much with my head pounding so hard. Besides, that would have been telling on Mother, on *them*. I'd never do that, not even if I was dying.

You know what I thought then, in that cool, still room, where other faces were appearing now, like masks hung on the white walls. I thought that if I was really lucky it might be true. I might be dying and then it would be over. I wondered if Alice would come and join the other masks, but then I remembered that she'd had an upset tummy that morning and stayed home. Sometimes my sister Alice doesn't eat for ages. Mother says that's why she gets stomachache so much. Mother said she does it to get attention, starving herself. But I'm not so sure. Still, imagine being able to go without food for an entire day. Amazing!

'Fatty! Fatty! Blubber boy! Harry is a blubber boy! Nah, nah, sweaty Harry! Nah, nah, smelly Harry!'

It was Keith, Bobby and Andrew that morning. Following me around the playing field. They're like the wasps you get on picnics that just won't go away. Every few seconds one of them would dash forwards and push me, or try to grab the roll of fat that shows when my shirt rides up, or they'd run ahead of me, spin round and poke me in the tummy. It isn't so bad. It doesn't really hurt. Sometimes I even like it, because . . . well . . . because it makes me feel alive, the pain. Anyway, they usually get bored after a while and go away. I can read the signs, clear as the time on a wristwatch. The jeering is loud

51

as can be to start with, like a football flying in the air and everyone screaming cos they think it's gonna be a goal. Then, after a bit, their voices start to drop, as if they know this next shot is going to miss. I name it 'the game-over slump', wait for it, cos I know it will come, eventually. After that, with a few more feeble taunts, they slouch off.

Nah, I don't mind them really, the boys. It's the girls that make me go burning red, and want to cry so bad that it takes everything I have to hold it in. They never touch me. They don't have to. Their bright eyes slide over me, over my pockets of fat, over my thick arms, my wobbly tummy, my plump legs, my big bottom. Then they snatch little sneaky glances at one another and smirk. It's like a knife going in, that shared smirk.

I used to imagine it you know, a knife sliding into a slab of my flesh. I used to watch Ah Dang in the kitchen slicing the fat off some huge piece of dripping, bloody meat, and I used to dream that someone could do that for me. Lie me down on a chopping board and trim the oily fat off me, slash, saw, slash. And then I'd get up all slim and lean, and I'd have muscles, and one of those bellies that was hard and dipped in like the other boys'. Then, when we changed for PE, and I pulled on those bright green shorts, shrugged on that white cotton T-shirt, no one would giggle. They'd say stuff like, 'Hey Harry, want to be in our team?' or 'What about being our goalie today,' or 'We're sure to win cos Harry's batting for our side, so there!' Sometimes they'd row over me. They would. In my head, they'd squabble and say, 'It's not fair, you had him last week. This week it's our turn with Harry.' Instead of me standing alone in the playground cos no one wants to pick me, with them all rushing to get into pairs, into groups, into teams, just in case they get landed with the fat pig, Harry Safford. And then I'm paired up with the teacher, who makes it worse by pretending to be really pleased about it. You know, 'Lucky me, I get to be with Harry.' Oh yeah, sure! Nobody wants me. It's as if I stank or something. Ah, who knows, maybe I do.

Anyway, it was after the boys got bored and left that the accident happened. There was this roller thing in a corner of the field. I think they use it to flatten the grass. There was no one over there, and it looked kind of peaceful. The roller was all gritty-brown and grey, flecked with pearly-white too, like slithers of soap shining in the sunlight. Attached to it was a thick black handle, balanced up against the playground's surrounding wire-mesh fence. Round about were tufts of tall green and yellow grass, like it hadn't been moved for ages. So I wandered over. It was more impressive close up, bigger somehow, sturdier. I touched the handle. Ran a finger along the uneven surface. It was metal, iron I think. Then, for a while I just circled the roller, not all the way round cos of the fence you understand, but nearly, and then back again. It looked so heavy, like you'd need a giant or something to shift it. After a bit I sat down on it and stared out at the kids in the field, all playing their games, skipping and chucking tennis balls about, shrieking and laughing too, like they were having a really good time. And the girls' hair was flying all about, brown and black and blonde, and their white socks were glinting in the sun.

The roller felt very warm under my backside, through my grey flannel shorts. Not so hot you couldn't stand it, just kind of comforting. The flesh of my thighs spread out against it, like a cushion. I squinted up at the sun, right at it, something Mother says you should never do. 'Because if you do, you'll go blind, Harry', she liked to sing at me. But I didn't care. Then there were dark spots rushing at me and I was so dizzy. It was the way you get when you spin round and round with your arms stretched wide, and you have to throw yourself down on the grass, and the world just carries on spinning, tilting under you. That's when I decided to do it, stand right up on that roller, plant my feet squarely on the warm curve of it, and see how things looked then. I know it's daft, but I wondered if it might be different up there. Perhaps I'd pick out something I'd never seen before, and seeing it would change everything.

I hauled myself up on the hot hump of stone. It was quite difficult actually, higher than you might think. I had a few attempts before I managed it. At first my back was to the playing field, and I was balancing with my arms out. It was great. Just like I'd imagined it would be. Only I couldn't see the field, just through the wire fence

53

and across the slope of road. I glanced back over my shoulder. I couldn't help it, cos I wanted to see if any of the girls were watching me. Especially June Mullery. She is so pretty, June, with pale, yellow hair and soft eyes. She never teases me, and once I was sure she smiled at me. At least I think it was me. I suppose it might have been her friends behind me, but anyhow it felt as if it was for me. Her face lighting up and her eyes so sweet and kind. It made it hard for me to swallow, seeing her smile like that . . . At me.

So I tried to turn round but something blinded me, something like a bit of the sun glaring at me from the field. I lost my footing, and I was falling, falling back, and without thinking I made a grab for the iron handle propped up against the fence. Only it just fell away with me, like seizing a stick of bamboo in a landslide. I tumbled backwards on the field, and the metal bar chased me, the way the jeering boys had earlier. The long horizontal handle at the top of it, the thing they grip to push it about with I guess, came crashing down across the brow of my head. Then it was pitch black, with the sound of the bar striking me, tolling inside my skull, a great under-water bell clanging on and on. When my eyes opened next Mr Beecham was carrying me down the steps.

I didn't die. The doctor came and went. Mother took me to Queen Mary's for X-rays and that was quite fun. And the doctors there said I was going to be okay as well. That's when the laugh came back.

'You're not very good doctors then, are you?' came the cheeky voice I hear sometimes in my head, the voice that longs to speak out loud, but I know never will.

We're back at the flat now. Mother's fussing loads and kissing me, so that I have red marks from her lipstick on my face, and have to rub hard to get them off. I can smell her perfume as well and that's nice, warm and comforting, like the roller before it flattened me. Then later she smells of something else, something sour, the whisky I guess, and that isn't so nice, because then she gets a bit sloppy. She looks good. If anyone was watching they'd say, 'There's an excellent mother, a mother who really loves her son. The way she strokes and pets him! Oh my, and can you hear the lovely things she says to him.' But what they wouldn't know is that it's not real. It's pretend. Like acting. And you know before long the performance will be over, or the show will be cancelled because the actress doesn't feel very well, and has to go and lie down.

As it happens Mother does have to lie down after a bit. Dad is away, or working late or something. 'Course Mum said she rang him straight away. She said he was terribly worried, but very relieved later to hear his only son was going to be fine. She's always calling me that. 'Only son!' As if that makes such a big difference to how much I'm worth to them. Like, if there were more sons, if say Alice had been a boy, they couldn't possibly have loved me as much. Who knows, if she had been, perhaps they wouldn't have had me at all?

'Harry, you have to know your father would have raced home if it had been serious,' Mother says, staring straight into my face and looking all grave.

And I understand what she means. That if I'd been going to die or if I had died even, he'd have come; my father would have come then, no question.

'He was frantic, Harry,' she tells me, her finger stroking the side of her glass. 'You know how much he loves you. He wanted to come, darling, of course he did. He's so busy. Important, clever men like your father always are. But I told him you were being a brave little man, *our* brave little man, and that there was no need.'

She puts down her drink, then gives me one of those funny hugs of hers, a bit awkward, as if she doesn't quite know where to put me. It lasts longer than normal of course, on account of the accident. By then she's on her second drink. Afterwards she holds me at arm's length.

'I'm so proud of you,' she tells me smoothing back my hair, careful not to touch the raised purple line, where the bar struck me. 'My precious only boy.'

'If it had been really bad, you're sure Father would have come?' I want to know. I can't meet her eyes. I might cry if I did, like with the girls at school, might make a big baby of myself. Hmm . . .

55

Mother would hate that. She doesn't like you to show feelings, not real ones in any case.

'Of course he would have, darling!' she says now, her eyes, that glow amber like a cat's sometimes, wide open. 'You know he would have, Harry.'

I want to say that it might have been too late, if I was dying or worse, already dead. If he'd come then, after I'd died, after my heart had stopped beating and I was all white and icy, well . . . there really wouldn't have been much point, would there? But Mother has turned away by then and the drink is in her hands again. We've had supper but that doesn't matter. I'm still hungry. I'm always hungry.

They've got this creepy festival here – actually they've got lots of weird festivals on the island, but this one is the spookiest. Yue Lan. The Festival of the Hungry Ghosts. It's the end of May now, so I guess it'll soon come round. Anyway, for a few weeks in July the Chinese believe that hungry ghosts, the ghosts of their dead ancestors, and people who've been murdered, or died at sea, or in a war and haven't had a funeral or been buried properly, will come tearing back to earth. And these ghosts who swarm back down here at Yue Lan, they're are not just hungry, they're starving, ravenous even. All the stuff they didn't get in life, like marriage and children and love, and all the money and food and houses and cars, and junk like that, for these few days you see they've just got to have them. You know, like nothing will stand in their way.

Sometimes at night, lying in bed watching the orange stripes of light slide across the ceiling as a car drives by on the road below, I picture them, the hungry ghosts. It's bit like the stampedes you get in cowboy movies, the image in my mind. Hordes of ghosts charging towards you, the air thick with the dust their trailing misty feet are stirring up, and their mouths gaping wide open, like the mouths of caves. Gigantic, black, frozen, empty caves, with those gleaming icicle things hanging down and reaching up at the opening, rows of razor-sharp teeth, waiting to gobble you up, to gulp down your blood. They save your still beating heart for last, a special treat. Then crunch up your bones until all that's left are a few splinters.

56

I expect they'd be delighted to find me, Piggy Harry, oink, oink; that I'd make a really tasty meal, keep them going, well . . . for a bit anyway. I see their eyes in my nightmares sometimes, like balls of fire, and the whites of them showing, only they're a dirty green colour, rolling about and all wild and scary in their smoky heads. I understand their hunger, like there's a living thing eating away at them, like they have to feed it, have to! Cos I feel it too, feel I can never cram in enough, that no matter how much I stuff into my mouth, chew and swallow and chomp and gnaw, it'll never stop the hunger, it'll never fill up the hole.

The Chinese do some neat stuff to frighten them away though: they make these brilliant paper models, like three-dimensional kites of all those things you need in life. Then they pile them on huge bonfires and burn them to ashes. They say you have to be careful for a whole month, but that the days in the middle are the most dangerous. They steer clear of the sea as well, stay indoors, and get the kids home early, in case the ghosts jump out and get them. Beaches are especially dangerous over Yue Lan. The spirits lurk everywhere, in the curl of a breaking wave, and in the currents that pull swimmers out of their depth, and in whirlpools that swallow up boats. They leave them food and pray, and burn joss sticks, but as far as I can tell they do that all the time anyway. Those joss sticks really smell if you ask me. Make my eyes water. As if that would satisfy them, with the kind of hunger they've got growling in their tummies. It wouldn't satisfy me, that's definite.

Mother is miles away now, on the phone to Beth next door, making her voice all dramatic, the way she does, describing what happened to me. She's talking about me but . . . well . . . the crazy thing is I feel left out, like I'm not really part of her story, that it's another 'only son'. I mooch into the kitchen and tell Ah Dang I'm hungry, and can she fix me something. She likes that. Makes her feel all needed. She always grins and wags her head, as if she understands the appetite I've got, what a beast it is, and her gold teeth glitter sort of magically.

While she's getting a plate together, Alice comes in. Up till then

57

Mum's kept her away. She's always trying to do that, keep Alice and me separate. You'd think Alice was some kind of snake full of poison. And it's true, my sister goes into these fits sometimes, yowling and moaning, and you do tend to feel a bit jumpy about her, cos you don't know what's gonna come next. But I get it. I know where all that noise comes from, all that rage. I'm jealous of Alice cos I want to scream too, scream until they all cover their ears, and screw themselves up. But I can't. I just can't.

'How are you feeling?' Alice asks then, and she smiles in that shy way she has.

'Oh not too bad,' I mumble, glancing back at her. I don't think Ah Dang put very much butter in my sandwich and it's bothering me.

'Ah Dang can I have some more butter please?' I ask. I'd like to talk to Alice, but if I take my eyes off Ah Dang, even for a moment, who knows what she might skimp on?

'*Ai ya, ai ya!*' mutters Ah Dang, peeling back the top of the sandwich and starting again. She isn't really angry. She fakes it. She tosses her head, making her plait whisk all over the place, and her hands fly about, and she gabbles in Cantonese, but you can tell. In her eyes she's still smiling.

'That's some bruise you're going to have, Harry,' Alice says.

I guess she must have seen it when I turned round. Ah Lee appears then through the back door. She sees all the food out, and me looking worried, and Ah Dang slamming things about. And she gives one of her silly hysterical giggles.

'*Ai yah! Ai yah!*' she echoes Ah Dang, and pinches my bare arm. '*Fei zhai! Fei zhai!*' she squeals, and she's off again.

I know what she said. Fat boy. I hear it lots. The Chinese can't resist my chubby arms. Can't stop themselves from pinching me. Even strangers. Pinching me and grinning, '*Fei zhai, fei zhai*'. I might as well be back at school. You know what it makes me think of. The story of Hansel and Gretel. When the witch locks Hansel up in a cage and every day she brings him lots of food, because you see she's fattening him up. Fattening him up for the day of slaughter, when

58

she's going to kill him and chop him up, and pop him into her huge cauldron, and cook him over her roaring fire till he's all tender and delicious. I like closing my eyes and imagining the witch's cottage, imagining being with Gretel, deep in the heart of the dark forest, then suddenly the two of us coming upon it. I think about how hungry we'd both be, our bellies rumbling, hungry and tired, with nothing to eat but dandelions and grass. Then we'd step into this clearing and together we'd gasp.

My cottage isn't made of gingerbread though, because I don't really like it. It's built of cake bricks, chocolate, and plain sponge flavoured at least six different ways, toffee and orange, and lemon and mint, and strawberry and coffee. And the bricks are cemented together with butter icing, and jam and cream. The windows are huge glacier-mint squares framed with marzipan. The front door is made entirely of caramel, and the doorknob is a shiny ball of liquorice. As for the roof, it's tiled in thick slabs of chocolate, milk and dark and white. There's even meringue smoke coming out of a butter-scotch chimney. The biggest problem we have is where to start. I run up to it and take the most enormous bite off a corner brick of rich, moist chocolate. Gretel, she walks nervously up to the door and starts licking it, as if it's a ginormous lollipop. In my version we've virtually polished off the entire building before the witch appears; there's only a few spadefuls of cake crumb rubble, and some broken chocolate tiles left. While Gretel and I are clutching our stuffed stomachs, the witch throws back a hatch in the floor, made, incidentally, of royal icing, and pounces.

'*Fei zhai, fei zhai*,' squeaks Ah Lee again. Pinch, pinch.

And I want to ask, in that voice inside me that never speaks up, 'Am I ready now, Ah Lee? Am I ready for the pot? Is my flesh plump and juicy enough yet? Are you sharpening your knives ready to slice me up? But I don't of course. I glance at Alice. In the story Gretel saved her brother, made him hold out a twig to the short-sighted, croaky, old witch instead of his finger, so when she pinched it she thought he was still all thin and stringy. Still, that's a story isn't it? Not real life. Not like it is here in the flat on The Peak, where none of us can do anything to put off what's coming. I think Ah Lee's finished her pinching now. She's wiping down the sink.

'Hmph!' I grunt. Ah Dang's only put one slice of ham in my sandwich and barely any cheese at all. At this rate I'll never be ready for the pot. 'Ah Dang, I'm hungry!' I wail. I try to imagine what a hungry ghost would sound like. 'I'm really, really hungry! HUNGRY! There's not enough filling in my sandwich, Ah Dang.'

Then Ah Dang's cursing me in Chinese and pounding her drum tummy, and picking up the butter dish and hurling it back down, and going at the lump of cheddar as if she'd like to murder it. I look back at Alice and our eyes meet. And Alice gives a 'hup' of laughter, and then she claps a hand over her mouth and tries to stifle it. Well, that only makes it worse than ever, because now I'm laughing too, a great boom of a laugh that make my tummy jiggle about under my shirt, like it's alive and it wants to escape. Alice falls back against the fridge and she's helpless now, arms limp, head tipping about, and that makes me lose it completely. I shuffle over to her, and my sides are really splitting, my shirt busting at the seams, and Ah Dang's screaming and brandishing the knife with the butter on it, like she's going to stab us both. And just for a second I let my throbbing head rest on Alice's shoulder, and the peals of laughter rock from her into me and back again. It's good, so very good laughing like that with my sister Alice that I want to sob.

Ghost – 1967

I watch many children come and go before Alice arrives. I observe them through the grid of an air-vent set high into the wall of the morgue. Their heads are dull and ordinary, and I know they cannot sustain me. True, I am curious. But when Alice comes I am spellbound. She appears one afternoon when all the other children have gone, and lies back on a patch of scrubby grass. She is a slip of a thing, pale as a creaming wave, her long hair always moving, her eyes moons of contemplation. It does not seem to worry her that the building above her is growing silent, that soon she will be alone. For a bit she stares up at the sky, follows the occasional fleecy cloud. Then she rolls over and sits up. As she does so, the golden-haired boy in the shadows fades away, as if he had never been.

Suddenly she notices the yawning mouth of the morgue, for the door is partly ajar. I cannot tell how long her eyes are trained on it, but the shadows are lengthening when at last she climbs to her feet. She walks straight to the entrance and shoulders open the rusty-hinged door. It shudders and grumbles and sticks a bit before swinging back. Alice slips through, under the nebulous mantle. She takes a few steps, and then waits for her eyes to adjust to the gloom. She inhales a long, slow breath of stale, dead air. She fixes stains on the floor with her perceptive eyes. She let her fingers linger on walls where the paint is flaking, where the bricks are impregnated with the transience of life. As she listens to echoes of the past, I slide into her and instantly feel my strength returning. I become the scum in her blood.

I garland myself with ropes of silver-stranded veins. And in the resonance of each heartbeat I know her every thought, her every memory, her every experience, her every twist and turn of emotion, often before she does, as if they are my own.

When at last she leaves, I go with her. We dawdle along Bowen Road. We wait for the Peak Tram, a funicular green cab with the cream roof to come and haul us up The Peak. We leave the terminus and stroll up a long road, past a shop called the Dairy Farm, then along a path to Alice's home. All this is new to me. The people hurrying by, their clothes, their colour too, for up here most of them are white-skinned, the cars and buses and lorries, the houses and the flats. Hers is a top-floor flat, as large as a palace. Surely, I think, several families live here. But I am wrong. There is only one. The flat is filled with beautiful things too, the kind that an emperor might own. Carvings and paintings, jade and ivory, snuff bottles and fans, books and carpets, and shelves crowded with fine porcelain. But there is no emperor, just Alice's family, the Saffords, and some servants to care for them, Ah Dang and Ah Lee. When I was alive there was only my father to care for me. And even then, as far back as I can recall, it had really been my job to look after him. Like me, Alice has a father, Ralph, but unlike me she has a mother too, Myrtle. And Alice has a younger brother, Harry, and a small dog she calls Bear. Alice has two sisters as well, who are being educated in England. It seems strange to me that, with so many people about, Alice should be lonely. But she is. I feel it. Still, it is lucky, because it means that she will probably welcome my company.

Together we decide that we do not like attending classes in the school that has been set up in my old army hospital. This is not because I believe education has no worth. My father was a wonderful storyteller and valued learning above all things. When we returned from a night's fishing I would lie down, the rising sun warming the deck under me, and he'd sit beside me. He'd puff on his clay pipe and after a bit the stories would come. He taught me to read and write too, and together we delighted in the words of the great poets and philosophers.

But the smell of death emanating from the morgue has started to make me fret. No, it is life that beckons to me now. I find myself wondering if the novelty of being alive again, albeit through the medium of Alice, will ever wear off. Somehow, I doubt it. So we abandon dusty studies in favour of exploration. We have to be careful where we go, for there is trouble on the island. The tense atmosphere reminds me of the weeks leading up to the outbreak of war. I overhear Alice's father saying that some of the Chinese people are unhappy about working conditions, and that they believe the British are taking advantage of them. Some days there are riots, people shouting slogans and fighting, even bombs exploding and causing dreadful injuries. It seems strange though that this time the enemy is not the Japanese, but the British.

Despite these disturbances, Alice and I do not curtail our outings. We visit the Tiger Balm Gardens, or we take a ferry to one of the outer islands, or we walk the length of Shek O Beach, or Silvermine Bay, kicking up the sand, or we catch a bus to Aberdeen and watch the boat people, my people, for a while. This last stirs up memories of Lin Shui for me. Sometimes I am certain I spot my father, scrambling about the rigging of one of the great junks, the rust-brown sails flapping and rippling under him, his long, silver hair swept up into a bun and skewered with a netting needle, as was his habit. Sometimes I see a young girl, just like me, her life shrunk to the wooden decks that enfold her, her days spent riding the waves, mending nets, patching sails, cooking, washing pots and pans, and doing her family's laundry. And I wonder if she realises how fine this life of hers is, if she values it as she ought. Sometimes too, I see the shadows of my ancestors and I know they are lying in wait for me.

Of course there are some advantages to being 'undead', for example I no longer feel hunger. I share with Alice what it is to need neither food nor drink. She joins me, fasting for long periods, till her head is light as a feather, and she trips about as if she is stepping onto clouds. When she grows dizzy and black shapes detonate before her eyes, I have to remind myself that Alice is only human and must eat to live. I prompt her then to feed, reminding myself that I am leasing her body. But while Alice fasts, her brother Harry feasts until none of his clothes fit him.

The flat on the Peak is emptier than I thought it would be, reminding me sometimes of the morgue. Alice's father is rarely at home, working constantly. Alice's mother, though sometimes in the same room, feels far away. I am envious of Alice having not one but two sisters. But I find even this, when they return home for the holidays, is not as I imagined it. Late one night we chance upon Jillian in the kitchen. She is surrounded by tins and packets and jars. She is stuffing food into her mouth, slices of bread slathered in chocolate spread and jam and peanut butter, cramming in biscuits and cakes and crisps and chocolate. In between mouthfuls she is gulping juice and milk, and brightly coloured drinks that bubble and fizz, as if infused with life force. I amuse myself by causing one of the tube lights in the kitchen to flash for a time. Jillian barely glances up. Instead, as it flickers, Alice's oldest sister looks as if she is jerking about like a gluttonous puppet, her blonde hair flying. Alice is po-faced, but I think it is very funny.

All the while, fearless nocturnal cockroaches scuttle about. Emerging from the drains they feast on smears and crumbs. Most are on the floor, though a few, braver than the rest, scrabble around on the work surfaces. Their antennae swivel. They are well fed these cockroaches, the size of Hong Kong dollars. Their beetle-brown bodies gleam in the glow cast by the fluorescent tubes. Fine hairs sprout from their busy, spindly legs. The wings of one that is trying to clamber up the slippery sides of a glass whirr madly. It lumbers into the air and flies about, rebounding off cupboard doors and tiled surfaces, before landing to gobble afresh on a fast-melting square of chocolate. They look as shiny as vinyl. Alice flinches. Jillian pauses in her gorging, just long enough to bring a clenched fist down on it. We hear the 'squish' as its mushy body is crushed. Jillian glances cursorily at the base of her fist. She wipes off the stuff that looks like yellow pus on a kitchen towel, and starts guzzling again.

'What are you doing?' Alice wants to know, the juices running into her own mouth at the sight of all that food.

Startled, Jillian jumps and turns on Alice. She cannot have known we were here, watching her. 'Shut up,' she hisses, a chocolaty dribble running down her chin. 'Shut up and get out.' The face of one of the amahs appears like a ghostly apparition at the window in the back door. It is Ah Dang, her plait unravelled, the top buttons of her tunic undone. She looks first sleepy-eyed, then amazed, as if she thinks she might still be dreaming. Despite this, her face registers concern, probably at the prospect of the morning's clean-up job. Meeting Jillian's incensed glare, wisely she elects to creep away.

'You'll make yourself sick if you eat all that,' says Alice prophetically.

And that is exactly what Jillian does. When she has eaten so much that she seems barely able to walk and keep it all contained, she flicks off the kitchen light, staggers through the dining room, and down the long, dark corridor to the bathroom. We follow her and see her stumble inside, slam the door, and switch the light on. A thin, yellow stripe at the base of the door filters into the dimness. We hear Jillian lock it behind her. Then she begins to retch. For a long while she vomits and chokes. The sounds are harsh. They splinter the night. I am amazed that no one wakens at the din. Alice crouches in the murk listening to her sister disgorging herself, and her mother snoring. A few times Bear approaches her, but then he senses my presence and slinks away again, hackles high. Several of the corridor windows are open, and a welcome breeze is cooling the flat. The cicadas trill. Their song rhythmically swells and then subsides. The taps snort out water. The toilet flushes. Then silence. The cicadas too are momentarily still, as if in anticipation. The bathroom door slams open, hitting the wall with a resounding 'thwack'. A square of light falls into the darkness, with the silhouette of Jillian squinting at its centre. She is not wearing her glasses.

'Bitch,' she fires into the corridor. She stinks of bile. She wipes the back of a hand over her mouth, gives a brittle laugh and flicks off the light. The darkness springs back. I remember what it is to be starving, the acid ache of it. I remember not knowing if I would eat again. I remember that food haunted my dreams, that it had the power to bewitch me. Jillian feels her way like a blind man past Harry's bedroom to her own, goes in, the door thumping shut behind her. Still Alice huddles in the blackness. Bear growls softly. Some time later, after several unsuccessful attempts, a key turns in a lock and scratches the dark. The front door swings open. Nicola appears with a boy in tow, silhouettes in the lobby light. Entwined they fall back against the front door, closing it with their bodies. They tumble onto the Persian rug in the shadowy hall. There is a lot of grunting and struggling. Clothes are tossed aside. White bits swim into sight. Buttocks, an erect penis, a breast, an upright V of splayed legs. They are made luminous in the moonlight, these infrequently seen body parts. The dog watches cocking his head in puzzlement.

'For Christ's sake stop fucking about and put it in,' snarls Nicola. The tone of her voice is bored and irritable. There is a bit of adjustment, then a good deal of rocking and panting, followed by a breathy cry. A few seconds pass. 'Get off me, Mick. I think I'm going to be sick,' groans Nicola. The boy, Mick, leaps up obediently. He begins tugging on his jeans. Nicola is slower to get up. She pulls on her pants and smoothes down her skirt. 'I'm tired, so can you just fuck off now,' she says opening the front door, unceremoniously showing the boy out, and shutting it firmly behind him. Without bothering to put on the lights she weaves her way down the corridor, never noticing Alice hugging the blackness to her. She vanishes straight into the room she shares with Jillian.

Alice's mother, Myrtle, is on next. Her bedroom door opens slowly, and for a few seconds she stands swaying in the doorway. Then she steps gingerly into the stream of moonlight. She is wearing a pale dressing gown. There is a metallic sheen to it. Her hair is loose, falling about her shoulders. Her gait is unsteady. She finds her way to the bamboo-clad bar in the hall. She also seems to want invisibility, and does not bother with the lights. She fumbles with the sliding door of the bar, grabs a bottle, unscrews the top and takes a greedy gulp. With it clutched to her chest, she treads with the care of a tightrope walker back to her bedroom, and quietly closes the door.

'While my father is away,' whispers Alice, whose father is on a business trip in Singapore, 'the mice come out to play.'

Later Alice drags some pillows and blankets into the corridor, and nestles by a bookcase that borders one of the walls. She cannot see the titles in the half-light, but she touches the hard spines of the books, and follows the contours of the lettering printed on their covers with an index finger. Much later, when I levitate out of Alice to glide along the ceiling, until I am floating just above the drinks cabinet, Bear cautiously nears my host. He sniffs her bedding warily, until he is satisfied it holds no trace of me. Then he nudges his way into the makeshift bed. Not satisfied with his proximity to Alice, he nuzzles at the bent arm at her side. Alice, half asleep, starts, her eyes springing open. Then in a wave of recognition she enwraps Bear, her dog, and draws him close to her. At length they sleep, Alice dropping off first, Bear rolling his eyes upwards and baring his teeth at me once, and then again, before finally settling down. I peer at them with bafflement at first, and then with something very like resentment. Alice's face is calm, like still water. Her arm rises and falls gently as the dog's lungs fill and deflate. Soon their rhythmic breaths interlock, fitting together like pieces of a puzzle, and their two hearts fall to beating in unison. I am covetous of their shared warmth, their joint slumber. Seeing their bodies spooned together makes me recall the taste of the Chinese speciality, Bitter Melon.

On the bar is a cut-glass decanter. Dipped in moonshine, the diamond panes glint like silver sequins. Although the decanter looks heavy, I am positive I can shift it. I condense myself and slither between it and the smooth, plastic surface of the bar. I radiate heat, drawing it from Alice, from the dog, from the air, and concentrating it, as you might do with a glass concentrating the energy of the sun to make fire. I distil the moisture of the night, sucking it up from the dew-soaked air. Soon the plastic is wet and slippery. I feel the decanter move then, just an inch or so. After that it is easy, one inch more and more and more. Now nearly half of the crystal sphere hangs over the edge of the bar. The liquid inside it sloshes and slops, a storm in a bottle. I draw every drop of it into the unsupported half of the glittering bulge. The bottle vibrates a moment. Then it arcs and plummets, splitting into pieces against the wooden floor with a heavy crash. The liquid bursts, liberated briefly before it pools. The dog snarls. Alice shifts drowsily. I hear a whimper coming from one of the bedrooms. I think it may be Harry. Then the hush slowly unfurls again.

In the morning though it is anything but quiet. A shaft of sunlight falls on the jagged pieces of the fractured decanter. It makes a wondrous dazzlement of them. I am delighted by the eye-catching trinkets I have brought into being. Surprisingly, Alice's mother is not impressed. She shrieks at Alice. The dog scurries away, head down, tail between his legs. The amahs raise their hands to their mouths, and insist they know nothing of how the decanter came to be broken. But when Ah Lee hunkers down and begins to pick up splinters of glass, Alice's mother grabs her shoulder and gives it a little shake.

'Alice will do this,' she cries. 'She will collect up every bit of it in a bag, and when her father comes home she will show it to him.' She lets go the shoulder and swoops on Alice. 'You will tell him what you have done. Do you understand me, Alice?' Myrtle Safford's face looks flushed. It is fast becoming the colour of raw meat. Her fingers work busily at the embroidered sleeve of her blouse. She is bound to pull a thread if she persists in picking at the fine handi-work, I think.

'I did not break the decanter,' Alice says, on her feet, head held high, facing her mother. She repeats this several times.

'Do not lie to me,' Myrtle interrupts her. Her eyes look dry and sore, the lids drawing in sharply, as if the bright sunshine is hurting them.

Jillian materialises wearing one of her father's old shirts. Her apathetic flint-grey eyes scan the tableau, amahs askance, mother enraged, Alice defiant. She wags her head slowly, knowingly from side to side. 'I have a sore throat,' she grunts, her hand stroking her collarbone. She yawns expansively, steps carefully over the broken glass, pushes past the amahs, and on into the dining room. 'I need some breakfast. I'm starving,' she mutters over her shoulder.

I cannot help wondering if she will throw it all up again later on. Nicola does not make an entrance. I expect she is tired after the previous night's exertions. Harry peeps round his door, surveys the scene, and vanishes like a timorous mouse. It is plain to me that Alice is agitated. She does not seem the least bit thrilled with my achievement. She stoops and picks up a piece of glass. While her mother is shouting, she pushes the ragged point of it into the tip of a thumb. Ah Lee bursts into a fit of nervous giggles.

'*Mo lei tau!*' Ah Dang mutters.

Alice looks down and notes there is blood on her hand. Her brow creases in confusion, as if she cannot imagine how it got there.

Days later Alice's father returns home and is presented with a bag that rattles when he lifts it up. It is full of my pretties. He asks Alice to join him in the lounge. He tells her that he is not angry with her, but he needs to understand why she has broken the decanter.

'I didn't break it,' Alice insists. Her thumb still hurts, though of course it is no longer bleeding. She rubs it unconsciously.

Alice's father looks so tired. He has dark smudges under his eyes. He presses the heels of his hands into his eye sockets for a long moment. I make the chips of glass in the brown paper bag resting on his lap, chink and tinkle. Hearing them sing he drops his hands, and his weary eyes rake the room. They alight on a book, a statue, a carved lantern, a record player, a television, on the Chinese carpet that covers most of the floor, finally coming to rest once more on the crumpled, open-necked bag on his lap. He looks, I observe, as if he has just discovered that life is not what he expected it to be. He looks as if he is staring down, not at a shattered decanter in his lap, but at his own shattered dreams.

'I didn't do it,' Alice reiterates. Her little fingers are crooked now, her face clouded. I explain that I did, but only Alice hears me. Her eyes dart about the room. At last they settle on her father's drooping head. 'I'm going to be good now,' Alice says.

Ralph – 1967

My first night home this week, I've been sleeping in Central, down at the office. It could erupt at any time, with each passing day it seems we come closer to the point of no return. And what will become of us then, us few servants of Her Majesty Queen Elizabeth, holding the fort while the Apaches circle? I don't hear the approach of the cavalry. We're on our own, chaps, with only our shadows for company. Myrtle has poured me a large whisky. Don't ask me how, but I know this is a prelude to one of her talks. I am colourless with exhaustion. My wife is making yet more demands on me. At the end of this God-awful day, she wants the only thing I have left, my attention. I feel the finger of scotch stroke the back of my throat. I wonder if Myrtle realises that I may very well be a target, on some kind of a hit list, that we all might be come to that. She is talking . . . talking about our daughter, about Alice.

'She has a violent temper,' she accuses bluntly. 'She is destructive.'

I haven't the strength to contradict her. There is violence breaking out everywhere downtown. Real violence. The blood, injury and death kind of violence. The once peaceful streets of the colony blossom with exploding homemade bombs, known to locals as 'boh loh', Cantonese for pineapple. Huge banners fly high, damning the British for the pathetically low salaries of the indigenous people, for their draconian working hours, for water shortages and increasing prices. Curfews that transform the colony into a ghost town, tear-gas, even the threat that troublemakers breaking the restrictions will be shot on sight, serve only to contain the mêlée. But for how long, dear God, for how long? My neck aches and the base of my spine too. I need a hot bath, a good, long soak. There aren't any showers at the office, and I am aware of the stale odour of a couple of days' sweat coming from my armpits, my back, under my collar, between my thighs. On and on she goes, damning our ailing daughter. There is the heavy tick of the clock behind us in the lounge. We are on the veranda. It is early autumn, but still warm enough to sit outside for a short while. I used to love the tick of a clock, used to find it comforting. But now it is just a reminder that time is running out. My eyes are stinging and my eyelids are heavy. I am so shattered that I am breathless. I am sitting down, and I am gulping in oxygen as if I am running a race.

'Frankly, Ralph, I'm not at all sure the Island School is such a good idea for Alice. In the few weeks since she started there her behaviour has been worse than ever, more erratic, more . . . well . . . Peculiar. Quite honestly I feel I can't cope much longer.' Myrtle pauses to assess the effect her words are having on me. Then, judging it to be safe, with a swift, flirtatious smile, she proceeds. 'I know you may not altogether agree with me, but please Ralph, hear me out. I really do feel that the structure of boarding school might be just what she needs. Alright, I will concede that perhaps the convent wouldn't be suitable for Alice. But that doesn't rule out boarding school entirely, now does it?'

The cicadas warble. There is the distant hum of passing cars. A horn sounds a long way off. A dog barks and is echoed with an answer. From where I am sitting I can see at least three cars winding their way up the Peak, and twice that many going down, yellow cones of light sliding along the curling tape of grey road that binds the slopes. There is a double-decker bus too, chinks of warm yellow light threading through the dusk, on route to the Peak Tram terminus I expect. I wonder idly if Myrtle wants to get rid of all our children? Will she carry on until we have none left? The answer is swift, light as warm air, and just as stifling.

She will carry on until Alice is gone. I sip my scotch and watch the coloured lights of Aberdeen harbour winking busily below, and the lambent stars and moon, poised and rigid above. I am so very weary these days. And I am lonely too. It eats like a maggot into my heart, this loneliness of mine. I nod and try to look as if I am taking it all in, as my wife's voice winds around me. I frown pensively. See, my expression says, I am cogitating, entertaining your suggestion, weighing up the merits of such a course of action.

In reality I am far off. I am reliving the unrest, the coiled spring of tension that lies in wait for me with every breaking dawn. I am thinking about the riots, the faces, distorted and ugly, the gaping mouths that stamp out words, hateful, vicious words, those bent on bloodletting. I think about Central, where often I have enjoyed a coffee at the Hilton, or lunch at the Foreign Correspondents' Club. I think of the Cosmo Club too and the Christmas parties we have had there, of the raffles and the paper hats, and of the turkey and Christmas pudding, the thick, steaming gravy, and the viscous yellow custard, so absurd in this land of sun and bamboo and sea. I recall those evil drinking games that I have tumbled unwittingly into after a Cantonese meal, games that have left me legless and the world spinning. I think of my Chinese friends, these men I have grown to love, who understand me better than any Englishman ever could, these men with whom I have spent my precious hoard of free time lavishly, and never regretted a cent of it. I think about the joy I have had rummaging in the alleys, fingering treasures in dusty boxes, imagining who could have created such beauty, such perfection in a past world. I think about the Star Ferries, their dark prows knifing through the sea, how the thrill of that journey over to Kowloon has never quite evanesced for me. I think of the banks and the money rolling in, the obscene amounts of money. And then, I think of the poverty of the locals, of the workforce, the poverty that in truth I have done little to ameliorate.

Finally the image of a small, thin, naked girl, hair, face and flesh ablaze, forces everything else out of my mind. It is a photograph on the wall of the Foreign Correspondents' Club, in its multi-storey setting, high above Central. There are other pictures alongside it but they do not register. It is black and white, this image of the flaming child. The lack of colour does not lessen the horror, rather the stark contrast seems to highlight it. I think she is Vietnamese. I think it was taken during the Vietnamese war. But it really doesn't matter. It might have been anywhere. Her face is split with anguish. Her mouth is racked into an 'O' of agony. She is staring straight into the camera lens as she staggers along the muddy path. Flames lick upwards and outwards from her core, they roar through her silk-black hair, they spark her eyelashes and crackle over her eyebrows, they crust and blister the jelly of her still seeing eyeballs. She holds her hands out pityingly towards . . . who? The cameraman? The soldiers? God? I cannot free myself of this vision tonight. She haunts me this little girl as she staggers forwards, her arms full of fire, offering up all that she has, offering it up to whoever will take it, offering up her hell on earth.

My wife is speaking again. She talks of the pressure I am under in my job during these unsettled times. She maintains it is vital that I am fit for the task of subduing these red rebels, that both Queen and country are relying on me to restore order to the colony.

'You cannot afford to be distracted by Alice at times like this,' Myrtle insists. She takes a slow meditative swallow of her drink before she speaks again. 'Neither can I. How can I support you, Ralph, if I am drained dry by our daughter,' she wheedles, her voice as velvety as moss. 'And it's not just that,' she continues. 'She is putting such a strain on our relationship, darling. You must see that. We need time to ourselves, time free of endless worries and arguments about Alice. Besides, I am very concerned that her disruptive behaviour may eventually rub off on our son, on Harry.'

Now she is praising a school she has found in the Highlands of Scotland, of all places, an establishment founded on strict principles of discipline and regulation. She is describing its location as if she were selling me a holiday home. The cadence of her voice is very nearly poetic. She paints a scene of rolling heather-covered mountains crowned with garlands of mist, spotted with strutting stags, of the blue-black lochs, ice-cold liquid bodies stretched out for miles, mirrors to the scudding clouds above, of the swarms of midges, and of the banks of virgin snow. I picture Alice in this setting, and marvel that Myrtle believes a remedy can be found for our turbulent daughter so far away, as if geography is the answer.

I turn my whisky tumbler around and around in my hands. The peaty aroma I inhale seems most apt. As the marauding gangs charge through the streets of Central, their war cries a united tirade against colonial rule, my bowels loosen and my legs turn to water. Perched on high in my office I watch the Hong Kong Police, their arms linked, like playground children at their games. Red rover, red rover, let the rioters come over! A human wall barricading the road, poised for the impact that will surely come. A couple of days ago, peering though my binoculars at this brave force, this force whose job it is to repel the wrath of mighty China, I focused on the face of a boy . . . he was no more than a boy I tell you, a Chinese boy, pitting himself against the rabble, against his own people. For this I know he will earn the title of 'Yellow Running Dog', for he has sided with the 'White-Skinned Pigs', the European interlopers.

Music thunders out from loudspeakers in Central District, the volume at such a high level you can hear it in the flat on The Peak, as if it is coming from the next room. It drowns out the slogans and propaganda, being broadcast from the communist-owned buildings. People are being attacked. They are being murdered. And a Chinese boy wearing the khaki uniform of the Hong Kong Police Force stands erect, head held high, and blocks their path, while I, Ralph Safford, representative of the British government, look down from my safe offices in the sky, my bowels liquid, my heart pounding too fast, and my hands slick with sweat.

'Damned communists!' I recall saying conversationally to a colleague on one of the darkest days. I peered down at the advancing, boiling mass, at the bracelet of police standing firm. They were advancing on the Hilton Hotel. If they break through, I thought, terror jerking at my heart, perhaps they will pour up Garden Road, past St John's Cathedral, and the lower Peak Tram terminus. Then higher, why not, half of the bloodthirsty rabble peeling off up the slopes to Government

House to lynch the 24th British Governor of Hong Kong, Sir David Trench, the rest continuing their march on Victoria Peak, where they knew we lorded it over them in luxury.

'Damned Red Guards with their "Little Red Books",' I blustered, trying in vain to steady my voice. I gestured at the angry crowds beneath our windows. 'Not exactly what we Brits would call a Cultural Revolution, eh?' I managed a chuckle, but the sound was hollow. 'We simply can't have this sort of thing. After all, these fellows are making trouble on British territory,' I said, sounding like the stereotype of a stoic British officer in a bad war film. I tried to instil outrage into my voice, fury at this insult to my sovereign Queen. And I very nearly pulled it off. But the sudden slump of my colleague's shoulders made it clear I was fooling no one. About now, I thought, the film camera should pan to the skies above, buzzing with British warplanes come to put an end to this rebellious nonsense. I glanced upwards, a clear, blue sky, a disarmingly beautiful day on the island of Hong Kong. I wondered if the Chinese boy in his man's uniform was glancing up too. I wondered if he was thinking that it was a good day to die, to become a *sei chai lo*, a dead policeman, with no clouds to impede his soul's flight.

My mind slides forward in time and I am back on the veranda with my wife. I raise my glass and toss back my drink. Myrtle takes it from me. She doesn't even ask me if I would like a refill. She busies herself with the new decanter, with the ice bucket. I hear the cubes of ice clunk and rattle as they are agitated with the metal tongs. Looking down, I see a brochure Myrtle has deposited in my lap for a boarding school in Argyll. I flip through the pages. They are full of snaps of Amazonian girls with flushed cheeks doing wholesome things. I pause at a shot of one leaping in the air, arms outstretched, hands spread wide. The netball she has just shot is arcing earthwards, about to slip through the goal ring. Her thick black hair is crushed back by the wind. The expression on her face is vicious. I will mow down anyone who gets in my way, it bugles through slit eyes, ballooning cheeks, a funnelled mouth and gritted teeth. There is a malignancy about it, I decide, that I find decidedly distasteful. I toss the brochure onto the drinks table. Myrtle notes my gesture and quickly hands me my drink. She has poured me a stiff measure. If I down this too fast I shall fall asleep. My lips curl upwards longingly at the thought of slumber, of drowning in slumber.

I wonder where it will all end? I overheard talk today of the People's Republic of China seizing control of the island, taking back Hong Kong from right under our noses. Once a remote, even a ridiculous, idea, this now feels tangible, a very real probability, a probability I am living with every day, down there in Central District. Up here on the Peak, to a great extent the family is insulated. As I listen to Myrtle prattle on about how difficult life has become for her, I smoulder with resentment. I cannot help it. I am in the firing line, the thick of it, not her. For the time being at least, she is tucked up safe in the flat on The Peak, with amahs to care for her. Still, foolish though it may be, I like to believe she's safe, that Harry and Alice are safe, that the communist agitators will draw the line at charging up The Peak and laying siege to the flat. After all, we are British subjects. I am fighting the urge to laugh at this notion, this notion that because we are British subjects, servants of Her Majesty Queen Elizabeth the Second, they will tread carefully around us. It will not make an iota of difference to the raging mob down there. No. I take that back. Of course it will make a difference. It will spur them on till they have butchered all the 'White-Skinned Pigs'.

I must stop this. What with a couple of swift ones before leaving the office, and the hefty measures I am getting through now, I've had far too much to drink on an empty stomach. I am growing maudlin. I ignore my own caution and take another slug of scotch. I bare my teeth at the night sky. I can't concentrate on my wife and her tribulations, tonight of all nights. Why is Myrtle bothering me with this, when what I need is pause, time to regroup, to prepare for the next onslaught, for most certainly it will come. How can I think about Alice's future – when I'm not sure if any of us even have one.

'I think it's for the best,' Myrtle says again, taking a gulp of whisky herself. Then, when I turn to her, my face blank, she adds a reminder of the subject under debate, 'Sending Alice to boarding school in Scotland.' She takes up the brochure, leafs through it, and seizes on the very page with the grimacing netball player that I stumbled on. She brandishes it at me, stabbing a manicured fingernail at the action shot. 'Just look at that,' she urges. 'That girl wants to win. That could be Alice in a few years from now. Think of that!'

I do not tell her this is the very thing that I am thinking of, this is what I am afraid of. I am too spent to argue. Besides, Scotland seems a long way away tonight, as does England. Sometimes I think I have forgotten what England is like, forgotten that it is home, my country. I feel as if I have been trying to create a little England, here, on the doorstep of China, and that anybody who really considers this will see that it is an impossible task, the work of a lifetime. For what? In just three short decades, as the century closes, China will reclaim her island, and she will probably do a very thorough job of obliterating all evidence of the British, as speedily as she can. And who would blame her?

'Ralph? Darling, are you listening?' Myrtle's voice sounds in my rambling thoughts. 'About Alice? Scotland? What do you think?'

From somewhere I find the might to withstand my wife's determination to dispense with Alice. I take a shuddering breath and meet her eyes, my gaze steady.

'No. It wouldn't work out for Alice. She would never settle in a boarding school.' My voice is unwavering.

'But how can you know that, Ralph, when—' Myrtle persists.

'It's too late,' I interrupt. 'She has started at the Island School. She has her uniform, her timetable. She may have already made new friends.' This last seems an absurd objection even to me, considering she doesn't have any old friends to speak of. But I plough on regardless. 'Moving her now would cause havoc.'

Again Myrtle, eyes alight, starts to argue, and again I break in.

'That is my final word on the matter, Myrtle. The subject is closed. Alice stays where she is.' I lower my head and stare broodingly into my glass, daring my wife to speak again. When several seconds pass and she does not protest, I glance up. She is staring moodily ahead, chin up, mouth set. She is furious and I do not care.

The year is drawing to a close when I hear at last that an order has come from Beijing, reining in the insurgents, effectively curtailing the violence and bombings for the present. It seems the riots, that will come to be known as the Colonial Riots, have finally subsided. I feel as if I have been holding my breath all this while, and now I can release it. Again I am looking down on the streets of Central and they are blessedly safe. Of course there is the accustomed bustle of this overcrowded island, but the faces I spot are benign, and the scurrying people are devoid of menace. I indulge myself. I dare to think the troubles are behind us, that the structure is still solid, and that Her Majesty's Crown Colony has been delivered back to her safe and sound.

I try not to dwell on the lives lost, or on those men, women and children whose futures will forever be blighted by this appalling time. I try to do what I can to improve the lives of ordinary Chinese citizens, driven now by guilt at what I know were the intolerable conditions they had to survive under. I admit, if only to myself, that corruption in both the ruling classes and the police force has been rife. I use what influence I have to combat this. My motives are not entirely altruistic though. I am driven on by guilt.

I have felt the immense might of China bearing down on me, on this tiny island of Hong Kong. And although this servant of the British Empire stood his ground waving the Union Jack, in reality I know that, like King Canute, trying to halt the rising tide, we never had a chance of holding the colony if China had really wanted to take it. Who knows what deals were done behind the scenes to persuade China to stand down when she did. But no matter the reasons, China has decided to let the British play 'I'm the King of the Castle' for a short while longer. There is no question in my mind that we are only able to continue with our precarious little lives on her say-so. For years I will toss and turn through sleepless nights, my dreams crowded with the ghosts of people killed and wounded, while I was on duty. I will wonder if I might have done better, if my actions might have been speedier, if more lives could have been saved. When the pats on the back are a distant memory, I will wonder truly if it was all worth it.

Brian – 1970

I cast Alice Safford in the role of Abigail in Arthur Miller's *Crucible*, because I thought it might bring the kid out of herself a bit. As Head of English and Drama at the Island School, the annual play is my baby, as agreed when I took up the post. I select it, direct it, produce it, sort out scenery, costumes, lighting, programmes, and just about anything else you care to mention. In short, I live it for a term. With the school only open three years, there was a lot riding on this first spring production. I couldn't afford mistakes. But I just had a feeling that fourteen-year-old Alice was up to the job. She's so much more grown up than the other girls in her year – intelligent, observant. Even at that first reading there was something in her voice that made me think she could pull it off. Which is more than can be said for Trevor Lang playing John Proctor. But then again, what he lacked in talent he made up for in enthusiasm. And frankly I didn't have much to choose from, well nobody actually. He was the only boy who showed up to the audition.

Alice was captivating from the outset, endlessly changing, one moment the seductress, the next spitting like a cat, then all wide-eyed innocence. In the court scene, where Abigail drives the other girls into a frenzy, she actually had the hairs standing up on the back of my neck. We even had a few visits from worried parents complaining their children were having nightmares, questioning my choice of play. But if I'd hoped that acting was going to help her overcome her shyness, or curtail some of the strange behaviour she'd been exhibiting at school, I was to be sorely disappointed. Throughout rehearsals and following the success of the play, Alice continued to prove difficult.

She's not a favourite among other teachers, that girl. And recently, I can't deny her conduct has been challenging. But what the heck, I like Alice. I don't mind admitting it either. I like her. Now when I say that, I don't mean I want to fuck her. Not like some of the older girls. And can you blame me? Sun-tanned legs peeping out from under those flimsy, striped, summer shifts. The zip down the front, with the metal ring through it, that looks like the ring-pull on a can of lager. God, the times I've dreamt of easing those zips down, of glimpsing those lacy, little-girl bras, of touching those firm young breasts and . . . The winter uniform's not much better either, with the chocolate-coloured skirts, so short that you can sometimes see the crease in the girls' thighs, and a hint of their curved buttocks beneath the fabric.

They know it too! Ah, believe me, they know what they're doing to you, as they sashay about this wreck we're having to make do with. A decrepit army hospital full of ghosts. Well, that's what the kids say anyway, whispering horror stories to one another about the morgue. Oh yes, we have our own morgue here at the Island School, very handy if any of the kids expire before close of day. Actually most of the students won't venture anywhere near it. Even Melvin Furse, the Head, hates it, says he can't wait to have the wretched thing demolished.

I've wandered around outside it once or twice, but I've never had the desire or the nerve to enter. There is something really menacing about that place. Gives a whole new meaning to the nicknames the Chinese have for us British. *Gweilo.* A dead corpse that has come back to life, a ghost man, or *gweipo*, a ghost woman. Apparently, so I'm told, years of oppression earned us such unflattering sobriquets. Still, it's easy to see how the Chinese populace first coined them, staring amazed as their new white rulers paraded before them like the living dead. The Chinese are a superstitious race. They believe in ghosts. As for me, before I came here I would have said it was all nonsense. Now, I'm not so sure. This entire building has an unsettling atmosphere you simply can't ignore, a mausoleum, smelling of damp and mould, paint peeling off walls, loggias open to wind and weather. Completely impractical. Furse keeps promising it won't be long before the new premises, currently under construction on the terraced slopes above us, are completed. Though quite honestly there have been so many delays, I am beginning to feel it will be little short of miraculous when it's finished.

And yet, I maintain there's something rather sensual about seeing a lovely girl stroll around this ancient ruin. Echoes of the dying and the dead, screams of agony, groans and sighs, rattling last breaths, mingling with the quick footsteps, fits of giggles, yelps of excitement, and whispered secrets, of ravishing young beauties hurrying to class. Like a film set: the girls playing the leading roles, the ghosts providing all the atmosphere. After all, I'm only flesh and blood, and surely there's no harm in just looking. Honestly, what man wouldn't let his eyes rove a bit with those slim hips swinging ahead of him, those breasts glimpsed from open-necked shirts, through the grinning teeth of an undone zipper. Seeing those swells of warm flesh lifting and falling, beads of sweat adorning them like crystal necklaces. They do it deliberately you know. Leaving one too many buttons undone, innocently hooking that ring with a curved little finger and easing it down a few inches, leaning forwards on purpose so that you can't help but look. What can I say? I'm a good-looking, testosterone-fuelled, young man. But don't get me wrong. With Alice it's never like that. She doesn't flaunt herself, not like the rest of them.

Alice has always been quiet, even from that first day in September when the school opened. Worryingly quiet if I'm truthful. But lately . . . well, sometimes I think she'll disappear, drift away if someone doesn't anchor her down. It's peculiar. Every teacher has a different story to tell about her lately. But they all agree on one thing – that Alice is skiving classes regularly, and that, when she does deign to show up, inevitably there is trouble. In maths they tell me she's proving obstinate and unpredictable, that she walked out of class for no reason last week and hasn't been back since. In French apparently she's been deliberately obtuse, pretending she can't understand a word. Last week she smashed a bottle of ink. I'm told it was all over her dress and hands, and that she just stood there staring at it, as if she was in some kind of stupor. At least that's what Christine Wood the French teacher said. In chemistry she very nearly set fire to her desk a month ago, and now Frank Devine has her sitting at the front of the class, where he can keep an eye on her. In art, her still-life painting is anything but still, I'm reliably informed – things flying about all over the place.

Only last week in the staffroom, Karen Manners, her art teacher, cornered me. I was gasping for a coffee and in a hell of a rush too. But when Karen wants to talk, getting away from her is no easy task. Anyway the upshot is that she told me Alice is always painting the sea, junks and boat people, even soldiers. Japanese, she thinks, she recognises the uniforms. I countered this with some crack about women loving a man in a uniform, which Karen swatted down without so much as the suggestion of a smile.

'I find that remark inappropriate. This is no joke, Brian. It's dreadfully serious,' she flared.

These women! Christ! The trouble is they have no sense of humour. Mind you, I've always wondered if Karen mightn't be a lesbian. That would explain her dour exterior. As Head of English the teachers naturally come to me when they have a problem. I understand that. Though sometimes the stuff is so trivial, I can't help wondering why they can't work it out for themselves. Handholding. They all seem to need their hands held. But I have to concede that this time the problem, Alice, is a substantial one. I like to tackle things head on, so I naturally went straight to her.

'Alice,' I said, 'if you keep skipping classes you do realise that it's going to have a detrimental effect on your grades, perhaps even your O levels when you come to take them.'

I'd caught her at the end of the day, hovering in her classroom, after everyone else had left. I don't even think she was listening to me. She was staring out of the window, eyes dreamy and distant.

'Alice,' I tried again, 'where do you go?'

Perhaps I should have said 'where are you now?' She just looked right through me, as if . . . as if she was stumped by the question, as if she honestly couldn't remember where she went when she played truant.

As a last resort I called in her mother. And that was the weirdest thing of all. Oh, she came immediately. She didn't try to put me off the way some of the parents do. She was punctual, too. Smartly dressed, stylish, you know. A belted, pale yellow shift, with a faded rose print in blush pink and gold. It was silk, I'd bet on it. Not Chinese, but that rough Thai silk. Over it she wore a white, short-sleeved jacket with embroidered sleeves. Her shoes were white as well, with very high heels. Not all women could carry off heels like those, but she could. And she had make-up on; not so much that she looked cheap, but applied subtly, giving her class. She was well-spoken too. I can't help but appreciate when an effort is made. It sets the scene I always think. Gives a meeting a professional air. A few of the parents I know, rolling up in jeans and flip-flops could learn a thing or two from Mrs Safford. She was the finished article right down to her painted pearly-pink nails.

Niceties first. Must observe protocol. I began by congratulating her on the OBE Ralph was awarded earlier in the year, in recognition of his dedicated service on the island. I told her that I'd seen the wonderful pictures of him, in full regalia at the presentation ceremony, on the front page of the *South China Morning Post*. Her too. And was it their son Harry by her side? She smiled appreciatively and inclined her head. And that lovely shot of Alice with her father, very moving. All traces of pleasure instantly vanished. I forged on. Weather. Always a safe bet. Then a smattering of politics, perhaps not quite so safe considering the current climate among the natives. Just lately I'd say they were definitely a wee bit restless. Still, it looked as though the riots were behind us, thank God. Hardly surprising they're fed up, considering we've been bleeding them dry for decades. But naturally I didn't say that to Mrs Safford. No, no!

Then I informed her as tactfully as I could about Alice cutting classes, about her erratic behaviour, about her obsession – yes, her obsession with the sea – which seemed to be influencing all her work in art, and closed by voicing my anxieties over her tumbling grades. As I spoke, Mrs Safford nodded and made small sympathetic noises. She didn't try to deny any of it, didn't make excuses for her daughter. Didn't make excuses for herself, come to that. Finally, when she did respond, I was so taken aback, for a moment I couldn't speak.

'Mr Esmond,' she said, 'I appreciate you imparting your concerns to me. But,' she continued, her diction frighteningly perfect, 'I'm afraid there is little I can do about it. Alice can be . . . intractable. She doesn't listen to anyone. Certainly not to me.' She fixed me with her unreadable brown eyes.

She left me nowhere to go after that. I recall muttering something about hoping that we could work together from now on. And her response? Mrs Safford bent, lifted her white handbag from the foot of the chair, and delved inside it. She fished out her sunglasses, opened them up and dangled them by one arm. Then she let the other arm rest momentarily on her flame-red lips, the gesture deliberately provocative, before putting them on. Her eyes now concealed, she pursed those lips lightly together, then gave me the kind of supercilious smile that makes a man wither away.

'I understand your frustration, Mr Esmond. In fact, I empathise with it,' she said, rising so that I rose too without thinking, and automatically put my hand into her outstretched one. 'But thank you so much for alerting us to the problem and for giving up your valuable time. Naturally, I will do my best to impress the gravity of the situation upon Alice. And if you could keep us informed, I should be most grateful.' And with that she bid me good afternoon.

I even remember the feel of her skin. It was very soft and cool. And her nails, they were long and sharp like a cat's, one of them scratching my hand lightly as she withdrew hers. When she'd gone, I tried to get on with some marking, but my mind just kept skipping back to our meeting.

'I'm afraid there is little I can do about it. Alice can be intractable. She doesn't listen to anyone. Certainly not to me.'

Those words of hers played over and over in my mind. I've met enough parents now to expect the unexpected. But nothing could have prepared me for that. You see, what struck me so forcibly was that Mrs Safford had spoken about Alice as if she was not her child.

Myrtle – 1970

I am sorting through my box of newspaper cuttings, cards and the children's scraps. There is a write-up about the play, *The Crucible*, in the *South China Morning Post*. I'm holding it in my hands, letting my eyes run down the print, picking out the salient points. There is a photograph of Alice too. She is wearing a floor-length dark dress, long sleeves, a square white collar and a white cap. The colours stand out well in the black and white print. Her eyes are fixed upwards, stretched wide in terror at something they see. It is a good review. Well, it would be, wouldn't it? It's Martin Bishop's byline. Ralph's been friends with Martin more or less since we arrived on the island. They're drinking buddies too, so it stands to reason that he'd be extravagant with praise when it came to Alice.

"'Alice Safford's performance as Abigail Williams was electric. She lit up the stage. She was every inch the part.'" Hmm . . .

Actually, I thought she rather overdid it. You can do that you know, overact. They used to love it in Victorian melodramas. Hiss the villain. Great fun. All that screaming and hysteria. I might just as well have stayed at home. At least here it's free.

I screw up the review and bin it. I can't hang on to these things forever. I have other children you know. If I kept all these bits of paper I'd have a roomful by now. I glance down at the next snap. It is of Ralph being presented with his OBE at Government House this spring. What a day that was! I beam. He looks splendid, better than Sir David Trench I think. I've always thought Ralph would make rather a good Governor. I don't think I'll hang on to the one of him and Alice gazing down at the medal. No point really when there are so many others.

Since the play Alice has been worse than ever. Fancy that silly Mr Esmond trying to tell me what Alice has been getting up to. As if I didn't know. I live with her. Alice's bad behaviour is part of our daily routine in our flat on The Peak, I'm afraid. Doesn't he realise that if I could have waved a magic wand and put her right, I would have done it years ago. She's unmanageable. And he's out of his depth, though he probably doesn't realise it. Of course he is. Most people are with Alice. Why Ralph can't accept there's a problem I do not know. He's blind to it, and nothing I do or say or even show him makes any difference. Of course I told him about Alice's latest debacle, about being summoned to the school, about her playing truant. His rejoinder – she was going through a rough patch. Well, if she is, it has lasted fourteen years.

In any case it's not just Alice's scenes I'm concerned about now. She's infected my son, she's infected Harry with her spleen. He used to be such a nice boy, so good-natured and malleable. I need a drink. I know it's early, that the children aren't even home from school yet, but I need to speak to Ralph tonight. I can't put it off any longer. One drink won't do any harm. I'll fetch it myself. I won't ask one of the amahs to pour it for me. They're so mean with the measures. I wish this damn bar door wouldn't make such a loud noise each time you slide it open. It doesn't seem to matter how careful I am.

'It's all right, Ah Lee. I'm fine thank you. Mrs Safford fine, okay? I don't need any help. Not just now. You carry on with the ironing.'

Snooping about. She might spend half her life giggling, but I've noted those sharp, calculating eyes of hers. I know how these servants gossip. That's the trouble with having servants. No privacy. Nowhere is sacred. Damn. No ice. I just can't face going into the kitchen to get some. How many times have I told her to keep the bucket topped up each day? I'll have another word. Ah! That's better. Never mind about the ice. I'll take it into the bedroom. Shut the door. Give myself space to plan what I'm going to say to my husband. In here the sun has been beating down on the bed for most of the day. The purple satin quilt cover is baking hot. I've kicked off my shoes and I'm sprawling out, letting my bare feet slide. The glossy fabric is so slippery. Its touch burns. And the whisky – that burns too. The wound has been cauterised, the flow stemmed. Now I can cope.

Alice has rubbed off on Harry. He is following her bad example, mirroring it. And he's grown, well . . . fat. Harry has become fat.

'Harry is fat.'

There, I've said it out loud. I'd like to call it puppy fat, and believe that one day he'll grow out of it. But really I'm not so sure. He has a double chin now and you can hardly see his neck. I'm constantly having to buy him larger sizes. I can't keep up with it. I tell those stupid amahs over and over not to indulge him, but when my back is turned I know they do – biscuits, chocolate, steamed pudding with syrup, pancakes, fritters. Anyone would think we lived in the North Pole and needed some fat to keep us warm, not that we were roasting on a sub-tropical island. Of course he's being teased at the Island School. Only been there a couple of terms and already he's being picked on. You'd think that would motivate him to diet. But not a bit of it. They yell abuse at him, and at their signal Harry heads for the kitchen.

I've tried to tackle him about it. But that temper of his, charging about like an angry troll, throwing things about the place. And as if I haven't got enough to cope with, there's a problem at the convent. The headmistress believes Nicola and Jillian may be involved in some way. Personally I think it unlikely, but Mother's fuming of course. Let's hope it comes to nothing. I could close my eyes and drift off to sleep. Normally I don't like too much sun but today it's pure balm.

Harry charged a glass door the other day. I expect Alice drove him to it. She certainly makes me want to slam into a glass door. The two of them wound up in casualty. Both of them needed stitches, Harry's hands were in ribbons, and Alice had deep gashes in her leg and foot, and a cut to her face just above her lip. We're becoming quite the regulars there. They might as well book out a treatment room once weekly for the Safford family. What must they think? Still, that nice little Chinese doctor never says anything. And of course he must know who we are, who Ralph is. He always sees us straight away, no matter how many patients are waiting. I tackled Alice about Harry's rages.

'Alice, do you fully comprehend the effect your theatrics is having on your brother?' I asked her.

She was standing in the hall. She had just whistled up Bear and was about to set off for one of her rambles.

'Harry is not himself,' she hedged, not daring to meet my eyes.

'Harry is not himself because of you, Alice,' I qualified.

Then she did look up. Her eyes kindled into life. She was angry I think. Or perhaps, incredibly, amused. Though it's hard to tell with Alice.

'You are driving my son away,' I said, just so that there was no misunderstanding.

She put her head just slightly on one side then and gave me that measuring look of hers, eyelids half closed but their sense well and truly open. I despise that way she has of saying nothing and implying everything.

'You've no answer to that, have you?' I dredged up. The silent and plainly ludicrous suggestion that I might be contributing to Harry's exhibitions hung in the air between us. The bloody dog kept yipping, and I would like to have kicked him, hard. He's not been disciplined properly, that dog. Alice indulges him. Now of course, like everything else, it's too late.

'Just go,' I spat.

I wanted her out of my sight. I couldn't bear to be with her for another second. Before she left she had the gall to ask me if there was anything she might pick up for me at Dairy Farm while she was out, as if all this was normal.

I want to send Alice away. But I can't. Ralph won't have it. So because of her I am going to have to sacrifice my son, my only son. Otherwise she will poison him with her venom. I hear the sound of the front door and Ah Lee's greeting. Alice is home. And I know as I roll the empty tumbler on the quilt, and see the faint residue of gold still coating the glass, that it is to Harry I must say goodbye.

Nicola – 1970

Funny, now that we know we're leaving, I almost feel fond of the old place. There's no denying we had some laughs here. Jilly doesn't see it that way though.

'It is a vile, hateful school. It's been torture. The best thing they can do is close it down,' she told me yesterday, as we collected together our things. 'I want to forget it, forget we ever had to endure life here, forget it even exists.'

And it was true, there were moments when the wretched convent, with its flock of gloomy nuns trotting out endless catechisms, had me a little depressed too. But I wasn't one to let misery engulf me. So after the first few downtrodden years, I put on a happy face, and instigated a programme of near miraculous recovery. Jesus, Mary and Joseph! I like that oath. I've borrowed it from Shauna, one of the Irish students who uses it all the time. I can do a pretty good impression of her accent by now as well. It makes Jilly nearly wet herself laughing. Anyway so, Jesus, Mary and Joseph, let me tell you how I transformed the once dull Saint Mary's Convent into something rather like a film set for St Trinian's.

'The trick is,' I told my sceptical sister at the outset, 'not to get caught, Jilly.' I remember I uttered these words on our first midnight excursion. Jillian was already crippled with guilt. I never feel guilty. Things only seem awful when you put yourself in someone else's shoes. I never wear anyone's shoes but my own.

'What if we get caught?' said Jillian, brow pinched, eyes anxious, considering the consequences of our actions. I never do that either.

'We won't be,' I asserted with convincing surety.

We took two friends with us. I chose Margery Billingham, a plump girl with buck teeth and frizzy brown hair. My selection was to prove questionable, the window we all had to crawl through being quite small and Margery being quite large. Jillian picked her best friend, Jane Redwood. Jane was unnaturally slim, with a surprisingly narrow mouth set into her oval face. She had shoulder-length hair the colour and consistency of straw, and spots on her protruding chin that occasionally were, I couldn't help noticing, full of creamy pus. It made me feel nauseous just to look at them. I thought she was anorexic, as I never saw her eat anything, but Jillian said she just couldn't stand the convent food, and that she ate loads of chocolate in secret. Anyway, her thinness proved to be her redeeming feature that night. I had to admit two of her could have slipped through that window with no trouble, unlike wide-girthed Margery. The doors were all locked at night and the nuns kept the keys, so the window it had to be.

The window I keep alluding to was in the larder, the larder lay beyond the kitchens, and the kitchens behind the dining block. I had made careful notes on lock-down procedures at night, which nuns walked the beat and when. By midnight they were all abed and snorting through their dreams, so all we had to do was sneak out of the dormitories, climb down two flights of stairs, creep along the corridors past the classrooms, until we arrived at the dining hall. Once there we stole inside, wrinkling up our noses at the lingering, stewed-cabbage smell that seemed to permeate the walls, tiptoed into the kitchens, and from here made our way through to the larder. We climbed, one by one, on the broad, cold, marble shelf, and clambered out of the small window to the rear of it. It was always left open we learnt from Sister McMullen, head cook, in order to keep the air circulating and the food fresh, and the grid insert was easy to remove.

What I hadn't bargained for was how quiet 'quiet' really is, how sounds swallowed up throughout the day, with thumping feet, chattering voices and closing doors, were magnified a thousandfold at night. Nevertheless we soon got the hang of it. Shoes off, avoid boards that creaked, learn to sign, freeze and vanish at the first hint of trouble, and work as a team. The adrenalin rush on those nights was something else. It was like having an electric charge pulsing through me, all my senses heightened, razor-sharp. From the start, getting Margery through the window was a struggle. In the end, Jilly and Jane went first. It seemed the escape route I had picked had one great advantage. Beyond the window, only feet from it, was a bank of earth, and that meant there was no drop. With a combination of pushing and pulling, in the end we managed to ease Margery through. And once I had joined the group, a quick sprint across the convent lawns, followed by a brief if ungainly scramble over the iron railings, and we were free.

From here we bolted around a bend of the road that took us away from the convent, and that's where the boys picked us up. We met the first lot hanging around outside Woolworths in Ealing, while we were staying with Gran one weekend. Darren, tall and mouthy, with sticking-out ears; James, the cute one, with blond hair and sexy blue eyes; Patrick, James's older brother who owned the car, a beat-up green Ford Anglia, not so good-looking but, on the positive side, much more experienced; and Boyd, a bit of an oddball, chubby, a gingernut with crooked teeth and bad breath, who we decided would do for Margery. James and Boyd were still at school, but Patrick worked at the Walls factory in Acton and was very grown up. He had money, which after all was the only thing that mattered. Darren had dropped out of school and was just bumming around. He was constantly trying to scrounge off us. What a turn-off! Even when I was really drunk, I avoided fucking him.

They brought booze and condoms and fags, and we roared off in their car, sitting on their laps and snogging before we'd even pulled away from the kerb, listening to Radio Caroline or Radio Luxembourg, the Stones or the Beatles or the Searchers blaring out. Then it was a race to Richmond Green, or the towpath to Twickenham, or by the river in Kew, where we drank and fucked and smoked, in that order, rushing back to sneak in by 4:30am latest.

I didn't mind this physical contact. I don't know why really – if it was the darkness that made it seem thrilling, or the booze, or the nerves, or perhaps it was just that it was illicit sex.

In time the operation grew slick, cushions in beds, moving with all the stealth of panthers, even smuggling back contraband, booze, fags, rude magazines, and a bit of weed now and again. The Ford Anglia was slowly upgraded to a Jaguar, and it was no longer boys who picked us up beyond the school gates, but men. We dashed across those lawns in all weathers. Warm summer nights where the moonlight was impossibly bright, and we raced like fugitives over the cropped grass. Autumn, when we had to pick our way carefully over crunchy leaves, the wind for once a bonus, mercifully muffling our steps. Spring, where our dash was frequently accompanied by raw, spicy scents, the air pungent with newness. And winter, when we had to be extra vigilant if there had been fresh snow, treading only in the paths already mapped out by pupils and nuns during the day.

Apart from drifting off to sleep once or twice in class, and having to struggle through dismal, interminable prayers with thumping hang-overs, we certainly seemed to be getting away with it. Now we had something to look forward to on the long tiresome days, a soap opera peppered richly with sexual encounters, good and bad to talk over, feats of ardour to compare, lewd and gross behaviour to smirk about. Meanwhile, during school hours we kept up a discreet campaign of disruption, hiding books, stealing small personal possessions that we knew the nuns shouldn't have, scribbling rude words over the pages of bibles in indelible ink: fuck, cunt, prick, fellatio, cunnilingus, mas-turbation, pudenda; even necrophilia. The effect was staggering. Nuns whispering in the corridors, timetables disrupted, classes cancelled, and an atmosphere of disorientation and chaos spreading even to morning assemblies. I learnt that it was easy to be duplicitous, easier still to manipulate people, oiling the wheels with flattery.

Goodness knows how long it would all have carried on for, if it hadn't been for lumpy Margery. She was so fat anyway that I didn't guess, guess that she was pregnant. One night, no matter how hard

I pushed and the others pulled, she lodged fast in the larder window, and began to wail about how she was going to have this baby. She wailed so loudly that I began to wonder if she was going to give birth right there and then, and as I was standing next to the end where it would all happen, it was a bit of a worry. This is how Sister McMullen found us, me in a fetching purple miniskirt, low-cut blouse, fishnet stockings and tons of make-up, Margery screaming like a stuck pig, her vast stomach wedged in the window-frame, her legs kicking out as if she was swimming the crawl, a crate that had been on the marble shelf upturned, and root vegetables rolling about noisily around the tiled larder floor.

The next day Jillian broke down in the toilets, and wept over the retribution that she claimed would surely be swift. I handed her a loo roll, and gave her a play punch on the cheek.

'Don't panic, Jilly,' I reassured. 'This looks much worse than it actually is. It's all about the spin we put on our stories.' I was already gambling on the guilt card I would play to Mother. 'We can make all of this work in our favour.' After that, I went to considerable efforts to ensure that our stories tallied.

'If in doubt say nothing and leave it to me,' I advised my sister. 'You just cry.'

Jillian nodded. Tears were easy for her. I didn't bank on Mother Superior wanting to see each of us alone, but I heard Jillian bawling through the door so I wasn't too dismayed. I gave her an encouraging look as she emerged, red-eyed and snivelling. Then it was my turn. Mother Superior wanted to know which one of us was the mastermind behind our nocturnal wanderings. I prevaricated, making it clear how very uncomfortable I felt about telling on my friends, but at last, hanging my head in resignation, I confessed that Jane had goaded us all into it. I explained that I didn't want to get her into trouble, but that Jillian and I had just been swept along by her cunning. Mother Superior looked doubtful. Picturing Jane, gaunt-faced and stick-limbed, her big soulful eyes and her timorous voice, even I had to admit casting her as arch villain required a gymnastic stretch of the imagination.

96

'Nicola,' Mother Superior said, searching my face with those penetrating grey eyes of hers, 'you do know it's wrong to lie?'

'Of course, Reverend Mother,' I muttered earnestly, hastily dropping my gaze from hers. Mother Superior placed a finger under my chin and raised my face, until our eyes met once more.

'I cannot be sure what you got up to on these nightly escapades, Nicola, but I have a good idea,' she said, withdrawing her finger.

I sighed plaintively. 'Really Reverend Mother, it was just innocent fun until—'

Mother Superior interrupted me. 'Do you know just how serious this situation is, Nicola? Margery's pregnancy is a catastrophe for her. It might very well ruin her whole life.'

I shook my head mournfully. 'I know, Reverend Mother, I know.' I told her I sympathised, though I didn't add that I thought Margery was a bloody fool to get herself knocked up. Further, if I'd been her, I'd have popped off to get an abortion double-quick. But I'd been at the convent long enough to know Catholics were funny about these things. Trust that fat cow to land us in it, I reflected gloomily. Placing my hands together prayerfully, I added, in the tone of voice parents use to encourage a disheartened child, 'Still, a baby, the miracle of life. Sister McMullen says babies bring their very own unique joy into this world, each and every one of them!'

Mother Superior sighed with exasperation, and lowered her head, making it very hard for me to read the temperature of her reaction. Her next remark clarified things a bit though.

'I'm going to expel you and Jillian from St Mary's Convent,' she announced in clipped tones.

I thought about this for a moment, and then shrugged. My gesture appeared to shake Mother Superior's composure, though I was unsure why. She seemed almost to fall against the edge of her desk, and waved me away with . . . well I might be wrong, but I thought it was something like disgust. As soon as I could, I tracked down Jillian in her dormitory, and broke the news. She flayed the air with her hands and, gasping, took a few tiny steps backwards. I told her to sit down and catch her breath.

'We couldn't have hoped for a better outcome, Jilly,' I told her firmly.

She hugged herself and rocked forwards and back. She muttered about Mother and Father, what they would say.

'I can handle them.' My words sounded glib but I was sincere. I gave her a pat on the back. 'We're going to be fine.'

Jillian looked disbelieving as she wiped her runny nose. But I was beginning to feel that familiar rush of invincibility. The summer was upon us. I was sixteen, Jilly, eighteen. Not long ago we had sat O level and A level examinations, half asleep, hung-over, and without any revision. But even the disastrous results I was expecting did not deflate my buoyant mood.

So there it is. Education gained at St Mary's Convent, England, zilch, experience gleaned, Jesus, Mary and Joseph, a lifetime's worth! We are heading back to Hong Kong, the disgraced Safford daughters, and who knows what delights await us there. Life, I've decided, is a bit like a game of cards, it's all about how you play your hand. And if you have to cheat a bit to win . . . Well, does it really matter?

Ghost – 1970

Alice buys herself a diary. The diary is bound in leather the colour of dried blood. It has the words 'My Diary' tooled in gold on the cover. It has a metal clasp and a tiny key. Alice pays out her words on its stiff, creamy pages, like a miser parting with hidden treasure coin by coin. She hunches over it when she writes her secrets, as if she thinks someone is watching her, as if she thinks she can hide what she is doing from me, as if she has a story separate from mine.

Today she writes: 'I don't think I am alone. There is something, someone with me. I want to tell but who would believe me.'

She is a strange little creature, my host. I tell her I am here, of course. I am always here. I scarf myself about her neck and mutter, soft as the rustle of bamboo leaves in the wind, 'Don't worry, Alice, you are not alone. We are cohabiting, you and I. Our tale is plaited tight, the strands of our lives forever interwoven.'

Alice frowns and slams shut her diary. Again she crooks a little finger, a sign I now know indicates her distress. Sometimes I find my host's behaviour a little bewildering. But there is no time to dwell on this, for we are spending today, a Sunday, on a friend's boat. It is the start of July. Conditions are ideal. The sky is the very palest of blues, marbled with milky translucent swirls. The sun, burning brightly, seems to swell as it rises in the sky. There is the barest puff of a breeze, that I know from experience will strengthen as we emerge from Aberdeen harbour. This, I understand, will be one of the last seaside outings for brother Harry for some time. In little over a month we are all to travel to Scotland, on the other side of the world, to install him in a boarding school there. On route we are collecting Alice's sisters from her grandmother's house. We are bringing them back with us to the island. So although the flat on The Peak is losing one resident, it is gaining two more.

The boat trip is to Lamma Island. I know it well. And as we set out, motoring past the walls of boulders, wind- and wave-breakers that protect Aberdeen harbour from the excesses of the weather, my spirit lifts remembering *Heavenly Sea*. This is not a junk though, it is a grand sailing yacht, owned by a commercial bank, Mr Safford says. Our host, Phillip Stubbs, is one of their most senior employees. The yacht is named *Seahorse*. There are four couples out to enjoy the day – the Stubbs, the Saffords, the Birleys and the Gibsons. So often have I heard the names of the other guests on our car journey rolling down The Peak, that by the time I meet them in person, I feel we are old friends. Alice and Harry are the only children present, the rest are away at boarding school, the summer holidays having not yet begun. There are two Chinese boat boys and a Filipino maid on board as well, and a banquet of food and drink. At first, Harry is morose, sulking in the cabin, but gradually he too seems to absorb the atmosphere of this perfect day and creeps out on deck.

Alice thinks that her parents look like movie stars, draped over the streamlined white *Seahorse*. In the flat there is a book full of photographs of Hollywood actresses. They strike glamorous poses in brightly coloured swimsuits. They clutch beachballs, hook arms through rubber rings and lounge on lilos. Alice's mother holds a drink. Sitting in the stern of the boat, a green and blue flowered headscarf tied at her neck, eyes mysteriously shaded with sunglasses, her mother looks like someone famous, Alice thinks, someone who signs autographs. She watches her mother deport herself like a model, whose picture might appear the next day in the *South China Morning Post*. While her father, Alice decides, is the image of Sean Connery in one of the James Bond films. She remembers the ceremony earlier this year, in which her father was awarded the OBE, Officer of the British Empire, at a grand ceremony in Government House. She pictures him now in his brilliant white uniform, how handsome he looked, and how proud she felt to be his daughter.

Ralph moves around the boat drinking a beer with quietly spoken Phillip, whose hair seems both prematurely grey and thinning. He shares a joke with demonstrative Mike Gibson, his neatly trimmed dark beard, moustache and horn-rimmed spectacles giving the impression of intelligence. He discusses politics with wiry Jack Birley, whose shrewd eyes roam ceaselessly, and whose large nose is made still more prominent by its generous coating of white suncream. He stretches out on the sundeck next to Christine, Mike's wife. The heavy make-up she has applied seems much more suitable for an evening engagement than a boat trip. Petite Pippa Birley, her hands forever patting, stroking and even squeezing her body, as if needing to reassure herself that it is still there, sips a glass of white wine and sidles up to Myrtle. She begins chatting animatedly about her sons, Jeremy and Luke, both attending the same boarding school in Oxford, and both, she explains to Myrtle, achieving outstanding results.

Though, of all the women on board, it is Amanda Stubbs who commands most attention, and yet who does the least to win it. Her shoulder-length gold hair is worn loose, the sun imbuing it with fascinating strands of light, from coppery red to an almost greenish citrus yellow. She is attentive to her guests, moving gracefully about the craft. Her voice is disarmingly gentle and kind, so kind in fact, it is impossible to imagine a vindictive word falling from her full lips. However delightful, it is a very foreign concept to me, this idea of coming out on a boat and doing nothing. Distantly, I recall the work was never over on my father's junk. Yet here the Saffords and their friends lounge in the sun, while the boat boys run the *Seahorse*.

Amanda Stubbs spends most of the outward trip in the cabin organising the food. Occasionally she does put in an appearance, checking if anyone needs their drinks topped up, handing out nuts and crisps, and speaking with the boat boys. Alice is drawn by the dazzle of her sunlit hair. Unlike the other women she doesn't have on a hat, headscarf or sunglasses, just a wide magenta hair band. She wears very red lipstick, and a floaty, diaphanous, cream dress over a turquoise bikini. The dress keeps blowing up in the sea breeze, and once or twice she holds it down laughingly. Alice thinks she resembles Marilyn Monroe, in a film she once watched called *The Seven Year Itch*. Yet even when she laughs, Amanda Stubbs's watery blue eyes seem glassy with sadness. Alice has produced her diary again. As we skip over the waves, she steals off to the very front of the boat with it.

'I like Amanda Stubbs but she has sad blue eyes. They look as if they have had all the fun rinsed out of them,' she writes, letting her feet trail in the sea.

The cold sea spray and the frothy bubbles of the breaking bow wave bursting over Alice's bare feet make her feel exhilarated. I am not sure if the curve of her left arm is designed to shield her diary from the sea, or from me.

'Harry seems very moody today. I do not think he likes the idea of boarding school. I am not sure that he will be happy there,' Alice continues, though with the roll of the boat her writing is a bit of a scrawl.

We buck over a large wave. As the *Seahorse* slaps back down, salty droplets freckle the page. The spindly letters bleed into one another and the words blur. For a second, Alice, whose face is also spattered with salty wet spots, thinks it looks as if tears have splashed onto her pages. She slams shut the diary and hugs it to her. Perhaps the thought has occurred to her that I could easily send it flying into the deep green depths, never to be seen again.

The sails are up now and flapping in the wind. The motor is stilled. The deck has stopped vibrating. Apart from the creak of the rigging and slap of the sails, it is surprisingly peaceful. The boat has slowed and the sea appears calmer. Alice scans the horizon, taking in the sparkling sea and the grey-green islands in the distance. She imagines them as the shoulder of a giant, or the belly of an enormous sea monster recumbent on the seabed, staring up through the watery depths at the strange airy world above. For a long while we sit like this. Then the wind drops and Alice is vaguely aware of the boat boys taking down the sails. In minutes we are under motor again, and the chug of the engine seems to rattle through Alice's head.

Rising cautiously, diary clutched under one arm, her other hand feeling its way along the deck rail, Alice moves to the stern of the vessel. Here her attention is caught by her father's antics. He scoops a handful of ice cubes out of the bucket that Amanda is carrying, and strokes her mother's bare thighs with them. Myrtle has pulled up her bottle-green cotton skirt to tan her legs in the sun. Now she gives a little scream as the ice slides along her warm inner thigh. She shoves her husband's hand away. The ice cubes fall to the deck and skitter about. Alice sees one of the boat boys hurrying to retrieve them. Her father grins at her and gives her a little wave. Then he sinks down next to Myrtle, and lays an arm casually about her shoulders. Myrtle pretends to ignore her husband, but Alice can see she is pleased. Amanda Stubbs, whose back is to Alice at that moment, turns to go down into the cabin. Alice locks eyes with her. Amanda turns the corners of her ruby lips up in a smile, but the smile does not reach those sad eyes.

We anchor in a bay off Lamma Island. Alice stows her diary away safely in her beach bag in the cabin. Soon lunch is served on deck by the Filipino maid and the boat boys. Today even Alice wants to eat. The sea air has given her an appetite. She manages a chicken drumstick and some salad, as well as a small bowl of ice cream. After lunch all the adults seem sleepy. No one is very keen when Alice's father suggests a swim to the beach and a walk. Eventually, Amanda pinches her hips with mock dismay and says she could do with the exercise. The two of them dive off the roof of the boat, their bodies darting into the green depths, shining and opalescent beneath the translucent lid of the sea. Myrtle does not like swimming. Alice cannot remember the last time her mother went swimming. Myrtle claims it makes her ears hurt, and that the doctor has said she must not get them wet.

As Alice watches, her father and Amanda strike out for the shore. Their arms plough rhythmically into the water, their legs just breaking the surface as they kick, a spool of white lace unravelling behind them. Alice feels a strange current of apprehension tingling along her spine. She shades her eyes and tracks their progress. She sees them shrink, until they look as tiny as the porcelain figures in her father's lacquer cabinet at home. At last they clamber out of the water. They look so far away now, Alice is unaccountably frightened she may lose them. With her forehead crinkled in a frown, she follows them walking up the beach. Amanda turns back and waves, as if she has suddenly remembered they have an audience. Alice returns the wave, though she is not sure Amanda notices. Then the two of them, her father and Mrs Stubbs, take a path that vanishes in the undergrowth.

Replete after lunch and dozy with drink, Myrtle Safford reclines on cushions in the stern, under the shade of the canopy. Phillip Stubbs sits reading the paper, and smoking contentedly a few feet from her. Mike Gibson and Jack Birley, in deckchairs set up on the foredeck, are engrossed in talk of business. Their wives sprawl on mats, laid out on the roof of the cabin. Christine Gibson appears absorbed in a book, little of her tanned face visible between the broad rim of her straw sunhat, and the rectangular screen of her open book. Pippa Birley's chestnut curls are caught up in a ponytail. She busies herself applying suncream with grim determination, and shifting her position with such alarming frequency, that she makes the curious occupation of sunbathing look exhausting. Harry has chosen to stay in the cabin, claiming that the sun is too hot for him, though Alice is certain he is preoccupied with thoughts of his imminent departure from the island.

We join him for a short while, and Alice tries to persuade him to come for a swim. But Harry wants shade and solitude. So Alice alone changes into her bathing costume, and shrugs on a baggy T-shirt. We find our way back to the bow. Alice nods briefly to the men deep in their chat of sure-fire investments, and then we climb gingerly down the rungs of the swimming ladder. Despite the scorching heat of the sun, or perhaps because of it, when Alice dips a toe in the sea it feels icy cold. She cannot face diving in as she saw her father and Mrs Stubbs do. For a time she clings to the ladder descending very gradually into the water. When Alice is submerged up to her waist, we jump, her cream T-shirt ballooning around us. The cold water closes over us. Then, to my relief, we stop sinking and rise back up. Alice's head bursts from the depths, a sheaf of silver water slipping from it. Her limbs flay. She swims a few strokes back to the ladder, and hangs there, half submerged.

For a while Alice listens to the slap of the water against the hull. She watches the anchor rope, the pale length of it seeming to waver as it descends, until it is erased in the green depths. She looks at the shoreline and decides that it is not too far, that she would be able to swim there if she wanted to. She calls up to Christine Gibson and tells her where she is going. Mrs Gibson leans over the edge of the roof. She lowers her sunglasses and peers at Alice bobbing below in the sea, as if she is trying to remember who she is. To Alice, Christine Gibson's face, hidden in the shadow of the large sunhat, is virtually invisible, a black disc against the white glare of the sun.

'Alright darling,' she says vaguely. 'Do take care, won't you?'

Alice nods. She is about to ask Mrs Gibson to tell her mother where she is when the disc, looming over her from above, rolls away and disappears. Alice hesitates for a moment and then we set off. The harder she swims, the further away the shore seems to be. Once she turns back to the boat, but no one is scanning the ocean, monitoring her progress. She imagines jellyfish, creamy yellow, and the living bruise of the Portuguese Man of War, gulping mouths rushing towards her, trailing their deadly stinging manes. Her heart races and hers arms lash at the sluggish sea. At last she can make out the blurred, trembling shapes of rocks beneath her. She can see her pallid legs bicycling furiously. She reaches out with them, trying to plant her feet on the slimy barnacled rock rearing up under her. But now she sees it is an illusion, that the rock is much deeper than she first estimated. She has to swim several yards more before she is able to stand. As she does so, rubbery, golden-brown seaweed fans brush her toes, and the soles of her feet. She finds herself anticipating sea urchins, black and spiky, concealed beneath the slimy curtains of weed. In the end she draws her knees up, and determines not to put her feet down until she sees the glint of yellow sand.

At last we stride from the sea and rid ourselves of its guile. As Alice sloughs off her wet skin, so her fright evaporates. The sand is gritty beneath her feet, and so hot that she has to hop and run to the path. And like her father and Amanda Stubbs, as we step onto it we are camouflaged by dusky foliage. Walking along the narrow trail as it winds up the small hill, we catch glimpses of the sea, its glittering belly heaving gently in leaf-fringed frames. Twice there is the flash of the boat, so white it makes Alice's eyes water. Higher and higher we climb, heading inland away from the beach, till eventually the small bay is lost to us.

We come to a temple, tiny, built of wood, with a steeply sloping roof, ornamented with strange wooden carvings at its apex and four corners. The small reddish-brown door, its paintwork splitting to reveal slashes of rough wood, is propped open. Ducking and stepping through it, Alice's nostrils are assailed with the scent of incense, heavy and acrid. The dusty air within is wreathed with smoky curlicues. It takes some time for Alice's eyes to adjust to the dimness, after the brilliance outside. She blinks back the wave of dizziness that washes over her. At last her pupils dilate sufficiently for the indistinct shapes to resolve themselves. At the far end is an altar, graced with a tall wooden statue, ferocious, unyielding, robed in forbidding red and gold, purple and black. There are offerings laid on the altar at the foot of the uncompromising god, oranges and lychees, a blue rice-pattern china bowl filled with sweets, each of them wrapped in shiny paper, and a wad of fake paper money. Tucked away to the right of the altar is a huge wooden barrel. Treading softly as a cat, careful not to disturb the fierce god, Alice approaches it. Glimpsing over the rim she sees the glint of water. Alice dips a finger in, withdraws it and sucks it. Salt. Seawater. At her movement, the silver face shivers into tiny ripples, and the walnut shell boat she spies in it bobs gently.

'Here is the sea, and here is the boat that sails on the sea,' Alice says softly. Her voice echoes in the still of the temple. 'In that boat is a fisherman, facing the angry winds and the boiling seas. And when he is away, through the empty black nights, his family come here and pray for his safe return.'

106

Then we step out of the temple and Alice readjusts to the unremitting fever of the sun. On a whim she decides to continue upwards. As we ascend, the path becomes more treacherous. Alice finds herself stumbling over rocks. Once she stubs a toe, and the subsequent stab of pain almost makes her cry out. The soles of her feet are scratched and sore by the time we crest the summit. The seawater has dried on her skin, and left a powdery residue of salt. It feels stretched, taut as the skin of a tambourine. Her eyes are smarting too, irritated by the sea, the smoky incense, and the blast of light beating down on her, and reflecting back up off the metallic greys of the rocks. Directly in front of her, Alice sees a large granite outcrop, flattened on the top and partly shaded by a giant fir tree.

'Standing atop this boulder I shall see everything,' Alice conjectures. 'If I rotate I shall see all around the coastline of my little island. I shall see the *Seahorse* tugging against its anchor rope. I shall see the roof of the temple that houses the angry god. I will be able to follow the shifting shoreline.'

We clamber up, Alice on tiptoe, arms outspread for balance on the flinty hot surface, and see none of these things. What we see instead is Amanda Stubbs straddling Alice's father in a clearing below us. They are both naked. We can see the white imprint of Amanda Stubbs's bikini standing out in sharp relief against her tanned flesh. The deep coral-pink of her nipples jewels the pale breasts. There is a golden haze between her legs. She is riding Ralph Safford as if he is a horse, thrusting her hips rhythmically forwards and back. And she is facing us, her spine arched, her head thrown backwards, her face raised to the blazing sky. Her hands are lost, entwined in her glistening golden hair. Her mouth is open, her eyes closed. Of her father, Alice can see only the top of his head, crowned with his crisp, black hair, and the expanse of his broad chest. He is ramming his groin upwards into Mrs Stubbs, his hands on her hips, grasping them firmly, the muscles in his arms standing out as she bucks against him. Alice recalls how many times those strong arms have encircled her. My host no longer wobbles on tiptoes. The soles of her feet lie flat against the hot rock, and she is oblivious to the searing pain.

Then Mrs Stubbs cries out, her head levelling. She opens her eyes, her watery blue eyes that have had all the fun rinsed out of them, and those sad eyes meet Alice's. They hold each other. Hearts hammer, threads of glittering sweat course down the flushed softness of hidden flesh. The instant shatters. Alice swings away, slipping down the side of the rock. I streak after her. She stumbles over the scree, immune now to the slashes and jabs of pain. She falls and grazes her knee. But she ignores the trickle of blood, and the grit that clings to the sticky wound. A branch whips across her face, and a twig lashes her eyelid. She winces. Her vision blurs. She rushes on, scarcely aware she is passing the temple. Finally, breaking from the sheltered pathway, we sprint towards the sea.

She craves its icy purity with her whole being. She is not conscious of the broken fragment of shell that has embedded itself in the heel of her foot. As she runs the shard is driven further in. The sand smudges with her blood. She flings herself into the water, opening her eyes to its coldness and salt smack with dreadful eagerness. Only now does she grow aware of her throbbing foot. For a moment she sculls the water, preparing herself. Then she holds her breath, bends beneath the surface, and takes hold of it. She feels for the ridge of shell protruding from the pad of her heel, grips it and yanks it out. Opening her eyes underwater, in the ring of her salt-excoriated, furred vision, she can make out the red tail of blood spiralling outwards. She pushes back the weight of water and bursts through the sea's skin. Blinking back hot tears, she screws her eyes up in disbelief. A white shape lunges out at her. It is the *Seahorse*, suspended over the vast dark green sea. We plunge forwards. Alice settles into her stroke, breaststroke, her legs and arms frantically describing circles. She tries not to harbour thoughts of grey shadows beneath her, her curl of sweet blood baiting them, drawing the monsters of the deep ever closer.

We are both thankful to tread on the solid deck of the *Seahorse*. The men in their deckchairs grunt a perfunctory greeting. We hurry past. Myrtle stirs, disturbed by the slap and vibration of Alice's wet feet. She glances up.

'Whatever have you done, Alice?' she remarks, spotting the blood oozing from the wound in her daughter's foot, as Alice hops into the stern. Phillip Stubbs leaps up looking concerned. 'You're leaving a trail of blood,' Myrtle Safford says with a sigh worn out by repetition. 'It may stain the deck.'

Phillip Stubbs is quick to assure her that this is of no consequence, and sees to it that the cut is washed and bandaged. As soon as his wife and Ralph Safford arrive back, he gives the order to weigh anchor and set sail. Alice is restive on the homeward journey, the confines of the boat claustrophobic. Her father notices the bandage, and probes the circumstances that have warranted it. Alice says that she swam to the beach and stepped on a broken shell. Her manner is offhand. She keeps her eyes lowered.

'We didn't see you there,' Ralph Safford remarks, his voice pitched with extreme care on a note that is both friendly and disappointed.

'No. I cut my foot the moment I stepped ashore,' Alice explains to her father. Her eyes move fleetingly over Amanda Stubbs, emerging from the cabin, dressed now in slacks and a blouse, rubbing her blonde hair vigorously with a towel. 'So I came straight back,' she finishes flatly.

Ralph Safford's blue eyes lighten a shade. 'What bad luck,' he says. And then, 'What a pity. We might have met up.'

'Mm,' agrees Alice absently. 'But it really hurt to walk on, so I didn't feel much like exploring after that.'

Her father nods his understanding of Alice's impossible predicament, and there is an almost perceptible relaxing of his broad-muscled shoulders. Once, perhaps twice, Amanda Stubbs seeks out my host with her sad eyes, but Alice has retreated to somewhere she cannot be reached. When we arrive home at the flat on The Peak, my host does not even bother to watch the sun set. She forgot to apply suncream, and now her face, forearms and legs are burnt, dark pink and tender to the touch. Even the cotton sheets seem to rub her raw when she lies back on them. Late that night she crawls from her bed and finds her diary. The curtains are tied back and moonlight is flooding in. Alice makes do without switching on the light. She sits at her desk, opens her diary, and takes up her pen.

'Today I saw my father and Amanda Stubbs fucking on Lamma Island,' Alice writes.

And then, before I have the chance to shuffle its cream leaves and make my host's diary dance for her pleasure, she hurls it across the room. It flies through the air, its pages flapping like the wings of one of the white cockatoos that gather in flocks about the island. The clasp catches the moonlight. It flashes like the parrots' sulphur crests. I am half expecting it to squawk when it hits the door of one of the built-in wardrobes, and with a final flourish of feathers tumbles to the floor. It is obvious after that, that any tricks I was thinking of performing for Alice's delight would be an anticlimax.

Harry – 1970

The cabin on the Stubbs's boat was an oven that day. It was like being cooked alive, sitting down there, dripping with sweat in that baggy T-shirt, feeling it pool where my thighs pressed together, between my buttocks, huge smelly patches of it below my armpits, and my skin slippery with it under my fat-boy breasts. The Filipino servant, fussing with bits and pieces, gave me a huge slice of sticky cake, and then stood over me while I ate it. I knew she wanted to pinch my arm, to squeeze the chubby flesh between her slim fingers till I cried out. But she didn't have the bottle. I suppose she wouldn't have said 'Fei zhai'. She'd have said something else, in her language probably. I heard Alice get back, saw the bottom of her legs through the cabin windows and her clambering into the stern, heard Mum scream at her cos she was bleeding onto the deck or something. Alice's legs looked burnt. Must have forgotten to put suncream on. The Filipino hurried away then, returning seconds later to fetch a medical box. And still I sat, baking in the cabin, wondering how long it would be before I was done to a turn.

I shut my eyes sometimes and try to recapture the feeling of that intense heat, the sweat, the awful stillness of the sea, flat as a mirror, but with all those things wriggling underneath it. In Scotland there are lochs and some of them are huge, stretch for mile after mile. But it's not the same. Not like the sea. It's okay though, because I pretend it's happening to someone else, all of it. I just watch, sit back and . . . well, sit back. Picking up Jillian and Nicola was the best part though. Mum and Dad and Gran in the back room, and me listening at the door, and Uncle Albert on the stairs waving his arms about, and taking a bow every so often. There were long silences and then raised voices, Gran's croaky one mostly.

'You have no idea . . . the goings on . . . the Reverend Mother was shocked . . . got herself pregnant . . . defiled herself . . . filthy . . . could easily have been . . . don't know what you expect . . . over there living it up.'

Dad made small sympathetic grunts. Mother's tone was haughty, and once or twice she even laughed, like a dry cough. With a wink of his eye, sinking down at the bottom of the stairs, Uncle Albert suddenly burst into song. 'How Are Things in Glocca Morra?' from *Finian's Rainbow*. I recognised it. I had seen the film the previous year. When I came out of the kitchen, with supplies of chocolate digestives and a milk moustache, he was still going strong. I licked my moustache, crammed two biscuits in my mouth, leant back by the bulldog umbrella stand, and waited for the song to finish.

'Why a boarding school in Scotland . . . you could have left . . . I'd have looked after . . . the boy needs . . .' Gran again.

'It's all settled.' That was Mother.

'All settled,' I echoed miserably through a mouthful of crumbs. Uncle Albert rose slowly to his feet and his voice rose with him. He was building to a crescendo, arms outstretched. I swear there were tears in his eyes. As the last note faded away he searched my face, desperately needing an answer to the lyric he'd been singing.

'Well,' I said, as truthfully as I could, quickly swallowing down the last of my biscuit and nearly choking on it, 'I'm not at all sure about Glocca Morra, Uncle Albert, but things are pretty crap here.'

Uncle Albert nodded as though he understood. I clapped a couple of times to show I appreciated his performance. He glowed a delighted pink at that. Then I ducked under his arms and headed upstairs where the girls were holding a conference—, well Jillian and Nicola were anyway. Alice was standing outside Gran's bedroom door, so Jillian must have lost it with her already. A bit later we all piled into the car and drove up North. We broke the journey in a B&B near Carlisle, and by then my stomach was churning. I reckoned it was how a condemned man feels the night before the execution.

'Eurrh, you're not going to have seconds?' Nicola was disgusted. She hadn't eaten any of her breakfast and neither had Alice. We could all hear the lady hawking and sneezing in the kitchen. I must say it was pretty revolting. But I still felt hungry. I could have eaten at least six eggs, twelve rashers of bacon and half a loaf, easy. Mother and Father went to settle up, Jillian and Nicola to get the bags, and then it was just Alice and me.

'Are you alright, Harry?' she asked, not in a soppy way, just straight-forward.

I sighed and cleaned my plate with a thick slice of white bread. 'I guess.'

'It might work out better than you think,' Alice tried.

I shrugged, sniffed noisily, and drained my cup of milk, then wiped my mouth with the back of a hand.

'Oh Harry, I'm sorry. I am so sorry and I can't . . . can't—'

I broke in there, and it ended up with me trying to make her feel better. The rest of the journey continued in silence, interrupted occasionally with the radio, or Jillian having a go at Alice, or Mother and Father mumbling to each other all secretively. By the time we arrived at the school outfitters it was pouring down with rain, and the sky was almost black. The woman in there, well, she was really thin and mean, and she kept tutting as she measured me, and saying that they didn't have such large sizes in stock.

'And the blazer too could be a wee problem. It's no good getting one that's a wee bitty tight. He'll only get bigger.'

She was on her knees with the tape measure in hand when she said this. Mother, she kept talking fast, like when you put a 33 record on at 45, and her face had this fixed smile on it, fixed the way a doll has. Father just looked uncomfortable. He started cracking jokes of all things. I tried to laugh, just to please him really, but honestly they weren't very funny. Alice kept fingering the tartan blankets, looking like she wanted to burrow down in one until she was invisible, while Jillian and Nicola were outside, heads together, probably trying to devise a plan. Once I'd gone, they knew they'd have to explain why they were being chucked out of the convent.

St David's Academy outside Stirling, that was where they all left me a few days later, journeying back down South. I rang and spoke to Mother just before they flew back to Hong Kong.

'Mother, please, please don't leave me here. Please, Mother,' I whispered into the communal pay phone. When I made the call there had just been me standing in the corridor, but now there was a queue. I cupped the mouthpiece trying to muffle my voice, so that the other boys wouldn't hear. I had brought lots of change with me but as it happened I didn't need it.

'Harry, darling, you're being so silly. You're bound to feel a touch homesick at first, but trust me, you'll soon settle in and start to love it.'

My silent voice spoke in my head then. It was screaming, screaming louder than Alice ever had. 'I hate it! I hate it! I hate it!'

'Mother, I'm . . . I'm begging you,' I mumbled, and it was like someone was inside winding me up tight.

The carrot-top behind me dropped to his knees, hands clasped, mimicking me. 'Mother, I'm begging you, begging you!' As he scrambled up they were all smirking and hooting with laughter.

'Now, darling, I simply must dash. I promise to write to you lots and lots. And before you know it, you'll be home for the Christmas holidays.'

There was a long pause then. I didn't say anything.

'Och come on, fatty. You've been ages,' carrot-top complained, giving me a shove.

'I've got to go now, Mother,' I said. I was drowning in the tears I could never shed.

Back she came, a famous actress delivering the last line in a play. 'Goodbye, my darling, my little man. You know how much we love you. Now make us both proud.' Then the click as the receiver was replaced. Carrot-top didn't even wait for me to hang up, just pushed me out of the way. 'Piss off, English piggy,' he sneered, giving me another dig with his elbow.

'Yeah, piss off, bog breath,' joined in the tall boy behind him. 'Piss off back to your mammy.'

Just as I shuffled off, the bell rang. Teatime. I started down the corridor. I could feel my buttock cheeks rubbing, because, in spite of everything, the seat of my trousers was rather tight, pushing them together. One of the masters stopped me and told me off, so I must have been running. I slowed down after that. I could feel the saliva rushing into my mouth and that hollowness in my tummy, and already I was imagining the texture of the food in my mouth, imagining it filling me up until I was rock hard. The boys' sniggers followed me down the stairs but I didn't care. I could smell the food now.

Ghost – 1970

It is the day of the party, the party Alice's parents hold each year on Boxing Day. Everyone seems preoccupied. Alice barely gives me a moment's thought. She is thinking about her father, that she will be able to spend time with him now he has a few days off. Over the past year he seems to have been absent even more than usual and Alice misses him. Because of this, she neglects me and I am hurt. That's why I upset the milk at breakfast. As Alice reaches for it, I tip over the large green and white striped china jug. It is very nearly satisfyingly full. The milk sloshes out soaking the tablecloth. Alice gives a gasp and snatches her hand away.

'Ah, so now I have your attention, Alice,' I tell her sweetly.

She pushes back her hair and rises, one of her hands covering an ear. She rubs it forcefully, as if she might like to pull it off. Alice's mother, too busy for breakfast she says, is a witness to my sleight of hand. All in purple, a shade so dark that when she moves into the shadows it appears almost black, Myrtle, on route to the kitchen, halts in her tracks.

'Alice, what have you done, you clumsy girl?' she cries, her voice so strident that I feel Alice's heart give a small jump, and her pulse quicken. She whirls about. Simultaneously, Jillian sitting on the opposite side of the table springs up with a horrified wail, as her lap gets a good drenching.

'I didn't do it,' Alice is quick to protest.

'Of course you didn't,' I tell her gaily. 'I did it. I've been so bored, Alice.'

'God, look at my skirt!' screams Jillian, her outstretched hands gripping the bunched, black-brocade hem of her skirt. 'This is new. Especially for the party. Now it's ruined!'

'Can't it be . . . be wa . . . ashed and . . . w . . . well dried in time,' Alice stutters anxiously. Her little fingers are tightly curled, that nervous habit of hers.

'No,' Jillian bites back, glowering at her sister. 'This very expensive skirt has to be dry-cleaned!' Her voice snags on the last word and is muffled as she clenches her teeth.

Nicola pokes her head round the dining-room door.

'I'm off. Taxi's here.' Her voice is upbeat. She scans the scene swiftly.

'Alice has soaked my dress in milk,' Jillian snarls.

Alice drops to her knees. She starts dabbing with a napkin ineffectually at the milk puddle appearing on the floor. She stares in dismay as the puddle widens, fed by a steady drip-drip from the sodden cloth above.

'Oh dear,' says Nicola glancing at her watch. 'I wish I could stay and help but I'm seeing Tom.' She turns to go, calling back to Jillian over her shoulder, 'You can borrow something of mine if you want, Jilly.'

A steady, if light dribble of milk, is also trickling into Alice's loose hair as she scuttles about, crab-like, on the floor. Alice's mother, surveying the scene, very nearly snorts with exasperation. The kitchen door opens a fraction and Ah Lee's head appears. It looks disembodied. Her white teeth show as she giggles nervously, taking in the upturned milk jug, and Alice diving at the milk puddles as they materialise.

'Missy Alice want me to—' But Ah Lee never finishes her sentence.

There is a loud bang, a very loud bang. It is so loud that this time everyone seems to jump. It emanates from the kitchen. Inside Alice, I flinch, remembering the sound of gunshots and what they importuned during the occupation. Ah Lee's head vanishes and we all

117

follow it into the kitchen. Once inside Myrtle Safford makes straight for the small chest freezer. The lid is open, propped against the wall, trails of frosty vapour billowing out of it. She pauses for a heartbeat before she peers over the brim, her hands scooping at the thick white mist that is bubbling out of it. I think she looks ghostly, standing there, bending over the chest, a few icy crystals clinging to the strands of her hair that have worked their way loose from her bun. She narrows her eyes until they are nearly sealed shut, and peers through the lashes. The contents of the freezer, at first lost in the smoky waterfall, slowly reveal themselves. Myrtle gives an anguished yelp, both hands closing over her mouth, and staggers back. Surely at the very least she has seen a mutilated body, the blood congealed, the flesh grey as dirty clay and hard as ice.

'What . . . is it?' asks Jillian cautiously, clutching her sodden skirt and inching forwards to take a peek.

Mrs Safford lets her hands fall away from her face.

'My magnum of champagne has exploded,' she says at last, her voice chiming out in plangent tones. 'It's . . . all . . . gone. All of it. Every drop.'

She rotates slowly, rooted to the spot, misty trails pooling now at her feet, like a stream of dried ice pouring onto a stage. Majestic. Livid. A frost queen.

'Alice.' She speaks the name slowly, to herself it seems. Repeats it as if she is impelled to let the dreadful resonance of it sound again in her mouth. 'Alice.'

Alice pushes her way past Jillian, leans forwards and looks into the open freezer, catching sight of a few clumps of frozen, golden champagne. She scrutinises the thousand slithers of green glass lodged in the icy crust that coats the freezer sides. 'They are like uncut emeralds,' she thinks, 'just lying in the snow.' She opens her mouth to deny all knowledge of placing the champagne in the freezer. Ah Lee giggles. Bear, lying across the back door that leads to the servants' quarters, yawns, stretches, stiffens and then relaxes. Ralph Safford bursts into the kitchen.

'What on earth is going on?' he demands.

Then all is bedlam, with Alice whining piteously that it isn't her fault, and Jillian screaming about her dress and the spilt milk and how it is ruined, and Myrtle, her face now disturbingly pale for one so angry, thundering that Alice has put the champagne in the freezer deliberately. Ah Lee accompanies this racket with bouts of unbridled mirth, her arms gesticulating wildly as she attempts to explain that she did it, she placed the champagne in the freezer, to keep it cool Mrs Safford she says. No one pays her any heed. Shortly after this Alice flees to her room and throws herself on her bed, her face buried in her pillow.

I listen to the sound of her frenetic breathing for a bit, waiting for her racing heart to steady itself. It is a couple of hours before we emerge. Alice climbs to her feet in slow stages, crosses to her dressing table, and fruitlessly attempts to draw a brush through her hair, but the milk has made it stick together. It is while she is thus occupied that Alice becomes aware of the front doorbell sounding several times. Eventually we slip out of her room to find the party happening without us. Alice nods to a few people she sees scattered throughout the corridor, glasses and platters of food balanced in their hands, chatting spiritedly.

'Alice, dearest,' says one elegant Chinese lady. She is wearing a silver-grey Cheongsam, with a carved, white-jade pendant on a heavy golden chain at her neck and a thick gold bangle encircling her delicate wrist. 'I was looking for you. I brought you a gift. I put it under the tree.'

Alice mutters her thanks and shoulders her way on down the corridor, through the steadily thickening pockets of guests. A few people embrace her, and one man, tall, with spiky dark hair, stops puffing on his cigar to peck her on the cheek.

'Alice, darling, I'm trying to persuade your father to bring you all to spend a couple of days with us in Macau. He keeps saying that he's too busy. We're all too busy, damn it. We have to make time for ourselves. Perhaps he'll listen to you.'

Alice nods, gives a quick smile and slides on by. We slip into the dining room. The room is transformed. Gone are the breakfast things, all traces of the spilt milk vanished. The table is laid with a fresh cloth, and piled high with joints of partially sliced ham, turkey and beef, wedges of cheese and bowls filled with golden curls of butter sitting on beds of ice cubes to keep cool. There are plates of biscuits and bread rolls, towers of fruit and several cakes. Ah Dang and Ah Lee dart to and fro to the kitchen replenishing supplies, scurrying around topping up drinks. We spot Harry filling a paper plate with crisps and wander up to him.

'Did you see what happened to Mother's magnum of champagne?' Alice asks, tugging at a knot of hair that the sticky milk has cemented together.

Harry grunts that he did. 'I think one of the amahs put it there, so you're off the hook,' he offers, uninterested. He shoves a handful of crisps into his mouth and drifts off.

Looking at the heaving table Alice feels a wave of nausea come over her, so we find our way onto the veranda for a breath of air. The jumble of conversation outside rolls over us in waves, reaching a deafening pitch. Then it seems to subside briefly, before once more gathering volume and fresh momentum. Spread hands slice the air, and fingers bend and uncurl, or swoop on some tasty titbit proffered by the giggling Ah Lee, or the solemn-faced Ah Dang, or they are jabbed emphatically, punctuating the speaker's intense dialogue. Spirals of cigarette smoke are ambushed by the breeze and stretched to translucence. Here too glass lenses catch the light as faces are raised, while mouths open and shut, and chew and pout and shake with laughter. The day is bright, and the sun, though thin, combined with the heat of so many bodies, generates a tolerable degree of warmth. Alice leans back against the veranda railing, taking in Jillian sitting on a rattan chair, smoking a cigarette and sipping a glass of wine. Her flint eyes have a brittle starriness about them, her eyelashes glued with blue mascara. She is wearing a dress of Nicola's, the scalloped neckline showing off her cleavage. And she is surrounded by friends all talking excitedly over each other. Myrtle Safford is clearly in her element, sweeping onto the veranda, clasping a glass of red wine. She moves through her guests, falling in and out of conversation with consummate ease. One moment she is gratifyingly amused at a joke she is told, the next, she is listening avidly to the retelling of some drama, her expression changing in perfect time with the altering mood of the speaker. Through the open glass doors that give onto the lounge, Alice sees her father mingling among his guests, always someone at his elbow vying for his attention. As the day wears on, the guests arriving dwindle in numbers, and one or two even prepare to leave.

Alice pushes her body off the veranda railing and strolls inside. Crossing the hall, she veers off her path answering the front door reflexively when she hears it. Phillip and Amanda Stubbs and their two children stand outside. Inside Alice the shock of recognition is palpable. Adrenalin surges around her body, her heart hammering, her mouth bone-dry, blood pounding in her ears. She reprimands herself silently for not expecting this meeting. The Stubbs, she knows, were invited to last year's party. She stands stiff as a scrubbing board and says nothing, while nestled within her, just like the freezing champagne, I am ready to burst.

'Hello, Alice,' says Amanda Stubbs in her low, kind voice. 'Merry Christmas.' Her husband grins amiably. Mrs Stubbs gives her children a little push forwards. 'We've brought Oliver and Jemima. Home for the holidays,' she says. Glancing at them, Alice can see that they take after their mother. Both are blue-eyed and golden-haired. The boy looks decidedly uncomfortable, hands thrust deep in his anorak pockets, shifting his slight weight from foot to foot. The girl has a dreamy set to her features, hiding behind her long fair hair. Still Alice's mouth remains clamped shut.

'We're not gate-crashing, Alice. We were invited. Promise,' Phillip Stubbs ventures, his eyes twinkling mischievously. He gives Alice a wink.

At this prompting she seems to remember herself and steps aside.

'Oh yes, sorry. Merry Christmas. Come in,' she says quietly.

As the family file in, Alice and Mrs Stubbs exchange a fleeting look.

' I . . . I . . . Mrs Stubbs I—' Alice stalls.

'Yes, Alice?' Mrs Stubbs asks, turning back.

'Your coats. I'll take your coats,' Alice mumbles. 'They'll be in my . . . my parents' bedroom.'

The Stubbs family shrug off their coats and hand them to Alice.

'What service, Amanda. Isn't she splendid?' Mr Stubbs says ingenuously. 'Oliver, Jemima, I hope you're watching this. Thank you very much, Alice.' He waves at a few friendly faces he has spotted across the hall.

'Yes, thank you, Alice,' Mrs Stubbs says softly. Jemima is hanging back, fingers resting lightly on the back of her mother's arm. Amanda Stubbs turns to plant a swift kiss on the top of her daughter's head. Oliver moves to his sister's side protectively.

Alice clears her throat. 'There's food in there and . . . and drink.' She nods in the direction of the dining room. 'Mother's on the veranda and . . . and Father's through there, in the lounge.' Phillip nods. Just before he steers Amanda through the open lounge door, he hesitates.

'If we have a really fine day, how would you like to come out on the *Seahorse* again, Alice? We had such a marvellous day last time. Do you remember?' When Alice does not reply immediately he adds a little uncertainly, 'You enjoyed it, didn't you, Alice?'

Alice pauses. 'Mm . . . well, yes.'

'Excellent. What say we make it just the Saffords and the Stubbs this time, and you can choose where we go, eh. How about that? What do you say, Amanda? The children would love it.'

'Sounds great, darling.' Mrs Stubbs's sad eyes are hooded. 'But you know Christmas is such a busy time. Alice is probably booked up.'

'Nonsense,' retorts Mr Stubbs cheerfully, already steering his wife through the lounge door with his hand pressed into the small of her back. 'I'll speak to your father, Alice.'

'Oh . . . thanks.' For a moment Alice stands still, then she starts to shoulder her way down the corridor with her armful of coats. She heaps them on her parents' bed with the many others already piled there.

Afterwards she goes to fetch herself a glass of water, and we walk in unwittingly upon her father and Amanda Stubbs in the kitchen. This time neither of them notices her. At first my host thinks they are looking for something in the kitchen cupboards, and then she realises they have found it. Alice's father and Amanda Stubbs are huddled between two open cupboard doors, and the only thing they are searching are each other's faces. Swiftly Alice turns on her heels and retreats to her bedroom. She sits on her bed in a patch of late afternoon sunlight. She stares at the pattern of wood grain on the parquet floor, sees the eye of a lion and the hooked beak of a huge predatory hawk hidden in the swirls. After a while there is a knock on the door. Alice looks up. Before she can invite the visitor in, the door opens and closes, and Amanda Stubbs is standing in Alice's bedroom.

'I was searching for the bathroom,' Amanda Stubbs says.

Alice snatches a hurried look at the immaculately dressed Mrs Stubbs, before casting her eyes down at the floor again. The image of Mrs Stubbs in a buttercup-yellow suit, a pencil skirt and matching jacket, her pale gold shoulder-length hair held back with a fawn velvet band, her lipstick freshly applied and very pink, burns on her retina.

'It's at the end of the corridor. Outside my bedroom door and just to the left,' Alice says briefly. She averts her gaze, fearing she might lose herself forever in those melancholy eyes.

But Amanda Stubbs makes no move to find the bathroom. Instead she comes and perches on the side of Alice's bed. They sit in silence for a bit. When Alice looks up she meets Amanda's eyes with hostility. Bear, who has sought refuge in Alice's bedroom from the hordes of people that the flat is currently teeming with, chooses this moment to crawl out from under the bed. He collapses at Amanda's feet with a sigh of fatigue so complete that it speaks for all of us.

'I'm not ever going to tell my mother, you know.' Alice is intransigent. In the distance the faint sounds of the party can be heard. Bing Crosby is crooning about a white Christmas, an unlikely event on the small island of Hong Kong, I muse, no matter how hard you dream about it. The chink of glasses and cutlery, peppered with sudden shouts of laughter or loud exclamations, drift down the corridor. This muted jangle makes the small quiet that now stretches out between Amanda Stubbs and Alice more marked. Alice casts about her bedroom for some distraction. She looks at the poster of the Beatles pop group, and at the small low table to the right of her bed crowded with dream pets, small stuffed animals all the colours of the rainbow.

'Mrs Stubbs, I know you want me to . . . you want me to tell my mother,' Alice says haltingly. Her diction is very precise, the consonants sounding with frightening crispness. 'But I shan't tell, not ever. If you need her to know, if . . . if you need my mother to know that you and my father are . . . you and my father . . . are . . . are fucking, then you must tell her yourself.'

Mrs Stubbs makes a sound, a smothered cry that dies in her throat. Her hands clasp over the nape of her neck seeming to drag her head down, her golden hair sweeping forwards, obscuring her face.

'You can't have him, Mrs Stubbs. You can't have my father,' Alice says. 'Well, I'm not going to give him to you anyhow. If you want him you have to take him.'

Mrs Stubbs's hair glistens in the white winter sunshine. The scent of her is carried on the air. It is a clean, fresh smell. Bear whines in his sleep and paddles his paws against the floor, a bad dream.

'Oh Alice—' Mrs Stubbs starts, breaking off suddenly, her hands falling away, her head coming up fractionally, her wistful blue eyes seeking out Alice's. There is a pause. The metal arm of one of Alice's bedroom windows, propped open a few inches, rattles softly. The draft lifts a few strands of Mrs Stubbs's golden hair. Then she speaks again. 'Help me. Please. Help me.' It is a monotone, lifeless.

Alice stares into her eyes. She sees they are no longer sad. Now they hold a chilling vacancy. Mrs Stubbs reaches a hand out to Alice, but when she touches her lover's daughter lightly on her arm, Alice recoils. Amanda rises to go.

'Why didn't you tell my father that I saw you, that I saw you together that day on Lamma Island, Mrs Stubbs?' Alice asks as politely as if she is inquiring if Mrs Stubbs likes sugar in her tea. She detects the faint whiff of sour milk coming from her hair. Her gaze strays outside her bedroom window, losing itself in the pale wash of sky. She sees a bird hanging, seemingly suspended there, frozen mid-air, wings outstretched, feathers ruffling, dark eye narrowing in on its prey. A kite, Alice guesses, buffeted by the wind, riding the current.

Amanda Stubbs walks towards the bedroom door. She places her feet carefully as if she is very high up, and knows that if she makes one false move she could fall. She rests her hand on the door handle, leaning heavily on it.

'I didn't tell him because . . . because,' she whispers hoarsely, 'because Alice, it would make no difference. There was . . . no . . . no point!' The door clicks shut behind her. The bird drops like a stone.

Jillian – 1971

The Boxing Day shindig's over, thank Christ, and I'm just about as far away as I can get from everyone, waking up in a Macau hotel room, with a sailor snoring at my side. Of course Mother thinks I'm staying with a friend, not that she's bothered anyway. Since the party she's been a bit preoccupied. I should say a bit *more* preoccupied. You always feel she's not quite there, as if she's going through the motions, her voice rising and falling when it should, her expression changing in perfect unison. 'Oh dear, that is a pity,' she says, and, 'Oh darling, you poor thing,' and, 'Of course you look lovely, Jillian,' and, 'Yes, I see exactly what you mean.' Only she doesn't. She's never seen what I mean. No one has. Except Nicola, and even she gets it wrong most of the time.

The sunlight's filtering through the curtains now, fiercely bright pages slanting through the gaps. You can see sparkling dust motes spinning in it. I'm looking down at my body, quite naked in the bed. I hate my body. It's a bit like a copy of Mother's, only with her all the proportions are just right— tall, voluptuous, fine facial bone structure, a grace about the way she moves. With me everything's just off a bit: too much fat on the hips, the legs not quite as long as hers, cellulite like orange peel clinging to the upper thighs, the breasts big, but droopy. I've seen Mum's breasts. Oh, she didn't show them to me, nothing like that. Christ no! It was through the keyhole. Peering through the keyhole, like a peeping Tom, at her magnificent body all steamy and pink in the bathroom. I just suddenly had to

126

know how we compared, mother and daughter. God, can you imagine if I'd asked her?

'Oh Mother, would mind showing me your tits, your thighs, and actually while you're at it, I wouldn't mind having a look at your pudenda.'

I know all the rude words. We used to look them all up in the dictionary at the convent, before copying them in the nuns' bibles and prayer books. Anyway, that's what I'd say. 'Could I have a quick peek at your pudenda, Mother.' Then, when she looked a bit put out, I'd elaborate. 'You see, Mother, the last boyfriend I had said my labia majora are a bit thin, sort of flappy. I think that's how he described them. He said he liked them 'plump as pigeon breasts, squashy, wet lips you have to prise apart to find the treasure hidden within.' Very poetical don't you think? The bastard was pissed.

I'd spew all this out while Mother was resting with a tiny cup of strong coffee after lunch, still a bit tipsy from the drinks she'd had. And I'd be perched on the end of her bed rifling through a maga-zine, *Woman's Realm* or something.

'Of course, darling,' she'd say with that set intonation of hers. 'Nothing easier.'

And she'd leap up and rip off her clothes, and stand there quite naked, while I strolled round her, thoughtfully nodding my head and rubbing my chin. Now of all fantasies you can have, that's got be the most implausible. So . . . so I peeped. And like the eavesdropper who listens in on something he would rather not have heard, I see that unlike me my mother has a near perfect body, that her breasts, though full, moving as she lifts and dips her arms, creaming herself, have great support. At that filthy convent, Jane, my friend Jane Redwood, she said she'd read if you could get a pencil under your tit, and when you let go it stayed there, that you had shit support. Well I could get a whole pencil case under each boob. It didn't matter how many times I raised my elbows and swung them back and forth like a chicken, doing my support exercises, they still hung there like droopy socks. And now I've been told the flaps of my cunt are too thin! Well Jesus Christ, they're the only things that are, then!

One more bit of me to worry about, because some drunken git of a boyfriend decides to tell me they're a disappointment!

It was Jane who got me started on the bulimia business. Skinny Jane who ate so much chocolate she was just one great big pimple.

'I've got no willpower,' I told her once. 'I want to lose weight but I just can't.' We'd sneaked behind the woodshed for a quick fag.

'Jesus Lord, you don't want to go worrying about willpower,' she told me grandly. 'Eat what you want and then just chuck it all up again.'

I couldn't quite believe what she was saying. 'You mean . . . mean . . . vomit?'

Jane took a long draw on her ciggie. Her eyes crinkled and she pursed her lips.

'You laughing at me, Jane?' I demanded, stubbing out my own smoke in a fit of pique.

'Don't get your knickers in a twist,' Jane told me like a puffing dragon. 'I'm just surprised you hadn't thought of it yourself. Eat as much as you like, and then stick your fingers down your throat and bring it all up again. And never gain a pound.' My disgusted face must have said it all. 'Oh, it isn't as bad as you think. After a while you get to be quite tidy and quick. It's just like the way birds regurgitate their food. Peasy.'

Not that peasy I thought, when two weeks later I still hadn't got the hang of it. But practice makes perfect, isn't that what they say. And now, it's second nature. Not so much in the day, but in the evenings, if you've made a bit of a pig of yourself. Brilliant. Well, not exactly brilliant. My throat hurts sometimes. I get headaches too, and I hate that feeling, the compulsion, making you do it. I hate that you can't just digest your food like everyone else is doing. You've got to find a loo quick, and then make sure no one's about to hear you throwing up. Drinking helps. Not alcohol, just liquid, makes it come sliding out more easily. Just when I think I can't bear to do it again, I see Alice, slim, fragile Alice, my little waif of a sister, who never overeats, who never seems to eat at all in fact. A sparrow couldn't survive on the lettuce leaves she nibbles on. And there am

I, a big, ugly cow, stuffing my fat face, then spending half my life down a toilet spewing it all up again.

He's snoring, the sailor by my side, prone and snoring like a foghorn. His name's Jack. He's a bit hairy. You know, hair on his shoulders, all down his back, not much of a turn-on. And now he farts. Terrific! But he isn't bothered. He isn't lying there worrying about the size of his dick. Oh, you can be sure of that. He woke up in the early hours and wanted to fuck. And so, because it was easier just to give in, we did. But it was one of those times when someone's on top of you, thrusting away with all their might, and you just can't stop your mind from wandering. I lay there thinking about how it's going to be for me here in Hong Kong, thinking about Alice and how I hate myself for despising her, but how I can't help it. I started counting how many times I've seen my father looking at Alice, those steely-blue eyes of his overflowing with love. He's never looked at me like that. Not once. Not one single time. Doesn't matter what she does, Daddy loves Alice.

I rouse myself then and shake Jack. He gropes for me.

'No!' I tell him flatly. 'We're getting up now and we're going out. Take a shower.'

He doesn't argue, just gets up blearily and stumbles into the bath-room. A moment later I hear him pissing a waterfall, then the toilet flushing. We're too late for breakfast but it sort of balances things out. I didn't manage to throw up supper you see. No opportunity. I just want to get outside, get some air. Can't breathe in this stuffy little room.

'What's the matter with you?' says Jack, tamping down his springy brown hair. He doesn't say it nastily. He's got an Irish accent, soft, southern. His mother comes from Cork he says. He's an okay bloke. Off one of the British ships in the harbour, and wanting nothing more than to spend a bit of money and have a good time. I shrug and he rubs my shoulders. It's quite nice actually. Of course he's married. They're all married. Most of them don't even bother to take off their rings. 'You're beautiful, you,' he says, and pecks me on the cheek.

'Let's just go,' I counter, trying to keep the weariness from my voice. Think of Mother. She would never let the side down by giving the ugly troll skulking under the bridge a hand up.

We go for a coffee, and I'm really starting to enjoy myself. Then Jack says how great it is to have company over the festive season, and so nearly blurts out 'when you're away from home'. I visualise home then, his home, with his wife stirring something yummy on the stove, raising the steaming spoon to her mouth, tasting and smacking her lips. Then calling out to Jack, face aglow, that his dinner's ready, popping the baby in its playpen, and cooing at it, on and off, through the meal.

'I bet you count yourself lucky,' I find myself saying, pushing my coffee cup away. Suddenly it tastes very bitter.

'Sure I do, Baby,' says Jack on cue, reaching for my hand. 'This is,' he breaks off and nods emphatically, a little too emphatically actually, 'this is fantastic. Being here with you.'

But oh dear me, that troll is definitely coming out to play today, like it or not. Look away now, Mother, it's not going to be a pretty sight.

'I should think you're enjoying this a lot more than finding a whore to fuck in Wan Chai.'

Poor Jack looks poleaxed. He gobbles at the air like a turkey, before finally managing to come up with a line. And oh Christ, yes, he hesitates for a moment, just to make sure he's got the name right.

'Jillian, what's the matter with you?' he says, giving my hand, still clasped in his, a little shake. 'What are you suggest—'

But by now the troll is out, a knobbly-kneed leg already over the bridge railings.

'Though I expect I'm a little dearer than a prostitute. Though I don't know. I suppose it depends what kind you go to. A five-dollar fuck up against a wall, or a high-class, overnight, hundred-dollar, no holes barred orgy. I've heard that it can be quite expensive to have the works.'

Jack lets go of my hand. He won't meet my eyes now. He clears his throat noisily. He's a smoker. So am I, so I can't really complain.

And already his hand is fumbling in his jacket. He taps the packet on the table, offers me one and I decline. Today, for some reason, I am certain that first drag would make me retch. With his lips he pulls a ciggie out of the packet. Again he fumbles for matches, strikes one, holds it to the tip with a steady hand, and lights it. Then he is inhaling deeply, gratefully, oh so gratefully, poor bugger.

'I guess I'm what you call a high-class escort,' I limp on. But the fight has gone out of me, and the troll is already moving back into the shadows under the bridge again. Though I don't apologise. It's not much, but it's something.

Jack surveys me curiously, as if I'm an island native, as if he has never encountered anything quite like me before, even though he has travelled the seven seas. Then he grins, a dog's grin, the kind Bear pins on sometimes, the kind that says, 'I don't understand what the fuck is going on, but hey, let's just go for a walk, have a pee and forget all about it.'

Again that fractional pause. 'Jillian, I'm going to take you sight-seeing. Anywhere you want. You just say. After that we're going out for a meal. And we're having champagne, the best French champagne, none of that rice-wine shit. Then before we have to catch the ferry back, I'm going to take you to a market and buy you anything you want. How's that?'

He doesn't wait for a reply, slips the packet of fags in his pocket, produces a wallet, throws a bill on the table and off we go. And we do have a good time, for a couple of hours at least. We visit the Kun Lam Temple and the Ruins of St Pauls, though the Catholic façade freaks me out a bit. For a while I'm back in that gloomy convent, more like a morgue than a house of God. But I have to say we did have a laugh.

'Have you noticed how much weight Sister McMullen is gaining?' Nicola would hiss in an Irish accent. 'Oh mother of God, could she be eating for two?' And on down the line it went, Chinese whispers, Nicola hamster-cheeked by then, hand clamped over her mouth trying to contain her giggles. Or she'd be pencilling in moustaches, sunglasses, ciggies and anything else she fancied on all the pictures of saints in her bible, or surreptitiously passing a foil condom packet down the row. Before long we were all falling about laughing, and the nuns not knowing what it was all about, looking like rows of battleaxes. Nicola's great like that, taking the black stuff and spinning it, until it's as light and sweet as candyfloss. Trouble is, once you've woofed it down, once it's gone, the black comes crawling back. And somehow it's even darker, because of the brief spell of light.

Anyway, apart from that, my sailor and I do have fun. A great meal, and true to his word we *do* have champagne, and the bubbles go up my nose, the way they describe, only it rarely happens. Then sailor Jack, doing everything he can to make me happy, until I find myself thinking, never mind about the hairy back, hails a taxi.

'Market! Shopping! *Fai d La*! *Fai d La*!' yells Jack at the driver, and off we speed.

And just about then, for a short interval, I really believe that I am that girl on the big screen, on holiday with the boyfriend she's falling in love with, the one who can't take his eyes off her, that before long we'll sail off into the rose-pink sunset. As we get out I'm laughing, shouting with laughter. Jack's laughing too, and I notice he has really gorgeous green eyes, deep green flecked with dark gold. We link arms.

'You can have anything you want my darlin',' says Jack, and I think he's a little drunk because his Irish brogue is getting more pronounced. 'You just point, my sweetheart, an' it yours.'

And I do point. I point at a pale-pink, padded-brocade jacket, and a string of beads that the stallholder says is best green jade, but that I think is plastic. Still, who cares? Jack's paying, so who bloody cares? I'm about to point at a royal blue Cheongsam, when I see that my fingertip has found something else, something several stalls down from us, something very striking indeed. In fact, one of a kind. My divining finger has found my father. But oh no, not just him. It's found a woman accompanying him. I recognise the woman. She has blonde hair, and gentle blue eyes, and a way of smiling that makes you feel as if crying would be more in order. She came to the Boxing Day Party. It's Amanda Stubbs.

Neither of them sees me. I duck behind the row of dresses. My heart is running away and I can't stop it, can't contain it. Jack is distracted, fingering a tray of tacky keyrings on the stall across the way, with a pretty young Chinese girl trying to sell him all of her wares. I slip my hands between two silky Cheongsam, red and gold. My fingers and palms meet. To a passer-by I must look as if I'm praying. And perhaps, considering, that wouldn't be a bad idea. When I open my hands, and my eyes, for I realise with surprise they are closed too, my father and Amanda Stubbs are having some sort of altercation. Mrs Stubbs's slim white hands are flying all over the place, and she is not wearing her smile. She is talking urgently, and I am sure I see a tear spill from one eye. I'm sure because it catches the light and I see it move down her face, winking and sending out its SOS.

I can only see half of my father's profile such is the angle, though more of Amanda. People keep jostling past, blocking my vision. But then, in one of the gaps, another tear spills from Mrs Stubbs's eye, and my father turns so I can see his whole face. He leans down and kisses it, kisses her pain away. And it's like a needle being thrust straight into the centre of my eye, a slither of anguish which, I know no matter how many years I live, will never quite go. They turn. They are at a crossroads in the alleys, then they move off down another lane. It was only an instant, a splinter of time, glimpsing into my father's face, into those ice-blue eyes of his. They were rent with love those eyes. Now they are gone, and Jack is hovering behind me.

'Well my darlin' what would you like? You can have anything darlin', anything at all,' he says flamboyantly, his lips tickling my ear. I can smell the booze on his breath. It's not unpleasant, just there.

What would I like? Oh my God, my God, I would like someone, just once, for one brief moment in my sawdust life, to look at me the way my father looked at Amanda Stubbs. That's what I would like.

Myrtle – 1971

Amanda Stubbs is dead. She committed suicide last weekend. I am not as surprised as most. She was, as they say, of a fragile temperament. I'm sure some men found that attractive in her, but I found it irritating. Only weeks ago she was at our Boxing Day party with her children. I doubt she ever gave them a second thought. Phillip is desolate of course. Now I suppose everyone will want to know why she did it. They'll be ferreting about to see if they can find a reason, a reason why she would want to leap from a balcony of the Mandarin Hotel, plummeting to her death. I was talking it over with Beth Fielding yesterday, Wednesday. She popped round for a drink. I was all out of vermouth, Beth's favourite tipple, but as it happens it didn't really matter because what we both felt like was a stiff brandy.

'She was so beautiful,' Beth said mawkishly, helping herself to peanuts from a small lacquer bowl on the drinks table, flicking them in her open her mouth and chomping them up with distasteful enthusiasm. The whole process, from selection to consumption seemed somehow irreverent. 'Yes, very beautiful. No one could argue with that.'

I agreed, but added that some beauty was only skin-deep. And Beth, who was on her second brandy by then (we both were), seemed to know exactly what I meant.

'Perhaps she was having an affair?' Beth suggested. I shrugged, hands open, as if I thought it unlikely. 'Perhaps,' said Beth ruminatively, 'whoever it was wanted to end it?'

'Perhaps,' I echoed, draining my glass. I took Beth's brandy balloon, topped it up, and poured myself a third drink. Although it was lunchtime we had had a shock so I felt it was warranted. And Beth didn't protest, therefore I must have judged the mood correctly.

'Maybe he told her it was all over,' Beth hazarded, taking the brandy I held out to her. She then tried to eat and drink concurrently. The result was that she very nearly choked, her face scarlet.

'Would you like some water, Beth?' I offered.

'I'll be fine,' Beth croaked. She took a hefty gulp of her brandy. 'This'll do the trick,' she said. There was a hiatus in the conversation while her complexion faded from a fiery red to a florid pink. Then, with a sharp intake of breath, Beth suddenly grasped my wrist. 'Myrtle, do you think he might have been at your party, the man she was seeing I mean?'

I took a swallow of my own brandy. It was Courvoisier and it was good. But Beth did rather guzzle at everything. She couldn't help it, poor dear. 'Unlikely,' I speculated. 'Not with her husband there and the children. Too risky.'

'Quite right,' said Beth nodding thoughtfully, drawing a hand back and patting her brassy curls. 'But I wonder . . . I wonder who it is then,' she went on reflectively. 'You saw it happen, the tragedy?' she probed, her eyes bright with curiosity. Whatever people say, they have a keen appetite for ghoulish details in a situation like this. There seems little point to me in pretending otherwise. Beth certainly did and I was happy to volunteer the information.

I shook my head and explained that Ralph and I had arrived at the reception just afterwards. 'We were late, Beth. Dreadful traffic,' I elucidated as an afterthought. 'It was all over by the time we arrived. Poor Amanda was lying prostrate on the roof of the lobby. Probably just as well she jumped there. Over the lobby I mean. Otherwise she might have fallen on someone. Imagine that.'

Beth made a small grating noise at the back of her throat, and her doughy face crumpled. I patted her on the back consolingly.

'Whatever is that perfume you're wearing, Beth dear? It's simply divine,' I asked pacifically.

Beth looked pleased. 'Diorissimo,' she told me, her cheeks once more reddening, but with delight. 'Nigel bought it for me.' She had finished the peanuts, and her tongue probed busily for any morsels that might remain lodged in her teeth. The effect was that of a living organism seeking escape from the closed cavern of her mouth.

'He's a sweetheart, your husband,' I told her. Beth preened. 'Can you bear for me to go on?' Beth nodded decisively. Those curls of hers could certainly do with a bit of taming. When she shook them about and they landed all awry like that, she looked perfectly ridiculous. She took a swift gulp of her drink. I made a mental note to talk to her about her hair dye too. In the afternoon light the colour was an unfortunate chrome yellow, the effect of it cheap and tawdry. Misreading my expression of disapprobation, she lowered her glass and gave me her full attention.

I continued. 'Well, her blonde hair was steeped in blood. It was pooling about her head. She'd landed on her back, and although I'm sure her skull under all that hair must have been completely crushed, her face was untouched. It looked quite calm. Not a speck of blood on it. Her eyes were wide open, staring upwards. That was the worst part of it I think. Those blue eyes. Ooh, it makes me shiver just to picture them. She was wearing a long gown. Red it was, very fetching actually, with sequins sewn into it. It must have blown upwards as she fell. There would have been quite a draught you understand. It was all rucked up around her waist. It looked like a red serpent writhing about her. You could see her panties. Cream lace. Her legs were splayed and twisted at odd angles. Broken certainly. Well, they would be wouldn't they? One arm was hidden under her back and the other seemed to be reaching for something. She looked . . . indecent, her legs apart like that and the panties showing. I told one of the policemen to cover her up. He argued at first. Gabbling about it being a crime scene or something. Then Ralph stepped in. He said something in Cantonese, very curt. He can speak a bit of Cantonese you know. I didn't understand what he said, but they covered her immediately and after—'

'Well, Ralph wouldn't stand for any nonsense, would he, Myrtle?' Beth interjected.

I half smiled. My drink was finished and four really would be pushing it. I thought I might ask the amahs to bring in some more snacks to soak up the booze. Otherwise, I decided, not much would be accomplished that afternoon.

'How did Phillip take it?' Beth prompted, breaking into my reverie.

'He was distraught, naturally. Beside himself,' I said. 'He kept saying, all Amanda told him was that she needed a breath of air. She was popping onto the balcony for some fresh air. That she would only be minute. And that . . . poor man . . . was the last time he saw his wife.'

Beth was lachrymose. She shook her head and pressed the well-padded heels of her hands into her fleshy eye sockets. As she smoothed away her tears she smeared her foundation. It was a rather alarming orangey shade that looked even worse in streaks. She rippled the plump fingers of her hands on her equally plump thighs. Her rings, the white-gold wedding band, the sapphire and diamond engagement ring, and that rather fetching platinum eternity ring encrusted with yet more diamonds, looked tight and uncomfortable, as if she would only be able to remove them with the assistance of large quantities of soap and lubricants. And it was my feeling that some people should never wear slacks. Beth was doing herself no favours with her current wardrobe. They were salmon-pink too. Such a bold, attention-grabbing colour. Still, I've always believed that dress sense is something you're born with, not something you acquire. Some might say my observations on Beth were a trifle waspish, but I feel it is your duty when you have a friend making a fool of herself to bring it to their attention.

'How dreadful for Phillip,' breathed Beth, shifting from buttock to buttock and pulling down the legs of her slacks at the knee, presumably to make herself more comfortable.

'Yes, it was,' I acknowledged, leaning forward to rub at an old lipstick smudge I had noticed on my glass 'After the police had spoken to him, we took Phillip back to his flat. Thank God the children had gone back to boarding school.'

Beth nodded her agreement, clearly thinking of hers and Nigel's children, Christopher and Anita, neither of whom had been sent to boarding school. Briefly I recalled Beth's foreknowledge of the Island School, which she elected not to share with me, and reminded myself to proceed with caution. 'That was my first thought. Imagine trying to explain it to them? I poured us all a drink. I couldn't think what else to do. Phillip cried. Like a baby. It was very disconcerting. Racking sobs. His entire body shaking. Ralph held him. The sounds he made were awful, ugly, unnerving. He kept asking why. Over and over again, why would she do it. Wild red eyes. Ashen-faced. Skin sodden with tears, mucus and saliva. He looked ghastly. The doctor came and left Phillip some pills to help him sleep. Then between us we put him to bed. Ralph gave the flat a quick once-over, in case there was a note, he said. But there was nothing. Ralph decided to stay, said he didn't want to leave Phillip by himself. I called a taxi.'

'He's such a good friend to Phillip.' Beth picked up her brandy and for once sipped it contemplatively. 'Friends like him are few and far between. I heard she'd been having treatment for depression.'

'It wouldn't surprise me,' came my retort. The mantelpiece clock ticked heavily into the sudden silence.

'She never said anything to you about being depressed did she?' Beth's free hand strayed to an ivory pendant at her neck. She worried at it.

'Never. Amanda and I were not close friends. She hardly spoke to me at all.'

'But then she was a bit like that wasn't she? Kept herself to herself. Except of course at your party.' Beth's tone was breezy. I matched it.

'At my party?' I questioned, still rubbing at the lipstick mark on the glass.

'Yes,' said Beth, her hands sandwiched over the folds at her waist. 'I had to nip back across the way to get the address of my tailor for Christine Gibson. She loved the frock I was wearing. The green velvet. You know the one. She told me she wasn't that happy with her own chap. Anyway, Jillian was at the front door seeing off her crowd of friends, such characters I thought, and it seemed rude to elbow through them, so I went the other way. Out of your back door, past the servants' quarters and through to my back door. That's when I saw you, by the laundry rack, with Amanda.' I must have shot Beth a disbelieving look and she took up the challenge. 'Yes. Oh yes I did, Myrtle. You had your back to me, Myrtle, but I knew it was you, in that divine purple gown of yours. You and Amanda had your heads close together. Hatching a plot were you? Quite a conspiracy going on, I judged. If not that, then a disagreement perhaps? An altercation?' She stroked her belly and flicked me a smile. 'Some topic that you both felt passionately about, certainly. Though this is all guesswork you understand. I didn't listen in to your conversation. Well of course I didn't. I'm no eavesdropper. Besides, your voices were lowered and it was impossible to hear a thing, with the wind blowing through those funny little octagonal openings in the walls. But I do remember Amanda's face. It was white as a lily, with the oddest spots of red on her upper cheeks. And her eyes . . . that was so peculiar, because she normally has, I suppose I should say had, that serene look about them. No, that's not right. I mean pensive. Yes, that's it. They were pensive eyes. But not that day. Oh no, not when I saw her out the back with you, Myrtle dear. They were . . . ablaze. Mm . . . that's it. That's what I remember. Her blazing blue eyes.'

The ticking of the clock suddenly seemed inordinately loud. I had abandoned my attempt at wiping off the lipstick. I would mention it to the amahs. They were getting slack. Once or twice recently I had taken fresh glasses from the cupboard, and found them still bearing the faint traces of lipstick about the rim, or smeary fingerprints on the stem or the glass itself. It just wasn't good enough. 'Oh that,' I said at length, my tone insouciant. 'We were discussing boarding schools. Amanda said that they were having a problem with bullying at the one they send Oliver to. She must have been angry about it. In fact now I recall she was rather upset.'

I stood. I waited. Beth picked a speck of dust from the sleeve of her jacket and crushed it between her fingers. 'Oh I see,' she said, stressing 'see' needlessly I felt. 'I didn't think it was important. Not something worth mentioning to the police at any rate.' She gave a breathless laugh. She had a tendency to wheeze. I don't think her weight helped her out much there either. If she wasn't careful she could wind up asthmatic. 'I guessed it was something of that sort. Looks can be so deceptive, can't they, Myrtle?' Beth continued. 'There was I imagining all sorts of silly scenarios, and the two of you were just comparing notes on boarding schools.' Now Beth looked up, her greedy green eyes meeting mine.

I smiled a slow, lazy smile. I hoped to convey nothing so much as complete relaxation. 'I thought I would ask the amahs to bring in some snacks. I'm feeling a bit peckish. How about you, Beth?'

'What a horrible way to die,' Beth said. 'It doesn't bear thinking about does it? Falling through all that space and smashing to pieces on the lobby roof of a luxury hotel. Anyone would think, looking at her life . . .' she paused to draw in a husky, faltering breath, 'that . . . that she had everything. But something must have been missing to make her do a thing like that.' Beth suppressed a belch and thumped her chest with a fat fist. 'Excuse me!'

'There, you see I was right. You *are* hungry, aren't you, Beth?'

'I could eat something,' said Beth obliquely.

I crossed to the lounge door. 'How about a nice cheese sandwich, and I'm sure we have some of that delicious Christmas cake left?'

'Sounds wonderful,' Beth replied absently. Her focus had shifted to a copy of the *South China Morning Post* on the shelf under the drinks table. She drew it out, flapped it open and buried her nose in it. 'There's a wonderful article here about the Mayo Clinic Diet, Myrtle. Not that you need to diet. Rather a lot of eggs if I remember rightly. Have you read it?'

'No.' I opened the lounge door. 'I think we might even have a few mince pies that could be warmed up. And I know we have some cream.'

'Mm . . . I just fancy a mince pie.' As I stepped across the hall I

140

found myself musing that my friend Beth was quite a sleuth. My, my, what sharp little eyes you have, Beth dear! All the better to see you with, Myrtle. Hmm . . . And I'd never noticed it before. She'd probably read one detective novel too much. Still, perhaps it would be best to be a touch more guarded in her company. I wouldn't want to give any more fodder to that overactive imagination of hers. As I entered the dining room, making for the kitchen door, Beth's voice followed me.

'I'm not sure I could cope with all those eggs though, Myrtle. They do tend to bind me up rather.'

Beth overstayed her welcome that day. I would have liked her to go much earlier, but then it's awkward showing a friend the door, particularly in the light of recent events. Beth made it clear that she needed to talk, to express her sorrow. So I listened, and listened, and listened. I never thought I'd say I was extremely glad to hear Alice arrive home. Beth made tracks shortly after that, and I was able to steal into my bedroom, lock the door and have a bit of blessed peace. Ralph rang in the evening and told me he'd be late again. He's been spending a great deal of time with Phillip over the past week, helping with arrangements to fly the body back to England for the funeral and burial, dealing with the police and so forth. I told him he'd done enough already, that he needed an early night, but he didn't seem to hear me.

'I owe it to him,' he said tightly and refused to be drawn further.

He's not been himself lately. Actually I think he's having some sort of belated reaction to the strain of the riots. I know it was a long time ago now, but these things happen. All that stress was bound to take its toll eventually. But he's adamant he doesn't want to see a doctor. When he finally arrived home he refused dinner, said he had work to do and shut himself up in the lounge. Jillian stays with friends most of the time now. Nicola was out and Alice was goodness knows where, so at least I didn't have to warn the children off. I went in, took him a coffee and asked him if he wanted to talk about it. But he just waved me away and said he was fine. He was so late coming to bed that I fell asleep in the end. After all, it had been quite a day, what with Beth's extended visit. When I woke up and glanced at the bedside clock it was nearly 2:30am. Ralph's side of the bed was empty. I got up and slipped on my dressing gown. I had fallen asleep without drawing the curtains. I often do. Our bedroom is the first one you come to on the long corridor. From its windows you have an excellent view of the veranda jutting out from the side of the building. Naturally it was dark, but there was sufficient light spilling out from the lounge for me to be able to see Ralph clearly. He was leaning over the veranda railing, his eyes looking not outwards but downwards. His head was almost lolling on his shoulders. Honestly, for a moment I wondered if he had dropped off to sleep. Then he lifted his face to the moon, slowly, as if it was a great effort, and sighed. The windows were open. It was a fine night and the sound he made was clear as glass. It reminded me of a cat I found just weeks after Father died. It was lying in the road outside the house in Ealing. I think it had been hit by a car. Its eyes were pink with blood, and there was blood on its whiskers too, and a sticky mess of yellow fluid oozing from an ear. As I picked it up it gave a sigh, a throaty moan that seemed to have been drawn from its trembling body by some kind of external force. And with that it let go of life.

The following day I called the Public Works Department, the PWD. I had given the amahs strict instructions to tell Beth I was out if she called. I stood on the veranda where Ralph had prowled the previous night. I took hold of the balcony rail, my fingers curling around the painted white pole. It was cold and hard. I peered down. It was a long way to the ground. It seemed truly astonishing to me that I had never seen it before. Falling from it would be easy. Perhaps it takes a suicide, someone you know crashing to her death from a hotel balcony, to make you understand how close you are to the edge yourself. The gentleman I spoke to at the PWD was Mr Chen, a helpful man if a little dense. I had had dealings with him before. When the flat was being decorated last year, as it is annually, I selected magnolia, playing safe, and came home to find lemon yellow splashed all over my walls. He was very apologetic and sorted it out as quickly as he could. But nevertheless he owed me a favour.

'Mr Chen, this is Mrs Safford, Ralph Safford's wife.' He acknowledged me with his usual deference. 'I should like bars fitted to the windows of our flat on The Peak,' I said without preamble.

'Bars, Mrs Safford?' he queried.

'Yes Mr Chen. I am worried about the children falling out.'

There was a pause. The black telephone receiver seemed inexplicably heavy in my hand at that point.

'Falling . . . mm . . . falling out of the windows, Mrs Safford?' Mr Chen verified.

His tone of incredulity annoyed me a great deal. 'Yes Mr Chen. And off the veranda too,' I added for good measure. There was another pause presumably while Mr Chen took a mental inventory of the ages of our children, whom he had met on several occasions while supervising work on our flat. 'I know they're teenagers, Mr Chen, but . . . well . . . you never know do you?' I said in answer to his unasked question. 'Better to take precautions now, before there's a nasty accident, wouldn't you say, Mr Chen?' I tried to instil a ring of maternal zeal into my voice.

'Indeed Mrs Safford, but I am just surprised that you have not made this request until now.'

That made me fume. As if it was any business of his to second-guess me. I was Ralph Safford's wife and I wanted bars on my windows, and that should have been quite sufficient for him to get cracking having them fitted as far as I was concerned. Down the phone line he must have become aware of his own impertinence, because now he stepped in quickly.

'Of course, Mrs Safford. How many windows would you like fitted with bars?' I sighed crossly. This fellow really was slow on the uptake.

'Why, all of them, Mr Chen,' I rounded on him, my patience tried to its limit. 'It wouldn't be much good having some with bars and some without. The children could just as well tumble out of one as all of them.'

'Yes, I see that now, Mrs Safford.' Mr Chen sounded penitent and I felt marginally appeased.

'And the veranda too. I want a strong metal grid fitted from the veranda railing to the roof.'

There was a barely perceptible pause.

'But Mrs Safford . . . ' he tailed off, his courage I suspect failing him.

'Yes Mr Chen?' I prompted him edgily.

'It will make your veranda look a bit like—' This time he ground to a halt. I heard him take a quick gasp of breath. Then in a rush, 'It will make your flat on The Peak look a bit like a cage . . . a cage in the sky, Mrs Safford.'

'Never mind that,' I dismissed his objection peremptorily.

'And when would you like—' Mr Chen began, but I cut him off.

'Oh just *do* it, Mr Chen! Get your coolies up here as soon as is humanly possible and do it,' I snapped. Mr Chen assured me he would have a team working on it by the end of the week. And with that I had to be satisfied.

Ghost – 1971

Lots of Chinese men arrive and fit bars to all the windows. They secure a belt of wire mesh between the veranda railing and the roof. They make the flat on the Peak into a prison. Mr Safford seems to be the only one who barely notices the changes. Jillian corners Alice whenever the opportunity presents itself.

'See what you've done,' she hisses, or, 'This is all your fault, Alice,' or 'Poor mother!' Her eyes rake the length of the corridor repeatedly, taking in the tunnel of bars with a groan.

Nicola insists we all look on the bright side. She tells her siblings that, whatever accidents befall them, they may rest assured that plunging to their deaths from our flat won't be one of them. When Harry comes home for the Easter holidays he stares at the barred windows in puzzlement. He moves slowly down the corridor pausing to grasp a bar and give it a good tug, as if he doesn't quite believe they are fixed in place, as if he thinks he might dislodge them, as if he is contemplating escape. At mealtimes shadow bars fall across the faces of the Safford family ranged about the table. Alice takes to gazing out of the dining-room window, her brow furrowed. She watches the sun set through the barred bathroom window. She looks with undisguised envy at aeroplanes and birds and even insects. The amahs grow mutinous.

'Why putting bars on all the windows?' they demand daily as they bustle about the flat. For once Ah Lee does not think this is a joking matter. She wrings her hands and squints at the bars suspiciously, her high forehead screwed into deep lines, her mouth tightly crimped. She clicks her tongue, 'Tsk tsk,' and she shakes her head.

Ah Dang pauses frequently in her daily tasks, glaring suspiciously from one window to the next, her hands pulled into fists and resting on her wide hips.

'*Ai ya! Ai ya!*' she says. 'How I clean the windowpanes now. This is very, very bad sign. We trapped with a crazy *Gweilo* family. *Zao gao!*'

Even Bear looks shaken, trying to pounce on the ever-shifting slanted shadows, his paws always bewilderingly empty. He eyes them warily as they slide across the floor, growling and backing away from them when they come too close.

Myrtle Safford is the only one who does not seem to be struggling to acclimatise herself to our prison. She is in good spirits, humming and whistling to herself, satisfaction cloaking her face as she surveys the sturdy bars. Of course I can slip through them with ease but Alice is not so lucky. She keeps counting them. Surprisingly she did not seem pleased by the news of Amanda Stubbs's death. When her mother told her that Mrs Stubbs had killed herself, Alice put her diary into the metal wastebin in her bedroom. She struck a match and set light to it. The pages went up in a whoosh, but the leather cover only charred and smoked for a bit. I can still detect an acrid odour in her room. A good storm might clear the air.

Nigel – 1971

It is August the 16th. Typhoon Rose is heading for the colony. At around 5am the radio informs me that Signal No. 3 is being hoisted, that she is about 150 miles away to the south. Despite this, I set off as usual for work, as does my next-door neighbour across the way, Ralph Safford. I am hopeful I can sit out the worst of it downtown, overnight at the office if necessary. By 10am, Signal No. 3 has risen to the North-east Gale, Storm Signal No. 7. Rose, we are told, is compact and deadly. Just after midday the South-east Gale, or Storm Signal No. 8, warns that the gale-force winds have altered course. It is clear from forecasts that Typhoon Rose means business. During the afternoon my wife rings me three times, urging me to come home. I find myself wishing that the phone lines would go down.

'I've picked the children up from school,' Beth tells me. 'They say it'll really take hold this evening. At a time like this you should be with your family. Come home, Nigel.' This last is a wail.

I ask her if she has seen to it that the amahs board up the windows, put the antiques away, get the candles ready and so forth.

'Yes I have,' she says. Her voice is sulky, like a recalcitrant child's.

'Then you know the best place to stay is in the hall. Centre of the flat. Most secure. No windows to blow out.' Personally I feel a lot safer in the offices in Central during a typhoon than I do exposed on the top of The Peak.

'Ralph Safford is coming home.' Beth is resentful. 'Myrtle has said we should all go over there and shelter.'

147

Ah, at last we have it. Beth doesn't wish to be shown up, wants Myrtle Safford to know her husband comes to heel just the same as Ralph does. God, I think, we'll be packed like sardines in that hall! The way things are going we could be there all night rubbing up against each other. Besides, I can think of plenty of other places I'd prefer to while away the hours during a typhoon. But I suppose I will never hear the end of it if I don't go back. By the time I get there, a little after 6pm, Rose is just getting into her stride. The skies are black as night. The rain is sheeting down. The wind really is howling. Getting from the garage to the flats' lobby is a feat in itself. And it's not just the gale-force winds you have to worry about, but all the debris whirling through the air. You'd be surprised what those winds can pick up and toss around. Anything loose. Anything not bolted down. How must the hillside squatters, the ones still waiting to be resettled, feel? Poor blighters. At least I have bricks and mortar between my family and the tempest.

Anyway, battered and sodden I finally manage to get the heavy swing doors of the lobby open. Greeted by Stygian gloom I stumble in. A power failure naturally. It is a laborious process, feeling my way up several flights of stairs to the top floor in near darkness. Everything is rattling and groaning and creaking and sighing, as if the building is on the verge of collapse. As I climb I begin to experience that rather unpleasant disconcerting sensation of the floor swaying gently under my feet, the entire edifice yielding to the relentless drag of the wind. I know it's a safety measure built in by architects – that what bends won't necessarily break – but when you're the one rolling about in a vertiginous top-floor flat on The Peak, logic is cold comfort.

Myrtle Safford, an eerie sight, answers my thumps on the door. Her hair, normally swept up in a bun, is loose and flowing over her shoulders. I've never seen it like that before. In her hand she holds a flickering candle. There are more candles placed about the room, on occasional tables and on the bar. The dancing flames make a play of light and shadow on Myrtle's face, and on the surrounding walls. I recall the Garrison Players' production of *Macbeth* that we caught at the City Hall a couple of months ago. Ralph's wife looks the very image of Lady M. in her sleepwalking scene.

'Out, out damned spot, eh?' I jest as I cross the Safford threshold, and am rewarded with a winning smile. She is quite a woman, Myrtle Safford, just the sort who might think nothing of doing away with a king, if it enabled her husband's ascendancy. Or perhaps I'm just jealous. I have not been awarded an OBE like Ralph Safford. And it is just the kind of window-dressing that the in-laws back in old Blighty would love. I glance over at my wife, Beth. She is on her feet, and gabbling something about how worried she's been. Myrtle Safford – eminently, and in my opinion more admirably, pragmatic – hands me a towel and offers me a drink. This episode might be just bearable through a haze of scotch I think.

So here we all are, at the mercy of Rose, a mistress with an incomparable temper. And of ourselves, no doubt. Which force holds more malignancy? I ponder. Faces by candlelight. Shadow puppets. *Zhi ying xi*. Let the play commence. I take my seat next to Beth, who at last has stopped fussing. She makes herself more comfortable, leaving, I note, scant room for me, and testing the load-bearing capabilities of the elegant wicker settee to the very limit. Myrtle busies herself at the bar, pouring and mixing her potions. Watching her, I am unable to shake the theatrical from my mind. A witch perhaps? In a setting not so very unlike a blasted heath. I brace myself for the prophecies to come. Ralph, who arrived only minutes before me I understand, is slumped on a bar stool lost in his own world.

And what of our children? Christopher, ten and horribly precocious, moves about restlessly on the carpet, as if no position his infant contortionist limbs settle into is comfortable. Anita, seven, an insipid child forever on the brink of tears, squats in a corner with the Saffords' old mongrel, the perfect victim for her ceaseless ministrations. Harry, the Saffords' son, hovers by the bar picking at a bowl of peanuts. Nicola, their second daughter, is leaning back against the cloakroom door, wearing, I cannot not help but notice, a very revealing mini skirt. And her top is cut so low that if she raises her arms her boobs will probably fall out. Besides that, even by candlelight I can see she's plastered in make-up. You might be forgiven for mistaking her as a hooker if you saw her strolling in Wanchai. Little trollop! So is it my fault I find myself imagining what it would be like to do her? A white teenager. Oh, I have plenty of Chinese girls of course, who look as if they have just trotted out of school. But a bit of white flesh straight from the classroom . . . that is a different matter. It would be a real treat. Myrtle says the older sister is staying with a friend in Kowloon. So that just leaves the amahs, theirs and ours. I glimpse them through the open doorway. They are holed up in the dining room, ready to duck under the table if the windows blow in.

Myrtle comes forward and hands me a scotch. Nice generous measure too. I sip it slowly. Time passes. Conversation is desultory. Myrtle hands round snacks, sandwiches, crisps and chocolate. It does not take much to revive Beth's appetite, and she tucks in as if she hasn't had a decent meal for weeks. Harry likewise, losing his veneer of diffidence in an instant at the prospect of food. My eyes flick over Ralph's bowed back. It appears the indomitable Ralph Safford had a weakness after all. How touching that the tragic death of Amanda Stubbs should have affected him so deeply. I leave him to his own devices. At about 9pm, the radio, which has been quietly updating the news since I arrived, announces that Increasing Gale or Storm Signal No. 9 has been hoisted, and that Rose, 50 miles south-west of the island, is fast approaching. I mull this over, and am just draining my third drink when a thought suddenly occurs to me.

'Where is Alice?' I ask.

My words seem to give even the mad dog, Rose, pause for thought, and a momentary lull ensues. Ralph straightens up. Looking around the hall he appears to focus for the first time. Simultaneously Nicola smiles and I see the whites of her teeth flash. Then she gives a light whistle, audible in the stillness. Harry grunts, folds his arms and moves across the room, nearer the shadows by the front door. Myrtle, for once in her life, appears tongue-tied.

'She's in . . . well, Alice wanted to stay mmm . . . in her . . . there seemed no harm in letting . . . ' Her voice peters out and she takes a swallow of her drink.

'Oh my God,' shrieks Beth, grasping my arm with her podgy hands. 'She's not out there is she, Myrtle? She'll be killed!'

'Of course not,' Myrtle retorts scathingly. 'Don't be so silly, Beth.'

'Then where is she, Myrtle? Where is Alice?' Ralph demands, rising, pushing away the drink his wife holds out to him, his voice a dangerously low growl.

Quite honestly I begin to feel I have stepped into the middle of the story. Why on earth is everyone so absurdly uptight at the mention of Alice? Am I missing something here? As far as I know, Alice is the only one of the Saffords' offspring who keeps a low profile on this island, excepting Harry of course. But then he doesn't count any more, tucked away safely in boarding school for most of the year. Poor little bastard! Chubby as a roly-poly pudding. School will have taken him apart piece by piece by now. Still, he seems to find great solace in food. But as for Alice, she's faultless, isn't she? Maybe not. I wonder . . . I wonder what Miss Alice Safford had been up to? It must have been something delightfully wicked to warrant shutting her away in a typhoon. Well, I think, detaching my wife's hands from my arm and settling back on the settee, this might be a great deal more entertaining than first anticipated.

'She's quite safe,' Myrtle manages defensively, in gear at last after a bit of grinding. She draws herself up imperiously. She is wearing a diaphanous floor-length dress; the reflections of the sputtering candle flames wavering on the pale fabric. Still clasping the drink she offered Ralph, eyes wide, mouth jutting forward stubbornly, she seems ready to brazen it out. 'Alice is in her bedroom. By the time I thought to fetch her, several of the windows had blown in along the corridor. It had become a wind tunnel. Glass was flying everywhere. Impenetrable. It was . . . the most . . . the most sensible course of action. To leave her . . . to leave her where she was until the signals start to drop.'

I stare in the direction of the heavy, wooden, sliding doors that, if closed, divide the hall from the long corridor. The flats are identical, ours and the Saffords'. Of course, with furnishings and decoration we all put our individual stamp on them, but the shell remains the same. In the gloom I can see a fat sausage of rolled towels at the base of the shaking doors, to block the draft and mop up the rain-water that would otherwise be flooding in I presume. Behind those doors the fury of the elements batters and thunders, reminding us all how treacherous it would be to venture beyond what seems like an increasingly feeble barrier.

'I'm going to get her,' Ralph states, his voice still low, though a note of unshakable determination has crept into it.

Myrtle begins to say something and then abandons her sentence. Christopher, who is clearly bored, leaps up and volunteers to go with Ralph. I notice Harry shuffle even further back into the gloom. Beth nearly suffocates our son by springing to her feet and clutching him to her ample bosom. Anita, as I might have predicted, starts to cry. Nicola, whose eyes I now become aware have never left me, lets a hand move against a thigh, easing her already indecently short skirt up a few inches. Someone should take that girl over their knee and give her a good spanking, I decide. The erotic potential of this image rather negates its original conception. But I have little time to dwell on my prurient thoughts. Ralph pushes past Myrtle, through the open doorway into the dining room, where the amahs huddle round the dining-room table. I rise to follow him. Here too candles sputter, spilling their weak light into the gloom.

'Where are you going?' Beth's sharp cry rises above the maelstrom of the typhoon. I feel her hand pulling on my damp shirt. I had slipped off my sopping wet jacket when I arrived.

'For God's sake, Beth!' I push her off, perhaps a little roughly.

'Don't go, Nigel. It's too dangerous. You'll be injured and then what will we do?' she bleats.

The dog growls. Anita, picking up on her mother's distress, turns the volume up on her sobs. In a torrent of emotion she deserts the nervous beast and flings herself at her mother's feet.

'Christ,' I mutter, moving towards the doorway, my empty glass still clutched in my hand. And still that little tart Nicola is giving me the come-on, moving her thighs together and sliding her tongue slowly along her upper lip. Had we been alone, I would have got some respect out of that little bitch. 'Stop fussing, Beth. I'm going to be fine.'

Myrtle takes my glass from me as I pass by. For a brief second our eyes meet. Whatever his failings, Ralph Safford's wife is magnificent. The image of my fat, hysterical and, God-help-me, lifelong partner waddles into my head. Because that's what she is these days, neurotic and overweight. True, I have gone to seed a bit since taking up this post in Hong Kong as well. I am not able to run around Lugard Road as often as I like, and the once well-muscled belly has lost some of its definition. Though I like to think I am still in pretty good shape compared to the other pencil-pushers. And I'm not bad looking either, really. Distinguished, I concluded the other day, when I passed a critical eye over my reflection in Beth's dressing-table mirror. A fair, freckled complexion, for the most part unlined; red-gold hair, albeit thinning a bit on top; cool green, poker-playing eyes, a great asset when working for the British government. And still I only have to wear glasses for reading.

I haven't done too badly, certainly better than Beth. These days it is all I can do to manage to fuck her occasionally. She has put on so much weight. Eats too much and drinks too much. But, I console myself, she has money, or at the very least, stands to inherit it. Only daughter of an English lord with a landed estate. That thought never fails to give me a stiffy before I sink into her. When this party here is over (and let's face it, anyone with an ounce of common sense can see it won't go on forever) I intend to continue the fun. They may mock me now with my lardy wife, but they will soon sober up when they see what's waiting for Nigel Fielding back home. One day, my plump pig of a wife will be bringing home the bacon. I am relying on it. Oh yes, big Beth is my contingency plan, and I would be wisest not to forget it.

But you can't condemn a man for dreaming, can you? More and more these days I think of Cynthia Feng. She is sleek as an alley cat, her smooth skin the colour of milky coffee. The coal-black hair that streams down her back is so long she can sit on it with her shapely buttocks. She doesn't talk much. Too busy sucking the tip of my penis, deep, deep down, with such exquisite delicacy that it jerks of its own accord, as if imbued with its own life. Love-making with Cynthia is a journey into the unknown. Easing apart her labia with their curls of dark hair, soft as goose down, and taking her cunt in my mouth until the lychee sweetness of it trickles down my chin . . . sweet Jesus! And when she slips her big toe with its painted toenail, cherry-red or sky-blue or canary-yellow, always a different shade, always tantalisingly sharp, into my rectum, I am in heaven, heaven on earth. And that's good enough for me. As for love – love doesn't come into it. I pay and pay well, and Cynthia is discreet. Besides, my sessions with her make 'love' seem very ordinary by comparison.

I enter the dining room and see Ralph Safford in the wavering candlelight. He is pulling tablecloths out of the dresser drawers, and swathing himself in them, so that very soon he comes to resemble a cross between an oil sheik and an Egyptian mummy. Atop the dresser the water trembles in the aquarium. The fish are dark shapes, gliding through the tangled golden filaments of reflected flames. I can't help but feel marginally superior, when I consider the disaster Ralph's affair nearly catapulted him into. Just as well Amanda Stubbs was considerate enough to die when she did, unselfish to the last, silly cow. For that, I suspect, judging by the demeanour of Ralph lately, was the *real* thing, the genuine article, the stuff they write about. How do I know about Romeo and Juliet?

I work closely with Ralph. Observing his surreptitious behaviour, I soon guessed he was having an affair. I just wasn't sure who with, until Amanda did the decent thing and topped herself. Give them credit, they did an excellent job of hiding it, quite a feat on the island, though how long they could have kept up the charade I don't know. So long as the papers don't get a sniff of it . . . because that could be messy. As for me, I work for the British government. I keep it zipped, my mouth that is. We don't want to give these commie chinks any more ammunition than we have to. Sleaze and corruption amongst senior-ranking British government officials. A headline we can all do without, thank you very much. Those red bastards in Beijing would lap it up.

'Here, let me give you a hand, Ralph,' I tell him, very nearly shouting to top the roaring of the gales, noisier now we are in the dining room. Wave after wave of dense rain pelts the windowpanes, the din only fractionally muted by the barrier of wooden boards shuttering the windows. It must have been tricky putting them in place with those bars the Saffords have had fitted. Goodness knows what that's all about.

Ralph stands like a child being costumed for his big entrance in a school play. The amahs hug themselves, their Cantonese conversation stuttering on, their voices rising and falling with the pitch and fall of the storm outside. Suddenly there is a loud, splintering crash.

'*Ai ya! Ai ya! Ai ya!*' screams an amah springing to her feet. It's one of the Saffords' servants I think, her black plait lashing about almost comically, her eyes popping, the whites, ghostly amber in the glow of the candles. They are an unsettling sight, piercing our murky cavern as it pitches and rolls in the dark sky. The others pull her back down and jibber at her until she settles.

'Another of the corridor windows,' Ralph says, his tone so ordinary he might be identifying the ring of a telephone.

I am binding his arms. He can use them to ward off slithers of broken glass, as he battles against the wind, trying to carve a passage down the corridor. He might be a fool but I have to admit he is a brave one.

It looks as if his dalliance with Amanda will be contained after all, no note I understand. What a saint that woman was! Oh, far too righteous for me. I like my women a bit more earthy. But nevertheless, it has to be conceded, one of a kind, determined even in death not to be a canker to her living lover. Cherishing him from the grave. All a bit highbrow for my taste, but I have to admit I'm impressed. Ralph Safford. Lucky, then, as well as a fool.

From the hall I hear my wife's voice chiming in, the bell of doom.

'Nigel! Nigel! I'm scared, darling. Please come back. Stay with me. Stay with me and the children. I can't bear for you to leave me.' Then to Myrtle, 'Don't let the men go. Tell Nigel he has to stay. We

155

need one of the men here with us.' Anita is chanting a nursery rhyme over and over again in that high, jarring voice of hers.

'London Bridge is falling down,
Falling down, falling down,
London Bridge is falling down,
My fair lady.'

'Dad, let me come too,' pleads Christopher, materialising out of the dimness in the dining-room doorway. For the first time I notice that he has an odd-shaped head, the silhouette of it looking slightly lopsided. I hiss at him to return to his mother and he slouches off sourly.

'London Bridge is falling down,
Falling down, falling down,
London Bridge is falling down,
My fair lady.'

The dog howls wolfishly. Beneath my feet the floor tips. I bite back acid bile and fight an urge to puke. I might be standing on the deck of a boat tossed on the ocean. I overhear someone telling Anita to shut up. I think it's Christopher, though it might have been Harry, the voices are so hard to decipher above the wind. In the chaos I am dimly aware that Myrtle is uncharacteristically quiet. She is usually centre stage, taking control, managing events. Perhaps this business with Amanda Stubbs has taken its toll, presuming she knew about it. I rummage in the drawer for fresh cloths. All I come up with is napkins. I make do, folding them hurriedly on the diagonal and winding them about Ralph's forearms, then knotting them clumsily. I would never have made a nurse, I acknowledge to myself. Ralph's brilliant blue eyes peer out at me from his mummified face, as we hear that Hurricane Signal No.10 has been hoisted.

'Thanks,' he says.

'I'll come with you,' I tell him, knowing that he will refuse my offer.

'There are no more tablecloths, Nigel,' Ralph relays, giving a back-ward nod in the direction of the empty drawers. 'You can't.'

I don't argue. I help Ralph through to the hall, and we stand side by side before the sliding door. Looking back I catch sight of the amahs ducking under the dining-room table. The dog scoots past us and joins them, spooked by Ralph's appearance. I leave Ralph poised to make his exit into the mouth of hell, and marshal wives, children and all into the small alcove before the front door. I hem them in with the wicker settee and any cushions I can find. Then, fighting the astonishing pressure of the wind, a lethal vortex of swirling water and glass racing back and forth along the corridor, I manage to draw the door back a couple of feet. Ralph forces his way through, curved arms held against his face like a shield. The wind forges past me. The stinging rain drives into my face remorselessly. I struggle to slide the door closed. My fingers are numb and keep slipping on the wet groove of the metal handle. I feel a stab of pain on my cheek, before I finally succeed in shouldering the bloody thing shut. Later I will find that a blade of glass has slashed my face barely an inch from my eye. I will shiver thinking of what might have been. I will swab the blood up with one of Myrtle's silk scarves, smelling of her scent, rich and overwhelming, the only thing to hand. I will sit, drink more whisky, and watch the candles gutter and die. And I will consider how fortunate we all are to have got off so lightly.

Ralph – 1971

I keep my head tucked down, my shoulders hunched, my feet shuf-fling forwards, inches of rainwater sloshing over my shoes, glass crunching beneath my feet. I summon all my strength and plough ahead into the teeth of the wind. Alice's bedroom is the third I shall come to. I feel my way along the wall, a blind man stepping into the unknown. Already the napkins binding my hands and elbows are soaked through. Small things glance off me. Then something larger. It strikes the back of my head, and for a second I reel and nearly overbalance. I recover myself and move on. Progress is painfully slow. I think how many times I have crossed this distance in seconds. Now I must wage war for a couple of feet.

At last I reach Alice's door. As I push my bulky hand down on the handle, it flies open and inwards, slamming into the bedroom wall. The wind pins it there. It picks me up and jettisons me inside. I am panting. My heart beneath my tablecloth wrappings beats erratic-ally. I stagger ahead, trying to yell above the tumult that it is me, Daddy, that I have come to fetch her, to fetch Alice. But here there are no candles, the windows are boarded up, and in front of me is a blackness so absolute that I am unsure if my eyes are open or closed. The wind claws at my back, trying to reclaim me for its own. Now I am dimly aware of prongs of thin, pewter-grey light, cast from behind me through the jagged jaws of smashed windows. My eyes narrow, straining to adjust to the gloom.

Still I have not found Alice. I lurch forwards towards the bed, scattering some stuffed toys, treading down notebooks and files, snapping pencils, crushing pens. As I near it I leap back, for her bedding rears up like a savage beast challenged in its lair, knotting and twisting and writhing. Then the sheets free themselves and flap, stingrays of the storm. They grow pearly, translucent, insubstantial as mist. Revealed beneath them, I see clearly now the dark shape of Alice. She is lying on her belly, her head to one side, turned towards me. As I lean over my daughter her skin seems to shine. I touch her cheek with my exposed fingertips and it is icy cold. I bend over her, tell her that I have come to get her. She does not stir. Panic, cold and corrosive as gall, worms its way through me. I grasp her narrow shoulders and shake her with my bound hands. Her eyes are shut fast. She is limp and lifeless. Again I shake her, more furiously this time, and to my relief she stirs and props herself up on her elbow.

Slowly she opens her eyes and takes in my surprising appearance. Strands of damp hair cling to her face, like seaweed, slick on a rock after a wave has broken over it. Her lips are trembling. She looks disorientated but not afraid. Again I reassure her, yelling that I am going to bundle her up in her bedding, and take her down the corridor to the hall where she will be safe. She says nothing, but when I start to swathe her in blankets she does not resist. I heft her into my arms and am astonished at how light my daughter has grown, as if there is nothing to her, as if when I come to unwrap her in the hall later, I will find that I have returned empty-handed. But my fears are unfounded. For once back behind the sliding doors in the comparative safety of the hall, I open my parcel to find Alice is very much present, chilled flesh and chattering teeth.

Time has passed since our dramatic entrance. Alice says she is fine. She has had some hot chocolate from a flask and is swaddled in dry towels, hugging the dog under the telephone table. And I have emerged from my trappings like an insect shedding a cocoon, and am hunched in a chair sipping coffee. Nicola is sprawled on the floor, panting as if recovering after some great exertion. She reminds me of a harbour swimmer who has just finished the race. Myrtle and Beth are sitting together on the wicker settee, discussing prices at

159

the Ocean Terminal shopping centre. Harry has made a bed for himself with a few cushions to one side of the bar and, impervious to the storm, seems to be sleeping soundly. Nigel is leaning against a wall, smoking a cigar-ette indolently. I suspect he is bored. Anita has also given in to tiredness, curled up by Nicola's side. She snuffles like a puppy. Christopher lying on his back, legs propped up on the cloakroom door, is thumping it with the heel of one foot, at intervals that I judge to be not nearly long enough. Through the open doorway, I hear two of the amahs muttering in Cantonese, though what they're saying is a mystery. Another has collapsed on her seat, resting her head on the dining-room table. I think it is Ah Lee: it is hard to decipher in the dwindling light. Their candles are almost out.

Just after 2am, the eye of the typhoon moves over the flat and an unearthly hush descends. We are all tired and talk is sporadic now. The radio tells us that during the night, Rose will continue on a north-westerly trajectory towards Canton, weakening rapidly as she goes. Some time after 4am, Storm Signal No.10 is replaced by No. 6. At this, judging it to be safe, Nigel rouses Beth, their children and amahs, and together they stumble exhaustedly across the lobby to their flat. At 9:15am, while we are all gratefully enjoying fresh hot coffee and gingerly exploring the flat for damage, Strong Wind Signal No. 3 is hoisted. Finally, by noon on August 17th, this is lowered. Rose has done her worst and it only remains for us to count the cost.

Bear refuses to leave Alice's side. He keeps snarling and I see his hackles are up. I expect he is thoroughly out of sorts with the wretched experience. Judging it safe, Alice and I take him for a walk about The Peak in the afternoon. We pass trees torn up by their roots like so many weeds, mud-slides that engulf cars and sheds, bicycles twisted up like scrap metal. Stranger objects too protrude from the mud, or hang in the trees, or simply lie in the roads. Among the wreckage we spot an ironing board, a bent abacus, a fallen tree with a naked, one-legged doll sitting astride a withered branch, a deflated rubber ring, and a dead cat, its yawning pink mouth twisted in a rictus of terror, its teeth oddly grey, its eyes frozen open, a streak of blood seeping from one nostril. When we return several hours later, Alice is holding a temple carving of a Chinese god. The wood of the god's brow is split, a slice of glass embedded in it, and an arm is missing, the socket ragged with splintered wood. But the bulging eyes are unscathed I notice. We stand on the doorstep of our flat and ring the bell, now working again, and wait.

'Most of the paint has peeled away,' Alice says, holding the temple carving at arm's length, and studying her find. 'It might be impossible now to recognise exactly which god it is.' I nod. I am not inclined this afternoon to be choosy. These days it feels like any god who cares to listen will do.

Later, I discover the staggering cost of Rose's rampage to the colony – the vessels that went aground or collided, the hundreds of boats that sank, the hydrofoils and ferries that were damaged. I learn that the *Fat Shan*, a Hong Kong–Macau Ferry, capsized, and that only a handful of passengers survived. The hurricane gales swept away countless hillside huts, leaving more than a thousand families homeless. Buildings collapsed, and there was widespread flooding and numerous landslides leading to road blockages. The dead and the injured numbered in the hundreds. The huge loss of livestock, and extensive damage to crops and fruit trees, would have a crippling effect on the farming community. It would take months, if not years, to undo the spleen of Typhoon Rose. Next to this, whingeing about what we suffered in the solid secure confines of the flat on The Peak seems risible.

Nicola – 1972

It was high time that my little sister had sex, so I invited her to come along to a party in the New Territories. The summer was drawing to a close but the weather was still great, and the guy who was holding it told me his parents were away. It couldn't have been more ideal.

'Want to celebrate passing your O levels and come to a party?' I asked Alice, when at last I found her in the late afternoon.

She was playing on the swing in the communal gardens of our block of flats. It's a single swing and quite substantial as it happens. But even so, a sixteen-year-old on a swing! For a while I just watched her. Then I raised my voice above the *crick-creak* of metal and wood.

'Fancy coming to a party on Saturday?' I tried again. I was beginning to wonder if Alice could hear me, if she even knew I was there. 'Alice, slow down. I want to talk to you,' I shouted. At last she seemed to notice me, and let her legs dangle. The momentum ceased, the swing slowed and eventually stopped.

'It's like flying,' she said, her words tumbling out all in a rush, cheeks flushed, eyes bright. 'I can see everything. Aberdeen. Junks sailing out to sea. The slopes of The Peak. I'm on top of the world.'

I resisted the urge to sigh my impatience. 'I think it's time you had sex,' I said.

Alice nodded but I had the feeling her attention was elsewhere. She closed one eye and began squinting at the sun.

'Look Alice, Dominic, a friend of mine, is having a party next

162

weekend, out at his place in the New Territories, and I want you to come. I'm going to take you to Lane Crawford to buy something to wear, and we'll finish up at The Alleys to get you a new bag and a bit of jewellery. How does that sound?' If I had expected her to gush with gratitude, I was to be disappointed. Alice looked uneasy. She sucked on a strand of windblown hair that trailed over her mouth, then hooked it out of her face with a bent finger. I saw with annoyance she had chewed her nails since the last time I painted them. They looked dreadful, as if some small animal had been gnawing at them. I glanced down at my own perfect painted talons, and smiled smugly.

'I don't have much money at the moment,' she protested.

'Oh, don't worry about that,' I told her airily. 'I know where to lay my hands on some cash.' And I did. A few dollars here and there, Mother would never even miss it.

She frowned with concentration, then her face darkened. 'I don't know if I'd be very good at sex.' She ran a hand up and down the swing chain nervously.

'Oh, sex is simple. Nothing to it,' I assured her with authority. 'You just open your legs and he'll do the rest. Wriggle about a bit, make noises and pretend you're enjoying it. It's easy.'

Ghost – 1972

Even without studying the fortune telling sticks, *Kau Chime*, my advice to Alice is to skip the New Territories party Nicola wants her to attend. I see evil spirits hovering over the house. However, despite frantic efforts to communicate my black premonition to Alice, she allows herself to be alternately browbeaten and cajoled by Nicola into going.

She looks like a painted doll when she finally totters out on foolishly high heels to the maroon Hillman Husky that draws up outside the flat lobby to collect us. Nicola has chosen a lime-green miniskirt for her sister, and a skimpy, sleeveless, white T-shirt. She has lent her a cap she said she purchased in Carnaby Street, with the British Union Jack emblazoned on it. The outfit is finished off with white PVC boots that are a size too large, also on loan, and fishnet tights. She has painted Alice's face, applying a thick layer of shiny green eyeshadow above each eye, and stroking on so much mascara that her eyelashes clump together like dried mud. They feel heavy when she blinks. She wears a slick of crimson lipstick as well that makes her mouth feel all slippery. Nicola has dabbed scent behind Alice's ears and put three condoms in her sister's bag.

'Make sure he wears one,' she advises.

'Hop in,' cries a voice from the front seat of the car moments later. It is the driver, whose name Nicola says is Rory. Following Nicola into the back seat of the car, Alice recognises Alan, her sister's newest conquest, and another boy who introduces himself as Scott.

Nicola sits on Alan's lap and they disappear in a clinch, only stopping to come up for air. Before we reach the end of the drive, Scott lifts a bottle out of a rucksack at his feet and offers Alice a swig. Alice raises it to her mouth and gulps. Then she coughs and splutters, and as the bottle is handed round they all laugh amiably. The sensation of warmth and well-being now radiating outward from Alice's stomach is a new experience for her. The back windows of the car are open and the warm night air pours in. The stars seem very large to Alice as the car races down The Peak. They are spinning in the firmament, their silver cores dividing. Then Alice finds herself on Scott's lap. She is kissing him, and he is kissing her back. He has soft, fair hair, and lips that, when she sees them made gold in the aureole of a street lamp, look as if they have been sculpted. Scott's tongue probes inside her mouth. It is rough and dry, and she likes the sandpaper rub of it.

We cross to Kowloon on the Star Ferry. In between kisses, Alice stares at the myriad colours weaving over Victoria harbour. They are reflections of the neon advertisements that decorate the waterfront buildings. They slither over the black fabric of the sea, a basin teeming with phosphorescent eels. They make Alice feel a little light-headed. Minutes later we dock and thread our way on through the busy Kowloon streets. We pass shops open for business despite the late hour, pavements heaving with people. A night sky criss-crossed with poles of laundry hovers over us. Gradually the blocks of shops, businesses, and flats thin, the hubbub of life is quelled, and the lights are extinguished. We seem to have been driving for a very long time when at last we arrive at the party. Rory pulls up on a triangle of grass at the centre of the double driveway. Alice's bottom and thighs feel numb from sitting on Scott's bony knees for so long. We tumble out. Alice's PVC boots crunch on the gravel. The house is grand, Alice decides, her eyes sweeping giddily from ground to rooftop. Light pours from the upstairs windows. Alice's gaze travels unsteadily downwards to the pillared porch. The front door is wide open, music streaming into the night.

At first Alice is with Scott, pushing her way into the throng, but she soon loses him. Inside the house the ground floor is dark, darker than outside it seems to Alice. And the music is loud, so loud you cannot talk. It feels to Alice as if she is descending into a sea of interlocking people, who have to undo themselves to let her through. At first she tries to search for Nicola, but it is too crowded to spot her. Someone pushes a bottle of beer into Alice's hands, and she drinks it without tasting the liquid. She stands by herself, her back against the wall and sees shapes moving on the settee close to her, and shapes moving on the floor in front of her. Then Alice's head is wheeling, and her cheeks and ears are on fire, and her eyes are watering with the smoke from so many cigarettes. There is a song playing with someone whispering French words. It feels as if the singer is standing next to Alice, crooning right into her ear. A boy takes her empty bottle away and pulls her into the middle of the room.

'You're lovely,' he says.

He is much taller than Alice and speaks into her hair. She reaches up and realises her Union Jack cap must have fallen off. She wants to go and look for it, but the boy she is dancing with holds her close. She can feel his hands running up and down her body, touching her shoulders, the small of her back, her bottom, leaning over her. Then he is easing his hand into the groove between her buttock cheeks, and on between her thighs. The room is baking hot, like a lit oven. Alice feels sweat pricking all over her body. Her heart is thundering. She feels as if she is being squeezed dry. The boy clamps his mouth over hers. The taste of his tongue is sour. He thrusts it deeper and deeper into Alice's mouth until she feels she might gag.

'Sweet,' says the boy huskily. Then, 'Let's go outside.' He tugs us after him without waiting for Alice's reply. She stumbles in her overlarge boots, tripping over sprawled limbs. She hears someone swear at her. Outside, the cool air meets her hot cheeks like a splash of water. She notices two people by the side of the porch kissing, and someone, she is not sure if it is a boy or a girl, hunched in the shadows by the drive smoking a cigarette. When they draw on it, the tip glows orange in the blackness. Alice wants to pause to take it all in. But 'he' is still pulling her, gripping her wrist, dragging her over the gravel, around the side of the house, through the back garden. We pass under a lamp and Alice sees that he has a mane of red hair, this boy who is leading her she knows not where. It glistens in the lamplight. It looks magical, like the hair of a sorcerer, hair that has been dipped in molten copper. Something brushes across her face and she swipes it away. We come to a narrow path that leads downwards. I plead with Alice to turn back.

'The evil spirit, I can feel him here, Alice, with us. Go back before it is too late!' And Alice is suddenly afraid. She freezes in her tracks, and tries to dig her white boots into the dirt path. She wishes to retrace her steps.

'I want to go back to the house,' she says, her voice lifting on the night air.

'Don't be silly.'

He draws us further and further down the path. Alice keeps losing her footing in the treacherous boots, slipping and sliding after him.

'I don't know you,' she calls out, but her words feel gummy and unwieldy.

'Of course you do,' the boy retorts gruffly, halting and rounding on her. Then his voice changes. It becomes soft and malleable, the way I know he wants Alice to be. 'I'm Warren. And I know who you are. You're Nicola's sister.'

Alice nods but she doesn't feel very sure, with the party still reverberating in her head, and the French words ringing in her ears, and the velvet blackness all about her.

'You're beautiful,' says Warren. He runs a thumb pad along her heart-shaped jawline.

But Alice still resists, shying away from him, trying to free her wrist from his clasp.

'This path leads to a beach, a small beach so pretty it will take your breath away,' coaxes Warren, looking down on her. His face is in shadow. Alice cannot see his eyes. 'Come with me, Alice.'

Then Alice goes, and she is not sure why she does, except that he called her name. The path winds down quite steeply in places, and sometimes Alice feels she is falling. But Warren catches her and steadies her. And when at last we are there, stepping into a tiny cove, a small sickle of sand studded with a single boulder, and sea frills ruffling and sighing on the shore, Alice's breath does leave her body for an instant. She wants to stop. Nothing more. Just stop and be.

But Warren is impatient, urging her on. And soon Warren is lying on the sickle of sand, and he is wrenching Alice's arm until she topples over in the ill-fitting boots, twisting an ankle. She gives a cry at the sudden pain. But the cry is muffled, for now it is hard to breathe, with the weight of Warren pressing down on her. She wants to push him off but he is too heavy. She is scared she may suffocate. The breath is coming to her in tight little gasps, and she has to fight to expand her lungs and draw it in. Her hands flay in the sand, scattering it like a crab bent on burying itself, seeking the sanctuary of a sandy grave. But she is trapped there. Warren's large hands are all over her now, prising her apart like the two halves of a shell, looking for the soft inside of her. He is between her thighs, plucking at her spider web tights, tearing them off, pinching at her flesh. A wave of rage so intense blooms in Alice suddenly, a primitive rage, a rage born of some other place, of some other time: the rage of a small Chinese girl who will not relinquish life.

'No, I don't want to,' Alice screams into the night, expelling every atom of air she possesses.

'Shut up!' snarls Warren, rearing up over her, one hand freeing his sex, the other ripping at her pants. 'Are you a little prick-teaser, Alice Safford? Is that what you are?' Warren shouts as his sex tears into the dew-soaked essence of her, thrusting again and again.

Alice's lips move but no sound comes. His red hair in the moonlight is incandescent, and when he rocks back, a crown of stars adorns his head. From the boulder a little way off I watch. I want to weep, but I am bound in a place where no tears are shed. When it is done, Warren rises to his feet quite calmly. He fumbles with his trousers and zips his fly, standing over Alice.

'Prick-teaser!' he mutters again. Then he saunters off, up the path and back to the party.

For a long while Alice lies still, while the moonlight slides across the surface of the dimpled dark water, and the stars glitter down. She listens to the lap and plash and hiss of it, and breathes in the pungent air, flavoured with salt. She is aware of the blood trickling down her inner thighs and soaking into the sand. It hurts when she sits up. She hugs her knees, her little fingers tightly curled. At last she scrambles onto all fours and retches bile and beer, until her stomach is empty. When she is finished she wipes her hand over her mouth, and sits back on her heels. She looks beyond the tiny beach, at the ink-black line of the horizon, where water and air seem to fuse. From here her eyes rove over the sea, across the arch of sky, and along the curve of sand. Warren is right, Alice thinks, this is a lovely place.

When she is able she stands. Her boots have come off in the struggle, and now she peels off her shredded tights and her pants. She lifts her lime-green miniskirt and bunches it at her waist, holding it there. She steps into the sea, and squats in the spume. With one hand she washes herself, cupping the seawater to her. Her secret tender places sting and smart but she is anaesthetised to it. Finally she dashes water on her face, and then she steps out of the sea. She stoops for her tights, scrunches them up and places them between her legs to soak up the blood. She pulls her tattered pants up over them. She collects up her white boots, bends stiffly and climbs into them. And as she turns towards the path, taking slow careful steps over the sand on her wobbling legs, I slip off the boulder where I have been perched. I weave round her shaking shoulders and gather her in.

Ghost – 1972

The first time I hear it, the sound is as light as the 'plink' of a raindrop falling into the sea. I dismiss it, for bodies can be noisy places to dwell in, the thunderclap of the heart that reverberates through organs and flesh and muscle, the 'shush-shush' of blood endlessly circumnavigating the body, the bubbling of gastric juices. It is a hive of activity day and night. But even so . . . even so, I hear it distinctly, the isolated drop plinking into the sea, there to be swiftly swallowed, and another falling after it. This sound instead of fading away grows in volume. It swells imperceptibly at first and so I take no real account of it. But then the drop in the sea becomes a drop in a lake, and the drop in a lake becomes a drop in a bath, and the drop in a bath becomes a beat, a second heartbeat! Its relentless rhythm jars on my spirit. On further investigation, I discover the interloper burrowing into the rich red lining of Alice's womb. It might look innocuous with its dumpling head and its seahorse tail, but I soon discover it has barbs sunk deep into my host. I know this, for when I stir up the pocket of water it dwells in, and wrench at the slippery tail, it holds fast and will not budge.

To my consternation, as time passes the minute creature more than doubles in size. It takes all Alice's reserves of energy for nourishment. There is nothing left for me. My host's body turns in upon itself. It is transformed into a cocoon, and this thing is the pupa encased within it. I tell Alice there is a parasite blockading itself inside her, making her body an impenetrable fortress. While she gives it sanctuary, I warn, it plots her undoing. And, more importantly, I feel certain it seeks to obliterate me.

My host is staring at a fish when first she feels the parasite quicken, the flutter of tiny limbs pounding the elastic walls of her uterus. Perhaps now my host will do something to stop this impending disaster, I think. So while Alice follows a fish, as it glides through the water of a tank on the Sea Palace floating restaurant in Aberdeen, within her another fish stirs. The family is attending a special dinner held by Mr Huang, Ralph Safford's boat-builder. Ralph is the guest of honour. While everyone settled themselves about the table upstairs, we slipped away. We are downstairs watching the fish that customers will select for their meals, their fate, an eminently suitable end for our little fish, I conclude sourly.

'There is a baby swimming in a tank inside me,' Alice whispers, the fingers of her hands pressing lightly on the glass side of the tank.

'Soon,' Alice marvels silently as we journey home that night, 'it will be Christmas, and Harry will be home, and there will be another party with mother glittering like a dragonfly, and darting from one guest to another in a wave of perfume. There will be a feast and gifts, and Jillian will scowl at me, and Nicola will bring home new boyfriends. And all the while the child within me will grow and grow.'

Does my host not recall how this squatter came into being? Can she not see that the coming of it does not bode well for either of us? But like a stubborn child who does not attend to the omniscient parent, Alice refutes my truth. Meanwhile I settle back and brace myself for the quake to come, a seism that I know will shake the shared foundations of our world.

Myrtle – 1972

It is a fine day. There is a mosaic of sunshine on the tiled veranda floor, grouted with wire mesh shadows. Very pretty really. I intend to make the most of it, though I did pop on a cardigan before venturing outside. I am sitting back on a wicker chair browsing through a recipe book, trying to come up with a few fresh ideas for the Boxing Day spread. I am really looking forward to it this year. Of course, one or two familiar faces will be missing which is sad. Phillip has already spoken to me and explained that he cannot face it. Entirely understandable I told him. Still, such a shame. He will be greatly missed. But who knows, by next year he may be feeling his old self again. You can't go on grieving forever I told him, with just the right balance of sympathy and pragmatism in my voice. Poor dear Amanda would never want that, I assured him. She would want him to go forward and be happy, if only for the children's sake.

For some unknown reason I am feeling elated today, as heady as a girl having her first taste of champagne. Christmas does that to you, doesn't it? The thought of family and friends all together celebrating the festive season, and nobody to spoil it, no cloud to blot out the sun. I must stop rambling and concentrate, plan menus and list ingredients, then explain exactly what I want to the amahs, make sure there are no misunderstandings. I can't afford any disasters this year. Ralph says Charles Yeung the film director is coming, he even hinted the Governor might look in. Mr Gao has promised that my dress will be ready in time, and as I know he won't want to lose my custom I can afford to be optimistic. Ralph wants me to wear the black pearls he bought me for my birthday. They'll finish the outfit off perfectly.

I do hope recent events don't jeopardise the success of the party. It's been a trying fortnight. I had to let Ah Lee go. Such a shame because she's been with us for a good many years, since we arrived now I come to think of it, seen the children grow up. But I simply cannot have a thief in my home. Despicable as it is, Ah Lee has been stealing from me. Goodness knows how long it's been going on for, but I first became aware of it at the close of the summer. And now two hundred dollars gone from my purse! Two hundred dollars! At the start of last week I withdrew it from my account at the Hong Kong and Shanghai Bank. I wrote it up on my chequebook stub (I'm meticulous about that kind of thing), and tucked it away for the Christmas shopping trip I was planning on the Wednesday with Pippa Birley. Imagine my shock when I fished in my purse to pay for the cab, and found it was missing. Well, I simply could not let that go.

How could I tell it was Ah Lee and not Ah Dang? Easy. Ah Dang was away. Her mother who lived in Shanghai was very ill, and Ah Dang begged leave to visit her, leave I felt obliged to grant despite the inconvenience. Sadly, I believe she did pass away. I'm not sure Ah Dang made it in time to say her goodbyes. But at least she was able to see the rest of her family and be there for the funeral. So you see there can be no doubt about the identity of the culprit. Actually I have always had my doubts about Ah Lee's integrity. Ten dollars here, twenty dollars there. It niggles at you, but at first you tell yourself you've been careless, forgotten an expense or two. After a while though it becomes clear that it's more than that. Of course I didn't rush in accusing her until I was certain. I double-checked my purse, my bag, even my coat pockets and the drawers of my dressing table, before I confronted her.

I called her into the lounge and made sure we were not disturbed. I had my purse open on the coffee table when she came in and I caught the unmistakable flash of guilt in those devious, slanted eyes.

Still, she denied it of course. Well, she would wouldn't she? Standing there wringing her hands and looking penitent. Quite pathetic really. I think I would have had more respect for her if she'd owned up immediately. But these servants are continually thinking they can hoodwink their employers. I am beginning to believe that it's an inherent condition. Of course I'm no stranger to servants stealing from us. I recall Aden only too well, Ralph simply avoiding the issue in the hope it would disappear. This time I intended to deal with it head-on.

'Mrs Safford, I not take your money. Please, it not me who did it,' she wailed when I asked her outright.

By now tears were streaming down her face, and really I began to feel sorry for the pathetic woman. But I had to dismiss her all the same. It was an impossible situation. I can't have someone in my home stealing from me and lying to me. Think what effect it might have on my children, being exposed to that kind of immorality. I know the silly woman has probably had no education, that as a result she may struggle to distinguish right from wrong. But I can't help that. Perhaps after this she'll acquire a more discerning nature. I told her I was sorry, but I was giving her notice and I wanted her out within the week. I was extremely generous actually, sending her off with an entire month's salary. But as for the reference she begged me for, it was more than I could do in good conscience. How could I write a letter of recommendation for her, when that would be virtually giving her a helping hand in securing another placement, and an opportunity to carry on with her thieving – possibly in the home of someone I know? Simply out of the question.

'I send money home, Mrs Safford, to my family in China. Please, please let me stay? I very sorry, Mrs Safford. I will work harder. No holidays. Please please. If I cannot get job, Mrs Safford, how can I live?' she begged. No giggling now, I observed dryly.

Well, she should have thought of that before she started pinching cash from my purse. I was firm, I had to be. I'm not a heartless woman, oh no. But there are limits and I'm afraid Ah Lee pushed beyond them. The consequence of this is that a new amah, Ah Wei, starts on Monday. And all this with the party coming up. Quite honestly it's a nightmare for me. But I shall just have to muddle through.

Suddenly I am aware that Alice is standing on the veranda, her back to me. Her arms are stretched wide, the fingers of her hands poking through the wire mesh. I find myself tuning in to the noises that surround me. The murmur of traffic, the distant sound of machinery as some building project goes forward. A dog barking. The lingering notes of a xylophone struck by a Chinese pedlar in the field below. The banter between two coolies returning home down The Peak after a day's manual work. And the patter of Alice's light voice. She stops speaking abruptly, and I realise it is the absence of her speech and not the presence of it that startles me.

'Stuffed pork. It might be nice cold with pickles for Boxing Day. What do you think, Alice?' I ask, with no expectation of a reply, jotting down a few notes on the pad I am resting on the open pages of a large cookbook.

'Mm. I'm going to have a baby,' says Alice.

What strikes me first about this reply is that is does not fit the question I have posed. Both question and answer revolve slowly in my head. Side by side they are incongruous, an antithesis to each other. Cooking and procreation. The harder I try to match them up, the less sense they make.

'I'm going to have a baby,' Alice says again.

'You're going to have a baby,' I parrot stupidly, following the inton-ation of her voice exactly, as if I am repeating a lesson with the assis-tance of a language tape. Why does Alice always have to talk in riddles, I muse? Why can't she just say what she means? I sigh testily, close my book, sandwiching both pad and pencil inside it, and set it down on the glass-topped table at my side. I slip off my reading glasses and let them dangle on the gold chain to which they are fastened. I have been rather enjoying the winter sunshine, the prospect of the party, and of Harry's homecoming for the holidays. But Alice just has to ruin it. 'What are you talking about, Alice?' I demand, my tone nettled.

Bear, who is basking on the warm tiles, stirs in his sleep. Alice withdraws her fingers from the wire mesh, lets her hands crawl like spiders over it for a moment, before spinning round to face me. She repeats for the third time, quietly, and one might almost say pedantically, that she is expecting a baby. I solve the riddle. I sit forward, my back suddenly rigid, as if a steel rod has been thrust down my spine. My hands, resting in my lap, stiffen, the joints lock. I glance over my shoulder to make sure no one is near, not Jillian or Nicola, or one of the amahs eavesdropping, for despite them playing dumb, I suspect they understand a great deal more than they let on. I even stand and check that Beth is not sitting, sunning herself on her veranda next door, as we all know to our cost what sharp little eyes and ears my neighbour has. Then I retake my seat and address Alice.

'How do you know?' I say in a tone low but distinct.

'Because last night at the restaurant I felt it move,' Alice reveals.

She turns away from me again and appears to be looking down on the Chinese pedlar, while her fingers orchestrate his silly little tune. There is a draught. I shiver and do up the cardigan buttons at my neck. My eyes bore into Alice's back and then veer from head to toe. I reappraise my daughter, for clearly while I was not looking she has changed. I observe her jeans, pale-blue denim stitched in strong, white cotton, and note that her legs look extremely thin, giving the impression that they are out of proportion with the rest of her body. My eyes rove over the sweatshirt she wears.

It is a black and purple tie-dye which I believe I saw Alice making. I recall her peeling back the lids of small silver drums of dye, and emptying the powder into an old fish kettle, swirling the liquid about with a wooden ladle, a ladle now permanently stained the colour lips turn after eating a surfeit of blackberries. I remember too how she tended the livid brew, simmering it slowly over the gas stove. With my sharp intake of breath, the vinegary dry smell of boiling dye returns to me. I even have a vague recollection of seeing her sitting earlier at the dining-room table, knotting glass marbles, clear but for a spiral of primary red, yellow or blue, into the white jersey cotton.

I take in her plain brown hair as well, loose, unkempt and dull. She is, I conclude, just an ordinary girl. There is absolutely nothing remarkable or even memorable about her. And yet, as I look on my daughter grown into a teenager, I feel a band of ice tightening about my heart. The years peel away, and I am in the delivery room of a hospital peering into her creased, newborn face for the first time, the same wintry dread closing over me. My hands flutter to my hair, and fidget with a small tortoiseshell comb tucked there.

'Are you . . . you . . . quite sure?' I falter.

'Yes,' replies Alice, head tilting, ears straining, as if keen not to miss a single note played by the pedlar far below. 'Can I throw him a dollar? He's playing so nicely?' She seems unwilling to tear her eyes away from him.

I tell Alice to stay where she is. I go inside and pour myself a large scotch. I catch sight of Ah Dang in the dining room. I instruct her that I am not to be disturbed under any circumstances, that she is to keep watch over the lounge door. She nods, folding her arms solemnly and moving to stand sentry in the hall. Then, drink in hand, closing the lounge door resolutely behind me, I cross to the centre of the Chinese carpet, and stare out through the glass doors at Alice. I take a slug of scotch. While I wait for it to take effect, I glimpse a future in which Alice does not cooperate, where she has the child, destroys our standing in the community, makes our family the hot topic of gossip on the island, wrecks her father's career, and consigns the Safford family to obscurity. For this is truly the scandal that will bring us all down, down to Alice's level! I glimpse myself too, spending the remainder of my life looking after a brat Alice has spawned.

And all this because my daughter has cheapened herself with some lout. You cannot even guarantee he is white. It will be in the papers. Everyone will know. The Governor will be informed. My role as a mother will come under scrutiny. And because the stigma will never vanish, the shame will always be with us. As for my mother, I can already feel the dark, pebble eyes turning on me with triumphant contempt.

I am determined. I stride forward and open the veranda door.

'I think you'd better come inside,' I tell Alice.

'But the man playing the music,' Alice prevaricates, 'shan't we throw him a dollar as he's trying so—'

'Never mind the pedlar, Alice.' I slice through her words smoothly. I take pains to keep my voice steady, cordial. I take my seat on the settee and gesture for Alice to take hers on the armchair opposite me. 'Sit down and shut the door,' I direct her. Alice does as I bid. And even when she springs up immediately to let Bear in, who, realising he has been deserted has begun whining and pawing at the base of the door, still I keep my sang-froid. I set my tumbler of scotch down on the coffee table. To my surprise my hands are rock-steady. I flick my tongue across my lips and manage a taut smile.

'Alice . . . you have been unfortunate and possibly naïve,' I say.

There is a pause. The clock on the mantelpiece ticks. The tiny porcelain, jade and ivory people in the glass-fronted lacquer cabinet by the lounge door seem to have braced their Lilliputian limbs, waiting for something to happen. Alice, intent on running her fingers like a comb through Bear's coat, picking off any burrs she encounters there, makes no response.

'Who . . . who . . . um,' I begin, and then almost immediately flounder. 'Doesn't matter,' I chirp up, as if the identity of the father is a mere technicality, a minor detail of no real import, which is in fact the truth. For the child, as far as I am concerned, is not destined for this world. Child! It is merely a ball of cells, the result of life getting out of hand, proceeding unchecked. The father's name is entirely immaterial. 'No, no, it really doesn't matter.' My splutter of girlish laughter strikes the wrong chord. I try to attain gravitas in my timbre. 'But you must see, Alice, there is no future in this either for yourself or for the . . . mm . . . ' The notes of the xylophone come stretched and distorted, tinkling through the closed glass doors, refusing to be excluded. 'But I'm sure you have already come to accept this, Alice, and so . . . and so quite rightly you have come to me, your mother, to assist you in . . . well, in sorting this little problem out. You have been sensible, Alice, and I commend you for it,' I throw

178

in recklessly, remembering the value of flattery when dealing with rebellious progeny.

'So I have been naïve *and* sensible?' queries Alice. I should like to have slapped her then, hard, across that ordinary face of hers.

I breathe on a smile, but it fails to ignite. I continue, undeterred by this less than promising start. 'I'm sure you must see what a disaster this would be for your father, Alice, in the important position he holds in government in the colony. And not only that, what a disaster it would be for *you* at such a critical time in your education, were you to continue in your . . . condition.' My eyes keep straying to Alice's waist, trying to detect a thickening there. But I can see nothing and this fuels some scrap of hope that it is all a fabrication, a malicious ploy to inflict distress upon me. Though even as I try to latch onto this comfort, intuitively I know this is no sham. 'Alice, this could ruin your father's life. You can't want that.'

Alice says nothing. 'Children, Alice, require enormous self-sacrifice,' I state feelingly. 'Not to mention the financial cost of rearing a family. I'm sure when you are ready and you have found yourself a nice husband you will have a child, well . . . children, if that is what you really want. But surely you see that this is not that moment,' I finish persuasively.

Finally it appears that I have Alice's attention. No doubt the mention of her father has penetrated, even if she is immune to the misery she will inflict on me if she is obstinate. I see the flicker of uncertainty in her face and seize the advantage. 'Alice you don't have to worry about a thing. I'll arrange it all. The sooner the better if you ask me. The first step is to fix up an appointment with a doctor and get it all confirmed, and then of course have it dealt with speedily.' In the silence that follows I sense it is incumbent upon me to conclude matters with a show of maternal understanding.

'I'm not unsympathetic, Alice, honestly I'm not. These things happen. You're a young lady growing up fast. It's good that you told me.' Alice rises, her eyes registering nothing. 'You leave it to me to explain to your father.' I take her mute show for acquiescence. 'And Alice,' I caution her just before she goes. 'No one is to know about

179

this. No one! Your father's reputation depends on it. Do you understand?

'He's stopped playing now, the pedlar,' Alice comments regretfully. 'It's too late.'

'Alice! Do you understand how imperative it is that you tell no one?' In this if nothing else my voice is unequivocal.

At the door Alice turns back. 'Oh yes, I understand,' my daughter says. 'I understand everything, Mother.'

'And you mustn't concern yourself you know. This kind of procedure is very commonplace these days. It's all quite safe, and it'll be over before you know it.' I have been running a finger around the rim of my crystal tumbler. The eerie whine it suddenly emits takes me completely unawares. I jump and pull my hand back as if I have been stung. 'Alice, this is for the best.'

But when I glance up, Alice has left, closing the door silently behind her.

The next day, following a thorough examination of Alice, I am given alarming news. My daughter's pregnancy is a good deal more advanced than first suspected, I am informed by Johnny Sheung. He is the gynaecologist I decide it is prudent to deal with, having shown himself to be most circumspect in the past. We are at his home in Causeway Bay, the nature of the meeting meriting complete privacy and confidentiality. While I speak to Mr Sheung in the seclusion of his study, Alice waits in the hall. Any hope I might harbour that Alice's pregnancy is all in her mind, the result of wild, teenage fantasies, is summarily crushed when he delivers his pronouncement.

'I estimate that your daughter's pregnancy, Mrs Safford, is of at least sixteen weeks' gestation, maybe more. To terminate it at this stage will be a complicated procedure,' Mr Sheung tells me gravely in his sibilant voice, his elbows propped on his leather inlaid desktop. He laces his long, graceful, effeminate fingers together under his dimpled chin. I shrug, indicating that it cannot be helped. Mr Sheung nods his understanding of the delicate situation we find ourselves in.

We discuss the transfer of a considerable sum of money from my private account, with the Hong Kong and Shanghai Bank, to the account of Grace Sung, Mr Sheung's married sister, avoiding any direct link between us. In addition to this, I obtain Mr Sheung's personal pledge that he will never divulge to Alice's father how far advanced her pregnancy was at the time of the termination. He also gives me his personal guarantee that all records of the procedure will be destroyed. Then Mr Sheung hands me a slip of paper with an address in Kwun Tong, Kowloon printed on it. He tells me to deliver Alice there, late on Friday night.

To my cursory inquiries as to both the calibre of the equipment to be used, and the standards of hygiene employed in the operation, Mr Sheung gives me first an offended look, and second, effusive assurances. Losing Alice, I tell him pithily, is not an option. Finally, well pleased with Mr Sheung's grasp of our predicament, I close by telling him that I feel quite certain that government funding for the building of his new birth control clinic will be approved. Further, I give my personal guarantee that the right people will be acquainted with the importance of his project. At this a smile passes between us. We both know that an understanding has been reached.

And to Alice I say after the appointment, as I pull out into busy traffic, 'Mr Sheung informs me that it's all going to be fine. Now, isn't that splendid news?'

Ralph – 1972

It is a crisp, clear night. The chauffeur-driven car purrs round tight bends as it ascends the Peak. I lean back in my seat and sigh tiredly. I am bone-weary. You have days like this in my job, days when you feel nothing more can be wrung out of you. How many times have I repeated this journey home, my mind wrestling with the dilemmas of government office, discarding one problem by the roadside only to gather another, domestic this time, as the car shifts down a gear, the slope steepens, and I near the flat on The Peak. Tonight I can just make out the dusky shapes of the mountains beneath the night sky. It is hard, looking at these curves so redolent of the dips and swells of a human body, not to imagine the island alive, a recumbent colossus, ready at any moment to gather up the folds of his garments and shake us all off, into the oil-black ocean. How whimsical I am tonight, as if I am still resonating with the extraordinary events of the day. I rake a hand through my hair and lightly touch my furrowed brow. Glancing at my faint reflection in the polished glass window, I confess to it that what has primarily absorbed me over the past ten hours are not matters of state and government, but the nigh on impossible task of keeping the secretaries in my office happy. Am I a fraud I wonder?

Bands of amber light slide over the car seat as we move beneath street lamps. It is soporific. I close my eyes and picture my personal secretary, Vivian Yau. She has thick black hair, always drawn back in a ponytail or a bun. It is surprisingly lacklustre, this hair of hers, as if it has been frazzled after one too many perms. Her face is broad, her eyes set a little too wide apart. She wears thick-rimmed, round-framed glasses that rather exaggerate this feature. Her complexion is wan. Occasionally her face erupts into a rash of spots over the bridge of her nose, or under her chin. She looks in dire need of fresh air and fun. Neither is in plentiful supply in government offices however. I recall her as she stood before my desk some weeks ago, arms folded, tight-lipped, glasses propped on the end of her nose, humourlessly peering over the rims. I asked her to sit down and gestured to the chair in front of her. She declined stiffly. I loosened my tie slightly. The temperature was definitely rising in my office. I gave her a brief, questioning smile and was met with an onslaught.

'Mr Safford, my family has very bad luck since we moved to these new offices. My nephew, he breaks his leg falling down a hole, and the doctor says now there are complications and recovery may take long time, several months even.'

'Oh dear, I'm sorry to hear—' I began, my stomach already in a knot, a sense of foreboding growing in me.

Vivian rushed on. 'And now my father feeling very bad, and coughing all the time, and having to go to the hospital for X-rays, and my sister Christine, seven months pregnant, says the baby not moving last week. The doctor very worried. My brother as well, he loses lots of money on the races at Happy Valley, and he never loses, always wins.' Vivian paused to draw breath and blinked accusingly at me. 'What you going to do about this, Mr Safford?'

I twiddled my cufflinks and made an effort to assemble my features into a suitably grave expression.

'I am very sorry for your troubles, Vivian, truly I am, but I fail to see—' I sallied forth bravely.

Vivian interrupted with another volley of complaints. 'It is this office, Mr Safford. Very bad luck place.' She revolved slowly, her eyes narrowing as they roved around the newly decorated walls. With a sneer she took in the paintings of Hong Kong island as it was when the British first arrived, bought so recently and hung as a finishing touch, the wide window giving on to fabulous views of Hong Kong's skyline, and the harbour, with its busy sea traffic all jostling for space in the crowded waters. She took in the stylish mock-antique filing cabinets, her sharp gaze finally coming to rest on the expensive plush carpet, fitted only a month ago. She lifted one shoe and examined it carefully, as if she had inadvertently stepped in dog's mess. 'Not good fortune in this office. Better fortune in last office,' was her unwavering conclusion.

Good God, I railed inwardly, one hand kneading the back of my neck. Does Vivian really think I can be held responsible for her nephew falling down a hole, and all her other family mishaps? And if, incredible as it seemed, she did consider me culpable in this tale of woe, what was I supposed to do about it? Did she expect me to vacate the stunning new premises we had been allocated? Was I supposed to insist on moving back to our former, shabbier, far less attractive offices, smack in the middle of Central, hemmed in on all sides?

'You do something, Mr Safford, or I don't know what happen,' Vivian told me curtly, barely veiling the implied threat. She turned on her heels and exited, making it clear she had delivered her ultimatum. If I did not want to find my office in turmoil, I had better act, and fast.

Before the day was up, I had visits from two more secretaries, Valerie and Cynthia. Valerie was complaining that she had been plagued with stomach cramps every day since our arrival at the new offices, and that her landlord had suddenly told her he would not renew her lease. While she spoke, she fingered a mysterious rash on her arm that she said had only just appeared. In her wake Cynthia tramped in, reddened eyes welling up with tears, to declare that her fiancé had postponed their marriage for a year.

For the remainder of the afternoon reports lay unread, letters unwritten, and incoming callers were advised that Mr Safford was in an important meeting. In fact I was fully occupied tracking down a geomancer. He assured me he would divine the cause of our troubles at the government offices, and remedy the situation, bringing us *zhu ni hao yun*, good luck. A mutually suitable time was arranged for his visit, though to be honest as the days passed, so uncomfortable was the atmosphere at the office, I would have been prepared to put off the Governor, Sir Murray MacLehose, to restore equilibrium.

So this morning my office was visited by a geomancer, Mr Lee. He was a wizened old man with rheumy eyes, the pupils consumed in his brown irises, a wispy white beard trailing from his pointed chin. He was clad theatrically in a silky black Kung-Fu outfit, and he carried a battered leather bag which I was to discover was full of instruments. These tools of his trade, I found somewhat disappointingly, resembled nothing so much as the protractor and compass I once possessed for use in Maths class at my childhood school. Without further ado he walked portentously around the office, observing the position of window, doors, desks and filing cabinets, and measuring the angles between them.

He then announced self-importantly, in a surprisingly deep bass, that the plate-glass window must be partially covered with the large portrait of Queen Elizabeth. He had been eyeing this where it hung on the wall since he arrived. He also demanded that my desk be moved, so that when seated at it, I no longer enjoyed fantastic views of Hong Kong harbour, but rather gazed out at an expanse of grey wall. When I set my jaw at this ridiculous suggestion, the geomancer suddenly became very animated. He circled his arms expansively, inhaled deeply and produced a high-pitched nasal hum, reminding me of a mosquito.

'Not cover window, not move desk, bad fortune stay,' he finally proclaimed, hastily packing instruments back into his extraordinary bag.

As the secretaries led by Vivian bustled in, however, I relented. I summoned two colleagues, who I have no doubt were conjecturing privately that I had lost my wits, to help heave my large desk into a dark corner, facing nothing more exciting than several yards of grey emulsion. The portrait of Her Majesty was then set up on the windowsill, blocking much of the view and most of the light. I was then asked to part with a considerable amount of cash for the

185

privilege of having this trickster disrupt my offices. As I wrote out the cheque, I swear that the delight Mr Lee was taking in my wretchedness was palpable. He sucked on his crooked front teeth impishly. Then he snatched the cheque from me with one hand, while with the other he smoothed a long whisker that protruded from a mole, growing to one side of his prominent hooked nose.

'Stay like this, very lucky,' he declared magisterially, giving the whisker a final twang, his eyes raking over the office one last time. Finally, to beams of approval from the secretaries, and a promise of a return visit, just to check the fortuitous angles were being maintained, the wily Mr Lee took his leave.

That is the trouble, I reflect, as we round the last bend and start up the long incline of the driveway. I like to think I perform well at times of crisis in government. Riots downtown, bodies washed down the river from China, landslides that cut off the Peak, where supplies have to be airlifted up to the residents, a flu epidemic, a visit from the Beatles or a visit from the Pope, both having much the same effect of public hysteria – these events I can cruise through. But it is the mundaneness of life I cannot handle – the plodding, the pettiness, the fusses over nothing, the superstitious secretaries. As we draw up outside the lobby and the chauffeur, a new chap, likeable enough, leaps out to open my door, Amanda puts in an appearance. She does that from time to time these days. Not content with haunting my dreams, now she materialises at the most inappropriate of times.

'Goodnight Sir,' the chauffeur peals out, cap under his arm, his head lowered to me in respect. I shuffle past with a wave, glancing at my watch and being surprised by the lateness of the hour. Amanda follows me to the lift. In the confined space the air is permeated by her scent, that intrinsic yet inexplicable fragrance that is as indescribable as it is particular. I hurry to drink it in, strangely more jealous of her in death than I think I was in life, increasingly unwilling to relinquish my ghostly lover.

As the lift progresses through the floors, we are joined by Alice, this not the anxious teenager to whom I normally return home, but her younger self, stepping out of the past. I see her clearly, as she was then, a small girl. She stands, potbellied, clad in nothing more than a bikini bottom, a turquoise background with an orange fish print, her mouse-brown hair lifting, flying, rumpled by the breeze. She gambols down Stanley beach, her legs seemingly too long, her motion coltish on the stretch of hot sand as she nears the sea. Then suddenly she stops and looks down at the briny wash, bubbling and ice cold, rushing at her feet, tickling splayed, stubby, pale toes, toes that plough in answer into the pliant, compact, wetly golden grit. Her narrow shoulders hunch, her chin juts forwards, her lips part, and seed-pearl teeth chatter in delight.

While others strike out for the raft or hover around the smoking barbecues, drinking and eating, engrossed in conversations too trivial to retain, my tiny daughter plays in the shallows, holding court with herself, her treble tones so soft that no one ever hears what she babbles. A miniature heathen, her hair strewn with seaweed, her hands full of shells, her face radiant, enchanted by sea and sky. Later, I rub her cold, small body vigorously with a towel, the way I have seen vets do with a newborn calf to bring it round, to remind it that it is of this world, that it must relinquish that other place from whence it came. And Alice reaches for me, bridging the gap, her anemone fingers flowering inside mine, their chill, wrinkled, tentacle tips suctioning against my flesh.

The lift doors spring open and I step out, crossing to my threshold. I insert my key in the lock and pause. I am overtaken by an immediate desire to cry. I try to name the emotion that floods through me, and am stunned to know it as grief. Unaccountably I am overwhelmed with grief for my youngest daughter, for Alice. Soon I will know that the girl on the beach is a woman, and that the swell of her belly is an indication of the child that grows there. And as I struggle to grasp this, my wife tells me that arrangements are already afoot to abort the foetus, that this is without question the best way to proceed, not only for Alice but for all of us. I learn that Johnny Sheung has agreed to perform the operation privately, and that I may rest assured that his discretion can be wholly relied upon. My hesitant questions about the identity of the father are discouraged. Myrtle insists that as Alice does not want to keep the child, excavating further is unnecessary. I drink down the scotch that Myrtle keeps pressing on me too fast, the stillness of the flat ringing in my ears. She bowls smoothly on, like a leading barrister delivering closing arguments, while my offerings are piecemeal, stilted and eventually even slurred. As the lounge clock chimes 1am I rise unsteadily and stumble to bed.

'So I take it we are agreed,' Myrtle says just before I drift off.

My lips are sealed. I roll away from my wife; my throbbing eyes latching onto the bars of the bedroom window. They have guillotined the full moon into wedges. I trail the silver segments as they fracture and twirl, as they liquefy and dribble into each other, then sink downwards towards the floor. Perhaps, I reflect foggily, in the morning I shall find them in a tangled heap under my bed. This is my last conscious thought before I pass out.

Ghost – 1972

This morning I am carefree. I feel as if I might almost rise up from Alice, as she lies inert on the bed, ease the metal-framed window open, slide out and ride on the thermals to soar above the island, as I once did so long ago. I nearly believe that I am alive with joy, for this very day the parasite is to be removed from Alice. Soon it will be just the two of us again. We will nurture the perfect synchronism that drew us like magnets from the first. I tell Alice this, I coo it lovingly into the flesh-pink whorl of her ear, the way when I drew breath I whispered into shells. But Alice is oddly unreceptive, merely turning away from me into her pillow. Undiscouraged I try again.

'No matter how deep the barb has been sunk, Mr Sheung will loosen it and draw the creature from you, Alice,' I tell her know-ledgeably.

I have heard the gynaecologist speak of his plan to annihilate the leech, with such supreme authority that even I am convinced, and would, if I could, submit to his skilled hands gladly. I smooth Alice's brow, for it is slick with perspiration. 'Then, oh then, Alice, your strength will return to you. You will recover yourself. And as you do, you will recover me too.' I very nearly add that I have been increas-ingly poorly of late myself. As the 'thing' has grown, each day staking out another claim on my Alice, I have been ousted, permitted less and less access to the landscape of my friend. The heart that beat so generously for me has grown hostile, shaking me off to ensure 'it' flourishes. Still more perturbing, the shrunken monkey buried deep in Alice has been thriving, increasing in size at a rate that is plainly designed to intimidate me.

I call it a monkey for that is what it has come to resemble, with its wrinkled flesh coated with fine, carrot-gold hairs, and its skin smeared with some waxy, noxious grease. I have scrutinised its bloated head, disproportionate to the shrivelled, tiny body that dwindles into toothpick limbs. The hairs sprout thickest over the dome of that skull, like tufted grass. Its bead eyes are hooded with veined lids, no thicker than rice paper. Its nose lacks definition too, and squats like a pimple on the pellucid flesh. Its mouth is similar to that of a fish – a slit, swollen lips gaping open and shut as it gulps greedily at the fluid in which it basks. Between its hairy spindle thighs, I spy a scrotum dangling like a pair of cherry stones, and I have seen the cord of its monkey penis stiffen and stir, rippling the wetness. Just lately it has taken to sucking on its nib thumb, so contented is it, so secure in Alice.

The room we are in is very dull, white floors, white walls, white ceiling, white blinds. Unremitting whiteness. A nurse appears and tells Alice they are nearly ready for her. By this stage I can barely contain the excitement I feel. I am tempted to send the ceiling light into a paroxysm of flashing and sputtering. But then, I tell myself severely, such behaviour might inadvertently trigger a chain of events, the final link of which could well be the postponement of the operation. And that would never do. Alice has been given an injection that has made her drowsy and silly. She is attached to a drip that feeds a drug into her blood. I sense the sharpness of it as her cells jostle one another, and her womb tightens and then relaxes. At first this tightening is sporadic, then it increases in frequency and intensity. Soon Alice is starting to draw her legs up beneath her in the bed, squirming at the growing discomfort. Within her the monkey winces and gobbles all the harder at its thumb. Alice is wheeled along a corridor into another room, equally white. But this one I am interested to see is filled with equipment. Buzzing machines and enormous, blazing lamps, making the room unbearably hot and bright. I feel rather like an actress making her first entrance onto the stage at the start of a play, a shiver of adrenalin scissoring through her. And look, there is a tray covered with shiny instruments, like silver treasure trove.

There are four of us in attendance on Alice during the extraction, two nurses and Mr Sheung, all dressed fetchingly for the occasion in pale-blue cotton, and myself naturally. I intend to make sure everything goes by rote for Alice's sake, and for my own of course. Although I am increasingly distracted by how very queer my host is starting to look. Her eyes have grown unsettlingly large, and her lips are so dry that they have cracked. She bites down with such a vicious intensity on them that specks of blood fly up. Poor Alice! I home in on Mr Sheung, try to let him know I am watching him hawk-eyed, that he had better not make a false move. Alice's feet have been lifted into stirrups. With her pale white legs akimbo it is easy to peek inside her and look for the coming, or perhaps I should say going, of the shrunken monkey.

There is an effervescent atmosphere in the room. I am infected with it and can hardly keep still. So it appears is Mr Sheung, chatting away excitedly. He tells Alice that her cervix is dilating nicely. Alice is not very appreciative of this remark I am sorry to say, and just moans. This could be why from now on Mr Sheung and the nurses speak only in Cantonese. I offer to translate for Alice, but she does not appear the least bit interested. In the end she misses all Mr Sheung's enlivening jokes, a passable story about foot-binding, and some entertaining flirtation betwixt nurse and surgeon, with a great deal of eyelid fluttering. Such a pity!

Alice writhes and groans for what feels like hours, until I begin to feel quite alarmed. Then suddenly the place becomes a hive of activity. The nurses rush about, their shoes tap-tapping officiously on the floor. Alice begins to scream. One of them hurriedly administers another shot of something. Not a moment too soon, I find myself thinking. Alice's pallor has taken on an unpleasant green tint, her eyes are bloodshot, and her cheeks, despite their pallid hue, are boiling hot. As the drug races through her bloodstream, thankfully the smouldering coals of my host are smothered, as if by a damp blanket. Yet still her arms flay, and she fights to lift her chest from the bed. The nurses work in tandem to hold her down.

Mr Sheung clucks like an old mother hen dealing with a wayward chick. My attention is seized by a flash of silver. I see the medicine man slide his sensual hands over the spread of treasure. Of course he is wearing rubber gloves, but they cling to his sculpted, graceful fingers like a second skin. The brilliant lights bounce off them and bestow a mesmerising sheen upon them. It makes Mr Sheung look as if he has shiny worms writhing where fingers once grew. A second later and the sac that the monkey swims in is ruptured. A lake of crystal water starts to seep out, veined with seams of crimson blood. Silver changes hands. A nurse takes the crochet hook from the doctor, the argent metal glinting wickedly beneath the jellied, crimson gobbets that cling to it. She passes on, in return, something I can only liken to an instrument of torture, that she names as forceps. Then Mr Sheung virtually disappears into Alice, foraging about with them, until he manages to grasp one of the monkey's toothpick legs.

'I am turning it into a breech position,' he announces with grandiosity, and both nurses look suitably impressed.

And even I am a touch awed, when, like a conjurer, he pulls both of the spindle legs out of the birth canal. I follow him as he selects a new instrument, sharp as a miniature rapier, and makes a tidy lunge into the base of the monkey skull. This cut he widens by sliding in minuscule scissors and snipping away like the most dextrous of tailors. Next he calls for a suction catheter. I am at a loss as to what purpose this gadget fulfils. But all is soon revealed as he sucks out the monkey brain, as efficiently as Ah Dang vacuums dust off the floor in the flat on The Peak. The skull caves in, and for a second I am worried that Mr Sheung may have made an error. But the appreciative grunt that accompanies what looks a bit like a balloon deflating must, I feel sure, mean that all is going according to plan.

'This will enable the foetus to continue its journey through the birth canal, slipping out as easily as a greased turd,' quips Mr Sheung, and the nurses titter behind their masks.

Blood burnishes everything now – the floor where the nurses

have trodden in it with their rubber heels, and spread it with their efficient steps; it blossoms on their starched cotton robes, and thickly coats their shiny gloves. It is even spattered on the white walls like an abstract painting, and coagulates in heavy, sodden swabs piled high on gleaming trays. It pools about Alice, trickling from her gaping vulva, tattooing her bleached belly and thighs with the print of death. There are even two smears of it on Mr Sheung's convex cheeks, which despite being lopsided, give a jolly and avuncular set to his face. Alice has stopped thrashing now, though at intervals she emits a peculiar, feral, guttural cry.

All the dynamic action is hidden from Alice by a small cloth curtain that divides her upper and lower body. I feel this is rather a shame, and may be why Alice is behaving so irrationally. Perhaps she feels left out, I hazard, abandoned, even isolated? Momentarily Alice is dumb and quiet descends in the room, a quiet punctuated only by the beep-beep of some piece of equipment, and my host's rasping breaths. Into the quiet falls a surprisingly loud sound. It is the 'slap' of the tiny monkey body, as it is deposited in an enamel kidney dish. Even if Alice cannot see, she hears very well I console myself. The mess of it reminds me of the mounds of factory waste I have seen in Aberdeen. I picture the twisted plastic limbs of reject dolls poking out of them, some melded together, some bent into curious contorted shapes, some spattered with dribbles of red paint. Alice draws jagged breaths into her lungs, as if she cannot bear to taste the air, air that is spiked now with an odour both salt and sweet and rancid.

I thought things were proceeding well, but now, as my host's eyes roll upwards until all I can see are their whites, I am not so sure. There is no sense of any kind in her now, I realise fretfully. So concerned am I that I scarcely notice Mr Sheung poring over the remains of the monkey, jabbing and prodding it with some steel instrument. Then he turns his attention back to Alice, taking pains to remove the bloody nest from her body, and making sure it is intact. I relax a bit when I see him lift his mask and smile beatifi-cally. I hear him tell the nurses that it has all gone very well indeed.

Shortly after this Alice is wheeled back to her room. My host sleeps as the nurses scurry about, and Mr Sheung pops in and out, keeping a check on his patient. And even when, some time later, my host does awaken, she seems to be in some kind of torpor. She goes through the motions, cooperating with Mr Sheung and the nurses, pliable as wet clay, but apart from this, shows no sign at all that she is present.

Believing that the monkey has been dealt with, we return to the flat that crowns The Peak. However, on our first night back, my attention is suddenly drawn by a dazzle of golden-red. We are in Alice's bedroom, the lights off, my host fast asleep. Turning from Alice's chalky face, I do the spiritual equivalent of a double take, for jiggling before me is another ghostly visage, spectral emanations streaming from it. I recognise the monkey instantly. Of course I do. That hallmark carroty hair, inherited from the beast that fathered him, cannot be mistaken. On closer inspection, I pick out the familiar toothpick limbs grasping at the air, the golden-red down coating the shrivelled body, and the tuberous genitals. Lastly, I take in the deflated-balloon head. It has grown fluorescent, like a glowing light bulb. The onionskin face is pierced with bottle-green glass-chip eyes. They are curiously open, and keenly scanning Alice's bedroom. It lies at the foot of the bed, and then, clearly aware it has an audience, shows off by levitating a few feet in the air and turning three somersaults in quick succession. I am scandalised.

'I thought we got rid of you,' I spit at it.

Its retort is simply to gurgle and chuckle, and grip its glimmering limbs, flexing them with glee. Obviously reasoning with this little ruffian is useless, so I try a more considered approach.

'Anger binds me to this life,' I inform it haughtily. 'And you? What persuades you to loiter here?' I make every effort to quell the animosity I am feeling at the unexpected arrival of this infant demon, this nursery vagabond.

'Guilt,' comes the burble of the miniature orang-utan. 'Hers not mine,' it adds with a mischievous wink.

'I am not sure how long we will be able to accommodate you,' I notify it icily. 'Things are quite tight here already.' The cheeky thing just chuckles at this. I decide to speak plainly. 'It might be better for all involved if you simply left.'

Alice tosses in her sleep, and we are both jolted out of what might have developed into an extremely robust altercation. The monkey indicates Alice with a waggle of its head.

'Can't go until she lets me,' it chants happily, giving an apologetic shrug of its slight shoulders.

'Then we had better make the most of things until she dispenses with you,' I tell it acidly. My words, meant to sober the malignant gnome, serve only to increase its mirth. The creature locks its fibrillar fingers behind its head, crows, and begins blowing frothy scarlet bubbles at me.

For the time being apparently the monkey is here to stay. Meanwhile, as Alice lurches back to life, I am thankfully far too preoccupied to fuss about it. Instead of celebrating our new freedom, my host is saturnine. She refuses food, seldom speaks and spurns her family. She does drink though, imbibing large quantities of alcohol, as well as taking any drugs she can get her hands on. She no longer washes either, is unwilling to change her clothes, and her skin has grown sallow and mottled. There are deep smudges under her eyes, clusters of sores around her mouth, her teeth are furred, her tongue discoloured and her breath sour.

Now we see next to nothing of the school that was once my home. At the flat on The Peak, Alice's family are wary of her, as if they are living with a tiger. Alice's mother has become still more remote, and though Alice's father seeks her out repeatedly, he is always rebuffed. The only member of the Safford household apart from him who does not repudiate Alice is Bear. He alone stays by her side when he can throughout the day, and sleeps with her at night. So closely knotted together are the two of them, that sometimes, fixing on them from above, it is hard to see where Alice ends and Bear begins.

Then one memorable summer night it nearly all comes to an abrupt end. Taking advantage of the fine weather, the PWD decide to repaint the exterior wall of the flat. Men come, and scaffolding rises up from the ground. It is like a monstrous stick insect that each day grows fresh joints, bound together with twine. From these joints new limbs shoot, reaching higher and higher into the sky. Before long the bones of scaffolding are rising above the top floor, so that the flat seems to become a cage within a cage, the metal bars of the windows now enmeshed further with thick bamboo poles. Alice stares at them blankly, at the men scaling them with the ease of trapeze artists, unencumbered it appears by their pots of paint and their brushes.

In the dead of night, Alice rises from her bed, shutting Bear in her bedroom, and creeps down the corridor, through the kitchen, past the amahs' quarters and up to the roof. Hovering before her, leading the way like an overgrown firefly, is the monkey. I shadow the pair of them. The door that opens onto it from the back stairs has been left unlocked by the workmen. It is a sultry night. The tumult of the cicadas fills the air. Dusty moths bumble towards the floor lights that trace the circumference of the low roof wall, only to rebound, scalded by hot glass, seconds later. Slate-grey cloud tatters scurry over the face of a half-dollar moon. A handful of winking stars plot the night's course. So exposed are we on this towering perch that the warm breeze buffets us relentlessly.

The roof resembles an enormous insect. Two huge rectangular wings fan out from a central cabin, the blue rooftop door set into it. I estimate the wingspan to be several hundred yards, one reaching towards the west, the other to the east. These are bordered by a wall no more than a few feet high. Suddenly I am distracted by Alice, scampering along the west wing, the one that effectively runs above the ceiling of her flat. Ahead of her flies the shiny copper sphere of the monkey. When she reaches the wingtip, the wall that is flush with her bathroom window, to my horror she springs onto it. Her arms reach upwards, the panting wind flapping at the baggy shirt she is wearing.

'Alice, get down,' I urge, trying to lasso her slim, bare legs, to hold them fast.

But Alice does not get down. Before her, suspended mid-air, the monkey jigs, all gummy grins. Below her the scaffolding rattles and creaks, the bamboo arms eager to be free of their bindings. Alice swings her head to the left in the direction of Aberdeen, drawn by the sprinkle of lights. She sways precariously on the narrow lid of the wall, then inches her bare feet forwards and slides her eyes slowly down, through the dizzying heights to the field below. She counts the blocks of light that pour from the illuminated bathroom windows.

'Skip, skip, one, two, skip, three. On the ground floor the Everards have left their light on,' Alice whispers. 'I wonder, if I land in his garden, will he come up to complain with bits of me all squashed and muddled, lying in the palms of his hands, as Nicola said he did with the onions. And will mother glide up to the door making sympathetic noises, and take Mr Everard to the bathroom to wash me off, before fixing him a large drink.'

Alice rocks very lightly on her toes. She roots her eyes to the hibiscus bushes that ring the ground-floor flats, their foliage, iron grey, their huge veined flowers, dark apricot, transformed in the eerie light cast by garden lamps. Alice turns, crouches on the wall, grasps the inner lip of it with both hands, and eases herself over the edge. She swings her legs until her feet contact the first of the horizontal bamboo poles. Once she has found a foothold she frees a hand, and gropes for the strut of a second vertical pole, that rises like a stilt to her right. As she grasps it she lets go the other hand, then circles it in the blustery air, as if testing it for resistance. She leans back as far as she can, out into empty space, the free hand scooping the air, as if she might swim to the ground.

'It would be so easy to just . . . let . . . go,' sings Alice, 'like Mrs Stubbs did.' Her words scatter like autumn leaves on the night's breath. She starts to loosen the fingers of her hand on the hard, smooth surface of the thick bamboo pole.

Instantly I snap Alice's fingers back down, locking them in place. For a long while we battle, she trying in vain to open her hand, while I fight to keep her muscles taut, her digits bent, her palm curved, a job made harder because by now her hands are slippery with sweat. By the time Alice finally relents, the first lance of dawn

197

is streaking across the horizon. Only then does she permit me to guide her benumbed limbs like a puppeteer. I yank her body back from the brink and fold it over the low wall. I take first one hand then the other, make claws of her fingers, and see that they find purchase on the wall's inner lip. I heft her over it, and finally she lands in an untidy heap on the rough surface of the roof. Not until Alice is safely tucked up in bed do I rest. Only then is there time to consider how close we came to losing our life, how vigilant I must be.

Myrtle – 1974

I cannot believe it. Ralph has insisted that Alice accompany us to the Rotary Club dinner tonight. The dinner is being held at the Country Club, located between Aberdeen and Deep Water Bay. Ralph is the guest of honour and will be making a speech. The event will be packed with important people. Alice will be a liability. I tell Ralph as much, but he will not listen to reason.

'I want her there,' is his reply to me. 'I want her to hear my speech. I want her to tell me what she thinks.'

I do not like to shatter Ralph's illusions about Alice entirely. I do not want to describe her moronic attitude, prevalent for over a year now, as well he knows. Nor do I wish to remind my husband that our daughter has dropped out of school, that she spends her days loafing about the house, looking like a tramp. We both have eyes to see and ears to hear. Alice is incapable of uttering a single intelligent word at present. These undeniable facts all evidence the likelihood that our daughter will think very little of her father's speech, if anything at all. But Ralph seems to be blinkered when it comes to Alice. And as I have just seen her emerge from the bathroom, in some ill-fitting garment, so loose she might as well have pulled on a bin bag, it looks as if it's all settled.

'Ralph, I think we should be going,' I say, as my husband paces in the corridor outside Alice's door like a fawning spaniel.

'I'm just waiting for Alice,' he replies, as if she is the guest of honour tonight!

So, because I cannot trust myself a moment longer not to say something I will regret, I dash into the bedroom to give my appearance a final check. The dress, floor-length, royal-blue chiffon with a beaded bodice, my most recent acquisition from the Swan Emporium in Central, looks fabulous. I am wearing my lapis lazuli and gold necklace with matching earrings. My hair, though swept up into its usual bun, is worn in a softer style, with tendrils permitted to escape and frame my face. My make-up is perhaps a touch stronger than I normally like it, with silver-blue eyeshadow, plenty of mascara and rouge, and poppy-red lipstick. But in the evenings a little extra goes a long way. As I think this, I have no idea just how far it will be expected to go tonight. I give a dab of perfume to my temples, take a tissue from the box on my dressing table and blot my lipstick lightly with it. I am looking at the imprint of my red mouth on the pale-pink tissue, when I hear Ralph summon me. I hurry out of our bedroom, briefing Ah Dang on our late return as I pass her standing in the dining-room doorway. I note with some displeasure that her white tunic looks a little creased, and make a mental note to speak to her about it later. Incredibly I find my husband and my daughter in the lobby outside our front door, pawing at bolts of fabric. Standing in the background beside the pedlar, her baskets bulging with yet more bolts of cloth, is our chauffeur. Quickly he removes his hat and lowers his head.

'Good evening, Mrs Safford,' he greets me. I ignore him.

'What on earth are you doing?' I ask my husband angrily, glancing at my watch, and stepping gingerly over the yards of material strewn about the cream-tiled floor.

'The lift's not working,' Ralph tells me conversationally, not bothering to look up from a piece of mauve and turquoise brocade he is fingering, as I reach my hand towards the button.

'What do you mean?' I demand, pressing the button several times anyway. I note with exasperation that it does not glow red, and that no approaching hum can be heard.

'I'm afraid the lift has broken. Apparently it's been down for some time according to Ah Dang,' Ralph fills me in, seemingly unconcerned despite the late hour.

'What do you think of this fabric?' Alice asks, either oblivious to my growing sense of frustration, or delighting in it. I am not sure which. She holds a length of lavender fabric embroidered with silver flowers against herself. Ralph starts to tell her how well it suits her pale complexion. Unable to contain myself a moment longer I explode.

'We do not have time for this now. Are you mad? Ralph you are the guest of honour. You cannot be late!' I add that I am going back inside the flat to report the fault with the lift to the PWD. In the same moment the Fieldings' front door swings open and Nigel appears. He is attending the Rotary Club dinner as well, and Ralph has already told me he has invited him to share our car. Beth will not be joining us as she has a meeting of the craft club she attends, making tat as far as I can tell – oven gloves, aprons, cloth bags and the like, for the Cathedral's summer fête. Just as well, considering that Alice will now be swelling our numbers.

'Myrtle darling, you look gorgeous,' Nigel says, picking his way nonchalantly across a sea of fabric towards me, and pecking me lightly on the cheek. He is immaculately dressed as always, in a black suit, crisp white shirt and Rotary tie. The crease in his trousers is razor sharp. He has the edge on Ralph whose own trousers, now I observe them, look in need of a good press. It is very remiss of the amahs. I will have a word with both of them tomorrow. You can't let your guard down for a second with these servants. 'You smell gorgeous too, Myrtle,' Nigel compliments me, providing some much needed salve for my smarts. 'Ralph, you don't mind if I steal your wife tonight? Mine seems to have deserted me.'

Ralph opens his hands in a 'be my guest' gesture. Nigel links his arm through mine, at the same time noticing Alice wafting about, like some sort of deranged fairy, stroking the lengths of material spread about us.

'And Alice too,' Nigel cries, feigning delight I have no doubt. 'This is my lucky night. Damn inconvenient about the lift, but I've rung the engineers and they promise they'll be here within the hour. I'm afraid that still rather leaves us in the lurch though, so the sooner we start our descent the better really.' Nigel indicates the stairs with a cheery smile.

Trust Nigel to be on top of things regarding the broken lift. I cannot help but be drawn under Nigel's spell. Practised charm it might be, but nevertheless it does the trick, smoothing my ruffled feathers. The feeling of gloom that has been hovering over me ever since I learnt that Alice is to join us this evening dispels rapidly. I begin to feel that Ralph could learn a thing or two from his colleague. Yet even Nigel's charm does not succeed in luring Ralph and Alice away from the pedlar's wares, until they have purchased several pieces of cloth. The fabric will, I feel sure, simply sit at the back of a cupboard for months on end attracting moths, until in the end I have to pass it on to the amahs. At least the pedlar has the good grace to stand back and let us leave, before she starts trying to negotiate the stairs with all her bundles.

The journey is mercifully uneventful. Nigel sits in the front and we three huddle together in the back. The proximity of our bodies feels uncomfortable. It is cool for the start of April and a squally shower is falling from a louring sky. But I am not overly concerned about the weather. We are members of the country club, and I know that the car is able to draw up under a sheltered colonnade at the entrance, so none of us need get wet.

Despite my worries the evening seems to get off to a good start. Alice drifts away and as far as I can see, though quite honestly I am far too busy socialising with friends to keep close tabs on my errant daughter, she appears to be adopting a low profile. And that is good enough for me. The upstairs clubroom, where the reception is being held, has been beautifully decorated, with lavish floral displays of orchids, arranged artistically about blocks of wood, gleaming metal and lighted candles, all very Ikebana. I am in the middle of a fascinating discussion with Martin Prowse, Chief Fire Officer, on the difficulties of battling conflagrations in multi-storey buildings, and he is in the middle of eyeing my bosom admiringly, when we are called into dinner. Naturally, as guest of honour, Ralph is seated at the head of the table with me at his side, but the late notice means that Alice

202

has been placed towards the table end. Secretly I am very relieved at this, and, as I see that Nigel is sitting next to her, I rest assured she is being well supervised, and give my sole attention to my husband and the splendid meal.

I am just finishing off an absolutely delicious chocolate soufflé, and settling down to listen to Ralph's speech (he has decided to give it on the resettlement of squatters, an admirable topic and one which I feel sure will draw much interest) when Nigel catches my eye. There are at least sixty guests at the dinner, so he is seated some distance from us. At first I am not sure quite what he is trying to communicate, with his raised eyebrows and his sideways tilt of the head indicating Alice at his side. But Ralph is speaking so I put my concerns on the back burner. Things appear to be going splendidly with Ralph just reaching his peroration when we flounder unexpectedly.

'There is no doubt in my mind that the alternatives we are offering to squatters are a first-class um . . . are a first-class um . . . er . . . are a—'

Ralph breaks off. There is some kind of disruption occurring at the other end of the table. To my horror I see that Alice has spilt a glass of red wine down the front of that frumpy green dress she is wearing, and that she is rising unsteadily to her feet and applauding loudly. All heads turn from Ralph and swivel in the direction of our daughter. The chair she tries to push back falls over, and a waiter rushes forwards to right it. Nigel is on his feet. Deftly he restrains Alice's windmilling arms, leans into her ear and whispers something. I realise that he is guiding Alice, as best he can, in the direction of the door. I stand. I lean into Ralph, assure him that I can deal with this, urge him to continue his speech, and move speedily to Alice's other side. I know I am blushing.

My daughter may be drunk but she is surprisingly strong, I find.

'Let go . . . go . . . . of me, Mother,' she slurs. 'I am . . . I am . . . I'm perfectly alright. If only you would leave me . . . be . . . and not keep trying to stop me.'

By the time Alice finishes what she is saying, or trying to say,

Nigel and I have steered her successfully from the dining room into the reception room, closing the door firmly behind us. Ralph, I can just hear in the background, has resumed his speech. We lead our struggling charge from here into the corridor and down it to the lift. This one had better be working, I think caustically, as we manoeuvre Alice into it. The lift-attendant fixes his attention on the bank of buttons ahead of him, as if he carries drunken girls up and down all day long, and has grown so accustomed to them that he is effectively blind. I wish this were true, but I feel sure Alice has yet again set tongues wagging and dragged our name into disrepute.

'Where are we going?' Alice blurts out, a touch too loudly, squinting at the panel above the double doors, as it indicates our descent with a sequence of lighted numbers.

She collapses against Nigel. He supports her gallantly, and prevents her from slipping into an undignified tangle of limbs on the floor. I wrap my arms around my waist to prevent them from striking her.

'Nigel, I'm so ashamed—' I begin. But Nigel cuts me off genially.

'Myrtle, don't say another word. All teenagers go through it. Not that mine have reached the dreaded teens yet. But I feel sure Beth and I have all this to look forward to. It would be odd if adolescents didn't test you a bit, eh?'

I want to hug Nigel for his understanding attitude, but Alice is sprawled all over him. As we clamber out of the lift Nigel speaks to the attendant in Cantonese, and I presume he scurries off to fetch our driver. Sure enough, by the time we reach the lobby doors he is there, the car's motor thrumming. He leaps out to open the passenger door, and somehow or other we manage to lift Alice into the back seat. But oh no, she cannot leave it at that, she has to do more damage before we speed away.

'You have lots of red hair growing . . . growing out of your nostrils,' she tells Nigel, her head poking out of the rear window. I am crippled with embarrassment. 'You should . . . should trim it.'

And I'm afraid it is out before I can censor it.

'Just shut up, Alice, for God's sake!'

I take several deep breaths subsequent to this, while Alice withdraws her head back inside the car, like a tortoise disappearing into a shell, from where she mutters something thankfully incomprehensible. Repeatedly Nigel offers to accompany us home. But I refuse graciously. I cannot bear for him to witness another second of my humiliation. I explain to Nigel that I will send the car back for him and Ralph, before thanking him profusely and settling myself in the front seat. My neighbour waves us off and we execute the most graceful move of the whole evening. Our exit.

Alice dozes on the journey home, her head rolling on her shoulders, while I add the tally of this night's exhibition to Alice's already weighty account. I ponder as calmly as I can, how many people have seen the Saffords' youngest daughter, blind drunk, making a spectacle of herself at the Rotary dinner, at which her father was the honoured guest. I allow myself to consider, in addition, those she may have spoken to prior to the dinner, and what she may have let slip in her inebriated state. I let the names of some of those important guests, names that carry with them influence and power on the island, run through my head. I try to calculate how long it will take to repair the damage done, how many weeks, months, years!

Alice has been through an awkward period, and I imagine the process was a little difficult for her. But she should have done something about it the moment she suspected she might be pregnant, instead of letting time slip by, like some gormless halfwit who thinks it will all go away if she forgets about it. She was lucky, her family stood by her. I personally financed the sordid business. And now that it is over I think she owes it to us not to heap more ignominy upon our undeserving heads. I have had just about all I can stomach from my third daughter. By the time we reach Mount Nicholson, I find myself unable to resist the urge to compare Alice's track record with that of her sisters. Apart from a brief spell at boarding school, where clearly they fell in with bad company, Jillian and Nicola have been a credit to us. Whereas Alice, who if anything has had an easier time of it than her sisters, seems to feel that a terrible injustice is being wrought upon her.

So absorbed am I in my reflections, that it comes as a surprise to me to find we are ascending our drive, and pulling up by the exterior lobby doors of the flat. Alice is asleep. The sight of her spreadeagled on the back seat, eyes shut, lost it seems in a guiltless slumber, enrages me almost more than anything else has done this night. Having ensured the evening is a misery for everyone else, now my daughter is set to enjoy her dreams. Well, not if I can help it. I tell the driver to wait, take the lift upstairs, noting cursorily that it has been repaired, and shake the equally dopey dog from its sleep. I ride back down, a confused, mildly disorientated Bear at my side, and tell Alice that we are going for a walk. With the help of the chauffeur, I manage to eject Alice from her seat and get her on her feet. She sways precariously as the car pulls away, the taillights fading into the night.

'I think I . . . I shall go to bed,' Alice mumbles, her voice thick as glue, groping for the brass pole handles of the lobby doors. Bear, a bit more lively now, prances at her feet.

'No, I think a bracing walk round Mount Kellett with the dog is a better idea,' comes my tart rejoinder.

'I'm . . . too, far too tired to walk,' Alice breathes heavily, her hands still grappling ineffectually with the door handles.

'I want you to walk,' I repeat with more emphasis, prising Alice off the door and giving her a shove in the direction of the steps that lead down to Homestead Path. At my prompting Alice at last begins to stagger forwards. 'You'd better grasp the railing,' I tell her as we make our way down the steps. I am damned if I am going to carry her drunken weight for another minute. 'You need to sober up, Alice.' It is a misty night but at least the rain has eased off which is something. 'You have to pull yourself together,' I advise my daughter as she shuffles behind me. She is dragging her feet, stumbling every few steps as we approach the end of Homestead Path, and the start of the road that skirts Mount Kellett. Neither of us is wearing suitable shoes for this trek. Our high heels click on the wet tarmac. In the stillness the sounds seem to multiply, as if instead of just the two of us quite a crowd is tripping about The Peak, while the invasive fog hangs over them. 'You can't carry on in this fashion. It was a very important evening for your father tonight, *and* Alice, you mortified him with your drunken behaviour.'

Alice makes no reply. I can hear the 'rasp, rasp' of her breath, see the pale vapour of it coming in little puffs on the cool, dank air. Now we stand at the side of the road, and gaze at a car coasting past us and on round the bend ahead with a hiss, its headlights briefly searching out our faces. We begin our faltering progress around Mount Kellett, following in its wake. At intervals we pass sweeping drive-ways that branch off the main road. These wind up and down the slopes to flats and houses, from where rectangles, and squares, and circles of light spill into the gloom. Just beyond the street lamps, lines of bamboo stand out in bronze relief. The smooth trunks and droopy leaves gleam as if varnished, wavering on the outskirts of the tangerine tepees of light. I hear a dog yap in the distance. A pair of eyes, lumi-nous, golden beads, burn out at us from the gaping, dark hollow of a hillside drainpipe. From time to time the moon emerges from behind the clouds, and a weak trickle of watery silver light filters across the sooty pavement. We pass a patch of grass that like the bamboo is bronzed with lamplight. Here wooden slatted benches are set out. From this viewpoint on a clear night we would be able to see Pokfulam, and beyond it the sea. But not tonight. The mist seems to be closing in and it begins to feel as if this road, this mount, is all that exists of Hong Kong, that the remainder of the island has been sponged away by the waterlogged clouds.

'Do you understand what I'm saying to you, Alice? Things have to change. *You* have to change. We cannot go on like this.' My voice seems to come from a long way off, as if it belongs to someone else.

Again, Alice does not respond. She has picked up the pace a bit though, so perhaps her reticence is a sign that she is coming to, that the consequences of her night's antics are beginning to dawn on her. She pauses momentarily beneath a street lamp and our eyes fuse. The whites of hers are made yellow in the glow. Her hair is frosted with mizzle and sparkles as if dusted with gold. Damp strands cling to her skin. Her dress is as soggy as mine, if not more so, for Alice has no shawl clasped about her shoulders as I have. It cleaves to her body like a second skin. The green of the dress has been transformed too. It is the colour of mud. The wine stain over her chest has grown black as blood. It looks like an open wound. The dog darts about, now fully awake to the scents released by the moist earth. He seems blithely unaffected by this bizarre nocturnal outing, though from time to time he freezes and growls, his tail stiffens and the hackles rise on his back. It is almost as if he believes we are being followed. But I can see nothing, so perhaps the fog is spooking him as well.

'Do you have any idea how stressful your father's job is, Alice? Do you comprehend how hard he works and how worried you are making him? He has a position to maintain on the island and you are not helping him to do that, are you, Alice? You are hindering him every opportunity you have. I know you've had a bit of a rough time lately, but you have to put it behind you and start afresh.'

We have left Pokfulam behind us now and passed Matilda Hospital. We have nearly reached the railings that border an exposed curve in the road, from where ordinarily we would be able to see Aberdeen harbour. Here the mountain slope falls away sharply. I begin to wish in earnest that I had grabbed our coats from the flat. The whisky which has provided me with an illusion of warmth for most of the evening is wearing off. I am shivering. I can hear Bear panting, but I can no longer see him. Along with the coats, it dawns on me that I should have brought the dog-lead. But it has to be conceded in my defence that I was distracted. Besides, Bear seldom runs off these days, and so far the night seems preternaturally still. Then the dog is suddenly barking, the shrill percussion rattling the darkness. He must have picked up the scent of some small mammal, or a cat, or another nocturnal prowler. Alice halts abruptly at the sound. I stop too, a few feet ahead of her. We are standing adjacent to the stretch of railings. They run for several yards, falling between two lampposts. I lean back against the cold bars. I screw up my eyes and peer into the blackness. The dog is nowhere to be seen.

I sigh in exasperation. 'Whatever must Nigel think of you?' I say. My tone is bitter.

'Oh, I know what he thinks of me,' Alice retorts. My jaw, clenched tightly shut, slackens at this. 'He thinks I am a drunk. He told me so. He leant over . . . me when I was . . . standing clapping Daddy's speech tonight, and he whispered . . . it into my ear. Alice you're a drunk, he said.' Her speech is laboured but clear as a bell now. It is as if the words are being forced out of her.

The breath leaves my body in a narrow visible funnel and dissipates. I feel as if someone has struck me a blow in the abdomen. But I am quick to rally.

'Well?' I challenge my daughter. 'What do you expect. That's what you were tonight, a drunk.'

'He said something else,' Alice continues. And suddenly I want very badly for her to be quiet, to swallow her words, to draw back from the abyss. But Alice has never drawn back and so she drives on. 'He said, you're a drunk and Nicola's a whore.'

My slack jaw drops open, and I try to scream but just like in nightmares no sound comes, only an aspirate whimper. It falls into silence. I take two slow ragged breaths. Only then do I feel able to speak.

'You are a wicked, wicked girl, Alice,' I tell the black silhouette of my daughter, her outline rimmed with gold. 'You have a filthy mouth. It is not enough that you are in the gutter, is it? Oh no, you have to bring the rest of us down with you. I will not listen to your vile lies.' I push off from the railings. Absurd as it may seem, I have an overwhelming impulse to run from my daughter, to stoop down and slip off my strappy evening shoes, and gather up the billows and folds of my chiffon dress and race away. I need to escape from this place, from the girl whose every action, whose every word, eats like a cancer into my life. From Alice. At that precise moment Alice turns from me towards the road and her voice rings out, steeped in terror.

'Bear!'

In the same splinter of time a car roars round the corner. A small solid body is paralysed at a point ahead of it, where the two cones of its headlights merge. An insect frozen in liquid amber. The pools of his dark eyes lock, not on approaching death, but on Alice, arms outstretched towards him. There is a screech of brakes. The dog glances off the car's wing with a barely audible thud. The driver does not even register that he has hit something. The car streaks on past, vanishing as quickly as it materialised. For a long moment we listen to the purr of its engine fading away.

Alice is the first to move. She totters off the pavement and into the murk. I can just decipher the outline of her crouching down, her arms gathering up a dense black mass. Then she is rocking on her heels. She is making strange keening noises. I take a few steps towards her, bend over the two of them.

'He's been hit. He's injured. We need to get help,' Alice says.

Intuition tells me it is too late for help.

'I think,' I tell her slowly, reaching a tentative hand towards the dog, 'that he may be dead.'

'I've checked and I'm almost certain there are no broken bones,' Alice hurries on, her voice brittle as glass, as if she has not heard me. 'Why did I call him? I don't know why I called him. I didn't hear the car. There was no reason to call Bear then. At that . . . that precise moment. He wouldn't have come if I hadn't called. He's warm, but I'm not sure how long that will last. Shock leads to a drop in temperature, doesn't it? We need to wrap him up. Don't his paws feel like sandpaper, and they're so large too. Out of proportion kind of. I've always thought that. And for a small dog just look at his barrel chest. His muzzle is soft as velvet. Softer. Have you noticed the tear in his ear? Of course you have. It was like that when we got him.' All the time Alice speaks her hands move over the dog, her touch soft as a caress.

Then she opens out her arms as if inviting me to make a closer inspection. I note that the grizzled fur of the barrel chest does not stir.

'He is not breathing, Alice,' I tell her. 'Bear is dead.'

Still Alice does not seem to mark my words, or if she does they are meaningless to her. One milk-white hand probes the canine skull. She holds the hand out to me, and I see it is covered with blood, black as tar.

'This is where the car caught him. Look. I will need to clean him up to see how bad it really is. Sometimes, once you've wiped away the blood . . . even if it seems very bad . . . you realise it's no more than a scratch.' She is hiccupping in her breaths and her head is shaking fractionally. 'He makes a terrible fuss about pain, Bear does. He's quite the hypochondriac. He's heavy too. Overfed I think. But if we carry him . . . between us we should be alright. We can phone the vet's emergency service . . . as soon as we get him back.'

'Alice, he's . . . dead,' I say flatly. 'You better give him to me.' Alice staggers to her feet still cradling the dog. His crushed head slips from the circle of her arms and dangles, then swings from side to side as she walks towards the next lamplight. Blood drips slowly from it and splashes onto the bronzed pavement stones.

'What are you doing?' I ask her, catching up, then moving in front of her to block her way. Alice does not answer so I speak again, more loudly, more forcefully. 'What are you doing with the dog, Alice?'

'I'm taking him home of course. I'm taking Bear home.' Alice has begun humming tunelessly. 'We can't leave him here in the cold. He'll be frightened. He hated this stretch of the walk anyway. Did you realise that, Mother? The stretch near the railing. As if he knew, always knew something . . . something bad might happen here. We have to get him away you see. Where he'll be safe. We have to look after him.'

'What are you talking about? Bear's dead, Alice. The dog . . . is . . . dead. Nothing can be done for him now.' I do not add that Alice might just as well have been driving the car that killed him, that all this is all her fault. But I think it.

'Hush hush,' Alice croons, and I am uncertain whether this is directed at the dead dog or me.

'What's the matter with you,' I snap. 'Bear's dead. No one can make him better now.'

'I know it,' says Alice, her tone that of mild reproof. 'But we need to take him home now.' I have had enough. I step forwards and wrestle the body out of Alice's hands. For a split second I consider what a devil bloodstains are to remove. Then I lift the dead dog in my arms over to the railings.

211

'Don't!' cries Alice, who is beside me now. 'Please don't!'

As Bear's head rolls against my hip, I experience the sensation of warm, viscous fluid soaking into my frothy layers of chiffon. I hoist the dog up over the highest railing, letting the metal pole shoulder the weight of him for a second or two. Then I thrust my arms forward and cast the body out as far as I can, hearing the thud of it as it lands in the brush below.

'Come on.' I am brisk. 'The dog is dead. The thing is done. It cannot be changed. Snap out of it!' I take a few steps, pause and look back. In the dim light Alice lingers by the railings. She is prattling. I pick out the word 'tree' and 'branch' and 'soldier' and 'dogs' and something about her father and shame. That much I understand but the rest is all nonsense of course. I move quickly to her, deliver a swift, hard slap across her face. I take hold of her shoulders and shake her. I grab her arm and drag her forwards. In this manner we finish our walk and arrive back at the flat on The Peak.

We stagger panting into the lobby and stand facing each other. Both our dresses are blotted in blood and so are our hands. Alice has a smear of blood across one cheek, and the flaming imprint of my bloody hand emblazoned on the other. There are crimson drops spattered on her white arms. I resist the urge to look at my own reflection in the gleaming brass panel where the lift buttons are set. Better not to know. I summon the lift and, when it arrives, wordlessly we step inside. Just before the doors close we are joined by Fred Macready from flat six, who heads up immigration services. The doors shudder to a close. Like the lift attendant earlier this evening at the Country Club, Mr Macready stares fixedly up at the lighted numbers indicating which floors we are passing. He clears his throat.

'Evening Mrs Safford, Alice,' he greets us with a brief nod. Automatically I lower my eyelids and dip my head. I gather up a few loose strands of hair that have tumbled free from my bun, and make a failed attempt to secure them.

'Good evening, Mr Macready. Inclement weather,' I say.

'Mm . . . mm . . . so it is. Damned mist,' mumbles Mr Macready.

Then silence as the lift ascends to the third floor. The doors spring open and Mr Macready gets out. 'Goodnight to you both.' Again he nods courteously but without meeting my eyes. Then the doors shudder closed behind him and we continue up to the top floor.

Ah Dang greets us. Rapidly she appraises our dishevelled appearance, the blood on our clothes, our hands. She cranes her neck, her eyes raking the foyer over my shoulder.

'Where . . . where is Bear, Mrs Safford?' she inquires tentatively.

'Bear is gone,' I reply brusquely, sweeping past her. 'Bear is dead!'

I leave Alice to her own devices.

Only when I have peeled off my blood-soaked garments and handed them over to Ah Dang, whose broad face remains impassive as she bundles up the soiled chiffon, only when I have poured myself a very large brandy and sit nursing it at my dressing table, only when I am meeting my own eyes in the silver mirror, do I let the darkness that has been with me since the accident crawl towards the light. I relive the car speeding around the bend and the thing freezing in its headlights. Only . . . only . . . the shape I am seeing is that of a teenage girl clad in a dull green dress, wearing a wine stain like a wound over her chest, hair wild, eyes huge, just before the moment of impact, when her body will rocket in the air, bounce on the bonnet, then roll off it, landing crumpled by the roadside, quite, quite dead!

Ghost – 1974

We have returned from a surprise late-night stroll around Mount Kellett with Alice's mother. It was, if I am truthful, a disappointing ramble, and this not just because of the damp and the fog, or Mrs Safford's unwarranted hostility. Unfortunately there was an accident. Bear is dead. He was foraging about in the scrub when Alice called him. As he stepped into the road a car rounded the bend and struck him. Alice wanted to bring his body home, but Mrs Safford flung it over some railings. So now my host is sitting on her bed hugging her knees. Although one of the amahs finally persuaded her to take off her dress, she has not washed or changed into clean clothes. She is wearing a bra and pants, both stained with red blotches. Her concave belly is smirched with yet more of Bear's blood. At first it was sticky but now it is dry and looks, when she drops her knees, like an enormous flaking scab. The bedroom light is off, but the room is not dark. The sky has cleared, and the moon is shining with indecent brilliance considering the funereal atmosphere.

Because Alice seems rather glum I play jester and try to lighten her mood. I make a supreme effort, sliding the glass of water on her bedside table around and around in tight circles, slowly speeding up until the liquid splashes out of it. And when this does not even elicit a smile, I push it over the edge, causing it to smash into lots of sharp pieces on the floor. They look so pretty glinting in the moonlight but Alice barely glances at them. I undulate the curtains next and start to inch them closed, giving up halfway when Alice's only reaction is a gusty sigh. Not to be outdone the monkey performs so many aerial cartwheels that I begin to feel giddy. Then it sucks on each of its ten effulgent toes in turn. But Alice, head slumped back on her pillow, only blinks in apparent boredom. She turns away and stares robotically through the gap in the curtains at the barred window-pane.

So here we all are. The jackanapes has given up and is snoozing under the bedcover. Worn out from my exertions, I am draped over the foot of the bed. This is when we hear it. A rapping noise coming, I think, from one of the windowpanes partially hidden by the curtains. Alice, whose eyes are closed, now opens them. I straighten up. The monkey gives a hollow little gasp and starts vibrating like a purring kitten. As Alice clambers to her feet and moves in the direction of the sound, the knocking increases. She pushes back the curtain, grips the bars and peers out of the window. I join her, while the monkey, curiosity aroused, drifts over to perch on her shoulder like a jaunty parrot. Staring out at a rapidly brightening sky, at first I conclude the events of the previous evening have frayed all our nerves, and left us with overactive imaginations. There is nothing there. A sinking moon and a few pale stars, the colour draining from them as if they are fluxing.

Then Alice peers downwards, though it is hard, thanks to the bars. Nevertheless, as she screws up her tired eyes forcing them to focus, there can be no mistake. Monkey and I can confirm it. Bear! He is only a few feet away. His back paws are suctioned to the wall. His front paws are sliding up the window. He raises one of them and bangs the glass pane. I realise the noise that alerted us initially was the soft thump of his paw pads, and sound of his claws scratching against the glass. He has almost drawn level now, and his feathery tail is waving enthusiastically. His fur, coarse and wiry with the odd patch of mange in life, has acquired a rutilant sheen in death. His eyes, cloudy on good days, opaque on bad, and frequently crusted in the corners with the dried remains of a glutinous discharge, have become a dazzling shade of ultraviolet. The tear ducts glitter like diamonds. The surrounding lids are copper bright, and as clean as if they have been ferociously scoured. Of course the back of his skull is flattened. This gives a curiously two-dimensional look to his face.

Bear, it appears, is dead but not gone, so it seems I shall have to go on sharing Alice. Inwardly I admit to feeling a little envious of Bear's dramatic apparition. By contrast my own disembodied form verges on a dowdy monochrome. But I feel sure that an intelligent observer would consider the wolfish poltergeist rather vulgar. The test of a superior phantom, I console myself, is knowing when to stop, when to set yourself sensible boundaries. Although I have come across only two other entities thus far in my crepuscular existence, I decide both are of the special-effect ilk. On first encounter my discreet luminance might not grab the eye in quite the same way, but I maintain it embraces subtlety and endurance, qualities of which the dog and the monkey can only dream.

Eyeballing each other through the glass, Alice is the first to speak.

'Bear! Oh Bear! How shall you come in, Bear, when the windows are barred?'

Bear shakes from head to tail, the way he used to do in life when he came in from a shower of rain.

'Bars are no problem for me now,' he says in a comfortable sort of growl.

Alice sees that he is right. Bear crouches, and then in one fluid motion jumps straight through the glass and the bars. He lands on the bed with far more elegance than his live self was capable of doing. The monkey and I join him, letting our emanations fuse for a thrilling moment. Alice gives a sharp intake of breath. She returns to the bed and sits back down on the side of it, a touch timidly. I like to think this is the moment that she has her first glimpse of me. What am I saying? I know it is. There I am, scorched on the back of her retina, a Chinese girl with short, black hair, naked but for a British soldier's jacket several sizes too large for her. Apart from the broken teeth and the bruises, I think it is quite a comely face. Alice tears her gaze away and lets it rest on the dog.

'I was certain,' she says gently to Bear-as-Was, who is rolling one scintillating violet eye, and making a futile attempt with scrabbling

216

forelegs to dig a hole in the mattress, 'that you died last night?'

'I did,' returns the sparkling, ruby-red visitant. 'I was hit by a car and then your mother threw my body over the railings.' He yawns hugely and it is like looking into a furnace, black teeth jutting out of molten fuchsia gums like chips of glittering coal.

'I'm so sorry, Bear—' begins Alice.

But Bear, scratching some kind of spectral itch, interrupts. He insists there is no need for Alice to apologise.

'Does it hurt?' Alice is curious to know.

'Not now,' says Bear with a throaty chuckle.

Alice's voice sinks respectfully, and she indicates me with a discreet tilt of her head. 'Do you know who she is?'

'I've got a hunch but I can't be certain,' Bear confides, rolling over on his back, and offering up his tummy to be tickled. 'I think she's been floating around for some time now.'

'Mm.' Alice nods as if in recognition. After all, it would be odd if she did not know me, considering we have been living together in fairly cramped conditions for several years now. She ripples her fingers nervously over the gelatinous coruscations of Bear's belly, then watches hypnotically as the surface of it breaks and shivers. The dog writhes in ecstasy. At length she glances up at the banana-flesh glimmer of dawn, rising from the depths of a charred sea.

Now the canine spectre sits up and stretches his neck towards the horizon, his nose gleaming like black onyx. 'I have to go,' he says regretfully, as if reminded of some duty he must perform. 'But don't worry, I'll be back.'

'Wait,' calls Alice, as the resplendent, filmy Bear bounds through the bars. 'When will I be able to cry?' But Bear has gone.

The first I hear of the move is later on in the day, when Alice, still neither washed nor dressed, shuffles into the kitchen to fetch a fresh glass of water. She has shrugged on an old dressing gown, far too long for her, and keeps tripping over the hem.

I am not sure how she has concealed it from me, but she has. Perhaps the idea occurs to her on the spot, even as the words form on her lips.

'I'm going away, Ah Dang,' she announces. She drains her glass and sets it down by the sink.

Ah Dang, who is busy rolling out pastry on a wooden board, looks up. She puts down her rolling pin.

'You going shopping, Missy Alice?' Ah Dang asks.

Alice draws the back of her hand across her mouth. 'No, I don't mean that, Ah Dang. I'm leaving Hong Kong.'

'Where you going?' Ah Dang demands suspiciously, narrowing her eyes and raising a floury hand to cup her chin, so that when she takes it away she looks as if she has grown a white beard.

'I'm going to England to live with my grandmother,' says Alice. 'I'm going to live in the red-brick house in Ealing.'

Something about the set of my host's mouth makes it apparent that this is no idle threat. She wanders down the corridor ignoring her sisters as she passes them. Clearly they have been summoned home so that they can be told of Bear's untimely demise. I shadow Alice, still reeling from her announcement that we are leaving the island.

By nightfall any hopes of mine that Alice will change her mind are dashed. She has at last washed, and dressed in jeans and an old shirt. She skips dinner, finds her parents drinking coffee in the lounge and declares her intention to them.

'I'm going to go and live in England for a while.' She stands before them on the Chinese carpet, her voice bold, her stance determined, feet apart, straight-backed, arms folded and head held high.

'Where will you stay?' comes her mother's stunned rejoinder.

I give the proceedings my complete concentration. This affects me personally, something Alice has failed to take into account.

'I thought perhaps I could live with Gran, just for a couple of months, till I find my feet.'

To my relief, Alice's father looks aghast. He begins objecting immediately. It is a very different way of life in England. Alice's grandmother will impose much stricter rules than Alice is used to. Alice will be terribly homesick. And besides, what would she do anyway that she might not do here in Hong Kong? Had I been able to, I would have clasped Ralph Safford to my shredded bosom. However Alice's mother, after a moment's thought, seems to take a sudden liking to the madcap scheme. Yes, she says, deliberating out loud, Alice might do very well in England. It would be a new start, the perfect opportunity for their daughter to develop a bond with her grandmother. What, she wants to know, does Alice plan to do by way of employment?

'I'm not sure exactly, but I think I'll start in the retail industry, just to earn a bit of money. Then, when I'm ready, I'll see about taking up where I left off with my A levels.' Alice's tone rings with verisimilitude.

'Oh,' Myrtle exclaims on an upward inflexion. 'That sounds an excellent idea to me,' she enthuses, setting down her porcelain coffee cup in its saucer with a resounding clack. 'A chance to strike out on your own.' What Myrtle Safford does not seem to appreciate is that Alice will not be on her own. I will be with her, and I have no doubt that so will the mischievous monkey, along with the miasmal *canis familiaris*. It is one thing for Alice to live abroad, but a poor Chinese girl in a threadbare jacket, a foolhardy monkey, and a dog with no road-sense? That is another matter entirely. But Myrtle Safford smiles now, the corners of her mouth twitching. I stare at her in bafflement as Alice's plan ferments. The voices about me grow louder, the gestures more expansive, and the clock on the mantelpiece chimes. I hover predatorily over the ivory carving of an elderly man set on a corner shelf. How intricate the work is, his flowing robes engraved with a pattern of flowers and fruits. I cave in, as if I am being compressed into a box far too small for me. When I spring out it is with the speed of a striking cobra. The ivory carving falls to the parquet floor. It breaks into four pieces. The sagacious old head bowls away and vanishes under an armchair. There is an immediate hush.

Ralph – 1974

It is a perfect June day. The sky is a brilliant blue. I shade my eyes against the glare. Turquoise? Azure? No . . . sapphire perhaps? I narrow it down to forget-me-not, an ironic choice as it happens. Here and there the blue is broken with eddies of white cloud. The effects of a blinding sun, which might otherwise be unpleasant, are eased by a palliative cool breeze. The driver has just dropped me at Kai Tak airport. I am here to see Alice off. She is leaving today, flying to England. She will be living for a while with her grandmother.

A plane roars overhead. I can feel the percussive vibrations of its engines pulsing up from the underfoot asphalt through my body. I meditate on the death of the dog. I think that it was, of all possible ways to end a life, not a bad one really. I told Alice as much. I sat on her bed one night a few days after it happened. I said, 'Alice, he was an old dog. He would not have lasted much longer.' I said, 'What happened, him being hit by a car like that and his life being snuffed out, was a mercy. Some might say a blessing.' Alice sat hugging a pillow, her eyes fixed on mine. She didn't blink. I noticed that. She didn't blink. Not once. Not while I was speaking. I said, 'In time we might have had to put him down. It would have been horrible. At least this way . . .' Then I tailed off. Alice wasn't buying it. I sighed. I wanted to take her in my arms and hug her to me. I wanted to tell her how much I loved her, would always love her, had always loved her. I didn't. Before I left she said she was sorry. Sorry for what? For being a teenager, for being here, for being alive?

I am inside the airport now and I'm seeing stars. My eyes haven't adjusted yet, coming from the brilliant sunshine into the shade. In a moment I will look for a small girl with a large case. Myrtle will be with her chattering away I have no doubt, filling up the silences. God forbid that we should ever have a spell of silence in the Safford family, for then the questions will surely come. I find myself thinking about a man I saw this morning. He clutched my arm and said he couldn't sleep because of the colour of his cell walls. I was visiting new secure accommodation for the mentally ill out at Stanley. This kind of thing is part of my duties as a Justice of the Peace. He had a bald patch, this man, and was pulling out his remaining hairs one by one. He was selecting them carefully, then giving a trial tug, before he plucked savagely at the follicle. When it came free he held it out victoriously for me to see. The officer showing me around started to intervene and send him away, but I held up my hand.

'It's all right,' I stalled him.

Then: 'I am going mad. The walls are sending me mad.'

This is what the balding man said to me. He spoke in Cantonese of course. I tried in vain to follow what he was saying, but one of the attendants in a white coat stepped forward smiling, and translated.

I scrutinised the hair held delicately between the balding man's thumb and forefinger for my inspection. I observed that the root had a tiny plug of brown flesh attached to it. I nodded sympathetically, and asked him what colour the walls were. I was not sure what to expect. Mustard yellow? Magenta? Khaki?

'White,' he said, his face contorted in revulsion at the mere thought of all those blank walls encircling him. He was suffering from etiolation, I concluded, the walls leaching the life out of him. I empathised. I watched the man shuffle off, busy again, rifling through his thinning hair, and picking the one destined to be shed, the one that was dispensable. As I watched tears sprang to my eyes and I had to blink fast, move on, start talking before I drew attention to myself. Filling up the silences. Not so very different from Myrtle then.

Myrtle – 1974

We are sitting on a low, rectangular, cushioned bench. It has been thoughtlessly upholstered in black plastic. In the heat it sticks to your legs like glue. You have to virtually peel yourself off it. The sweat trickles between my thighs. My flesh feels as if it is expanding. Even my hands stick to the surface of the seat when I lean on them. I fold them in my lap. I have waited here to see Jillian and Nicola and Harry off. I have waited here for Jillian and Nicola and Harry to arrive home. I have never waited here to see Alice off. Despite the difficulties of extricating myself from this horrid seat, I am up and down like a yo-yo. I am restless. Ralph is late. He is hurrying here from a prison-visit out at Stanley. If he doesn't make it, I am afraid . . . I am afraid Alice will hesitate, and will not go.

'Nicola and Jillian said they would try to make it,' I tell my daughter cheerfully. Alice's face, angled at a plug of chewing gum squashed flat on the floor, comes up at this. Her audible exhalation of breath does for a reply. We both know they are not coming. Things have been awkward between the girls since the death of the dog. I know they didn't see Bear that much, but they were devoted to him all the same. It was a dreadful blow to lose him that way. Jillian wanted to know how Alice could do such a terrible thing, and Nicola just shook her head and said how much she would miss the dog, how she had adored walking him, when she found the time of course. I told them there were extenuating circumstances, that they should not judge their sister too harshly, that she never meant it to happen.

222

'But it did happen,' said Jillian. And I had to concede she was quite right.

Alice is wearing jeans, and a blue sweatshirt with a swirl of sequins on the front. The sequins reflect the fluorescent tube lighting set into the airport ceiling. They keep drawing my eyes, the sequins, green and orange spangles of light. I would have thought she'd be sweltering in it (the air conditioning in this place is less than useless), but she insists that she feels cold. She is wearing a small rucksack on her back, packed with a few things for the plane. I buy her a magazine and a couple of packets of fruit pastilles.

'Make sure you suck them during take-off, won't you? It stops the ears popping,' I say, handing them to her. Her head is down as she takes them, her eyes veiled by hair. I notice her hands in her lap, that she's been biting her nails. They look chewed to the quick. I start to say something, and then I think, why bother. Alice nods in thanks for the sweets but never looks up. I glance at my watch. It is already midday. We have checked in her luggage at the BOAC desk already. I thought it was judicious.

'Let's do it now before a queue builds up,' I suggested. Alice shrugged. I led the way and Alice trundled after me with her case. Asked whether she packed it herself, Alice was non-committal.

'She only means I helped her,' I told the smartly dressed ground stewardess with a fixed smile. And I reminded myself Alice would soon be lifting off. By tomorrow she would be on the other side of the world. I bit my tongue. 'And are there any seats by the emergency exit?' I requested, defiantly upbeat. 'You'd like a seat by the emergency exit, wouldn't you, Alice?'

'What, in case we crash?' Alice said. I scratched the palm of my left hand with my right, pushed Alice aside and took the initiative. I secured her a seat just behind the emergency exit. I thanked the stewardess and hurried Alice away as fast as I could, explaining chirpily that these seats had more legroom.

Now we are just waiting. I decide to take advantage of this time alone together to give Alice a little advice.

'You will be careful about Granny,' I say. I reach a hand towards

223

the tresses of Alice's hair, loose down her back. I am going to stroke it. Then Alice wheels round and faces me, and I change my mind.

'What do you mean?' Alice demands bluntly.

I rub the palm of my right hand before I respond. 'I wouldn't mention the . . . well . . . you know?'

'No?'

'She's an old woman. She doesn't understand these things.'

'What things?'

I raise my eyebrows suggestively, tuck in my chin. Alice stares blankly back at me. My legs are saturated. I am sure that when I stand up there will be a wet circle on my rear. I might even get a prickly heat rash where my thighs are rubbing, and that is so uncomfortable. I probably have patches of sweat under my arms too. I would love a cool bath now, a cool bath and a cold drink.

'What things?' Alice is mulish. Around us people struggle with their luggage. There is an endless chorus of murmuring voices. From time to time a few notes bounce off the white walls and the tiled floors, played I think on a xylophone, announcing the arrival or departure of a flight. The atmosphere created is similar to that on an ocean liner, when the passengers are summoned to a meal or an activity. It's odd that airports seem to affect people the way churches do. They all lower their voices and go about looking terribly sheepish. I need a drink. As soon as Alice's plane has taken off I will have a double whisky. The remainder of the day will be spent placating Ralph, I forecast gloomily. I will need fortifying. Perhaps I will have two. 'What things?' Alice prompts me yet again.

I clear my throat and speak in hushed tones, as if I too am being subdued by the reverential atmosphere, rather than discussing my daughter's squalid abortion in a public setting. 'The termination,' I whisper.

'Oh . . . that,' says Alice, her whisper of the 'stage' variety. I do not imagine it. She is being deliberately insolent. I wait for her to continue. She slips her rucksack off her back and fiddles with the buckle, but offers nothing more.

'Granny might be upset if you told her. Surely you can under-

224

stand?' Why doesn't she say something? Is she enjoying this? Revelling in my embarrassment. 'Telling her . . . well . . . it wouldn't serve any purpose now, would it?'

'Wouldn't it?' Alice returns wide-eyed.

I chew the side of my cheek, then rally. 'And come to that, I'd be inclined not to tell her about the death of the dog either.' My words, delivered with deceptive sweetness, hit their intended target. A flicker of emotion lights Alice's eyes. 'Of course we all know it was an awful mishap that could never have been predicted. But being elderly these things can be disturbing.' Alice looks away and nods simultaneously. Her movements are so lethargic, it is as if she can hardly be bothered to execute them. 'And Uncle Albert, I shouldn't—' I decide to quit while I am ahead. I swallow and remember how dry my mouth is. 'Oh never mind. I know you won't let me down, Alice. I'm so happy for you at the start of this great adventure.' I make to grasp Alice's bony shoulders in an embrace, but she stands up. My hands slip off her, unable to find purchase.

'Dad!' she says.

Turning, I see Ralph striding over to us in a grey business suit, his tie askew, the fingers of one hand combing back his dark hair. They sit, huddle together a short space from me, and talk. I might just as well not be here for all the notice they pay me. But as I hear them call Alice's flight, I chastise myself for being miserly with my husband. Surely I can afford to be generous with these minutes, for soon, very soon, she will be gone, and I will have him all to myself. Even so, by the time we listen to the final call, I am on my feet and pacing about the bench.

'Shall we wander over?' I say, trying my hardest to sound casual. 'Best not to leave it too late. We don't want a horrid rush.' Ralph is fussing about money, passport and goodness knows what else. I want to interrupt him. I want to say we have been over and over this a hundred times. But I contain myself, and let this pointless dialogue run its course. At last we troop over to the departure gate. Prematurely I bend to give Alice a peck on the cheek. I miss my mark and find myself kissing my daughter's ear. I delve in my

225

handbag for a handkerchief. Clasping it, I try to wipe away the smudge of red lipstick I have left on Alice's earlobe. My daughter flinches. I shrug, and pop the hanky back in my bag. I feel very cross and quite ridiculous. I hear an odd snicker of laughter and realise it is coming from me. I stand aside while Ralph enfolds Alice, and, making what I cannot help feeling is an unnecessary spectacle of himself, clasps her tightly for at least a minute.

'If it doesn't work out you know you can always come back,' he says, releasing her reluctantly. I hold my breath and wait for her response.

'I know,' says Alice blithely, but she is looking at me, not Ralph I am pleased to note. Then I release the air from my lungs and greedily gulp a breath. I smile at my daughter. We understand each other.

'Do take care, won't you, darling,' I call after her as she vanishes through the departure gates. I tell Ralph that I want to see her plane take off. I do not add that I will not believe she is gone until I see her airborne. We make our way to the outside viewing platform on the second floor. The heat is coming in waves off the runway, making a shivering mirage of it all. We have to wait some time before we catch sight of Alice, stepping off the bus that has ferried her out to the plane. She walks up the mobile steps to the aircraft entrance. She turns then and waves. Ralph is grasping the wire-mesh fencing. He looks as if he would like to scale it, clamber down the other side, run over to the plane and fetch Alice back. Glancing from Ralph to Alice, my eyes are stabbed with a momentary flash as the sun catches on her sequinned top.

It seems ages before the plane takes off. The doors have closed yet nothing happens. In order to see it, we are forced out of the narrow block of shade we have found. My throat is parched. The viewing platform is sheltered, and without a breeze the sun is nigh on intolerable. I have forgotten my sunglasses. What with my thirst, my throbbing eyes, how sticky my skin feels, and how fatigued I am, the kind of fatigue an actress experiences after giving the perform-ance of her lifetime I think, I am almost overcome with impatience.

Why doesn't it go? Is something wrong? Is there a fault with the engine? Or is there a passenger who is feeling suddenly unwell? A young woman who has changed her mind, and says she wants to get off?

And then, thank God, the engines start up, a rumble that drowns out the thunder of my own apprehension. And suddenly I do not feel the heat or the clammy sweat. I lace the fingers of my hands and shelter my eyes from the glare. I inch forwards. My skin brushes against the hot metal of the mesh fencing. I breathe in the scent of fuel, mingled with dust and sea. I follow the plane as it taxis out to the start of the runway. I stare at the runway strip. From where we are standing it looks no more than a fragile plank stretching out into the sea. The plank sits on a wall of enormous boulders. The sides of the wall splay as they vanish beneath the glittering water. The plane is hurtling down the plank now, picking up speed and then . . . then it lifts off. I can feel the fencing trembling with the force of it. In its own way it is awesome.

'Well, well,' I say, following the jet's trail in the air. 'It looks like Alice is safely away.' Ralph is as taciturn as his daughter was minutes ago. I smile and gently prise his hands from the fence. I link arms with my husband and lead him in the direction of the airport lounge. 'Let's have a quick drink before we dash off,' I suggest. Ralph shakes his head. I start arguing with him. 'What with the heat and—' I begin, and then break off. When you have won you can afford to be magnanimous.

Ghost – 1974

On our arrival we are met with the news that space and privacy in the Ealing house is to be at a premium.

'I've taken on a couple of lodgers, so you'll be sharing with me for bit,' Audrey Lambert, Alice's grandmother says, forcing her voice out through the cracks, as she leads the way up a gloomy flight of stairs.

Alice wrestles with her suitcase. She is red-eyed, her skin dry and papery, her mouth inflamed from licking her lips repeatedly in the dry atmosphere of the plane. Having purchased two bottles of vodka in the duty-free shop before leaving Hong Kong, she has taken periodic nips of the stuff throughout the flight. Now, struggling up the narrow staircase, she glances over her shoulder. Her head wobbles, her eyes stretch wide, and her mouth gapes, for here we all are, the dog, the monkey and me, like a bridal train sweeping behind her. The monkey, having slept for most of flight, is just waking up, green eyes crossed in puzzlement as it surveys the scene. Its illuminations flicker weakly, as it bowls hesitantly up the banister. The dog, never one to make a fuss, trots upstairs after Alice, snuffling the worn carpet at her heels with mild interest. I glide decorously after him. From one of the front rooms, Alice's Uncle Albert can be heard, having what sounds like a conversation with himself. He is a flamboyant character, his robes reminiscent of the elaborate garments I have seen actors wear, when they give performances of Chinese opera.

'*Carousel*,' identifies Audrey, wheezing and patting her chest, as we gain the upstairs landing. She pauses for a moment outside her bedroom door to catch her breath, and gestures to another door adjacent to it. 'The lodgers' bedroom. They really are very nice girls, Geraldine and Yvonne.' She takes in Alice head to toe and sniffs. 'Very nice and very respectable. The smallest bedroom has been converted into a kitchenette for them, and the largest bedroom, well, that's their sitting room now.' Alice nods dully. Her eyelids are heavy, and although it is only lunchtime she would dearly love to go to bed.

George is waiting for us in Audrey's middle-sized bedroom. George is Audrey's budgie. I loathe him from first sight. In the main he is covered in iridescent lime-green and vivid yellow plumage. Sprouting from these opulent colours are two speckled, dirty-grey wings. This grubby pattern extends upwards, capping his silly domed head. He has a curved honey-coloured beak, a blue cere with dark pin-prick nostrils set into it, and a pair of beady black eyes, rimmed in oyster grey. His cage is suspended from a short chain. This in turn is hooked onto the overhanging metal arm of a stand. The stand is set between quilted twin beds. Eyeing us suspiciously, George squawks and flaps against the shiny silver bars of his cage. He lights on one of three wooden perches skewered through it, dips his long tail feathers, and defecates messily on the golden gritted paper that lines his tray.

'Remember George?' Audrey says, crossing to the cage, and blowing kisses through the bars at the bemused bird. 'He's a treasure, isn't he?' Alice looks impassively at George. 'Perhaps I hadn't got him when last you visited. But I don't know what I'd do without him now.'

'Mm . . . does he . . . sleep here?' Alice inquires haltingly setting her case down, and watching as George makes his wagging way along a perch. He moves, she observes, with surprising alacrity, speeding to his feeding bowl, from where he seems to do a far better job of spitting birdseed all over the twin beds than depositing it in his feathered belly.

'Oh yes. I'd be lost if he wasn't by my side at nights,' Audrey says. 'He's such good company. Irreplaceable!' She is temporarily overcome with emotion. Her glasses have misted over. She removes them, polishes them energetically on her pinafore and places them back on.

229

Over the next few days as Alice tries in vain to catch up on her sleep, we find out just how good George's company can be. Alice observes through smarting eyes that he never seems to tire, that he keeps up his screeching chatter throughout the night. And this, despite her grandmother putting a cover over his cage, signifying that it is time for all living things to rest. While from the back room that looks out onto the tiny walled garden, or booming out from the environs of his downstairs bedroom, or declaiming satisfyingly in the splendid acoustics of the upstairs bathroom, Uncle Albert can be heard mid-script, mid-song, mid-performance. During the meals that are eaten around a small oak dining table, seated on yellow formica chairs, the recitals continue. And they continue through television programmes and radio plays. One morning, washing up in the small kitchen, Alice asks her grandmother why her Uncle Albert no longer performs for a living, while we are lucky enough to be entertained all day long by him.

'He jumped on a nail when dancing in a pantomime, dear,' Audrey says, agitating the few bubbles that float on the surface of the warm water, in the white enamel sink she hunches over. 'He was barefoot you see. The nail was rusty. Fate, my dear, that's what it was. Very nasty. All that talent. Such a waste. Now he works part-time selling tickets for the Royal Opera House.'

From the dining room Uncle Albert can be heard blissfully warbling.

'*Funny Girl*,' Audrey sighs, her chest swelling with pride, her gnarled hands occupied scouring out the grill pan.

Then one Sunday evening after a soggy weekend, in which the bird and Uncle Albert compete with one another to see who is the more voluble, Alice announces she is off job-hunting in the morning. I experience an immediate rush of excitement wondering where this hunt will lead us. However, our search proves to be a wretched affair. Fruitlessly we tramp the streets for several hours, being told repeatedly that there are no vacancies. Just when I think Alice would do well to give up, she accepts a job as a shop assistant at a small supermarket in the high street, Harrison's.

'I'm just learning the ropes. Of course, I shan't be a shop

assistant for very long,' Alice informs her grandmother over coffee later that night. Audrey shoots her granddaughter a mistrustful look. Alice takes a gulp from her cup and scalds her mouth. After a bit she says lamely, 'They're going to train me up for management.'

Recently we have all grown jittery. And can you blame us, considering. The dog hides in the dark cupboard under the stairs, or paces the tiled hallway, claws clicking, or skulks about at the back of the garden shed, leaping out when you least expect it. The monkey mewls through the nights, compounding Alice's exhaustion. And even I, ill at ease in this cold grey country, finally boil over. The first day of her new job, my host scrambles out of bed to see the stand for the birdcage empty. The chain is swinging gently from side to side. The cage is lying upside down on the floor, under the bay window. There is birdseed showered all over the room, water spattered up the newly decorated bedroom walls, papered in a rose trellis design, and a cuttle-fish lodged in the light fitting. The bird cowers in a corner under a torn bit of soggy gritted paper, heart rattling, wings flapping ineffectually.

True, he has lost a bit of plumage and his remaining feathers are a little ruffled. But apart from that no real harm has been done, certainly nothing that warrants the kind of reaction Alice and her grandmother have seeing George's little mishap. My host screams as she stands over the empty cage, and then begins to jabber unintelligibly, arms thrashing the air. At the sharp cry Audrey's tired eyes spring open, and veer confusedly from the upturned cage to her granddaughter. She flings back her covers, climbs from the bed and totters over to Alice. The lizard skin on her arms and neck trembles violently. Her flaccid face darkens to a bruised purple. Her brow puckers into ugly, uneven ridges. She sucks in her lips and her eyes flare.

'George, my baby! What have you done to George?' she howls.

Audrey – 1974

I do not have insomnia. If my rheumatism would only let up, I know I would sleep and sleep. It's the pain that keeps waking me. It settles in the joints. My knees are the worst, then my hips and then my hands. I am wearing my glasses, kept to hand at my bedside. I scrutinise my swollen knuckles. They look like witch's hands now, twisted as the trunk of some old tree. I've put on my sidelight, but I'm afraid it's got George going a bit. Chinks of light must be getting through underneath his cage. He's started chirping, very softly it's true, but I'd best go downstairs if I can't rest. Across from me Alice is asleep. I shall not say fast asleep, for she tosses and turns and mutters.

My hands are bad because I began a letter to Myrtle yesterday. When you are young, you cannot contemplate a world where writing a letter could levy such a high price from you. I did not finish it. Alice returned home, and as the subject of my missive was sensitive enough for me not to want my granddaughter to see it, I put it away carefully in my writing folder. Not satisfied with this I came upstairs, and tucked the folder in the bottom drawer of my dressing table, beneath my undergarments, hidden from sight. No one saw me.

Then in the middle of the night my pain woke me. Even turning on the bedside lamp was a struggle, but I managed in the end. In the subdued lighting, at first I could not believe my eyes. Items of my underwear were strewn across the room. My writing folder was lying wide open on the floor. The two pages of my letter lay screwed up a yard or so from the bin, as if someone had aimed to toss them in, missed and left them scattered, wide of their mark.

I did not cry out. I am getting used to such happenings. I made my slow way over to the bin, bent painfully and retrieved them. I returned with them to my bed, eased myself down on the edge of it, smoothed out the creased paper and read.

'Dear Myrtle,

For some months now I have been deeply worried by Alice's behaviour. I have tried to keep my anxieties from you, but we are rapidly descending into mayhem. I feel the situation can no longer be ignored. Do not misunderstand me when I say that Alice's manner is a cause for concern. I do not mean that she is rude or difficult. In every respect she appears compliant and polite.

However, although I have never caught Alice making mischief we live daily with the consequences of her actions. Lights fuse, the bath floods, the toilet refuses to flush, the television has broken down no less than five times.

I have done all I can to help you in the past, Myrtle, and this, despite the problems with Jillian and Nicola, and us having very different ideas about family life. But something's not right with Alice.

I have just learnt that my sister-in-law, your Aunt Deirdre, now living in Haywards Heath, is gravely ill and has asked for me. I feel I would never forgive myself if I did not go to her.'

This was when I left off writing. Now I look at my scrawl on the crumpled sheets, and see that in some places they are very nearly illegible. I fold them and place them carefully under my pillow. I can't face copying them out again. I will try to complete it tomorrow or after I get back from Deirdre's. My eyes rove round the room. I do not have the energy to tidy away my undergarments for the moment. It will have to wait until morning. The shadow of the bird-cage looms large on the wall, and as I watch it begins to shift, just a few inches at first, and then more, until it is jerking and swinging.

My eyes snap back to the cage. Motionless. Alice, on her back now, looks as if she is trying to shift some heavy object from her chest. She grunts with the effort. Not for the first time I feel a finger of unease trace my spine. I climb laboriously back into bed and pull the blankets up. In a while I will snap off the light. Though in the dark, some nights I hear strange noises, the thump of a book falling perhaps, the scrape of a chair-leg, the clatter of a saucepan lid. Maybe it's the lodgers I tell myself? Still, why not just this once try to sleep with the light on, eh?

The following day, a Friday, I tell Alice about my sister-in-law, that I must go to her. I inform her that a cab is coming for me on Saturday at noon, and that all being well, I should only be away overnight, returning on the Sunday. I tell her I will leave a number by the phone in the hall, and that she can ring me if there are any problems at all. I add that the lodgers, Geraldine and Yvonne, are visiting their respective parents for the weekend. I have already spoken to Albert. Alice is very sympathetic.

Over and over on the morning of my departure I tell her to make sure the gas is switched off, that all the electrical appliances are unplugged. I tell her to be especially careful if she is cooking. 'Don't worry, Gran,' she sings out, as she waves me off and I leave my home behind, 'I'll take care of everything.'

Ghost – 1974

After Audrey leaves, the house seems very quiet, as if it is waiting for something to happen. Uncle Albert vanishes back into his bedroom. Though Alice pauses outside his door for a time, all continues silent. She goes into the kitchen and pours herself a glass of orange squash. She checks she has turned the tap off several times before she is finally persuaded that it is only dripping, not leaking. Then she sits in the back room, in her grandmother's wooden rocker. For what feels like an age she rocks her slight weight forwards and back, the motion reminding her of sitting on the swing in the gardens of the flat on the Peak. She thinks about England and how it does not feel like her home at all, no matter how much she wants it to. My host feels, she imagines, the way an immigrant does, coming here to settle, leaving their country far behind them, coping with a new life, new ways of doing things. And always searching for that sense of belonging, but not necessarily finding it.

As she rocks, Alice thinks about the Queen, pictures her sitting on her throne with her sparkly crown perched on her head, just like the portraits she has seen so many times in Hong Kong. Alice wonders what she might say to her if she was ushered into her throne room by a guardsman with a crimson jacket and tall bearskin cap.

'Your Majesty,' Alice imagines saying, after curtseying, 'although I know I'm British, at least that's what's stamped on my passport, I don't feel right here. I feel like a kind of non-immigrant, as if I should fit in but I don't.'

She is certain that the Queen would be very gracious about it, but explain in that special voice of hers that it cannot be helped.

'Alice Safford, you are a child of the colonies, and I'm afraid as my empire shrinks, they are vanishing fast. So, wee, wee, wee, my overseas subjects are bound to find their way home. In time, Alice, I feel sure you'll acclimatise and, just like a stick of Brighton Rock, feel British through and through.'

But Alice is not so sure. I remind her that if she is finding the adjustment hard, how difficult does she think it's proving for us! Eventually, brooding on this, she falls asleep. The preternatural quiet is harrowing. The dog and the monkey are nowhere to be seen. Even they would have provided welcome companionship at present. But deliverance from this enforced solitude comes from a surprising quarter, for it is Uncle Albert's singing that wakes Alice up. Still dazed, she looks at the clock over the mantelpiece and shakes her head. She stares at the lengthening shadows in the garden. Cool indigo fingers extending over the small expanse of grass, and over the beds, where late summer flowers bob their heads, and on up the brick walls that encase the small plot. Alice rises and we creep into the hall. She is barefoot, and the pretty tiled floor, a geometric design of cobalt blue, nut-brown, saffron yellow and cream, is cold to the flesh. Uncle Albert's bedroom door opens off the hall. Alice stands outside it. We spot the monkey sliding down the banister.

'Wheee!' it squeals.

'Shush!' hisses Alice, a finger to her lips. The daredevil monkey glowers and scampers up the stairs, vaults onto the newel post, and, pipe-cleaner legs astride, starts sliding down again.

Bear-as-Was shuffles out of the under-stairs cupboard, a woe-begone expression on his long face, tail between his legs. His nitid steely claws scrape over the tiles. Alice raises her eyes and shakes her head. Taking the hint, the dog slopes off back into the shadows. Then another sound rings out. It is Uncle Albert again. He is in good voice today. The lyrics of a light opera thunder out, interspersed with what sound like grating sobs.

Alice begins to obey a well-mannered impulse to leave her Uncle to play out his misery in private. She turns away from the door and takes a couple of steps towards the stairs. But we have never been in Uncle Albert's room, and I for one am curious. Without giving Alice time to think I steer her back again. By now, so abandoned is his weeping that it cannot be ignored for any reason. Alice taps softly on his door, and when this draws no response she knocks more loudly. Light comes in coloured shafts, blue and green and brown, falling through the small stained-glass panel set into the front door. It shifts over Alice's white face, giving her the look of a woodland sprite. The leaded panes make up the picture of a boat, making us both feel homesick.

'Uncle Albert, it's me. It's Alice. Can I come in?'

There is a hiatus in the wails, but no summons for her to push open the door. On a whim, for which I must take responsibility, Alice decides she will enter without an invitation. We shut the door in the monkey's naughty face. The scene that meets us could not have been more fantastical. The curtains are tightly drawn against the fading day. A glowing bulb, suspended from the ceiling, protrudes from a beaded pink shade. A bedside lamp set on a table, with a frosted-glass shade shaped like the petals of a flower, also illuminates the fair-sized room. The alchemy of electric light falling on the plain yellow satin curtains transforms them into bands of shimmering gold. In the room is a bed, one side of which is buttressed against the dividing wall, separating bedroom from hallway. There is a tall, ornately carved wardrobe, and a chest of drawers with a freestanding mirror set upon it. The mirror comprises three hinged panels, each framed in dark wood, and standing on clawed feet. Here light bounces between the silver planes, the reflections multiplying and fracturing, giving you the impression that the room is never-ending.

Uncle Albert lies supine on a decorative, flower-patterned rug, hugging his knees. His face is plastered with thick make-up, a foundation of peach greasepaint, cheeks rouged as red as ripe apples, mouth smeared with scarlet lipstick, eyes ringed with bands of peacock-blue and weighed down with thick, spider-leg lashes. His hair, which normally sits like a pudding basin over his head, dun grey, with a space for his face snipped out, has been tucked up into some sort of net, and clipped firmly down. He is shedding real tears. Seeing them triggers a distant memory of the sensation of weeping in me, the dragging feeling in the chest, the eyes brimming over unbidden, the lungs shuddering in painful breaths, desperate for air but unable to expand, as if squeezed by invisible hands. I follow the progress of Uncle Albert's tears, mesmerised as they roll, not down his cheeks but across them, such is the angle of his head. The tears cloud as they gather specks of black mascara, blue eyeshadow, peach foundation, and cherry-red rouge, coursing along the fleshy pads and bony hollows of his cheeks. Mucus is also dribbling from his pronounced Roman nose, and running into the colourful tears. Funny – the sight of his sorrow reminds me that I have never seen my host cry.

He is wearing a willow-green, full-length, mandarin-style robe, with copper fruits embroidered on it. Beside him on the floor lies a blonde wig, sprawled out, as if it has recently faced combat, and is now making the most of a few minutes' respite. Albert's bed is unmade. His bedding, together with a tangle of coloured shawls, tumbles over it. They spill onto the wooden floor beneath it. The mirrored door of his wardrobe is flung wide. Several outfits lie in a jumble at the bottom of it, fighting for space with brocade slippers, and pairs of glittery high-heeled shoes. A cigarette in a turquoise enamel cigarette holder, still smoking, balances on the side of a glass ashtray, atop the chest of drawers. Its pearly trail snakes up towards the ceiling. Alongside it are several well-thumbed scripts, and an open wooden box crammed with make-up. A drooping auburn moustache loops over one corner of it. Tubes of greasepaint are just visible, and two false beards, one black and one white. Piled in an oval china dish in front of the make-up box are glittering rings and bangles, shiny beaded necklaces, and pairs of spangled, dangly earrings. Set to one side of the mirror is another wig, a mass of electric-blue curls propped on a wig-stand. Scents of tobacco, incense, perfume and sweat permeate the air. It feels to me like an actor's dressing room, a place of disguise and magic, which I suppose, after all, is what it is.

Then Uncle Albert suddenly spreads his arms wide. Staring straight at the ceiling he gives a prolonged, nasal groan. As Alice approaches cautiously, her nostrils are assailed with the heavy odour of jasmine. When she reaches him she squats down, and leaning over him, speaks in a whisper.

'What's the matter, Uncle Albert?'

Uncle Albert gives another heartfelt sob. He tears his sodden eyes away from the ceiling, and rests them on his niece's features.

'Uncle Albert, do tell me what's wrong? I can keep secrets you know.'

Uncle Albert licks his clown mouth and says falteringly, 'I . . . am . . . I am in love.' Alice nods encouragement. 'I am in love . . . with . . . with a married . . . man.' You can tell he is an actor, I reflect admiringly. His modulation is perfect. He pauses. When Alice does not move, and her steady gaze does not waver, he continues. 'His name is Reginald and he has decided . . . decided that he must go back to his wife and his two children. He has left me, to return to the sham that is his marriage.'

Again the tears rush to his eyes, and his chest heaves up and down. But now he weeps silently, and his anguish seems so much more poignant for the entombment of its sound. Alice draws even closer, lightly touching his shoulder.

'I do not think I can bear the pain. I think I would rather die,' confesses Uncle Albert elongating his words dolorously.

'Perhaps,' says Alice, taking hold of her uncle's arms, and pulling him up with care until he is sitting, 'we should have a party.'

Uncle Albert slumps wet-faced on the floral rug, while he absorbs this suggestion. He is still sitting when Alice returns with a brand-new bottle of vodka.

'Let's have a drink, Uncle Albert,' she says, breaking the seal and unscrewing the top.

Uncle Albert has stopped crying, and is looking intrigued. Alice brings in a yellow Formica chair from the dining table in the front room. She goes back and fetches two cream and blue striped mugs. She sets them down on the floor. She pats the chair invitingly. She fills the mugs with generous measures of vodka.

239

'You sit here, Uncle Albert. I am going to touch up your make-up, and put your wig back on, and soon you will be all beautiful again.'

When Uncle Albert has made himself comfortable on the chair, Alice hands him a mug. She takes the other in her hand, and clinks it to his with a winsome grin.

'The devil take Reginald,' is her toast. 'Now down it in one, and then I'll pour us another.'

So while Uncle Albert drinks his vodka, Alice redoes his make-up with the utmost care. She decks him with beads and bangles and earrings, till he sparkles. She eases on his shoulder-length blonde wig. She selects a pair of glamorous shoes for him, and with determin-ation tugs them on his large, unwieldy feet. She chooses a mandarin-style jacket from Uncle Albert's wardrobe for herself. It is black, with huge, extravagant, roseate peonies appliquéd on it. She pulls it on over her shirt, and does up the fiddly cord buttons. Then she covers her own face with greasepaint, smoothing it on with her fingertips She dabs bright spots of rouge onto her cheeks, paints on eyeshadow, strokes mascara through her eyelashes. She sweeps lipstick over her mouth, and, as an afterthought, she seizes the electric-blue wig from the dresser, and pulls it on over her own mousy-brown hair. And when she is finished she tells Uncle Albert that now they are both ready for the party. Uncle Albert takes two long, thoughtful swallows of vodka, and the corners of his clown mouth turn up in a broad smile.

'Let's dance, Uncle Albert,' Alice proposes.

So Uncle Albert gets up and tries out a few experimental steps. His blonde hair swishes around his face. They push back the chair, lift the vodka bottle and the mugs onto the chest of drawers out of harm's way, link arms and jig about the floor.

'Let's dance the tango?' Uncle Albert proposes.

'I'm not sure I know the tango,' Alice says, frowning.

'It doesn't matter. We'll make it up as we go along,' Uncle Albert reassures her. 'Performers often fake it,' he adds with a professional wink of one heavily lashed eye. So Alice speeds into the garden and picks a late rose. It sheds a few flesh-pink petals as she rushes back with it, holding it in her clenched teeth. After weighing up the effect Uncle Albert nods his approval. Then, he grasps his niece in a clinch and they scissor to-and-fro across the floor. Ballet is next. Alice stands on tiptoes and totters around the room circling her arms gracefully. Uncle Albert does proper turns, executed with as much precision as he can manage in his high-heeled shoes. His eyes fix on a spot. Then he spins, his head flicking round and catching up with the rest of him in a flurry of blonde hair a second later. He wiggles and concertinas himself and jumps.

'I do not have the freedom I am accustomed to in a leotard,' he says apologetically. But Alice only applauds the louder.

Alice reveals shyly that she has always wanted to fly, and Uncle Albert tells her that it can be arranged.

'I did it once with the aid of a belt and wires in *Peter Pan*, Alice,' he says. 'It was simply stupendous.' He helps Alice onto the bed. When he raises his hand, the agreed signal that he is ready, Alice leaps into the air. Uncle Albert catches her, his open arms closing on her small, airborne frame.

'I've had to catch all manner of women in my time, and some of them weighed a ton,' volunteers Uncle Albert, wincing at the memory.

'I wasn't too heavy was I?' Alice asks anxiously.

'Not you,' replies Uncle Albert, dismissing Alice's concerns with a flowery wave. 'You are light as a bird, dear lady.' He bows genteelly and Alice giggles.

It is the mention of the bird that gives me the idea. They are having such a fun time, Alice and her uncle, and I am beginning to feel excluded. I watch them as they collapse onto the rug and share some more vodka together. I ruminate on how I might contribute to the party spirit.

'Reginald can be a pompous twat sometimes, and a bit of a killjoy,' Uncle Albert declares audaciously, finishing off his sentence with a loud raspberry, his tight red lips flapping as the air is forced out. They both shriek with laughter, making me feel even more keenly that I have been left out in the cold. The private joke just seems to get funnier and funnier. The two of them roll about on the floor and

241

laugh and laugh. They laugh until different tears course down their cheeks. I recognise them as tears of joy. I feel bitterly jealous then. That is when my idea becomes a compulsion, and I force it into Alice's happy head.

'Why don't we set George free?' Alice blurts out excitedly, topping up their mugs with vodka, taking up hers and handing Albert his. They both take several sips as they consider the idea. 'He must hate it cooped up in that little cage. He must want more than anything to spread his wings and fly.'

Uncle Albert listens to what his niece says with his head on one side, and his blonde hair spilling over one shoulder.

'That . . . that . . . is a most ex . . . excellent plan,' he concurs. His voice has become sticky as plum jam.

At last the two of them weave their way upstairs with much hilarity, having drained the bottle, still hugging their now empty mugs. The monkey at the top of the stairs scouts ahead. The dog slouches after them. I slide elegantly along the ceiling. Once we are all in Audrey Lambert's bedroom Alice switches on the light, and with a flourish produces a second bottle of vodka from under her bed. My host and Uncle Albert refill their mugs.

'I shall . . . shall endeavour to . . . to sing I am the very modern model mo . . . jor general,' announces Uncle Albert. But he keeps tripping over his words and spluttering with laughter. Alice, over-come with mirth as well, lies on the floor and kicks her legs against the floorboards, until the din of drumming makes the little bottles on Audrey's dressing table tinkle. The monkey sits on the edge of the mantelpiece over the small fireplace clapping its rubiginous star hands, and swinging its spindly legs. Bear-as-Was rolls on his back galloping his diaphanous crimson paws in the air. Then Alice rises unsteadily, and staggers over to the budgie cage. With my guidance she opens its door. George squawks nervously. He hooks his beak on the bars in agitation. He clambers round and round his cage three or four times, as if making sure it is still there, still safe. Uncle Albert says they should forget George, because he is making a drama of escaping.

'We haven't got all day to . . . to wait around for . . . for that daft budgie to take off,' he protests.

Uncle Albert is right because dusk is setting in. Soon the day will be gone and the night will descend. He slips off his high-heeled shoes, and with difficulty mounts Audrey's bed. He climbs unsteadily to his feet and begins to jump. Following his lead, Alice springs on her own bed. They try their hardest to get a rhythm going. The monkey thinks this is a great laugh and joins them, bouncing so high that once or twice it hits the ceiling. The dog makes do with racing round until he is so dizzy he flops down. And because I think it might be amusing I nudge Alice. She clambers dutifully off the bed, and fetches the packet of birdseed from the top of Audrey's dressing table. They fill their hands with hundreds of seeds, and while they bounce clumsily, they throw them up at the ceiling.

'It's raining birdseed!' Alice squeals, alight with merriment as seeds shower down on her head.

Uncle Albert even catches some in his mouth and pretends to crunch on them, as if they are really delicious. But Bear-as-Was and the ghoulish monkey are riveted by something else now. While it is raining birdseed they bound over to the birdcage, their ghostly eyes trained on George. Tempted perhaps by the flying feast, he ventures nervously out of the cage. He flutters around the room, a radiant flash of green and yellow. He trills happily, gobbling seed wherever he finds it. Alice and Uncle Albert are halfway through a rendition of 'Three Little Maids from School', which Uncle Albert says is from *The Mikado*, when they notice George has finally emerged. They point and gaze at the bird for a short period, as he circles the room. By now they are making substantial inroads into the second bottle of vodka, and both are beginning to feel a bit sleepy. Neither of them realises that there is a sizable gap at the bottom of one of the sash windows. I have been inching it up for some while now. I like to keep busy. By the time George discovers it and falls out, Alice and Uncle Albert are so drunk it is hard to think straight.

'George,' Alice slurs, 'has . . . has fall . . . fall . . . en oh . . . oh . . . out of the window.'

'Ah, that is . . . to . . . ooo bad,' is Uncle Albert's only comment, before he blacks out on the floor with a thud.

Alice stumbles over to the window and joins me, the dog and monkey following curiously. The monkey spies a walking stick propped up in a corner of the room, and uses it to pole-vault onto the window ledge. And the dog bounds up and rests his paws either side of the little imp. I mould myself economically to the window-frame. Alice takes up her unsteady position under me and adjacent to the dog and monkey. From here we spot George, illuminated by the bedroom light, sitting in a tree only feet away. It is a large magnolia tree with huge, waxy, dark leaves. Against them, George's dazzling plumage is shown off to great advantage, even in the waning light. Alice slides her hands under the gap in the sash window, and after several attempts manages to push it up at least another foot. She lowers her face to the rectangle of deepening blue, and talks into it in a murmur. She is fighting to keep her eyes open. The image of George keeps splitting in two, and Alice has to concentrate very hard to merge them back into one.

'Fly Georges, fly. Go on, fly away Georges.'

But George only swivels his head, blinks his beady eyes, and nibbles experimentally on one of the large leaves. Then Alice too passes out, close to her uncle, the empty vodka bottle rolling out of her hand, and over the seed-covered floor, before finally coming to a halt by the bird stand, where the empty cage swings gently. We three ghosts curl up beside her.

And this is where Audrey finds us, bathed in the dapple greys of dawn, her son Albert, in his make-up and blonde wig and robe of mandarin splendour, and her granddaughter Alice, crowned with a mass of electric-blue hair, the tips of it sodden from the pool of vomit in which she lies, and me lounging close by. Alice's face is wet with bile. It has soaked into her black jacket, and stained two huge pink peonies a sickly mud-brown. Audrey stands in the doorway and surveys the carnage of her bedroom, her spine rigid, her breath coming in harsh gulps, her heart beating erratically. She has rushed home early, driven by a dark premonition, she mumbles brokenly.

Sensing rather than hearing a presence in the room, Alice opens her eyes. Her throat is parched. Her head hurts and the taste in her mouth is vile. Her skin is crawling. Only inches from her eyes, floating on the brown pool of bile her head lies in, is a fluffy feather, yellow edged with lime green. Now her eyes swim up and beyond it. The first thing she fixes upon is her grandmother's face, puckered and pale as milk skin. Alice sees she is swathed in a coat, standing only feet away. She tracks a line of drool, running from the corner of her grandmother's slack mouth down her chin. Fleetingly Alice meets her pinched, agonised eyes, notes the sweat beading her brow, her eye sockets, her cheeks. Finally her gaze drops to her grandmother's cupped hands. The hands are angled towards her, the rheumatic fingers bent awkwardly about some treasure. The sight makes Alice think suddenly of the three kings presenting their offerings to baby Jesus in the stable. She stares at the gift, stares at the yellow and green plumage streaked red. She sees that George's head has been bitten clean away, a single drop of blood blistering over the ragged stump, swelling and swelling, till at last it is liberated and splashes to the floor.

Dear me, I think resignedly, what a very silly bird not to fly away when it had the chance. Instead it must have hung about, making itself easy prey for the next door's cat. Such a pity! The dog and the monkey at my side nod in agreement.

The very next week we move out, all five of us. Yes, five. It pains me to tell you, but as we climb into the taxi I see a flash of green and yellow in the wing mirror. It seems headless George intends to join us, regardless of how welcome he is. I am not overly impressed with our new domicile either, a bedsit by Ealing Broadway station. Apart from anything else it is very cramped, consisting of a small combined bedroom and kitchenette, and an even smaller bathroom. It is situated on the second floor of an old Victorian house. It is a hovel compared to the flat on The Peak.

Ghost – 1975

The day everything changes dawns like any other. Christmas has been and gone, with Alice refusing an invitation from her father to fly home for the holidays, claiming work could not possibly manage without her.

'I'm afraid Harrison's needs me, Daddy. I couldn't leave them short-staffed during their busiest period,' she told her father on the communal payphone in the hall.

It is January. In Hong Kong soon there will be celebrations for Chinese New Year, the volley of firecrackers in the streets of Kowloon, a riot of coloured fireworks bursting and starring the night sky, homes chiming with laughter, filled with the steaming aroma of appetising dishes, families and friends visiting with each other. Here, we are on our way to work. Overhead is a canopy of slate-grey cloud, from which drizzle has been falling for some hours. The streets are crowded with people bundled up in coats and hats. Some steer prams and pushchairs, hold umbrellas, or grasp baskets of shopping or briefcases, as they hurry by. Alice has forgotten her coat. She is shivering in her damp clothes, little puffs of her warm breath misting in the cold air. Cars and buses, their headlights raking the gloom, their spinning tyres sending up fans of muddy water, rumble noisily on by. Horns blare, brakes grind, engines grumble, voices blur into one another, and the lights from traffic and shops bounce and scissor over the dark puddles.

Predictably we are late arriving, my host looking unequal to the demands of her job. Hanks of damp tangled hair cling to her cheeks and forehead. There are blue shadows under her glassy eyes and deep grey hollows beneath her pronounced cheekbones. The sores at the corners of her mouth are weeping pus. She looks emaciated. Her clothes are creased and ingrained with dirt. Even her green overall has stains on it. She now slips the quarter bottle of vodka she always carries in her bag into the large pocket stitched at the front of it. Then she makes her entrance on the shop floor. The floor-supervisor, Janice, looks askance at her and steams over.

'You don't look well, Alice,' she observes economically. 'P'raps you ought to go home.'

'No . . . no, I'm fine,' Alice insists, swaying slightly on her feet, and pulling on a lump of matted hair at the back of her head.

'You better stay out of the way this morning then, and do a bit of shelf-stacking. Aisle three,' Janice orders. And then, when Alice hesitates, she tells her to be quick about it. As Alice wanders off, she follows her stilted progress with disapproving eyes, and a shake of her head.

Sure enough, in aisle three we find a trolley loaded with cardboard boxes. Alice prises them open and lifts out the cans she finds, one by one, her muddled brain trying to recall what she needs to do with them. Making painfully slow progress, she begins lifting them onto the shelves. But as she works the monkey does its best to sabotage her efforts, tipping them over. A few fall to the floor, and the dog bats them playfully about the aisle with his scarlet forepaws. Sensing sport, the bird puts its feathered shoulder to a packet of Weetabix, thrilling at the domino effect it manages to achieve. One by one, the entire row of cereal boxes tumble to the floor. I do what I can to curtail this ghostly horseplay, but they are incorrigible.

As we near Alice's lunch-break, my frazzled host can think of little else but the bottle of vodka in her pocket, and how badly she needs a pull on it. At this inopportune moment, a disgruntled customer accosts Alice in an abrasive impatient tone.

'Where are the tins of red salmon? I've been looking all over the place. I do wish they'd stop moving things about. It makes it very difficult when you're in a rush.' She pauses, her sharp mud-brown eyes absorbing Alice's slovenly appearance. She fingers the pearls at her neck irritably. 'I especially need red salmon for a Fanny Cradock recipe I'm making this evening.' Alice scans the tins, trying hard to focus on their labels. She starts ineffectually shuffling them about, then with a trembling hand offers one to the customer.

'No, no, that's tuna!' The lady is irate. Her backcombed grey hair sits on her head like a bird's nest, wobbling as her ire rises. Her voice climbs steeply. 'I said salmon, red salmon! Are you deaf? Do I have to keep repeating myself?'

Alice is contrite. She apologises, and after several attempts, thwarted yet again by the monkey, who is once more haunting the shelves, slots the can she is holding back in place.

'There they are,' the customer declares, pointing a manicured finger at the topmost shelf. 'Up there.' The monkey materialises among the cans of salmon she is indicating. 'You'll have to lift one down for me. I can't possibly clamber about in this skirt.'

The monkey grips the shelf edge with its spidery fingers, and peers down at Alice, devilry dancing in its refulgent green eyes. The dog stands on his hind-legs, and places his forepaws on the middle shelf, eager to help. The budgie who has been wheeling overhead, collides with a tower of special offer toilet rolls, and sends several tumbling to the floor. The sudden series of thumps as they impact on the tiles makes the customer jump. Returning her gaze to Alice, she appraises my host critically.

'Well,' she demands, 'are you going to assist me?'

Alice's head wobbles in assent. She eyes her goal blearily, working out she will need to stand on the bottom shelf in order to reach it. The monkey hides, crouching down behind the tiers of canned fish. I lean back against the shelves, spectral arms entwined, interested to see how this will play out. Alice clears a space for a foothold, and steps onto it. With one hand she grips the second shelf, with the other she reaches towards the third, and makes a grab for the can of salmon. The monkey's riposte is to pitch three tins back at her. One strikes Alice hard on the head, another hits her shoulder, and a third lands on her foot. She yelps, leaps back and ducks. As she bends, arms flaying, the bottle of vodka tumbles out of her pocket and smashes on the floor. Instantly my host dives after it.

'Nooooh!' she wails. Her head swings up. She holds the customer's stunned brown eyes with her own venomous ones. 'Look what you've done, you stupid cow!'

She is kneeling on the broken glass in a paroxysm of rage, more wild, unholy sounds streaming from her mouth. The monkey, emerging from behind a can, peers down in astonishment at Alice crawling on the floor. The dog sticks its beetle-black nose in a puddle of vodka, and crunches experimentally on a shard of glass. The bird, having succeeded in prising the lid off an egg-carton on the opposite shelf, squats hopefully on a large brown egg. The customer clutches at her pearls and starts screaming.

Then they are all running towards Alice, customers and staff alike. They come from the cheese and the meat counter, from the fruit and veg, from the bakery, and from the other aisles. Harrison employees in their green tunics, customers, men and woman, old, middle-aged and young, swell the numbers, wheeling trolleys and clutching shopping baskets and bags. Janice the supervisor is one of the first on the scene, almost as if she has been expecting an accident. She is followed by the manager, who in turn is followed by the new security guard, Bert. As they near Alice, they all freeze and stare. They are agog. My host is on her knees, groping about on the wet floor, among the jagged pieces of glass. The customer, who wanted the salmon for her recipe, slumps against a shelf whimpering. Somebody steps forward to calm her down. Suddenly Alice scoops up a fragment of the bottle that still holds some vodka. She raises it to her mouth and drinks greedily, lapping at it with her tongue.

'Do something, Mr Valler!' cries Janice, her eyes veering from Alice to the manager. 'For God's sake!'

But the manager stands as if paralysed, his mouth gaping open, his eyes glued to my host. As Alice's tongue whips about the fragment of the bottle, it is lacerated on the razor-sharp edges. It begins to bleed copiously. Blood and saliva dribble down Alice's chin, and plop onto her supermarket tunic. They spatter on the tiled floor, making patterns.

'The vodka . . . has gone!' Alice keens, tapping into a deeper register, the plaintive ululation sounding more like a growl. 'There is none left. Look. Can't you see, there's none left.' She sucks desperately on the ragged glass slicing the moist membrane of her inner cheek.

'What shall I do, Mr Valler?' begs Bert, shifting his weight uneasily from one hip to the other, looking anxiously for guidance.

Janice the floor supervisor tries to take command. She steps forward, arms folded. She stands over Alice. 'Get up!' Alice does not move. 'I think you'd better call the police, Mr Valler!' she barks. A baby starts grizzling. A child bursts into tears. And a guide dog, a golden Labrador, suddenly spots Bear-as-Was floundering beside Alice. The effect is instantaneous. His owner is knocked to the floor as the dog slathers and prances, a handful of customers rushing to his aid.

Alice, head bent, eyes raised, expression demonic, grins at Janice, widening her bloody mouth to reveal wet red teeth. Then she lowers her face to the floor and begins to lap up the spilt vodka, meticulous as a cat with a dish of cream. The dog, parodying his mistress, joins in. The monkey shimmies down a supporting shelf-column, seizes the cap of the vodka bottle, and scoots off through the crowd with its find. The budgie, flustered by the unfolding hysteria, sticks a clawed foot straight through the egg and gets soaked in yolk.

'Christ!' yells Janice. 'She's mad. That girl's out of her mind. Call the police, Mr Valler.' The look on her face is victorious, her cheeks flushed, her eyes radiant. 'If you don't call them, Mr Valler, I will!'

'What's happening to her? Mr Valler, call an ambulance! Why is the guide dog snarling? She's sick, poor thing. I've never seen the like in Harrison's. Has the girl flipped? I only called in for some jam tarts. Can't somebody get hold of that damn dog! Are you going to leave her in that state? For God's sake, call the police!' come a chorus of shouts from solicitous bystanders as my host continues to grovel on the floor. And then a strident voice booms out above the rest.

'What d'you want to go fetching the police for, getting this child into trouble?'

Her rich sonorous tones roll over us like breaking waves. Bear-as-Was immediately sits to attention, the monkey hurdles back over the sea of bobbing heads, to perch on his rosy brow. Even the budgie, still wrestling with the egg, feels the vibrato rippling through it. Rotating, eggshell hat over stumpy neck, it turns in the direction of the voice. The speaker is a tall, plump woman of middle years, with skin the colour of milk chocolate. Her face is open, her nose broad, her eyes percipient, the irises dark as burnt toast. These features are fringed with hair black as crow's feathers, thick and curly. There is a gilt clip fastened in it, fashioned in the shape of a butterfly, studded with green, yellow and purple plastic gems. She is wrapped up in a mauve coat with a fake fur collar. Her ankle boots, slick with mud, have left prints on the tiled floor of the supermarket. All eyes search her out as she hovers on the fringe of the circle, and in front of her a path clears. Even the guide dog is returned miraculously to its former placid self.

Alice's head comes up fast. She locks eyes with this mystifying woman. In that very second something snaps in my host. The stone heart thaws and the tears finally come. She climbs shakily to her feet. Glass particles adhere to the sticky blood at her knees and a crystal splinter protrudes from the palm of one hand. The woman moves closer.

'Help me. Please.' It is a barely audible whisper, but I see from the light that kindles in the woman's eyes that she has heard it. She strides up to Alice and folds her into her coat. She pays no heed to the blood which seeps into the mauve fabric, and which edges the fur collar.

'I'm going to call the police,' Janice declares, pointedly ignoring the remonstrations of this new arrival. 'They need to take Alice away, to sort her out.'

'There's no need for police here,' the woman retorts. 'I know this child. I know Alice. I'll take her home. There's no real harm done.' She starts to guide us all down the aisle.

After that things happen quickly. Janice, the manager and the security guard trundle after us, as do several of the customers. Alice stares blankly ahead. Our new chaperone maintains yet again that she knows Alice, that she is a friend, a good friend, that she will look after her. The manager seeks confirmation of this and, to my amazement my host nods vaguely. The monkey, atop the dog, the dog, walking to heel, shake their heads adamantly. The headless budgie, roosting on Alice's shoulder, makes a chopping gesture with its wings, signifying a denial. I bellow in my host's ear that this is a stranger who may lead us into terrible danger.

However, everyone seems so keen to be rid of Alice that they probe no further. In the confusion no one even asks this woman her name. At her request, the manager hurriedly shows the way to the ladies' room. Once inside 'she' lifts off the bloodstained overall, removes the glass splinter and cleans Alice up with paper towels from the machine.

'We do not know this lady,' we importune, all but the budgie. It simply bobs up and down frantically, in mute expostulation.

'It is insane to trust her. If we go with her who knows what might befall us,' I add, my ectoplasm streaked puce with panic. But Alice, still foggy with drink, docilely submits to this stranger's administrations.

'Don't you worry about her. She's gonna be just fine. And as soon as she's feeling better, I'm sure she'll come to see you, to sort this all out,' the interloper tells the manager presumptuously, as we emerge from the ladies' room. 'Oh yes, I'll look after her now.' She wags her head, and the plastic gems in the butterfly clip spark under the supermarket's pearly lights as if they were priceless jewels. Then she grasps Alice's arm firmly and leads us out of the store. My host trots along with her willingly. We share dismayed looks. In this unlikely guise, our expressions say, is a force to be reckoned with.

Audrey – 1975

'I said Alice is missing!' I shout into the mouthpiece of the phone. I find it hard to trust this business of long-distance phone calls, speaking to your daughter who is over 6,000 miles away as if she is in the same room. Although I am told it is unnecessary, I cannot break myself of the habit of raising my voice. I speak too with exaggerated clarity. Despite my efforts, Myrtle asks me to repeat myself and I do, even more emphatically.

'What do you mean missing?' Now my daughter's voice matches mine for volume.

'She hasn't been to work for some weeks. Alice's manager rang me, a Mr Valler. He said there had been some trouble, and so he thought . . .'

'You mean there has been more trouble since . . . since the accident with the bird?' Myrtle interjects.

There is a strange delay on these long-distance phone calls that peppers the conversation with momentary silences, or results in two voices sounding at once, speaking over each other. Sometimes I think an entire call is wasted simply trying to achieve sequential communication. I feel every one of my seventy-six years today. My back aches and I am so very tired. I sit down on the chair by the hall table.

'Mother? Mother, are you still there?'

'Yes. I don't really know the details, Myrtle. Her manager was a bit vague about it. I think she may have been intoxicated at work.'

I am sure I hear my daughter utter an expletive under her breath. 'Anyway, she cut herself or something. He said it was nothing too serious but he sent her home . . . well, to her bedsit, and some lady who knew her went with her.' I pause to take a breath. My chest feels tight this afternoon and every inhalation is an effort. My eyes prick too, particularly the left one. Perhaps I have the beginning of a stye. I am a little light-headed as well. I did not manage any lunch today. The talk with that 'Creepy Joe' landlord earlier on has left me feeling strangely disquieted, and yes, if am honest, marginally culpable in this peculiar business. 'Mr Valler said that he didn't call Alice for a couple of weeks, as he felt she might need time to recuperate, though what he meant by that I'm not quite sure. But when eventually he rang she wasn't there. He kept trying, always unsuccessfully. Naturally he became worried, and using her original details that he still had on file, he contacted me. And then . . . and then . . . ' Despite sitting down I am feeling dizzy. I lean heavily on the telephone table to steady myself.

'And then? And then *what*, Mother?' comes Myrtle's impatient voice down the line. Always minded of the expense of long-distance calls, I try to gather my thoughts.

'I took a taxi round to her bedsit this morning and her landlord was there, a Mr Fitch. A most unpleasant gentleman if you ask me. Anyway, he said Alice had been late with her rent, and he'd come over to see what was what. When she didn't open the door he let himself into her room. Well, Myrtle, he said it was empty. Picked clean as a bone. Those were his very words. He said there was no question in his mind that she'd skedaddled, leaving him out of pocket. He seemed to think I was going to reimburse him. The cheek of it. The thing is, Myrtle, she's not been in touch with me either. It's been quite a while since anyone's seen her. She's vanished.' My hand alights on my chest where I feel my heart fluttering wildly, a trapped bird. Remembering George, I shiver. 'I thought you and Ralph would want to know. Do you think I ought to go to the police?'

There is a pause at the end of the line all those thousands of miles away. It lasts several seconds. I wonder if we've been cut off or if there is some kind of interference. I shake the receiver clutched in my hand, hopeful that the line may clear. Then Myrtle's voice sounds again.

'No, of course you shouldn't go to the police, Mother. Don't be ridiculous. And we'll settle up with the landlord, so don't fret about that either. I'm sure it's nothing to be concerned about. She probably didn't like her job and, rather than do the responsible thing, she just walked out and found herself somewhere else to live. I don't doubt when she needs money she'll let us know. In the meantime please don't go upsetting yourself. Alice ought to be ashamed of herself. She's put you through quite enough. I am sorry I burdened you with her, really I am.' An audible sigh carries clearly over the line. 'You are not to worry, Mother.' This last comes to me like an order.

'If you . . . you . . . say so,' I falter. I am still uneasy. I should like to dismiss this as Myrtle has, but a deep-rooted instinct tells me there is something more sinister afoot. 'I'll let you know if there's any news.'

'I'd appreciate that. But don't you go getting caught up in this thing. Do you hear me, Mother? In the meantime we'll try to bring forward our leave. We'll be with you as soon as we can, and then hopefully we can sort Alice out once and for all. I'll ring you next week if I don't hear from you before then. Goodbye Mother.'

'Goodbye Myrtle.'

Carefully I place the receiver in its cradle. Throughout the afternoon I listen out for the ring tone of the telephone, feeling at one moment expectant, despondent the next. Albert is late home this evening, and listens with an unreadable face to the news I impart that his niece Alice is missing. My son barely touches his plate of food – rissoles, one of his favourites that I have prepared especially. He pushes it away and walks out of the room without uttering a word.

Ghost – 1975

Predictably the headless budgie is the first to take flight. No staying power, that chicken-hearted bird. We're better off without it, I console myself. Our kidnapper races ahead, dodging shoppers and pedestrians, Alice's arm tucked firmly in hers. I streak after them, while the monkey and the dog bring up the rear. I am the only one to spot it. Oh, it is no more than a quick burst of lime-green and butter-yellow, breaking the monotony of a dull grey sky. But I know that that flash signals we've been deserted by the headless budgie, that we ghosts are reduced again to a trio.

'Go on then. Scram,' I holler after it. 'You were never one of us anyhow.'

Then I turn my attention to Alice and plead with her.

'This woman could be a *mo gwei,* a demon in disguise. Who knows where she's taking us?'

But Alice, clutching a tissue to her still bloody mouth with her free hand, indicates her refusal to listen with a stubborn shake of the head. On we go, threading through the crowds, trudging past shops, until we sweep into Ealing Broadway station. Here this busybody purchases tickets for herself and my host, then hurries us onto a train. As we roll away, I realise that it is too late to turn back. The carriage rumbles and rattles along, first above ground, then whistling and screaming through pitch-black tunnels beneath it. It bumps us about until the monkey covers its eyes, the dog buries its muzzle in the grubby upholstery, and I . . . I huddle down into my army jacket and wish us far away. I lose count of the stations we pass through, until at last, when we grind to a halt and the doors judder open, she bundles Alice off. As we slither after them, a voice rings out telling us to 'mind the gap' between the train and the platform. It is a poignant reminder of how vulnerable we all are, how easily we might slip away into ether. We exchange worried looks and plough on through underground passageways. Before long we board another train. When this one screeches to a standstill the meddler hauls Alice out, and on we dash, moving upwards now. We come upon a girl with three shiny silver rings piercing her nose, and scuffed blue boots on her feet, plucking disconsolately on a battered guitar. The woman pauses and rummages through her bag. She drops a handful of coins into the open guitar-case. The girl, still playing, nods her thanks as we pass by.

At last we leave the warm fug of the tunnels, and enter a twilight world dotted with lights. We hurry along pavements hemming wide roads busy with traffic. Brakes scream, engines snarl, horns blare. Then these narrow and grow quieter, before we turn into a residential street that looks as if it has one long house snaking the length of it. I soon realise that the snake is divided into segments, and that each of these segments is a home. We stop before a black wrought-iron gate, and 'she' opens it and pushes Alice through. Frantically I try to penetrate Alice's woolly mind, to make her see sense.

'This woman,' I whisper persuasively 'could be a madam, a mistress of whores. She espied you, Alice, with your pliant young body, and plans to cajole you into working for her. If you go into her house you could be raped every day and never escape. Think of that!'

Alice hesitates. She frowns and blinks slowly. But already the woman has opened her front door and is beckoning her inside. I pull hard on each of my host's limbs in turn, trying to dissuade her from entering. The dog and the monkey cower under a low privet hedge which lines the front path, no help at all. Alice glances back over her shoulder. She follows the progress of a large red car as it purrs by and recedes into the distance, and watches an elderly man leaning heavily on a stick as he crosses the road. Her head rolls back. She stares up at a pale gold smudge of moon through a pearly film of cloud.

'Alice, come inside and warm yourself,' says our abductor.

And Alice, with the beginnings of a serene smile touching her lips, straightens up, walks forward and enters the house. Clearly a little abstracted, Alice shuts the front door in our lambent faces, and we have to push through it to join her. Lights have been switched on, two overhead and one standard lamp, illuminating our path. There is no hallway I note. We glide straight into a room much larger than the bedsit we have grown accustomed to. There are some hooks on the wall by the door where the lady's mauve coat now hangs, her muddy boots standing side by side on a shoe rack under it. A three-piece suite and a television are ranged about a fireplace at one end of the rectangular space, with a dining table and chairs at the other. It is ordered and clean with bright furnishings. A carpet patterned with swirls of gold and blue runs the length of the floor, lemon-yellow throws cover both the settee and armchairs, while the curtains, drawn back from the windows at either end of the room, are a shade of deep mustard flecked with white dots. The tiled fireplace is recessed in the honey-coloured walls, knotted newspaper and kindling laid ready in the grate. Above it, set on the dark wood mantelpiece, is a brass carriage clock surrounded by photographs. There are four in all, three of which have carved wooden frames. The largest is of a man in a suit and a woman in a frothy white dress and veil, both smiling widely. A wedding photograph I presume. Scrutinising it closely, I see there is the semblance of our captor about the happy bride. In the next picture she appears again, looking older, standing on a small bridge with a teenage boy on one side, and a girl, a little younger, on the other. Another image has at least a dozen faces crowded together, all of different ages, including a new baby wrapped up in a white cocoon. I have a terrible shock when I look at the last photograph though. Silver-framed, it is the colour portrait of a teenage girl with large brown eyes and long dark hair. Despite her skin tone, the likeness to Alice is uncanny.

'Why don't you sit yourself down, Alice, and I'll fetch us a nice cup of tea.'

Still reeling, I fly about to see the woman watching Alice. She is wearing beaded pink slippers now and an orange, brown and cream striped dress. She bustles through an open doorway at the back of the room, through which I glimpse a kitchen. Still dazed, Alice sits down on one of the four ladder-back chairs arranged round the square dining table. I scud speedily to my host's side, annoyed that I let my attention wander in such a potentially serious situation. I try to communicate my fears to Alice, but her eyelids are heavy and keep closing on me. We hear drawers scraping open and closed, the chink of cutlery on china, and that rich voice I am already learning to dread rising in song, before the whistle of a kettle seems to jolt Alice awake.

'By the way, my name is Reta, Reta Okello,' the women tells Alice, emerging from the kitchen with two steaming mugs of tea. She puts both of these down on the embroidered tablecloth, one before Alice, then turns and fetches a tin from a sideboard. Finally she takes her seat, joining Alice at the table. My host lowers the bloodstained tissue from her mouth and tucks it away in a pocket. Dried blood crusts her swollen lips. Her tongue is thick and her inner cheek is still tingling where she nicked it with the broken glass, though no longer bleeding.

The woman beams, the butterfly clasp in her hair giving its rainbow wink in the glow of the room.

'Much better,' she says approvingly, casting her eyes over Alice's drawn face. 'By tomorrow it'll be all gone. You see.' Cautiously my host fingers her mouth and gives a shy half-smile.

'That's if you live that long, Alice,' I glower. 'If any of us do. Of course it's highly likely that the brew she has made is drugged,' I warn my host, indicating the tea with a hyaline finger. The monkey, occupied inspecting the shiny tin, the dog, nose in the coalscuttle, nod together lugubriously. The dog, not surprisingly feeling insecure in these new surroundings, pads over and lies down at Alice's feet. Tipping Alice's mug over would seem a wise move to me at this juncture. But Alice disagrees, grasping it firmly with both hands the moment I tug it.

'I don't know if you take sugar, Alice, but as you've had a bit of a shock I popped a couple of teaspoons in anyway. It'll do you good,' Reta Okello clucks. Alice nods and blows shakily on the hot liquid. 'I want you to call me Reta, Alice. I'm your friend.'

'Alice does not need any more friends,' I shrill. 'Why on earth would she want you when she has us.' Judging by Reta's smug, self-satisfied expression, she does not hear me. Alice does though. She flinches. I am delighted to see the liquid in her cup slopping over the rim.

'Oh, I'm sorry,' breathes Alice hastily, her eyes immediately anxious.

'Don't worry about it. That's what washing machines are for, Alice,' Reta reassures, her tone easy. She leans forwards and pulls the lid off the tin, sending the unsuspecting monkey flying. It bounces twice and plummets over the edge of the table, landing on the dog's highly sensitive nose. He yelps, and bats the pest off with a paw, bowling it over the carpet. Alice's eyes widen at the spectacle, but Reta notices nothing. She offers Alice a biscuit. At least my host declines this. Then she studies Alice's face carefully for a long moment, reaches over the table and sandwiches Alice's hand in hers.

'You remind me of someone, Alice,' she says, her tone suddenly hushed. Even in her comatose condition I see a flicker of interest in Alice's red-rimmed eyes. After a moment Reta continues, although she does not appear to be focusing on my host, but on a spot a little way above her shoulder. 'Her name was Kesia, my niece Kesia. She was a wild child. Always in trouble. Always so angry with the world. We couldn't tame her, Alice. She found life . . . hard. I think you understand what that means, to find life hard.' Again Alice nods, as if very slowly the words she is hearing are penetrating her reason. 'My sister tried everything to help her daughter. We both did. But Kesia didn't want to be reached. We lost her, Alice. We couldn't hold onto her. She slipped away from us.'

Reta pauses and takes a deep ragged breath. She shuts her eyes, lifts one hand to her mouth and presses two fingers against her trembling lips, holding them there for several seconds before letting them fall away. Still she waits, swallows, takes a slow steadying breath. When she speaks her voice is flat with sorrow. 'I will never forget seeing her lying on that table. She was freezing, poor child. Her fingers were black with the cold. I told them, shouldn't we fetch her a blanket, rub her hands and feet, get the circulation back into them. I wanted to lie down next to her, give her the warmth of my body.'

'Dead?' I suggest to the dog and the monkey.

'Dead,' they chorus back enthusiastically. If there is one thing we three are experts in identifying, it is the signs of death.

'Such a light she had, Alice, such a fierce bold flame. I couldn't believe her fire was gone, that our Kesia played with ghosts.' She snatches a quick breath and her eyes spring open and come to rest on Alice. She gives my host's hand a little squeeze and grins, a crooked finger wiping moisture away from the corner of her eye. 'I think you would have liked her, Alice. I think you and Kesia would have been great friends. She looked a lot like you. I have a photograph of her on the mantelpiece. When you are feeling better I'll show it to you.'

Reta lets go of Alice's hand. She picks up her mug of tea and sips it thoughtfully. Alice tugs on a strand of hair, pulls it forward in front of her face, teases it apart.

Three times she takes a breath and tries to speak, frowning as she attempts to formulate words in her head, to anchor them down before they drift away.

'You mean . . . you mean,' she begins breathlessly, 'hmm . . . hmm . . . that your niece, Ke . . . Kesia, your niece Kesia is dead?' she asks at last.

Reta, arranging biscuits on a plate, pauses, nods her head and smiles sadly at Alice.

Alice scoops back the strand of hair and for the first time stares straight into Reta's face at the grief etched there. I know she is struggling to master speech, the heat of the vodka still melting her words, making her lips numb, her limbs heavy.

'And now . . . now Kesia . . . plays with ghosts all the time?' It is barely a whisper but it is edged with urgency. Again Reta nods and her shining dark brown eyes glisten anew with tears.

From the houses either side an undercurrent of muffled noise can be heard, the jumping beat of music, distant voices rising and falling, cars, engines firing, turning over, coughing. Underneath the table Bear-as-Was whines. The monkey, who has managed to scale a chair, now gains the summit of the table and takes a running jump into the biscuit tin. Alice's mouth falls open. Then she sees me, sitting at her side desperately trying to attract her notice. I shrink into my army jacket until my head disappears. Normally I would never resort to such silly tactics to get Alice's attention, but Reta, weaving her sad story to inveigle my host, is being unscrupulous. Now I pop my head up through the neck of the army jacket and give my best gap-toothed grin. At the very least I expect a giggle, but to my surprise Alice looks at me with huge frightened eyes, then hurriedly drops her gaze.

'Am I dead, Reta?' she asks quietly.

Reta Okello leaps up giving us all a nasty shock, rushes to Alice, leans over her and embraces her. The dog is on his feet in a flash, teeth bared. The monkey's squashed sorrel head inches into sight above the rim of the biscuit tin. I shudder. We all find this overt display of emotion embarrassing. Besides, this Reta woman has only just met Alice and cannot possibly care for her the way we do. I expect Alice to be appalled and shrug her off. But my host lets herself be pawed, and even starts to respond in kind, swivelling in her chair, her own arms reaching tentatively around the stout lady. The scene repels me so much that I have to look away. The monkey high-jumps over the rim of the biscuit tin and capers about the tabletop wobbling like a jelly. The dog groans, rolls his violet eyes and slumps down on the carpet in disgust.

'No, Alice, you are not dead,' Reta tells my host firmly, though why Alice has to seek confirmation of this from her, I do not know. She need only have asked us. We would have informed her she was very much alive – after all didn't we all depend on it? Reta starts stroking Alice's hair, a gesture of such intimacy that I want to slap her hand away. 'What makes you say that, eh?' She pulls back from Alice and looks at her with concern.

Alice squirms in her chair. She cannot hold Reta's penetrating gaze. Her eyes veer from her to us. The dog wags its magnificent maroon tail, the monkey waves and makes a vulgar noise, and I nestle closer to my host, lacing my misty legs. 'Because of the . . . the . . . the—' Alice gives a small frustrated cry.

'Because of what, Alice?' echoes Reta Okello.

'The gho-gho—' Alice seems to give up and slumps forward on the table, hiding her face in the crook of her folded arms.

She appears distressed. We exchange baffled looks. But Reta Okello straightens up. Her head wheels round slowly, and with half-hooded eyes she rakes the room. We three freeze instinctively. I cannot be certain, but when she looks in my direction for one weird moment I think she sees me. For a few seconds she is very still, as if she is not only seeing me but hearing me as well, tuning in to my ghostly frequency. I feel violated by this intrusive trickery. She behaves in an identical manner towards the others. Then she hisses through her teeth and with an index finger draws what looks like a five-sided star in the air.

'*Tano*. Five for protection,' she mumbles softly.

Slowly circling the table, she repeats this three more times. As she speaks and draws her stars, we find our ghostly skeins elongating, then tangling into each other and drawing into tight knots. What remains when she has finished her work is a globe of writhing spectral fibres, silver blue, flame red, scintillating foxy-brown, rolling about on the carpet. We are unable to divide ourselves into separate entities for a good quarter of an hour. And while we wrestle to free ourselves, buck and sway like a junk in a typhoon, that dreadful enchantress with her wicked fingertip magic, calmly settles down to drink her tea with Alice.

Despite my ghostly exertions, I force myself not to break contact with my host. A lapse in concentration could prove fatal. So as I arch and dip and gyrate, incessantly trying to gather up my frayed edges and plait them back together, I listen avidly. I discover that Reta is a nurse employed at a local hospital. Despite my uncomfortable condition, I spare a thought for the poor wretches she cares for, and wonder how many, if any, survive. Her husband, she explains pensively, was killed in a car accident many years ago. She lives here alone, though she has children – a son, Kosey, and a daughter, Subira. She tells Alice that she wants her to meet them both. She adds that her son lives in France where he runs a small business exporting fine French foods.

'He is coming to visit us quite soon. Isn't that lucky, Alice?' Reta says. Our enmeshed emanations let out a unified wail. We share the same horrified reaction. The spawn of this witch might well be more of a threat to us than she is. When we finally succeed in unravelling our ectoplasm, we overhear Reta telling Alice that she looks very tired, that she needs to rest.

Up the sorceress gets and off she goes, my Alice gullibly following her. Disorientated, I barely have time to gather my spirit-wits together. The dog, elated to be liberated from our ghostly quagmire, is currently in fruitless pursuit of his lashing burgundy tail.

'There is no time to waste,' I caution him. 'The witch is leading Alice upstairs. Don't you understand we are in serious danger of being annihilated.' He halts abruptly, buries his nose deep in his pelt and bites frantically on a spectral mite. This is not the reaction I had hoped for, and just serves to illustrate that all apparitions are not of the same calibre. I make a thorough search for the monkey. It is hiding under the table.

'Exactly what are you doing?' I ask, feeling the chances of us being routed increasing fast. The monkey glances up and blathers something unintelligible. I blink back frosty ghost eyes incredulously. The imp is parting chestnut hairs on its wee potbelly and picking off specks of glitter.

'At this rate we are done for,' I muse sombrely, as I shepherd the pair of flat-headed phantoms upstairs. Here, in a small bedroom, we find the hell-cat practising her sophistry on my host, distorting her mind, probing our secrets. I know she intends to destroy my relationship with Alice. But then she does not know how close we are, how insoluble are the ties that bind us. Surely Alice will not abandon me, any more than I will abandon Alice. But if it's a fight the hag wants . . .

She gives my host a nightgown, and I find myself wondering if she has impregnated it with poison. She draws the curtains with their striking pattern of green and red ellipses, and points out the location of the bathroom. While she waits we disappear into it and emerge moments later, my host wearing the nightie, holding her folded clothes. These she lays at the end of the bed before climbing into it. Reta leans over her and tucks the blanket in around her. The dog retreats under the bed, and the monkey wraps itself up in a fold of the curtains. When the witch makes to leave, pausing for a moment at the door, my host begins protesting. For once we ghosts are in harmony. Not before time, we concur telepathically.

'Reta . . . things . . . things come to me in the dark. Bad things.'

I am not quite sure what to make of this. But Reta does not seem phased at all. She gives a brief understanding nod, and as her eyes rake the gloom I am measurably diminished. Once more I experience the uncomfortable sensation that they are alighting on me, tracing my outline. Before I know it, she is revolving on the spot.

'*Tisa*, nine for protection,' she mutters, as her finger strokes the air. '*Nisaidi, tafadhalie.* Help me, please.' I see the number nine, red as blood, suspended in the air. Again her finger sketches a figure. '*Saba*, seven for protection.' And there it is, the number seven branded in front of me in a deep dazzling blue. Lastly, her hands move above Alice's prone body making the star with five points. '*Tano*, five for protection,' she whispers. The number five, black and threatening, extends its inky limbs over Alice, encasing her as if in a cage. 'Leave this place.' I am not sure if my host sees the ominous spidery scrawl looming over her, but her eyes, looking up, are peaceful, drowsy. Incredibly she is untroubled by this display of evil spell casting. But before I have time to react, I sense invisible flames rearing up from nowhere, starting to scroll across the bedroom floor. As they leap over me it is as if I have taken a sleeping draft. I feel myself sinking and condensing into a puddle. Although I make frantic efforts to whip myself up again, they are futile.

'Don't you worry yourself, Alice,' the crone's voice sounds above me. 'I'll sit with you while you sleep. I won't leave you, I promise.' I make one more attempt to rear up, vowing I will be a maelstrom roaring through Reta Okello's tidy house and leaving devastation in my wake, but to no avail. I manage little more than a ripple.

I feel Alice put her head down on the pillow, a great breath sighing out of her. Within seconds my host is drifting off to sleep. Soon Alice's breathing alters, becoming deep and rhythmic. A sensation of unimaginable relief settles on me as Reta Okello rises and leaves the room. But in minutes she returns clasping a small red velvet purse and a tiny pair of shiny silver scissors. I watch as she bends over the sleeping form of Alice and snips off a lock of her hair, then puts it into the red purse. Next, with immense care she clips a nail from the little finger of one of her hands outstretched on the pillow. This too she places in her purse. Now she rifles through the pile of Alice's clothes and snips a scrap of fabric off the hem of her skirt. She thrusts this into the pouch also, pulling the drawstring neck tightly closed. Then she lays it flat on the palm of her left hand and rubs it with a circular motion of her right, quietly speaking Alice's name jumbled with incomprehensible words.

Lastly she slips a hand between the bedhead and the wall, feeling for something. The glint of the iron nail is reflected on my mirrored surface. She hooks the bag on this before retaking her seat and dozing in the bedside chair. The greys of dawn are edging through the slits in the curtains before I am able to re-form. Having accomplished this I make a few cautious moves, rustling the sheets, flipping the pages of a magazine on the bedside table, levitating the floor rug a few inches, testing my strength. But every time those alert eyes of hers flash open, and almost as quickly she squeezes them into tight slits and pouts, then 'pahs' out a breath. It may not sound like a lot, but believe me it throws my concentration and I am all translucent thumbs. Meanwhile the dog and the monkey are of no assistance whatsoever. Despite my entreaties, they showed their cowardice by remaining cloistered throughout the night and beyond.

Over the next few days it seems to us that Alice does nothing but slumber. I overhear Reta saying to her daughter, Subira, on one of her frequent visits, that Alice sleeps like a baby. Well, if she does, it is news to us. The Alice we know roams through the nights like a caged animal. At first I comfort myself that when Reta goes to work we will have ample opportunity to undo the damage. But I soon find out that Reta never leaves the house without scratching one of her strange signs on the wall and muttering her rhymes. This is one among many unpleasant rituals the witch performs. Tiny gauze pockets of berries are hung from small golden hooks over the windows and doors, red dust appears sprinkled on the threshold of the house, pungent green leaves and soporific herbs are tucked in all the corners of the rooms. In addition to this, when Reta is at home candles burn continuously – candles with peculiar symbols carved into their wax. The results for us are cataclysmic. We loll about in sorry little patches of icy mist, unable to do anything except summon up a drip every so often. It is very worrying not having any idea what the future holds for Alice, for the dog, the monkey and me.

Subira starts to call Alice one of her mother's strays, hugging her as she does so. This enrages me. Alice is no stray. She belongs to me. She is my property, and Reta is as good as stealing her from me. But I am so lethargic, so attenuated that I haven't the energy to put up a fight. I cannot smash a glass, or make a light wink, or even turn on a tap. I am like the opium addicts I used to observe in Hong Kong stumbling out of their shady dens, dizzy and stupid with their poppy juice. I stew frostily as I observe, not once but countless times, Alice confiding in Reta in a way she has never done with me. Oh, I know everything there is to know about Alice. Her mind is transparent to me. But how much does she share willingly with me the way she does with Reta? She talks freely to her, a virtual stranger, about her family and how it was back in Hong Kong in the flat on The Peak. And Reta nods as if she empathises, though she cannot possibly understand the way I do. I was there, seeing Alice through every storm. Most of all, Alice talks of her father, what an incredible man he is and how deeply she loves him. She tells Reta that in time she may contact him, let him know she is safe and well. Reta seems overjoyed by this.

'I was visiting an old friend in Ealing and I popped into Harrison's for some teabags, and found you. How lucky was that, Alice,' Reta says, beaming. Watching them together my essence curdles.

Weeks slide by, and before long we cannot help but observe that Alice is changing. She bathes and brushes her hair daily. Reta pours nasty infusions into the warm bathwater – salt and vinegar, lavender, frankincense and sandalwood, marjoram and sage – until I can no longer detect Alice's distinctive bitter welcoming odour. Her clothes, for the most part lent to her by Subira, may be a poor fit but are clean and pressed. The sores around her mouth have vanished, and her complexion has cleared. Though still pale, there is hint of peach occasionally in her cheeks. She has found an appetite too and is in danger of making a habit of meals. While Alice apparently thrives within Reta's portals we decline.

I am exuberant on the morning that Alice returns to the bedsit in Ealing, convinced we are saying our goodbyes. Off we four go, and even if Bear-as-Was does look badly neglected, his coat hanging in greasy, lustreless strings, his tail between his legs, and the monkey is forever sulking, I refuse to be downcast. But it turns out to be a fleeting visit with some mad old lady who lives on the ground floor. Before we know it we are back in Reta's house, with no prospect of decamping. Unexpectedly the next day Subira arrives to take us out. As we strive to keep up, we overhear her telling Alice that she mustn't be nervous, that she will be made to feel welcome as soon as we get there. Instantly we become apprehensive.

Like her mother, Subira is tall. She has short wiry black hair, streaked with mahogany-brown, and a wide gap between her two gleaming white front teeth. She laughs a great deal and so does Alice in her company. They make an exhibition of themselves all the way to the church Subira takes us to. It is a dingy, antiquated building, the stone walls cloaked in lichen, vines, and unkempt rambling roses, though they are not yet in bloom. One or two tiles are missing from the moss-ridden roof, and likewise from the steeple that reaches up, weather-worn, into the sky.

I feel a touch constrained as we walk through the graveyard. I don't know what it is about the dead that both attracts and repulses me. We do not enter the church though, but loop around the back of it and pile into a small room. We are greeted warmly on the way in, though I say 'we' advisedly. The jolly woman in the purple pantsuit looks right through the dog, the monkey and me. Inside the room many chairs are set out in rows, all facing towards a wooden desk, while a further two are set behind this. School, I conclude confidently, remembering the Island School my host and I attended in Hong Kong. There is no disputing that it is a very nice school. The pupils are being handed tea and coffee through an open hatch in the wall, and offered biscuits from a plate. They are even permitted to smoke. I take an inventory of the other students. They are all different, in age, colour, shape and size. Some are smartly dressed, some of average appearance, and still others look scruffy and untidy, all mingling and chatting together.

Suddenly the two teachers take their places behind the desk, the remainder of the class filling up the surrounding seats. I float uneasily at the back of the room beside the dog. Disturbingly, he seems to have taken on the appearance of a cobweb, foggy and disjointed, with tiny holes appearing here and there. Seconds later the monkey joins us, its expression glum, its thumb very nearly chewed off. Then one of the tutors launches into a monologue, centring unrelentingly on his own life. Considering that his only major achievement, as far as I can fathom, was downing the equivalent of the South China Sea in wine, I am surprised he is so eager to publicise it. In any case, I am bored stiff, quite an achievement for a vaporous apparition I feel. I start to drift off, but, before I do, I observe my host's expression. There is no misreading it. She is enthralled. After what seems like an age, coupled with an unnecessary amount of kissing, hugging and hand-shaking, Subira leads the way to the door.

This is when I chance to regard the dog more closely. He has grown . . . well, invisible in patches, and this, not the healthy lucidity of a hale and vivacious entity. Even as I peer at him he starts to disintegrate.

'Alice! Alice look at your dog! There is something amiss with your dog. He's losing cohesion.' Alice marches past me without a pause. I chase after her, just managing to grab the monkey by the scruff of its neck, and bring it along with me. But by the time we reach the church gate the dog is nowhere to be seen. I glance back and see it hovering in the air over a holly bush. It is fizzing, dissolving, much like the Alka-Seltzer tablets Myrtle Safford sometimes popped into a glass of water, and drank down in the mornings in Hong Kong. There are no better words to describe the unfortunate process poor Bear-as-Was is undergoing.

'Hurry up,' I beckon, conscious that I cannot loiter with the pace Subira is setting. It shakes its ragged two-dimensional head, then turns dolefully away and slopes off, melting into the nacreous sky. I am sorry to see it go. I have grown accustomed to the old brute.

We repeat this unfortunate exercise several days later, and this time the sickly pallor of the infant monkey alerts me instantly. Moment by moment it is becoming more vitreous. Finally it flickers like a tawny sparkler for a couple of seconds, before fading away without so much as a charred wisp to mark its parting. Alice hurries down the church path, oblivious to me and to the unfolding tragedy.

'Alice,' I cry, tracking her with difficulty, 'the monkey has gone. We must search for it. We cannot possibly desert it.'

She pauses as if listening to me. I wait to see her face blench aghast, but to my astonishment she gives a tremulous smile. Then she links her arm through Subira's and with a jaunty step skips away towards the gate, very nearly leaving me behind too. Kosey arrives the following day. He is even taller than his mother and athletic in build. He has keen dark eyes, chiselled features and a fuzz of black hair cropped close to his skull. For two weeks his deep voice and rumbling laugh fill the small house. Subira seems to be over nearly every day. She is tickled when she finds evidence of her mother's sorcery everywhere in the house.

'Oh Mother, more of your nonsense,' she says, her face wreathed in smiles. She holds up a saucer full of shiny black shavings and glittering white crystals that she has found in the kitchen. The powerful potion has been sucking the moisture from me all day, until I feel as tough and salty as the strips of dried beef people chew on in Hong Kong.

'Black salt,' Reta says proudly, poking a finger in the speckled mess and stirring it about meditatively. 'Sea salt and black scratchings from my big soup pan, to keep us safe, darling.'

Subira smiles indulgently at her mother. 'If it makes you feel better.'

Reta glances at Alice, laying the table and sharing a joke with her son Kosey.

'It does,' she says, replacing the saucer on the kitchen windowsill and nodding to herself. From halfway up the stairs, gripping the banisters and peering out, as if from a prison cell, I grimace at the necromancer.

Reta, unlike me, is in her element. She cooks large meals, stirring her cauldron with glee, revelling in having so many to look after. She washes and irons and cleans, delighting in the fresh scents that are choking what little life there is out of me. She throws away the ingredients of old spells and speedily prepares new ones. And when I am not fighting for survival indoors, I am being dragged all over London by Subira and Kosey. Like their mother, they both seem fascinated by the similitude between Alice and their cousin Kesia.

'In this early evening light,' Subira says wonderingly, 'you could be her reflection.' We are sitting on a park bench – well Subira and Alice are. There is barely any room for me, so I am perching on one of the curved cold metal arms. Kosey is leaning his back against the trunk of a nearby oak tree, surveying us contentedly. Alice laughs doubtfully. 'No, really, you are so very like her. Even the way you talk – nothing for ages and then an excited rush,' Subira says, patting Alice's arm insistently. 'Kosey, doesn't that remind you of Kesia, the way Alice speaks?'

Kosey nods. He looks at Alice and I see a fond protective gleam in his eyes.

'You could be her twin,' he says. He covers the short distance between us, graceful as a cat, and gives a lock of Alice's hair a playful tug. 'If you weren't white that is.' They all laugh and the coldness inside me expands into ice.

Alice is not a reincarnation of their dead cousin, Kesia, someone for them to care for and pet as if she was their dog. They do not know Alice at all, the dark landscape that lies just beyond the horizon. They have excavated no more than a few inches of my host, whereas I have unearthed every cursed treasure. I am at home with Alice in a way they can never be. If they realised what demons lurk behind the innocent large eyes that look so very like their cousin's, they would run from my host. However tenuous my hold, I am still in possession of Alice. If they breach her walls they will find me waiting for them.

On one of these outings an idea surfaces. I am not sure whether it comes from Subira, or Kosey, or even, disappointingly, from Alice. It hangs over us this idea, like an indistinct whirling mass of grey cloud, before suddenly it shapes itself. Alice is going to stay in Paris for a time with Kosey. Now the small house is full of plans. Kosey talks excitedly of France, of the flat he has in Paris, how vibrant the city is, how wonderful the art galleries, of how much my host will love it there. The bright curtains in Reta's small house are drawn tight against the advancing darkness. Alice sits in the middle of the settee, Kosey one side, Subira the other. They are leafing through a photograph album, pointing, giggling, telling family stories, talking of cousin Kesia, of how much they miss her. Reta is humming happily as she brings in a tray of coffee and cake. They draw closer in the circle of cosy light. Tomorrow I am going to Paris. Hunkered down beside the front door, a draught knifing through me, a gelid mantle settling over my ectoplasm, I feel a sharp stab of homesickness for the island, for the flat on The Peak, and for *my* Alice.

Myrtle – 1980

'Mrs Safford, your letters,' Ah Dang says, holding out a small silver tray with the post piled neatly on it. Last week, she just bundled the letters on the breakfast table. I told her it wasn't good enough. She was to bring them to me on a tray as she had always done, and that was that. I am still at breakfast, taking my time enjoying my coffee. Ralph has dashed off to work. The flat, apart from the amahs of course, is gloriously empty.

'Hmm . . . thank you, Ah Dang,' I say, scooping up the wad of letters. Ah Dang nods and shuffles off. She has slowed down considerably recently and, though always given to plumpness, has put on even more weight. Her hair is streaked with white too and some days she doesn't even bother to plait it. If it wasn't so hard to find staff at the moment, I would probably dismiss her. I flick through the letters, a bill from my tailor it looks like, an invitation to a reception at Government House, a postcard from Beth and Nigel holidaying with the family in the Caribbean. I sigh longingly and glance at the last letter, airmail, postmarked France. And now I look more closely at our address, handwritten. I freeze. I recognise the style, the tilt, the looping letters, the distinctive swollen 'a'. It is from Alice. I cup my mouth and smother a cry. I rise too quickly from my chair and it rocks on its back legs, then comes down with a thud.

In an instant I slough off the five years since Alice went missing. Revisiting my daughter's life and its effect on all of us is like diving from a safe rock into boiling seas. It is the spring 1975 and we are

273

sitting in the front room of the red-brick house in Ealing. Three of us are present, Ralph, myself and a young policewoman, WPC Atherton. Mother is not with us. In the short time it took for Ralph and me to arrange our trip to England, my mother had a tragic accident. She fell down the stairs and hit her head. She died. Indirectly I hold Alice responsible. I know my mother was very worried about her, that she was preoccupied and no doubt consequently careless.

As I sit in the drab little room and listen to the constable talk, my mind keeps drifting off. There is so much to do, so much to arrange – the funeral, the guests, the flowers, the food, the drink. Whether to bury her or have her cremated? When I finally succeeded in getting Albert's attention, he seemed to favour burial. I am thinking about headstones, marble or granite, and what might be a fitting epitaph for my mother, when I notice that Ralph is close to tears.

I make an effort to concentrate on what the constable is saying, but as far as I can tell it is good news. She has visited Alice's bedsit in Ealing and met with another lodger, a Miss Roper, who saw our daughter only yesterday. She says that it looks as though Alice has been keeping a dog and flouting the landlord's rule forbidding pets. I raise an eyebrow. What a surprise, I think, as Ralph makes a curious little bleating sound. The policewoman looks up at him sharply. Then she goes to great pains to explain that in all probability this is why Alice has quit her lodgings. And no, she says, her voice steady and reassuring, she does not know where Alice is currently staying. Apparently she did not pass on that information to Miss Roper, only gave her a letter of notice and the rent she owed. When Ralph keeps demanding what the police are doing to find his daughter, WPC Atherton gently informs him that Alice is nineteen and, in the eyes of the law, an adult. She has committed no offence, and hard as it may be for us to accept, she is free to go where she pleases. Seeing Ralph's face crumple and his eyes brim over, she adds hastily that she is sure we will hear from our daughter very soon. I concur, unfortunately. As soon as Alice needs something she is bound to be in touch. But I am wrong. Ralph hires a private detective at great expense and I hold my breath, fully expecting him to arrive on our doorstep any day with Alice in tow. But the Alice-free months keep sliding by and the detective explains ruefully that the trail has gone cold. Then Alice-free months turn into blissful Alice-free years. Until now that is.

I summon Ah Dang from the kitchen and tell her I am not feeling well, that I am going to lie down for a bit, that I am not to be disturbed. She nods and her eyes slide down to the letter grasped in my hand, then, seeing the warning on my face, she quickly averts them. Once inside the bedroom, I fetch the key from my dressing table drawer and lock the door. Then I sit at my desk by the window, pick up the horn paperknife we bought in Aden, slide it under the letter flap, slit it and draw out Alice's letter. It is May, a fine day with sunlight slanting through the bars. I can see knots of cloud, the edges teased into gold by the rising sun, bowling along in the arc of blue. A shadow flickers over my face as a bird skims past. A swarm of flies hover in the air a few feet from the window. They do this, gather high in the air in the cool of early morning, before setting off to feast on whatever putrefaction they can find. Their faint buzz is audible through the open window. I drop my gaze and read.

'*Dear Father and Mother,*

I wanted to write just to let you know I am fine and living in Paris. I am very sorry if I have caused you pain and worry. It was never my intention to do so. The way I disappeared without letting anyone know where I went, I know it was wrong. Unforgivable maybe, but I hope not. All I can say is that it felt as if everything was crashing down on me, that if I didn't hide I would be crushed. I think of you both most every day, and of the flat on The Peak, and Hong Kong. Sometimes it feels so hollow this separation.

I have some exciting news that I just have to tell you. I am getting married. I expect you won't be able to believe it any more than I can. His name is Carl, Carl Napier. I am going to be Mrs Napier. Isn't it wonderful? So many exciting things have happened to me. I made friends with a wonderful family in London, the Okellos, and their son Kosey asked me if I would like to return with him to Paris where he lived. He said it was a beautiful city and that I would love it there. And I did. I do. We weren't romantically involved, if that's what you're thinking. He was just like . . . well, a big brother. But it was through him that I met Carl. They are in business together exporting luxury foods. It's only a small company but Carl says it's growing fast. Anyway Kosey introduced us and we began seeing each other. It wasn't serious at first. For a long time we were just good friends. But over the last year all of that changed. Still, when he asked me to marry him I couldn't believe it. I think you'd approve. He is very handsome, with green eyes and sandy gold hair. He's old-fashioned really, likes to look after me.

I have a job now too. I work in a restaurant. It's called Ramirez, after the owner, Pierre Ramirez. He seems very pleased with me. I started in the kitchen doing anything that was needed really, endlessly peeling and chopping vegetables, and washing up so much that I had dishpan hands for a while. But now I am serving tables. I speak French too. I took lessons at a college. I felt like I was back at the Island School again. It was hard work, but because I was having to speak it every day I soon picked it up. Carl and I live in a lovely airy third-floor flat on the Rue de Ménilmontant. It reminds me sometimes of the flat on The Peak. Of course it's nowhere near as special, but it's home for me now. We are nearby the fascinating Père Lachaise Cemetery, named after a Jesuit priest. It's simply vast and hundreds of famous people are buried there, painters and writers and politicians. I know it sounds a bit macabre but I love it, walking along the many paths, looking at the graves and the tombs. Some of them are like miniature houses, only without windows and some them are so grand, mansions, carved out of swirling marble and speckled granite with gold lettering. It's like a really peaceful park, with beautiful trees and benches to sit on in the shade, and birds and flowers. I have to admit Carl doesn't like me going. He thinks it's very strange that I should enjoy the company of the dead so much.

We are getting married next month. Of course I know how busy

you are and that you won't be able to make it. And besides, I
realise I have no right to expect it after everything that's happened.
But I just thought you'd like to know. I hope you are both well. I
picture you at home on The Peak. You're wearing a beautiful dress,
Mother, that whispers as you glide down the corridor, and lots of
jewellery and that perfume you love, Je Reviens. I close my eyes and
I can smell it, heavy and spicy. And Father has just got home from
work and slipped off his jacket. He's in the lounge staring at his
cabinet of snuff bottles and ivory figurines. Oh, and night is falling
with the sky a great mess of colour.

I've put my address at the bottom of the letter. I would love it if
you wrote back. But if I don't hear I'll understand why.

I miss you both and love you very much, Alice.'

I reread the letter carefully and then I go to the kitchen
where Ah Dang is already preparing lunch, beating batter for
the fish to be dipped in. I ask for a saucepan and matches.

'You want to do some cooking, Mrs Safford?' Ah Dang asks,
surprised, rinsing her hands under the tap.

'No.' Ah Dang stands poised, waiting for me to explain. I say
nothing, just cross to the unit of open shelves where the pots
and pans are kept. I select one, snatch up the matches from the
lacquer box they are kept in and return to my bedroom. A few
minutes later and I have quite a nice blaze going. If it was a
cold day just think what a comfort it would be.

Bear – 1986

I am floating in liquid blackness. It is very peaceful. The blackness purls about me. It is like the sigh before sleep. I hang on the ebb and flow of that sigh. I am inanimate. Here is where I stop, like falling in a well but knowing you will never reach the bottom. I am dormant, my being in a state of stagnancy. And a voice, a small voice, a voice that I thrill to, a voice that once when I had a heart made it dance, comes to me. It is Alice's voice. It says:

'Don't go, Bear. Stay with me a while longer.'

And so I wait. I do not go forwards. I do not go backwards. I wait for the voice to summon me.

What I notice first is that the black is not so black any more. It is while I am thinking about this that the black becomes the dark brown of rich earth. And before I have time to consider what change this might import it has transmuted to drab grainy greyness, like a faulty television screen. At first the grey appears even, an unending uniform fuzziness. Then the lines form, some vertical, some horizontal. They fill with light, dove-grey light. Two become more pronounced than the rest, stretching before me. The space between them glows like the mother-of-pearl I saw inside shells on the beaches of my island home. It glints invitingly. It is a path and I am moving stealthily down it. To either side of me are blocks, some tall and upright, some long and narrow, and some with triangular roofs. These last are like little houses. They have doors but no windows, and must be black as a starless night inside. Scattered among the houses are

278

stone people, a few with wings, their hands folded as if in prayer. I feel the wind scourging me. I hear the fiery whoosh and crackle of leaves. My path is bordered with tree trunks, straight and forbidding as iron bars. My eyes slide upwards, see them flow into fluid manes, undulating and tossing in the breeze. I move on. Above me the sky is like a length of silk, the colour of it shifting from deep navy to the metallic blues of slate and steel. I feel the drag of an ivory moon rolling through the night.

I do not know where I am, only that something is propelling me forwards. On and on I go, one track leading to another like the tree branches that surround me. It has been raining and sweet wet smells rise up from the damp earth, the mizzle still falling, glistening in the moonshine. Now I break into a trot, a growing sense of urgency quickening my pace. I round a bend and stop abruptly. Another scent permeates the air, a familiar scent, the scent of sadness. My head rotates slowly seeking the source. Beside me is a large rectangular marble box nestling in grass, and huddled on the top of it hugging her knees is the Chinese girl. She nods in greeting. I leave the path, pick my way carefully around it and come upon Alice. She is curled up in the shadow of the structure cast by the moon, though her long hair spills out into the opaline light. She is asleep, but it is a poor kind of rest. Her breath misting the air comes erratically. She whimpers and moans, and gulps now and again as if out of breath. She wears no more than a skirt and cotton blouse, and her pale skin is pricked with the cold. I lie by her side and nudge her. Automatically her arm encircles me, though still she sleeps. I have no breath so we cannot find a shared rhythm. But she must find some comfort in my presence for very soon her respiration deepens and she quietens.

'Bear. Bear.' Alice speaks my name from deep in her dreams.

'Welcome back,' says a voice from above. I swivel my head and roll my eyes upwards to see the Chinese girl peeping over the edge of the marble block. 'I wondered when you'd show up. I expect the others will be along sooner or later.'

'It's nice and peaceful here,' I comment sleepily.

Again she nods. 'Cemeteries usually are.' Then she settles down on her back, one arm draping down over us. 'I far prefer it here with the moon and the stars and the dead of course, than back in the flat with Carl. He's a brute, but you know that already don't you, Bear? That's why you're here.'

In this way I pass the night with Alice and the Chinese girl. Once a cat, white and black, hunting through the night, happens upon us. I bare my teeth and snarl. It freezes, its hair standing on end, and emits a low growl in response before scampering off. And once a tiny shrew pauses to nudge my spectral muzzle with its long dark snout. Its spray of silver whiskers twitch, then, like the cat, it too is paralysed for a second, before it scurries away into a forest of grass. As the moon fades and sinks and the sky shakes off the night, I slip out from under Alice's arm to stand watch over her still sleeping body. The Chinese girl rouses herself and stretches. She peers down at me.

'You going now?' she says.

Far off I can hear a city waking up, the birds, the traffic, the aeroplanes, all growing braver, challenging the silence.

'I think so. I'm tingling a bit. That's a sure sign.'

But only when the dew starts to sparkle and a faint ribbon of primrose yellow hugs the horizon do I feel myself start to fade properly. Again, though I will myself to stay with Alice, the absolute blackness engulfs me. It seeps into me and I am unable to resist its sweetness. This time the limbo seems short-lived. The blindness melts away and I find myself materialising on a busy street corner with people rushing past. I stare about me in confusion and then down the road I see Alice. She has fallen and is being helped up by a large man with a bushy brown moustache. She looks stricken, face streaked with tears, her cheeks blotched red, her lips chewed raw.

The Chinese girl stands close by her, while overhead the monkey swings on a telegraph wire. I sidle up to Alice and nod at the Chinese girl.

'I can't have children. I'm spoiled inside,' Alice mutters over and over under her breath when the man has gone.

I track them home, but before I can make myself comfortable

indoors I am smothered by the raven-black ocean. But there is no peace in it, only a whine to its voice that has me thrashing about, desperate to find my way back to Alice.

'You filthy whore . . . I had a right to know . . . I'm your husband . . . You should have told me the truth . . . How can I believe anything you say now? . . . I don't want you working in that place any more . . . How can you call it rape, you were drunk . . . What other lies have you told me? . . . You're my wife, you do as you're told . . . Where have you been? . . . It's not right wandering around graves day after day . . . This place is a tip . . . For Christ's sake, what's the matter with you? . . . I don't want you going to that awful cemetery any more. Do you hear me, Alice?'

The snatches of speech jump out at me, pouncing on me in the swirl of thick sooty dye. They jar on my sensitive ears. And with them come terrible visions. Once a hand splits the ocean, flying through space and striking pale flesh with a crack. Once the blackness fractures into a mass of fine hair. I feel the grip tightening on it, yanking it back, the jab of pain in her neck that makes her wince and cry out, the stinging sensation in her scalp as strands are torn out. Once the murk roils about me, sloshing forward and back, again and again. As he shakes her, vicariously I feel the confusion and growing disbelief, along with the swimming sensation of light-headedness, the black roses blossoming before the eyes. And once the blanket grows threadbare, and I become sodden with light. I am crouching at Alice's feet ready to spring. There is a man with light-coloured hair grasping her shoulder. His fingers dig into her flesh until she begs him to let go. He is shouting at her.

'Whore! Liar! You fucking liar!' Cloudy flecks of his spittle land on her face, on her bruised upper lip, on her hair, in her eyes. She flinches, tries to wrench free, to pull her body away from his. But he is too strong for her. I smell his rage. It is of the killing kind, a bitter rancorous stench that will not abate until her blood stains his hands. He clenches his fist and draws back his free arm. The impulse that sends it flying towards Alice's soft womb is murderous. Hackles up, muscles bunched, muzzle drawn back into a savage grin, auroral razor-sharp teeth bared, I spring. I bring him down as a lion would his prey, nail him to the floor. My claws rake his flesh. My jaws are snapping scissors ripping into his mouth, peeling back his upper lip until the bloody laceration vanishes into a nasal cavity already blocked with clots of thick blood and dark mucus. Then I am upon his arm, my gnashing teeth tearing through the fabric of his shirt. I am shredding the softness to a pulp, feeling his blood pumping out warm and wet, seeing the shaking limb bloom in glistening reds and purples.

He is limp as a rag, eyes closed against me, when finally I back off to skulk in the shadows. Alice is standing by the window. I think she is motionless, but when I study her more carefully I see that her head is moving. She is shaking it fractionally. Now, as well as the smell of sadness, her face is wreathed in sorrow. The man on the floor stirs. He is lying in his own sticky blood and seems unable to believe it. One hand moves to the red mash of his mouth. He gurgles in a shocked breath. He scrabbles to a sitting position and groans. Again with tentative fingers he explores the tattered bloody shirt-sleeve, the bite wounds on his arm. His cold green eyes grow round and wide with terror. Alice's head is to one side as she surveys him.

'I'm sorry,' she says quietly, almost to herself.

He staggers to his feet. His blood splashes on the wooden floor as he moves away from Alice, out of the room, out of the flat. The door slams and the stillness laps back in. Alice opens the French doors and steps out onto the tiny balcony. She rests her hands on the metal railing. Beside her stands the Chinese girl, barefoot, in her army jacket. Out of the corner of my eye I see something wiggling on the floor where the drawn curtains fall in soft folds. A moment later, and a tiny shape the colour of autumn leaves dashes over to join Alice outside, shimmying up the balcony railing. I steal out of the gloom and shuffle over to them scenting the crisp night air. There is a blinding streak of green and yellow and the budgie swoops out of the darkness and alights on Alice's shoulder, clawing at a strand of her hair. Alice glances down at me and I feel the leash tighten between us. I do not think I will be returning to oblivion for some time. I pad around to the Chinese girl.

'I'm back,' I say, nosing a ghostly bare calf.

She turns to me. 'Mm, so you are,' she smiles. She looks sidelong at Alice, busy plucking a loose thread from her lavender cardigan. Now she pulls and it starts to unravel from the bottom of the sleeve.

'It may be a long night,' the Chinese girl says.

Pierre — 1986

'Forget her,' advised my restaurant manager, Eugène, snapping a finger at the new waiter, Bernard. His thin lips twitched into a smile when the nervous lad dropped the handful of forks he was carrying and they clattered on the floor. 'I always told you the English girl would be trouble. And I was proved right, non? You can't rely on her any more. Most of the time she's drunk and what a sight! She's putting the customers off their food. Her hair all messy, her clothes dirty. She's bad for business.'

I sighed regretfully. We had all guessed that bully, Carl, was at the root of her problems. Hadn't we seen the bruises? But after all, he was her husband. If she wouldn't leave him there was nothing anyone could do. Eugène read my thoughts.

'She made a bad marriage. She was young, naïve. It happens,' he said with a shrug. 'But she is not your responsibility,' he added, his tone now grave. 'However sorry you feel for her, she is not worth the ruin of your restaurant.'

I knew he was right, that I must dismiss Alice and forget her. Still, I was delighted to learn from one of the waitresses some months later that she was going to divorce Carl.

Secretly, I harboured the hope that once it was all settled, Alice would return to work. Until the trouble with her husband she had been doing so well. I had really begun to believe she had a future at Ramirez. She seemed such a lonely young woman, with no family here to support her. Sometimes, when service was over, I would sit at my usual table in the window, hoping to see her. But the only thing looking back at me day after day was my own reflection, a short plump man overly fond of his food, his eyes set too close together, a prominent nose and a little twist of a moustache.

Myrtle – 1986

Ralph grips the wire mesh that cages in the veranda, just as Alice did all those years ago. Back then, our daughter told me she was pregnant, putting all our lives in jeopardy. Now, my husband says, 'Alice. I wonder where she is?' And I wonder, will I never be rid of her? 'I think of her, that this very second she is somewhere eating or sleeping or maybe—' He breaks off and laughs softly. 'Maybe even holding a child. You know it is possible that Alice has a family of her own by now.'

I pat him on the back. Oh yes, yes it is, Ralph. Only the letter I received last week told me that her marriage hasn't worked out. Such a pity, but hardly a surprise. Still, apparently this Carl fellow held out for a good five years. In my view, he deserves a medal.

'I should have tried harder,' Ralph sighs, pressing the side of one cheek into the galvanised metal mesh.

'Tried harder?' I query. It is a summer's evening and the ice is melting in my whisky. But if I go inside and sit down now, it might appear . . . well . . . heartless.

Ralph fixes me with those lucid blue eyes of his. 'Tried harder to find her.'

'You did your best,' I console him, giving his arm a squeeze. 'You couldn't have done more. The police. A private detective. All that money you—'

'Money!' Ralph pushes away from the veranda railing and starts to pace the length of it. 'I'd have spent ten times that much, a hundred times, whatever it took, if it brought her back.'

'Of course, of course,' I say soothingly. 'That's not what I meant. Just that you did all you could. You know Alice and I had our differences. There's often a bit of friction between mothers and daughters, isn't there? But I miss her as much as you do.'

'I know I'm not the only one suffering,' Ralph concedes with a backwards flap of his hand. 'I'm being so selfish. She's your daughter too.'

'Mm . . . so she is.' I glance at my whisky through the lounge doors. Would Ralph notice if I slipped in and fetched it? Ralph, who has his back to me, wheels round.

'Sometimes I just can't bear it, the God-awful pain of missing her, as if a limb had been severed. And, just like they say, feeling it there some days but having to accept it's only an illusion.'

'Oh . . . I know. It's dreadful, darling.' Ralph moves away from me again and slumps against a corner post of the veranda. He has sweat patches all over his shirt. He should shower and change. He'd feel so much more comfortable.

'Do you think she's altered very much?' he asks the night.

Not at all, I muse dryly. The letter, Alice's second letter, was a chaotic outpouring, full of errors and smudges and inkblots. No doubt she had been crying. Her marriage had fallen apart. According to her, Carl had become possessive, jealous, unreasonable, didn't want her to have any life of her own. Apparently she had pushed him over the edge and the poor man had become violent. *I am so unhappy. I rang Uncle Albert. I didn't tell him where I was or worry him with this. I just needed to hear his voice. I wish I could come home but I expect that's not possible any more.* That's what she wrote. How very familiar it all sounded. Horribly so, actually. Then there were some confused ramblings about spending the night in a cemetery, how she felt safe there, and about a dog attacking Carl and him having to go to hospital for stitches. God, the sordid images it conjured up.

'She'd be ten years older now,' Ralph says wretchedly, rubbing the dome of his head on the metal post. '1986. It's eleven years almost to the day that she went missing.'

'Oh darling, must you torture yourself like this?' I say. But I am slightly off key, sounding more baffled than solicitous. Thankfully, awash with emotion, Ralph does not seem to notice.

'Is her hair the same colour, the same length? Has she put on weight? She could have done with that. Far too thin. What about her clothes? Do you think she has a job?'

Not for much longer, if that letter is anything to go by, I muse darkly. Missing shifts and turning up drunk at that restaurant she was working at? Wasn't that what Mother said had happened at that supermarket in Ealing? Some people never change, do they? Ralph breaks down, sobbing. I cross to him and stroke his back. He swings about and collapses onto me, tears flowing freely now, his chest heaving.

'There, there, Ralph.' I feel the wetness soaking into my hand-embroidered silk collar but resist the urge to disentangle myself. 'You must try to be brave,' I urge. Ralph nods his head against me, pathetically.

The last thing my daughter wrote was that she thought they would divorce, that like everything else in her life her marriage had failed. What a revelation! It reeked of self-pity. Always the victim, that's Alice. Well, she isn't finding her way back here, not if I can help it. Life on the island these days is hard enough without coping with all her traumas again. Hong Kong is not the same any more. The children have married and gone, Nicola and Harry settling in England and Jillian going to America, of all places. I thought I'd enjoy the peace but in fact I miss them. The way things are, well, it's unsettling.

Anyone would think the Chinese were already in charge. You just don't get the respect any more. And would you believe it, Ah Dang told me last month she had decided to retire, said she was getting too old to work. I was aghast, after everything we've done for her, she deserts us when we need her most. I told her I couldn't find anyone to replace her at such short notice, if at all. No one wants to be an amah now. They all think they can do so much better. I explained with admirable patience that it is not as easy as she might think finding good amahs. She nodded at that, with a funny glint in her eye I didn't like at all. And then she had the cheek to say couldn't Mrs Safford manage with just one servant, Ah Wei? No, Mrs Safford could not, I told her. So grudgingly she agreed to hang on till the end of the year, or until I found someone, whichever came sooner. And do you know, I think she expected me to be grateful. Whatever happened to loyalty?

Once Ralph retires, I have no idea where we'll be living. The last thing I need in my life right now is Alice. Ralph's sobbing has subsided. I lead him into the lounge, sit him down and place the tumbler of whisky in his hand.

'Have a drink, Ralph, it'll make you feel better,' I direct him. While he sits nursing his whisky, I toss back mine, proving my theory. Immediately I feel more in control. My eyes flick over to Ralph, his body crumpled in the chair. Well, one of us has to be. Alice's second letter went the way of the first. I glance through the open glass doors at a sky sequinned with stars. There's a new moon. It glows a purifying snow-white. On such a night as this, optimism is called for. I take a deep breath and make my wish.

'Do you think . . . do you think, Myrtle, that she'll ever come back to us?' Ralph says lifting his wet blue eyes to mine.

I hold his gaze and sigh plaintively. 'I want to say yes, darling, you know I do. But perhaps it's time to accept Alice has gone for good,' I whisper resignedly. As I turn away to freshen up my drink, I cannot resist a brief smile.

Pierre — 1996

We are in a small fishing village in Brittany. We stroll along the harbour front, the wind whipping Alice's hair about, and flattening what little I have left. We find a small restaurant on the seafront. From our table we look out on the colourful fishing boats bobbing about on their moorings, their lacy brown and green nets piled on the decks. Beyond them, luring them on, sprawls their tempestuous mistress, the vast blue body of Atlantic Ocean. We order a seafood platter and, for me, a bottle of Chablis, chilled to perfection, for Alice mineral water. We gorge ourselves on the flaky white flesh of crab and lobster, on plump pink prawns, on slithers of grilled squid, on tangy golden-brown mussels, on round fat milk-white scallops with their half-moon orange corals, and on semi-pellucid oysters with the palest sensual hint of olive-gold in their wet gleam. I am drunk, not on wine, but on the sting of the salt breeze still lingering on my skin, on the colours, bold and primary, that rush at us through the little window, the blue and red hulls of the boats, the jagged spill of topaz yellow from the sinking sun, the sea banquet enchanting my palate.

I look across at Alice, the manager of my restaurant and my companion. She is laughing, her face intent on extracting the delicate meat from a lobster's claw, and I remember. I remember a bitterly cold January morning, the start of 1987, my breath misting the air as I hurried to my restaurant. I halted mid-stride at the sight of the restaurant sign, Ramirez, gold on black, and under it, hunched on the doorstep, a small woman shivering in a navy-blue duffel coat.

Alice. She scrambled to her feet at the sight of me. 'Hello Pierre. I'd like my job back,' she said without preamble, through chattering teeth, direct as ever: 'I can start straight away.'

She looked terrible. Her skin grey, dark sickles under bloodshot eyes, hair dull and tangled. I nodded and tried not to look too pleased. 'I see. Well . . . I don't know Alice. I have to—'

'I know I let you down before and I'm sorry,' she hurried on. 'But that's all sorted. I'm . . . I'm divorced now, living . . . living by myself. I thought I was doing quite well before . . . before the break-up.' She paused and bit her lip pensively. 'I'd really like another chance, Pierre.' I shrugged, then folded my arms. 'You don't want me back, do you?' said Alice, her face blenched and her shoulders caved in.

'What I want, Alice, is for you to step out of the way so that I can open the door to my restaurant. Then we can get inside in the warm and you can make us both a cup of coffee, hmm?' Alice met my eyes and grinned.

I am not going to pretend the early weeks were easy. Alice turning up to work in ill-fitting garments, the colours at war with each other. Alice struggling to chop vegetables without taking a finger off, her brow a tight 'v' of concentration. Alice trying to check off deliveries, the words and figures before her clearly a jumbled blur. Alice struggling with her now rusty French, so frustrated I thought she would dissolve into tears. But gradually she came back to me. Her pride in her work returned, and along with it her reliability, her confidence and her sense of fun. And when Eugène left to run a restaurant in the South France where his family lived, Alice got the job. She soon exceeded my highest expectations, rewarding my faith in her.

I am no longer a young man and my health is not good. I smoke too much and I eat too much. Alice scolds me continuously about these vices. But these days it is the simple pleasures I enjoy. Sitting at a street café in the sunshine, sipping an espresso and relaxing with a cigarette, strolling around the Louvre with Alice at my side, staring in wonder at the paintings, attending a concert together, savouring an excellent meal, drinking a fine wine. Pierre Ramirez, a man who lived too well. It is a good epitaph, non?

Ghost – 1997

I slip into each corner of the room in turn to see if the view is at all improved from another angle. Then I hover just above the bed in which Mr Ramirez is dying. But it makes no difference. Of course his death is not nearly as dramatic as mine, though with all Alice's weeping and the wailing, you would think it was. I tell her, he is an old man, and that anyway he brought this on himself. I draw her attention to the countless times she warned him to give up smoking those cigarettes. But Alice disregards my logic and remains distraught.

The budgie is absent from this death scene, as is the monkey. But I have spotted the dog's glittering feathery tail poking out from under the sick bed. If the officious nurse, her huge breasts rising with every indignant breath she takes as she bustles about, could see him, he'd be ousted. She's fretting about germs though it hardly seems worth it. Put plainly, Mr Ramirez is going where germs are of absolutely no concern at all.

He is sucking greedily on his oxygen now, fed from a tank through a tube, then a mask, into his suffocating body. In and out it goes, in and out, with an ominous rattle. That is the death rattle. We all recognise it. The grumpy nurse, head to one side, checking the pressure dial listens attentively, then sighs her acceptance. I shall miss the pernickety old boy. After all he did take Alice back to work at his restaurant when we fell on hard times. What's more he had an inhibiting effect on our ghostly menagerie, and that is quite an accom-

292

plishment. They didn't quite vanish but they kept a much lower profile, like naughty children when a parent arrives.

Alice is clasping his fingers now, and if I slip into her I can feel they are quite cold, and as stiff as if rigor mortis has begun to set in already. She is muttering her thanks, and tears keep squeezing out of her ducts and trailing down her pale cheeks. Such a show of anguish – what a pity he can't hear a thing. It is late June, and a summer shower is drumming softly on the windowpane. But, peering out at the gleaming Paris pavements I judge it will soon pass.

Mr Ramirez has left my host his restaurant, so he must think very highly of her. But even this, when I remind her of it, does not comfort Alice. The dying man gives a gravelly sigh that seems to fill the room. Then I observe his locked fingers unfurling ominously, as if giving a last stretch. Some machine suddenly stops beeping. Alice bursts into tears proper, and the nurse seizes her by the scruff of her neck and hoists her out of the way. She is busy with a stethoscope prodding and pushing and listening for some time, before finally she stands back and shakes her head, her long face lugubrious. At the very moment that Alice collapses, I am distracted by Pierre Ramirez's spirit rising up in creased white pyjamas, and starting to float gently out of the room. The dog peeps out from under the bed, flattens his ears and gives a low throaty moan.

'Oh for goodness sake,' I mutter. 'By now you really should have got used to the company of ghosts. In reply, Bear-as-Was bares his teeth half-heartedly and slinks back under the bed.

As for me, I waylay Mr Ramirez as he glides through the closed window.

'Aren't you going to put up a fight?' I demand scornfully. 'Some little show of outrage.'

He shakes his ghostly slicked-down locks with such force that they fly up in wispy curls.

'You do fully comprehend what this means, Sir?' I ask, clasping my ethereal hands before me.

Again he nods his head and turns his face away. The nurse clatters about like some old cleaning woman. You'd think out of common decency she could give us a moment's peace. Alice sobs and the dog snarls. It is pandemonium. The solution, I decide, is to ask Mr Ramirez to delay his departure and join our number.

'As you can see Alice is inconsolable,' I persuade with my chipped smile, arms stretched wide in a gesture of welcome. 'Perhaps if you joined us, the "undead", for a short while, it might soften the blow.'

Mr Ramirez turns back to me and I am struck immediately by his incandescent face, now a beacon of unearthly light. 'Won't you join us?' I wheedle. But yet again Mr Ramirez shakes his head and I see he is leaving! He casts one backward look over his opalescent shoulder. The expression I glimpse makes me feel that it is me and not him missing out on something. For the first time, I find myself wondering if perhaps remaining here, fastened to my host, clinging onto life with every fibre of my being, is not as clever as I first thought. Is it possible that far from cheating death, the only spirit I have cheated of that otherworldly uplifting light is me?

And this is not all that disturbs my emanations. Only a matter of days after Mr Ramirez's exit, my host and I are sitting together on the small settee in our Paris flat. She is sniffing and periodically dabbing her nose and eyes with a hanky. The dog is slouched on the floor snoring noisily. One flame-red leg rotates against the floor-boards, the scrabbling silver claws clicking like a typewriter. I suspect he is chasing ghostly rabbits in that great field in the sky. The monkey is skating on the coffee table, executing little pirouettes and every so often smacking its fish lips together in satisfaction. Aware it has an audience, it gives an improvised pyrotechnic display, a shower of tangerine spangles shooting out of its dented head. Meanwhile the decapitated budgie makes jerky progress along the top of the settee back, like the mindless cack-winged bird it is. You would think, without its beak it could not do much damage. But its destructive powers, now employed shredding cushions with its talons, are awesome. But I am distracted now by the images on the screen: before us is home, our home, the island of Hong Kong. In that instant I realise how much I've missed it.

'It's finally come,' Alice mutters under her breath. 'The hand back of Hong Kong to China.' I turn to my host. Her face is pensive, her mouth drawn, her eyes clouded. She looks all of her forty-one years. 'June the 30th 1997. The British are leaving and the Chinese are arriving.' Her lips barely move. I slide into Alice and feel the goose bumps all over her flesh, and the hairs standing up on the back of her neck. Her throat is constricted, as if someone has her in a stranglehold. And there is a wound inside so raw I can hardly bear to share it with her.

We listen to Prince Charles, in his admiral's white uniform, make a speech, while the skies spill fat drops all over him. Solemnly we follow the descent of the Union Jack, as it is lowered from its flagpole for the last time. We see the black arch of heaven blaze with a lavish display of fireworks.

'They're making sure we have a good send-off,' Alice says, in a reverent tone. 'There are lots of important people there. Look, Chris Patten. He is the last governor of Hong Kong, the 28th. Was the last governor of Hong Kong,' she corrects herself.

Then Alice scans the rows of dignitaries at the ceremony. I know she is looking for just one man. It is not the last Governor of Hong Kong. It is not even the future King of England. It is her father, with those piercing blue eyes that used to light up every time he saw her. Her eyes are trained with fierce concentration on the changing televised picture, hands pressed together in front of her, little fingers crooked. We see footage of the People's Liberation Army crossing the border from China, in their buses and open trucks, rolling into the New Territories, Kowloon, and Hong Kong island.

'It is the end of empire,' says Alice quietly. That night, we are both dreadfully homesick. The dark is pierced by the dog's plaintive howls, and the monkey's falsetto bawling, and the sound of ripping, as the budgie rends apart what remains of the curtains. At least the restaurant provides some diversion for my host. While Alice works, the dog, the monkey and the budgie stand sentry at the door.

But the seed planted that day takes root. Time and again we catch ourselves daydreaming, my host and I, visualising our island basking in the South China Sea. We stare out at the city, blind to the busy

Paris streets and the River Seine sliding inexorably towards the ocean. Instead, we conjure up a mountain range of skyscrapers clinging to the waterfront, their dizzying peaks nearly lost in the pipe-clay clouds. We see the thousands of windows throwing back the dazzling glare of the summer sun. Then, after sunset, we envision their long bellies glittering in electric shades of orange and red, purple and blue, pink and yellow and green, sending arrows of light quivering and zig-zagging across the stippled black waters of Victoria harbour.

Our ears are full of the never-ending cacophony of traffic, slith-ering through clouds of exhaust fumes, and the ding of tram bells, packed carriages rolling noisily up and down the length of the island. Alice breathes in air thick with remembered smells, fair and foul: the crisp scent of dawn, refuse and spices, the heady fragrance of orchids, all mingled with the aromas of food sizzling and popping in woks. But most of all, we recall The Peak, and the two of us standing as one on top of the world, gazing down the dusty green slopes into the jewelled depths of the sea.

Ralph – 1999

My mind has become a sponge. Most of the time I fall through the holes. The onset of this porous condition was gradual. It started after my retirement, when I had already begun to feel that it was no longer my island, but nevertheless could not bear to leave it. The embryonic signs were present when we said our goodbyes to the flat on The Peak and moved into the Girl Guides Headquarters, my last British bolthole. It seemed safe, to retreat to rented rooms in this remaining outpost of Her Majesty the Queen. The date of the handover was fast approaching. The mood on the island was changing. I felt like a guest who has overstayed his welcome. And yet I could not bring myself to go home. Home! Is it my home? England? Arguable. So the Girl Guide Headquarters seemed the obvious choice. An English oasis surrounded by increasingly foreign territory.

In the large meeting hall there was a portrait of Her Majesty Queen Elizabeth the Second on the wall. It was placed in such a way – centrally and high up – that it dominated the room. She struck a regal pose, Her Majesty, standing in an imposing dress with a full skirt, a royal-blue sash over the glittering bodice, a splendid crown sitting atop her brunette curls. Alongside her, placed respectfully lower down, were portraits of Sir Robert Baden-Powell and his wife Olave, founders of the scouting and guiding organisations.

Here I was able to recapture, for a short while, security and a sense of the familiar. But despite this, I knew that beyond these walls all was crumbling, all was changed, all was depolarising. I, who was awarded the OBE for services rendered to Her Majesty the Queen, had become obsolete. Dressed in dazzling white, gold buttons shining in a neat row on my jacket front, I knelt before the then Governor of Hong Kong, Sir David Trench, and became an Officer of the British Empire. He had been wearing full regalia too and looked even grander than I. He had smiled warmly, his eyes full of pride. His pewter hair, burnished in shafts of citrus light, was made steel. It had been a job well done and I knew it. I had steered a course through typhoons and landslides, through riots and flu epidemics, through influxes of refugees, through the trickle of swimmers prepared to pit their lives against the rigours of the sea for their freedom, and through periods of unimaginable transition.

When Mao Tse-Tung spearheaded his Cultural Revolution, and incited the Red Guards to embark on their trail of destruction and terror, I had been staunch. I had kept a clear head, standing erect in China's long shadow, and waving the union flag on Her Majesty's island enclave, never balking. I had claimed this small territory for Queen Elizabeth the Second of Britain, let those who challenged her authority do so at their peril. However foolhardy, this was what I did. And for these deeds and more I was given an illusory post – I was made an officer of her vanishing empire.

It was the spring of 1970, an unseasonably hot day, I recall. The interior of Government House felt pleasantly cool. My shoes tapped on the tiled floor of the ceremonies' room. Alice had been there, and Harry, and Myrtle, of course. My wife wore a white hat, with white feathers that curled around her face. She wore a dress with a pleated skirt, the fabric patterned with small white and pale yellow checks, white lace gloves and white shoes, while Harry wore a short-sleeved white shirt and white shorts. Alice was wearing a pink cotton dress sprigged with white flowers. She was wearing ankle socks and they were white too. Surely our audience was snow-blinded by the profusion of whiteness. Alice's long brown hair was drawn back in a ponytail, making her eyes look even larger than usual. I opened the dark leather box afterwards and showed her my medal.

'See, Alice,' I said, 'your father is an Officer of the British Empire.'

She stared at me with those big eyes of hers, slipped her hand into mine and held it tightly.

Eventually, after my retirement, we bought a flat in Quarry Bay. and moved out of the Girl Guide Headquarters. We ignored entreaties from Nicola that it was time to return to Britain, staving off the inevitable I suppose. The British flag, my flag, was lowered on the colony of Hong Kong for the last time on the night of June 30th 1997 amid torrential rain. I followed it as it slid down the high flag-pole where it had fluttered for one and half centuries. British rule had come to an end, and so I felt had I. Already the advance guard of the People's Liberation Army were triumphantly crossing the border from China into Hong Kong. Now the Union Jack was being super-seded by another flag, five yellow stars spiked against a red back-ground, the Flag of the People's Republic of China, while the Chinese national anthem, March of the Volunteers, swelled in the gleaming wet of the night. And with it, I knew, would fly the new Regional Flag of Hong Kong, the delicate white petals of the Bauhinia blakeana flower, standing out against its familiar crimson background. The island that marked the boundaries of my life was to be reabsorbed into its mother country, and all that I had known was evanescing. I had already lost Alice, and now I was to lose my island home.

'Alice,' I said, the voice in my head heavy with despair, 'they have come for Hong Kong. What shall I do?'

'You knew that sooner or later we would have to give it back,' Alice replied solemnly. 'It was never *ours*.'

Later that night, we visited friends who lived on Mount Austin on the Peak. Standing on their balcony, and staring out across the blurred mountain slopes, while above my head the sky shuddered, tinselling with fireworks, a thought struck me. In some place, in some pleat of time, there would be Alice and there would be Hong Kong, always. Alice roaming The Peak with Bear, while the sun shone, and the rain fell, and the mist swirled about. For a long time I stood on the balcony and stared out to sea.

The island was undergoing a process of vicissitude. Daily, it mutated into an increasingly alien organism. I disliked going about now. I, who had once been the honoured guest at the feast, found myself queuing for a table. Some friends left, relocating to Britain, to America, to Australia, to Canada, scattering to the far ends of the earth, and with them went my prestige. Once I was worth everything, now I needed to be worth *something*. Myrtle had her whisky. I think, more than anything, that blunted the transmogrification for her. Her greatest trial, as she often told me, was the nigh on impossible task of finding staff to cook and clean for us.

'What has happened to all the amahs?' Myrtle would complain frequently. 'How am I expected to cope without help? It really is *too* bad. Nobody wants a job in service now. I shall never manage, Ralph.'

But we did limp on with a series of unsuitable Filipino maids, who I suppose did their best. But they were no longer content and that was apparent. The compensation for us was a kind of camaraderie among the old retainers who remained behind, those of us who had served our Queen in this little outcrop of the British Empire and, now it was gone, would go down with comportment and the appropriate gravitas, waving our outdated flags. The young – oh they would weather the changes as the young always do, but we were dinosaurs and we knew it, all of us putting off the moment when we would lumber back to Britain, as out of place there as we now were here.

And as I said, it was around this time that I began to forget. It started with the odd word. You know what you want to say, the blasted thing is on the tip of your tongue, but it just won't come. Never mind, you tell yourself, later it will surface from the deep recesses of my mind. Only it didn't. I grew adept at substituting other words, at changing a sentence once begun, so I did not have to embarrass myself, floundering on the rock of some fugitive word. Finally we succumbed to Nicola's entreaties that we return to England.

'It's high time you came home. I'd love you to buy a place near us in Sussex. I'm on the lookout for something special. Besides, you can't stay over there forever. I imagine the island is quite altered now with the Chinese in charge. After all, Father, you *are* British,' she reminded me, 'so isn't it time you lived in Britain?'

Myrtle was reconciled. The novelty of a Hong Kong where she was no longer queen bee had worn off long ago. 'It will be lovely to spend some time with the children,' she coaxed me.

I made no response to this. I felt that in leaving Hong Kong I would be deserting Alice. I knew this was a nonsensical argument, entirely without foundation. Alice had vanished in England, and the chance of her having returned to Hong Kong in the intervening years was negligible. In the early days I had done everything I could to find her. The police had not been interested at the time. They had said she was an adult, that it was up to her if she wanted to keep in touch. In the end I had hired a private detective, a Mr Morris Cowie, a short, rotund, pedantic man, with a pointed nose and disconcerting weasel eyes. He maintained that, despite considerable efforts on his part, the trail had gone cold. You have to understand that this was not the age of computers and databases. The world seemed an altogether vaster place than it does today. Some years after she disappeared, Albert insisted he had had a call from her. But I wasn't so sure. After his mother's death Albert absented himself entirely in his plays and musicals, no longer, it seemed, able to distinguish between acting and reality. Nevertheless, I like to think it was true about the phone call.

I let things slide. That's what I must live with. I tell myself that there was little I could have done. I try to believe it. But the truth is it was just easier that way, to let her go. Age is a great leveller. It reduces everything to the mundane. It dulls the pain. But despite this, I believe I failed my youngest daughter. The burden weighs heavily on me now.

Nicola took us to view Orchard House outside Uckfield during our annual leave in Britain in 1998. It seemed overly large the house, Edwardian, stylish, full of period features, but the garden was rather too sprawling. We'd never had a garden, well . . . not one of our own. The gardens belonging to the flat on The Peak were communal, and all taken care of, except Peter Everard's treasured patch of course. Why should we want the millstone of a garden dragging us down, and one of such massive proportions as well, at our time of life?

There seemed no logic to it. But as Myrtle appeared smitten with it, I went ahead with the purchase.

It was during that trip to England that Albert died. He fell in front of a tube train during the rush hour. One onlooker said it was a deliberate act, that he threw himself onto the line just as the train hurtled into the station. He told the police he was convinced it was suicide, said Albert was humming at the time. A song from *South Pacific*, he said. 'I'm Gonna Wash That Man Right Outa My Hair.'

The following year we packed up our lives in wooden tea crates. Chris Patten had sailed out of Victoria harbour for the last time on the royal yacht *Britannia*. We followed in his wake on a Chinese cargo vessel, the *Jade Empress*. I thought a cargo ship might be a more genteel way of travelling than one of those awful ocean liners. This seemed entirely fitting to me. Manufactured in Hong Kong. Now we were being exported abroad.

Myrtle – 1999

I am sitting on a tea chest in the tiny flat in Quarry Bay. Our lives have been crated up. In a matter of weeks we will be back in England and living in Orchard House. The island was once such a gracious place to be. The old values stood for something. There was a sense of purpose, of direction. And now, as far as I can see, the Chinese are going to do their damnedest to wreck all that we have achieved for them. Oh, they'll skim off the cream, naturally, and take all the credit, while we are made to scurry back to England like whipped dogs. It makes my blood boil just thinking of it.

Is it really nearly two years since the handover ceremony? I suppose so. I recall it was a washout and the Chinese officials revelled in it, as if the gods themselves refused to mark our going with the panache we deserved. Speaking for myself, I can't quit the place soon enough. The humiliation of it and the smug delight of the locals that you meet at every turn. We couldn't get a table the other night at the Tai Pak. I told them who I was.

I said, 'This is Myrtle Safford, wife of Ralph Safford OBE. We have been coming to your restaurant for years.'

'Very good. I know who you are, Mrs Safford. But I'm afraid we have no tables for Saturday.'

'I don't think you understand—' I began. And he interrupted me. He *interrupted* me!

'I'm sorry, we are fully booked on Saturday, Mrs Safford. Perhaps some other night would suit?'

'No, it wouldn't. I'll go elsewhere. And you can be sure we won't be dining at your establishment in the future,' I said and slammed down the phone. Well, of course we wouldn't. Like so many others, we were joining the exodus abroad.

And it wasn't an isolated incident either. My tailor, the man to whom I had taken my business for years, told me he was too busy to run up a few winter dresses for me to take back to England. In Cloth Alley last week, when I tried to bargain, the stallholder laughed in my face.

'I offer you a fair price,' he said. 'Take it or leave it.' And he shrugged. So what choice did I have but to buy the silk from him? Even if it was overpriced. Glancing back I swear I saw him smirking at me. And yesterday a Chinese man pushed past me and took my taxicab. Well, I expect the place will fall apart after a few years without the British organising things. Then they'll be sorry.

Ralph is out buying luggage for the journey. The few pieces we have were in a sorry condition. He set off early. Just as well or he might have intercepted the mail. Since his retirement, I've had to be eagle-eyed about getting to the post before he sees it. I look down at the letter one last time.

'Dear Father and Mother,

I don't know if this will be forwarded on to you. Father will have retired by now. You might not even be in Hong Kong any more. You certainly won't be living in the flat on the Peak. Perhaps you've moved back to England already. It was selfish of me to pour out all my troubles to you when I wrote last, and I'm sorry for it. I just had no one to turn to. I was so unhappy and I missed you so much. But I'm divorced now and I put all that heartache behind me long ago.

I watched the hand back of Hong Kong on the television in '97 and ever since it has preoccupied me. It broke my heart. Not Hong Kong being given back to the Chinese, that was as it should be. But seeing the island again. As the camera scanned the crowds, I kept thinking you might be there. I looked and looked but I didn't see you.

My friend Pierre died that same year. If you received my last letter you'll remember he owned the restaurant where I work. It was very sad. He had been ill for a little while. I don't know how to fill the void left by him. He willed me his business. At first I thought I couldn't manage it alone, but I'm coping quite well.

I expect you're both feeling empty too, seeing the island go. It's strange isn't it? I think about it all the time now. It comes to me in great waves and then I recall the big things: the shape of the mountains on the Peak silhouetted against the night sky, the crescent curve of a beach, the endless moods of the sea. And sometimes it's the tiniest details that prick at me when I least suspect it, being woken by the heat of the sun, the feeling of ice-cold water sluicing down your throat on a burning hot day, rose velvet light lancing through a veined scarlet petal.

I would like so much to see you both. I really believe things might be different now between us. Please can we try? If you don't want that, maybe we could just talk. A few words, that's all, I promise. I've noted down my telephone number next to my address at the bottom of the letter. Sometimes I think I have forgotten the sound of your voices, the music of them, and that frightens me. Then, they come unbidden into the silences inside me. You, Mother, chattering on the telephone, sounding so wonderfully regal and authoritative. And Father, the way you'd insist with a groan to the pedlars that came to the door that you had enough rugs, or fabric, or china, or whatever else they were selling. And then, minutes later, be gleefully showing us your purchases.

So many years have passed. I expect an awful lot has changed. I'm a middle-aged woman now, not the girl who ran away. Perhaps I am only considering myself. Perhaps this is too distressing for you now. Perhaps you don't want to be bothered by it. And of course that's your choice. If I don't hear, I'll understand. In any case, I needed to tell you that I love you, Alice.'

The letter was forwarded first to the Girl Guide Headquarters and then to the flat in Quarry Bay. It seems wherever we go, Alice will find us. I treat it with the contempt it deserves. Mutia, our Filipino maid, is puzzled when I bring the pan of ashes into the kitchen for her to wash up. But she says nothing.

When Ralph comes home at lunchtime with a new set of suitcases, he sniffs the air and frowns. 'Do I smell burning, Myrtle?' he says.

'It's the toaster. Faulty wiring. I think we should sling it out,' I reply easily, opening a window and letting the draft clear the air. 'I've told Mutia to unplug it.'

'Best not to use it again,' Ralph advises. 'Far too dangerous.'

'Exactly what I thought,' I agree.

Ingrid – 1999

'Zandra, that's your third glass of wine.'

'Oh so what! Christ, do you *have* to be so anal, Mum?'

We were at a party to welcome home Ralph Safford, Lucy's brother. He had lived in Hong Kong most of his life I was given to understand by the elderly lady I cared for, Lucy Holiday. Now he had returned to England to settle down in Orchard House with his wife, Myrtle. I was in the kitchen, fetching Aunt Lucy a tumbler of water. I guessed the raised voices were coming from the next room.

'You're getting drunk. Making a spectacle of yourself. You don't want to go the way of your—'

'Oh Jesus, not that again. The way you keep dredging her up. It's like a monster in a fairy tale. I'm not a kid any more, Mum, so you're wasting your time.'

'I'm being serious, Zandra. These things can be carried in the genes. You want to be careful.'

Curious, I thought. Perhaps the Saffords have a dipsomaniac relative? 'Look, all I'm doing is having a bit of fun. For fuck's sake, leave me alone.' I heard a door slam, turned, and came face to face with Nicola Salway. She was Ralph's second daughter, I recalled, and Salway was her married name.

'Oh, it's you, Ingrid,' she said, somewhat ungallantly. 'I suppose you heard all that.'

I shrugged, hands spread, as if to say I couldn't really help it. 'I was just fetching Aunt Lucy some water. I think she's had a little wine and it's made her dizzy,' I explained raising the glass in my hand.

'Ah, I see,' said Nicola, her voice decidedly lacklustre. 'Zandra's such a handful. It wouldn't be so bad if her father shouldered half the burden but, oh no, he's far too busy for that.' She sighed in annoyance. She was wearing a dusty mauve pantsuit with a pleated flower-print scarf pinned at her shoulder, fidgeting agitatedly with its arrangement. The sunlight, shafting through the kitchen window, picked out the amber shades in her bangs. 'Why don't people warn you what it's like bringing up teenagers?'

She sighed and I smiled understandingly. 'It's a lovely party,' I mollified. 'And what a splendid house too.'

'Do you think so?' She sounded mildly pleased.

'Yes, quite splendid.' I tucked a loose strand of hair behind my ears and glanced out at the sunlit garden – the walkway shadowed by the pergola with its tumble of blush-pink roses, the buzz of lazy bees, the wavering butterflies, the buffet table weighed down with food and drink, the clusters of people all laughing and talking, and Lucy, red-cheeked and tipsy, propped up in her chair by a large bush of sage-green hebe. 'Quite a challenge for your parents to look after though,' I observed idly. I was surprised by Nicola's defensive reaction.

'They needed a big place. My parents are accustomed to lots of entertaining.'

'I see. Lucy did say something about your sister staying with them for a bit.'

'That's right,' Nicola said cagily. 'At least in a place this size they won't get on top of each other.'

'True,' I agreed. But in reality I was thinking about upkeep, heating and cleaning, and how Orchard House, however grand, was the last place an elderly couple would want to be ensconced.

'Anyway, if you'll excuse me, I must see to our guests.'

'Of course,' I said. 'And I must take Lucy her glass of water.'

I waited a moment, then followed Nicola through the door that gave from the kitchen onto the garden. In my absence, someone had given Lucy another large glass of wine, and she had nearly polished it off by the time I arrived.

'Lucy, ought you really to have had that?' I admonished with mock gravity, lifting it out of her hands.

'I feel . . . I feel . . . I feel—' Lucy waved her fragile hands about expansively, as if searching for the word.

'Drunk?' I supplied disapprovingly, realising I was beginning to sound much as Nicola Salway had with her daughter minutes earlier.

'Not at all,' Lucy said hoarsely. 'Actually I feel rather . . . rather . . . ' She tailed off, burped softly, then took a deep breath, and resumed. 'Rather wonderful.' I gave a little shake of my head, looking down at my rebellious charge. Lucy leaned heavily on one arm of her chair, raised up her vivid blue eyes to meet mine and flirtatiously fluttered her sparse lashes.

'Can I have another wine, Ingrid? Try the red this time?'

'I really don't think it's a good idea,' I advised. 'What about a nice drink of water?' I held the glass before her nose to which her face-powder had adhered in patches. The tip wrinkled in disappointment, but she let me bring the cup to her lips. Ten minutes later she announced she was feeling sick and thought perhaps we should go home. She did look very flushed, her eyes over-bright and her forehead when I felt it rather hot.

'Oh Lucy, I did tell you not to have any wine. You know it doesn't agree with you,' I reprimanded her, wheeling her towards our host to make her apologies.

Although Lucy, unlike Zandra, did not tell me to stop being so anal, I caught the flash of defiance and repressed a giggle at her septuagenarian schoolgirl spirit. Ralph Safford seemed a little confused as we said our goodbyes, as if he was having a hard time placing his sister. I had heard so much about this man, now with his hunched shoulders and his potbelly and straggly whiskers. The striking blue eyes were clearly a family trait.

'Come and see me again soon . . . ah—' He seemed about to go on but his brow suddenly furrowed as if he was trying hard to remember his sister's name. There was something almost desperate about the request, a sense that he was seeking some familiar anchorage in this foreign harbour he had unwittingly sailed into.

For most of the journey to Lucy's Hailsham home she slept, though for the last ten minutes she was suddenly wide-eyed and preternaturally alert.

'My brother Ralph is very forgetful these days. He used to have such a sharp mind,' Lucy declared portentously. 'It's very tragic.' Glancing across at her my lips twitched. Lucy's own memory seemed haphazard at best. 'You know, I don't think he ever got over it,' she added.

'Got over what?' I asked, my mind elsewhere. I had just come to a crossroads and was concentrating on pulling out safely.

'What happened . . . well, over the years it ate away at him,' Lucy added, fingering her belt.

'Oh Lucy, don't undo the strap,' I pleaded, knowing this habit of hers only too well by now.

'I don't like it. I feel trapped,' Lucy maintained pugnaciously, slipping the catch. 'That's better. Now I can breathe. He worshipped her, you see,' Lucy volunteered, her mind leapfrogging again.

'Who?' I was feeling a little tired myself. 'Ralph worshipped who?' We had just turned into the High Street.

'Al-ah!' I braked suddenly as a child dashed out in front of the car. Lucy, unbelted was shunted forwards in her seat.

'Lucy, are you all right?' I asked, looking aslant. Mercifully, there was no one behind us and we had been doing less than 30mph.

'No broken bones I don't think,' Lucy piped up but I could see she was shaken.

'Now perhaps you realise how important it is you keep your safty belt fastened, Lucy,' I said. I leant over to double check she was unhurt and refasten it, simultaneously scowling at the child now safely across the road and pulling faces at us. We had stalled. There was a lengthy pause as I fired the engine and accelerated away once more. 'Who did Ralph worship?' I prompted again. But Lucy seemed not to hear me.

'Shall we have fish fingers for tea,' she suggested brightly. 'All that wine has given me a fearsome an appetite.'

Ralph – 2003

A sense of transience persisted long after our arrival in Britain. I found myself eagerly anticipating my return home to the sunshine, where once I had lived in a flat on The Peak and been King of the Castle. Here, on this cold, desolate isle, it seemed I was no better than the dirty rascal. On the heels of this came the unpleasant thought that home, my home, had gone, that here I was to stay, here to die and, no doubt, here to be buried. The holes in my sponge brain were widening all the time, and the world about me was becoming a bewildering conundrum. Shortly after we moved into Orchard House, Jillian and her husband arrived, along with their son, Amos. The trouble was that they simply did not go. Then one day, don't ask me how, they were a permanent fixture, along with the furniture and the curtains.

But by then my thoughts had solidified into ingots of dull metal. They were exhausting to heave about. It seemed so much easier to simply set them down. Nicola suggested that she and Jillian might take care of our bills to lighten the load.

'You don't want to be worrying about paying bills at your age, Father. We can take care of it,' she reassured. And then I think she took me to a doctor. In any case she made me sign something she insisted would make life a good deal less complicated.

But it didn't, because one day a man came with boxes that he dumped in the hall, and he wanted me to sign something too. Then I was filled with terror, because I suspected he might want money as well my signature. You see I wasn't sure . . . sure of the value of the coins and notes I had, for the numbers on them were all tangled up and illegible.

'That is the Queen,' I remember telling the man. I jabbed a finger at the picture of Her Majesty on the note in my hand. There was no mistaking the value of her. 'She is the Queen of Hong Kong. Her name is Edwina, and I am an officer in her empire. What do you think of that, eh?' I barked.

But he just looked at me as if I was insane, and thrust a clipboard at me. 'Just sign 'ere, mate,' he told me. But what was my name? I couldn't remember my name. Perhaps, I thought desperately, if I scribbled something on his form, he would think that it was my signature. But then he was pushing a pen towards me, and I wasn't sure how I should hold it, in the middle or at both ends. 'All I need is a signature, mate.'

He was impatient, and he smelt of sweat and orange peel.

Suddenly I felt bellicose. How dare this man invade my house with his boxes, and try to make me do things against my will. 'Why don't you smile?' I berated him. 'You can smile can't you?' He didn't know what to say to that. Sure enough I had him there. 'What's the matter, you miserable little worm? I am Queen Edith's officer. Perhaps I should fetch my sword? I expect you'd grin soon enough with that pointing at you. Get out of my house!' That's when Myrtle and Jillian appeared, with Amos in tow, and everyone began shouting. The man with the boxes told Jillian that she should lock me up.

'What have you done now?' demanded Jillian, when the man had gone. 'What did you say to him? He probably won't make any more deliveries here.'

'Good!' I told her. Then I shoved the note with the portrait of the Queen at her. 'He didn't know his own Queen, Queen Eleanor the Second. I told him that I was her officer. Once I had a sword. Did you know that? I should have cut off his head. That would have served him right.' Myrtle started crying, so I patted her on the back. Everyone was so tense these days. Sometimes I thought it would be better if I left them to it.

I know a secret. I have told no one my secret, but I will tell you. Orchard House is shrinking. It is reducing. I explain this carefully to Larry one morning. I am sitting in an armchair, and I lean in towards him. He is lounging on the settee.

'When I arrived here it was a large house,' I confide in an undertone to my son-in-law. I make an effort to keep my voice steady. I do not want to alarm him unnecessarily. 'Now there is no space anywhere. I am being hemmed in, besieged. There are piles of papers all over the floor and,' here I beckon him closer with a curling finger, 'they are spreading. Soon they will infiltrate the entire house. We need to call someone, to alert the authorities.'

But Larry remains infuriatingly calm. He shakes his head slowly, and greasy strands of yellow hair fall over his eyes. When he pushes them back I see he is grinning. It is an unattractive, mirthless grin.

'Oh, they're just a few of my papers, old boy,' he tells me airily. 'I'll see to them when I can.'

I am about to tell him to pick up his fucking papers and get out, when I stop. I bite my fist. I am not sure any more whose house it is. Maybe it is I who should get out? But then where would I go? A staccato series of explosions brings my head up fast.

'The soldiers are on parade. I should be there,' I tell Larry. He rises languidly, and stretches.

'No, Ralph, old boy, it's just Amos jumping up and down the stairs. It's a new game he's got.' As he speaks, he sets down another pile of papers near the chair where I sit.

'How would you like some fish and chips for lunch, Ralphy boy?' he offers, tucking a straggle of hair behind a large ear.

'I don't like fish and chips.' I am firm.

'Oh yes you do,' he overrides me.

'No I fucking don't!' I thunder back.

'I'll get you a nice bit of cod,' he tells me, turning for the door.

'I've wet myself,' I bellow after him, vindictively.

I would like to bend down, take up the pile of papers, and fling them in the air. But it hurts too much to stoop these days. I cast a malevolent eye over them. I can feel my heart leaping in my chest.

Once my heart pounded. It was a mighty organ, and the boom of it was invincible. I think of the steady, heavy clunk of a grandfather clock, and the light runaway tick of an alarm clock. The latter best describes my heart now. What's more, I feel the alarm might go off at any moment. I allow myself a few minutes' reminiscence. You are entitled to one or two lapses when you are old. I bring to mind my last boat, *Ruby Red*. I am sitting at her helm, gripping the rudder in my hand, while the sail fills out and billows in the wind. My nostrils flare with the salty spume. I am scudding over the waves and steering my own path.

Myrtle comes into the room. She is wearing an orange and pink kaftan and some beads. She looks as if she is dressed for a party. Perhaps we are going out.

'Did I hear Larry say that he was getting fish and chips?' she asks, settling herself down on the settee with a newspaper.

'I hate fish and chips,' I tell her, my tone defeated.

'I know you do. We both do,' she empathises, knotting her beads around her fingers.

Then, 'Is Alice buried in the garden?' I say. 'Is she buried in the apple orchard?'

Myrtle closes her eyes. I guess that she must be feeling as tired as I am.

'You see the apples . . . the apples have gone rotten, Myrtle. They should have been picked but they have been left, and now they are riddled with wasps and worms. They are putrid with decay.' Again I pause. I concentrate very hard, tracing a swirling pattern on the upholstered arm of my chair. I refuse to let this thought elude me. 'Alice will . . . not . . . like that, you see,' I say measuredly. 'Being buried under all that . . . rotten fruit.' The smell of apples, sweet and buttery, permeates my nostrils, and I feel a strand of golden hair brush my face. 'Amanda?' I say, my voice thick with wonder and the joy of recognition. 'Oh . . . Amanda!'

I am jolted out of my reverie then by Myrtle. She expels the air from her lungs with a harsh grating noise. Looking up, I see her shudder involuntarily. In the silence that follows I swear I hear the buzz of angry wasps.

Nicola – 2003

I finally managed to lure Father and Mother back to Britain, persuading them to buy Orchard House, just far enough away from my rural idyll for me not to be bothered on a daily basis, but within easy reach if there was an emergency. I solved Jillian's financial problems, all down to that deviant gambler she married, in the same stroke. How? By relocating them of course, all three. Jillian, Larry, and costly test-tube baby Amos. Goodbye America, hello Blighty. And not just Blighty, but Orchard House, big enough for all of them. They have free board and lodging, and I have live-in carers for the parents and a lot less to worry about.

Of course I'd like to help more, but what with a husband, a daughter, a home to run, I have very little free time. True, Desmond spends the week in London, but nevertheless I have to keep things spic and span for the weekends. Actually I'm not terribly sure what my husband does. I think he sells computers or something like that. I've never taken much interest in his employment. So long as the money keeps rolling in, it really doesn't bother me what he gets up to.

Brother Harry has plumped for Kent, and easy access to the Channel Tunnel, so he's no use at all when it comes to shouldering his share. He's living on one of those estates where all the houses are identical, not to my taste at all, along with his wife, Carmen, a nondescript little thing, and their two children Edgar and Tiffany. As for Alice, nothing has been heard or seen of her for well over two

315

decades. She might as well be dead. Oh, there was that call Uncle Albert claimed to have had several years ago. Poor Uncle Albert, falling under a tube train. What a way to go. Still, I wouldn't be surprised if he made it all up. About the phone call I mean. Honestly, he was raving mad, a performer living in his own production. The preposterous thing is that Alice 'dead' seems to make her presence more felt than Alice alive, what with Father constantly drivelling on about her.

It may sound heartless, but Father losing his grasp of reality has been an unexpected bonus. When, his tone irascible, he demands why Jillian, Larry and young Amos are still houseguests, we simply tell him it is by his express invitation. His brow knits and he ponders this for while, before accepting it without demurral. Even more fortuitous, we managed to persuade him to give me and Jilly joint Power of Attorney. Harry was happy to leave us to it, though I have to admit we cut it very fine. He was just barely compos mentis when he signed on the dotted line.

'Success,' I recall telling Desmond later that evening over the phone. 'We now have joint Power of Attorney. Isn't that marvellous?'

'Mm . . . yes,' Desmond replied distractedly.

'Desmond, do you fully understand what this means for us?' I tried again.

'I think so. I suppose it—'

'You think so!' I interrupted crossly. 'It means that we now have complete control over Father's estate . . . over his capital, Desmond.'

'I see. That's . . . good. Look, Nicola, I'm afraid I can't make it home this weekend. I'm snowed under. We have that new contract to work on and—'

'That's fine,' I told my husband sweetly. We said our goodbyes, that we would see each other the following weekend, and hung up.

I knew that Desmond intended to spend the weekend fucking prostitutes in London, that work didn't come into it. I knew too that he did this on a fairly regular basis. I had no problem with it. Why should I? Frankly, those whores saved me considerable effort, for, it has to be said, very little reward. It seems odd to me now, sitting in my immaculate home, surrounded by valuable antiques, creations that are vastly superior to the creatures who fashioned them, that sex once played a major part in my life. And, I suppose, looking back, I wasn't so different from a working girl myself then. It was part of the deal and I seem to recall I fucked with gusto. It empowered me. It brought me what I craved – mastery. Though it used to infuriate me when Desmond and I first met that he visited trollops in Wanchai.

'Don't come near me, you stink of sex. If you think you're screwing me after you've fucked your prostitutes, forget it,' I would rage at him as he crept guiltily into our flat.

He would grin then, as if he had been no more than a naughty schoolboy, and try to nuzzle closer. Truthfully, I did find something stimulating about him when he came in reeking of 'eau de slut'. I would wonder what she had done, what she had sucked, what she had used, what acrobatics she had performed? Though of the two of them, the whore was always infinitely more tantalising. All the same, the prospect of what the seductive Suzie Wong might pass on to me via my husband was sufficient deterrent to curb my appetite for voyeurism.

These days, however, sex is no longer part of the deal. There is still a deal of course. There is always a deal. I keep the house impeccably clean and stylish, and bring up our daughter, an accomplishment in itself, and Desmond gives me lots of money. I have not aged too badly, a tendency to plumpness being my biggest downfall as the years slip by. However, the thought of sex with Desmond, flabby and pale as a raw chicken, with all the tugging, pulling and rubbing that it entails, quite simply revolts me now. Sometimes when I recline in the hall on my newly upholstered, wine-red velvet chaise longue, I fancy myself as a madam at the helm of a glamorous brothel. I sip a glass of chilled white wine and nibble on a chocolate, enjoying the fruits of Desmond's labours, while I visualise some other woman opening her legs for him, and putting up with all that panting and moaning and mess.

Lately the cottage is very silent. I am becoming increasingly aware of this stillness. I live in fear of shattering it. Our daughter Zandra was home briefly last night. She's not frightened of shattering anything. I think she may have inherited sister Alice's neurotic gene. She was drunk too. She broke an antique vase. She was trying to reach a book and she bumped it. She laughed when it rocked and I dashed forwards and tried to save it. It was one of a pair of Japanese Imari vases. They were very valuable. This morning when I came down, I found a small piece of the golden dog that sat atop the lid of one of the vases, lying under the corner of an armchair. I leant down to pick it up. I was feeling the sharp edge with the pad of an index finger when the phone rang.

'Father is playing up,' Jillian informed me peremptorily. 'You have to come. I can't cope.' I told her that as soon as I had finished cleaning the house I'd swing by.

The sun is shining today. It's already quite warm, although it's still early. The sunshine shows up the dust. That is the down side to it. There is such a lot of work to be done. I thought the house was spotless but the sun has put me right. Desmond is away again so that makes things a little easier. Still, the dirt behind the kitchen appliances kept me awake last night. You can't see it but you know it's there, nestling in crevices, coating surfaces, furring up walls. Bacteria. Germ transference. Cross-contamination. Multiplying all the while.

When I arrive at Orchard House later in the morning I step into an uproar. The place is a tip. There are bundles of dirty washing lying around, piles of books and papers, shoes and coats and towels strewn about the floor, and used crockery scattered throughout. All this fighting for space among an assortment of Chinese antiques of considerable worth. We must think about putting them in storage or, better still, selling them off. The smell of cigarettes hangs on the air too, one of Larry's vices. As does the smell of urine: Father's.

Father, who is standing at the dining-room table, propping himself up on a chair, looks decidedly damp about the crutch. Mother is sitting at the table, staring disconsolately at a plate of congealed fried fish and chips. She is wearing an orange and pink kaftan and a rope of amber beads. There is a tiny fly trapped in one of the beads. I know it is there. I've seen it. Mother told me it was very lucky. I'm not sure the fly would agree with her. Dotted around Father's feet are several soggy chips. There is a lump of battered fish in the middle of the table. It has left a smeary trail on the polished wood surface.

The trail leads to Father's plate. There is another lump of battered fish grasped in the hand father is not using for balance. The hand is raised as if holding a weapon seconds before an assault. Father is squeezing the fish so tightly that drops of oil are trickling down his wrist. As I near him, added to the smell of smoke and urine is that of fat and fish. Amos is lying on the settee, shoes muddy and still on, playing some sort of handheld electronic game. The game emits a high-pitched beep from time to time, a hit, along with a deflated whine, which I presume signifies a miss. Larry is nowhere to be seen. What a surprise! Jillian is standing in the dining-room doorway snivelling, and brandishing a tea-towel in her hand.

'Look what he's done to his dinner. Just look. He's thrown it on the floor,' bawls Jillian. 'I lovingly prepare dinner for him and see how he repays me.'

She has dyed her hair an alarming shade of mahogany red and, from the look of things, it is a recent job. There is a slight discolouration on the skin that borders her hairline.

'I hate fish and chips,' shouts Father, letting fly his handful of squashed fish and batter. It sails through the air and strikes the wall above the dresser, sticking fast to the red and white flowered wallpaper.

'What do you mean, Father? You've always loved fish and chips,' I say, trying to keep my tone calm and pleasant. 'Now apologise to Jillian, and let's get this mess cleared up.'

Amos sighs rudely, as if we are disturbing his concentration.

'I will not,' bellows Father, eyes popping.

'He really doesn't like fish and chips,' Mother adds unhelpfully, pushing her own food round and round on the plate. 'Jillian knows he doesn't like it. We don't like going to bed at seven o'clock either,' she adds daringly.

'That's not true. You take yourselves to bed early because you say you're exhausted,' shrieks Jillian, so impassioned one would think she had been accused of murder, and perhaps such a scenario is not as far-fetched as it might first appear. 'I slave day and night to cook your meals and—'

'But Larry fetched this from the chip shop, and your father told him twice he didn't fancy fish and chips,' Mother carps, her face flushing.

'Well, then, I'm sure Larry didn't hear him,' retorts Jillian acidly, bunching up the tea-towel as if readying herself to enter the fray. 'Larry tries his best and all you do is pick on him.'

Now I sigh, for it is perfectly obvious to anyone who knows Larry that never once has he tried his best.

'I hate fish and chips,' yells Dad. Then, just for good measure, 'Larry is a dickhead!'

'See! See!' Jillian is beside herself now. 'He delights in abusing my husband. Don't think I'm going to make you scrambled egg. If you don't eat your fish and chips, you can starve for all I care. I have better things to do than run around clearing up after you.' Amos rises, kicks the settee in temper, and storms out of the room, pushing his way past his mother, who barely seems to notice him. 'I don't know how much more I can stand. You're driving me crazy. I shall have a breakdown!'

'Why don't you do as you're told the first time then,' hollers Father, now turning a deep shade of mulberry. 'You never fucking do as you're told!'

'If you're going to swear at me I'm leaving,' Jillian shoots back, tossing her head of startling red hair.

'Why don't we all calm down,' I suggest with valiant optimism.

Jillian moves to stand menacingly behind Mother, looking as if she might like to smother her with the tea-towel. 'I'm tired. I am *so* tired,' she warbles.

I scratch my brow. 'How about a sandwich, Dad?' He shakes his drooping head. His expression is woebegone, his complexion paling to a chalky white, his sparse hair awry. He is unshaven, and his side-burns have almost met under his jowls and formed a beard. There is a blot of ketchup on his cream shirt, over his heart. It looks like a bullet wound.

But there is life in him yet. Up comes his chin for a second skirmish. 'Where's Alice?' he fires pugnaciously, lifting his chair a few inches and slamming it back down. 'What have you done with her?'

'Christ! Not that again,' Jillian shrills, leaning over Mother and whacking the table with the flat of her hand. A nervous tic jumps in Mother's cheek. 'Can't you shut up about Alice! Just fucking shut up!'

'Let's all be one big happy family again?' Mother offers pathetically. She mashes her fish meticulously with her fork, then with her knife spreads it thinly around her plate. We all look on with macabre fascination.

Jillian takes a deep breath, holds it for a second and then lets rip. 'We were never a happy family!' Then she turns smartly on her heels and flees the room.

'Where's the whisky? I want a whisky. Where has bloody Jillian hidden the whisky?' Mother wails, rising and moving heavily to the dresser, starting to open drawers and cupboards and rifle through them.

So preoccupied am I in the hunt for the golden cure-all, and in assuaging Mother's maternal anguish, that I do not notice Death sidle into the room. When I turn back, a bottle of whisky held victoriously aloft, Father is slumped in his chair, his eyes half-closed, his lips blue and trembling, beads of sweat breaking out on his cadaverous skin, one hand clawing his arresting heart.

Nicola – 2005

I was right about the dirt. When the removal men came and started shifting the furniture I saw it. And not just behind the furniture, underneath it as well. To think I had sat in the lounge and watched television, with all that filth only feet away. I am moving to a new build in East Grinstead. I would have preferred a place in Eastbourne, but it was just too expensive. And Jillian and Larry are moving to Hastings, a small two up, two down. Of course I've had to down-size a bit myself, though I have no complaints about the divorce settlement. Desmond was very generous when it came to it. He didn't seem interested in any of the antiques either. I wonder if he realises how much money they're worth. Still, he said he didn't want them. He said I could keep them. He said Selena didn't like old things. Oh, that's her name, Selena, Se . . . le . . . na. Much as I would have expected. Pretentious and unlikely to be her real name. I don't bear her any grudge now. Not really. In a way, I sort of admire her. She saw what she wanted and she took it. It's a laudable ethos in my opinion.

Don't misunderstand me. I did fight for my marriage. In the final months we spoke more than we had done for ages. I even tried to seduce him. Can you believe it? Not that it made any difference. Actually, I think he was shocked, couldn't scuttle away fast enough. Still, I'm a pragmatist. If our marriage was dead I wouldn't waste any more time trying to revive it. Every so often these rain clouds come along in life and threaten to bowl you over, don't they? I expect it happens to everyone. You can stand there and get wet, or go somewhere it's dry and sunny.

Having to sell Orchard House was another surprise. Of course I knew that eventually we would have to dispose of it, though I hadn't been anticipating the need for such an early sale. But I might have known that Larry, with his weakness for gambling, would be our downfall. I rushed over to Orchard House when I got Jillian's urgent summons. Larry was out and Amos was at school. Before we'd even sat down it all came out.

'We're in a dreadful mess,' Jillian sobbed, swaying on the soles of her slippered feet in the hall. 'Larry's been gambling. He's gambled away thousands, Nicola, online. All our credit cards maxed up to the hilt. The final tally is over £100,000. The money from Dad went long ago. The debt collectors have been round. I don't know what to do!'

When she finished speaking, her mouth carried on working. I took her by the elbow and guided her into that dismal back room. God, it was in a state, and it stank too. I tried not to think about the germs flying about spreading disease. As I pressed Jilly down into a seat, having moved the clutter off it first, I noticed that several of the buckets used to catch the drips from the leaking roof were spilling over onto the carpet. She's a slob, I thought, remembering how lovely I had made it before Father and Mother moved in – pretty soft furnishings, everything gleaming, fresh, clean. Still, we all have different standards I suppose. And some of us, I reflected, reluctantly turning my focus back to my elder sister, now weeping uncontrollably, have none.

I've got to admit that when she first told me, I could cheerfully have wrung Larry's neck. Of all the irresponsible stupid things to do. But after I'd composed myself, and Jillian and I had shared a drink, I began to see that this situation might be salvaged.

'You despise me, I know,' Jillian said, staring glumly into her empty glass, having downed her drink in one.

Inwardly I sighed. What could I say? Why did you marry that useless pillock? Why did you blow a small fortune on trying to have

323

a baby, when you could have picked up one at some adoption agency for free? Why didn't you keep a closer eye on your worthless husband, and put a stop to his nasty little gambling habit before it got out of hand? Oh, why didn't you just pull yourself together and make something of your life, instead of sitting back, like a useless victim, and letting everyone else do the work. Well, me in fact. Sometimes I wanted to shake Jilly till her teeth rattled. Nevertheless she was my sister, and even now, after all these years, hearing the desperation sound in her voice, I wanted nothing more than to find a solution to her woes. Gradually, as I stared at the bowls and buckets full of rainwater, a plan formulated in my head.

'We'll sell the house,' I announced to Jillian, crouching in front of her and meeting her tearful eyes. 'After clearing your debt, we'll split the proceeds three ways. Luckily we put the house in your name, so it should be straightforward enough. Besides, I could do with a bit of extra cash at present, what with moving myself. And Harry will be glad of the additional funds too, with his youngsters growing up fast.'

'But where will I live?' Jillian wailed pathetically, her hands towards me, palms outwards, in a gesture redolent of the statues of the Virgin Mary we had met at every turn in the convent.

At that, I told her to snap out of it, that she must buy a new home in a less expensive location. 'If you have any sense you'll lose Larry, but if you choose to hang onto him, you had better take away his credit cards, because if he does this again Jilly, I'm telling you, you're on your own,' I advised her, my tone sonorous, in an effort to impress the gravity of her situation upon her. My sister produced a soiled tissue from an equally grubby sleeve and blew her nose noisily. Hunkered down on my heels, my hands resting on her knees, I rose rapidly and retreated a short distance, remembering that the common cold is an airborne virus. 'And Jilly, this will be the very last time I'll bail you out. It will have to be,' I added as an afterthought, wagging an admonishing finger at her. 'Once we've sold the house there will be no money left, and nothing I can do for you.'

324

Having heard my plan she revived. The two of us were just talking about opening a bottle of some sickly liqueur Jilly had hanging about from last Christmas, when my sister suddenly rocketed out of her seat. 'What about Mother,' she shrieked, gesturing towards the ceiling, where Mother mostly stayed these days in her upstairs bedroom. 'What are we going to do with Mother?'

On the instant, I decided that it would be impossible for me to take her. I was moving to a new build where everything was immaculate. I cannot tell you how much I was looking forward to a salubrious, uncontaminated home, where at last I could sleep at nights without worrying about bacteria. Mother and that sleek, minimalist look were incompatible. I understood from Jillian's endless whining that Mother was fast becoming unpredictable, and most recently obdurate.

'You know, I wouldn't be surprised if she's gone the same way as her brother. Uncle Albert was barmy, don't you remember? Always mumbling lines from some old play or musical, or singing,' Jillian suggested. I nodded, recalling mad Uncle Albert, and his endless repertoire. 'Even if this hadn't happened, Nicola, I've been meaning to tell you that I didn't feel I could carry on for much longer. She's constantly wandering off. And half the time she just doesn't make any sense, going on about Hong Kong and Daddy and parties and people. And they're all dead. They've all gone.'

It was then, anticipating the care of Mother falling to me, Harry with his busy household not even being an option, that I began to ponder whether we could find a local care home for her. After all, she would be able to contribute her generous overseas pension towards the cost. Besides, with her deteriorating mental state, the council, I felt sure, had an obligation to look after her. The moment this idea struck me, I knew we had found the way forwards. Luckily, Mrs Diane Malloy from social services was sympathetic, having had personal experience in caring for an ageing relative. Doctor Hillman was also extremely helpful in confirming Mother's deteriorating mental condition. With their assistance I was able to secure her a place at Greenwood Lodge, a care home for the elderly outside Brighton.

We also found a buyer for Orchard House fairly rapidly. The chap from Golders and Packman Estate Agency, Ray Clegg, a stocky man with stringy grey hair, rabbit's teeth, and no scruples at all, was confident that a period property like ours, in need of a bit of work, would be a buyer's dream. And he was right. Within the month we were under offer, having achieved an excellent price for the ramshackle old house too. Time has simply flown by since then. I had the best of intentions, but sadly I haven't managed to get over to Greenwood Lodge very much. I have rung regularly though, and the manager there, a Mrs Bowker, has been most understanding. Besides, I see little point in feeling guilty when she tells me Mother is doing just fine. In any case, I know Ingrid, Aunt Lucy's carer, has promised to visit, so there's no need to panic. After the removal men have come and gone I might try to call in.

It is a lovely spring day. The sky is deep rich blue ribbed with filmy white clouds, like a ladder arcing overhead. The wisteria is just out. The cottage thatched in pale green and tasselled with lavender-blue looks like something off the lid of a biscuit tin. I am standing in the kitchen. My hands are rubbed raw. There is the lingering smell of disinfectant in the air. I drink it in. I'd have hated the newcomers to think I was dirty. I am staring out into the back garden and there is a thrush, a mistle thrush, hopping on the clipped green grass, looking for worms. Every so often it stops and swivels its small, grey-brown head, as if peering behind to see if anyone is following. It knows the worms are down there, burrowing through the crumbling earth, turning things over, mixing things up. It's biding its time.

I think suddenly of Zandra. Of course I love her very much but . . . well . . . she is so destructive. She's better off staying with her father. He's more patient with her than I am. Sir Walter Scott should have written, oh, what a tangled web we weave when first we practise to conceive. Desmond says she's been nurturing a secret love of art all these years, that she wants to be an artist. He said something or other about her going to art college. Well, if he's prepared to fund it why not? Personally I've never rated all those arty-farty careers.

And now, as so often, inexplicably I think of Alice. She is in the gardens of the flat on The Peak. I see her flying through the air on the swing. She is soaring upwards, her long brown hair trailing behind like the tail of a comet. In the rush of it she holds the mauve hills, and the shimmering sea, and the limitless expanse of blue sky. I want her to come back down, to stay with the rest of us earthbound mortals. I call to her but she can't hear me.

'One day,' she shouts from above, and her voice is seized by the streaming air, so that I have to strain to catch her words as they dash by, 'one day . . . I am going to go so high . . . so high . . . that I shall swing right over.'

Ghost – 2006

He comes in when there are just a few stragglers finishing off their meals. Alice, sitting in the same corner that Pierre Ramirez occupied when he was alive, glances up. Their eyes meet. I know she is going to say that service has ended, that she is sorry, that she hopes very much the gentleman will return another day. Then she is rising, gasping softly, fingers splayed across her mouth. She is not certain yet, but I am. He moves towards her. He is older of course, his tight black curls threaded with grey. The shadows have deepened beneath his eyes, below his cheekbones. His brow is lined. There are crow's feet at the outer corners of his eyes. Deep furrows run from the base of his nose to either side of his mouth. But he is still a tall imposing figure. He wears a grey winter suit, a beige shirt, a red and silver striped tie. He moves gracefully for such a tall man. He reaches the table and speaks quietly.

'Hello Alice.'

Alice's fingers slip from her mouth, drop to her neck. She is wearing a heavy silver chain and rolls it back and forth between thumb and middle finger.

'Hello Kosey,' she says.

She offers him a coffee. When he declines she leads Kosey Okello to her office in the rear of the restaurant, says they can talk undisturbed there. Once inside she closes the door, gestures Kosey to take a seat across the desk from her, and sits herself. There is one large window giving onto the courtyard through which a weak

328

trickle of grey light filters. It is January and already it is growing dark.

'It's good to see you after so long,' Alice tells him. She leans forward and presses a switch and the desk lamp blinks on. A pool of yellow light, reflected in the highly polished surface of the desk, lights up Kosey's features. 'You look well.'

'So do you, Alice,' Kosey says, returning her gaze. 'I asked around.' His eyes rove about the office. 'They say this place is yours now, has been for some time, that Pierre left it to you in his will.' He fidgets with a gold and blue enamel cufflink, adjusts the pin nervously.

'That's right, he did,' says Alice simply. Then in a lower voice, 'He was like a father to me in many ways.' I lean back against the wall, arms by my sides. I am suspicious, doubting already that this is merely a social call after so many years.

'Carl would have been livid. He hated you working here.' He gives a dry cough and smiles awkwardly. 'Have you heard from him, Alice?'

Alice shakes her head. She glances away, out of the window and remembers the cold green eyes, the furious face, the slaps, the kicks, the shoves, the dread. But now she does not feel afraid, she feels angry. Her back straightens. She holds her head up with dignity. 'What about you, Kosey? Has Carl been in touch with you?'

'Not since he left the company, and that was over a decade now.' He lowers his gaze to the desktop, taking in a neat stack of bills, a pot of pens, a large leather diary, a circular glass paperweight with a swirling orange and red flower encased in it. 'I was very sorry it didn't work out for the two of you.'

Alice shrugs. She asks Kosey if he is married and if he has a family. Now Kosey smiles in earnest as he describes his French wife Lorraine, and his twin daughters Sophia and Zoe, who will be sixteen in May. He talks a little of his new business venture as well, exporting select French wines, how well it is going.

'And what about you,' he says at last. 'Are you married, Alice? Do you have a family?' Resting on her elbows, my host plaits her fingers together. She takes a moment before explaining that she never re-married and that she has no children. Then Alice and Kosey tumble into an uncomfortable silence. Distant sounds from the kitchens reach their ears, pots clanging, muffled voices, the clatter of a something falling to the floor.

'How are your sister and your mother?'

As Alice speaks, Kosey's hand slips into a jacket pocket. There is the faint crackle of paper.

'That's really why I'm here, Alice.' His head sinks and he draws his free hand across his brow. When he looks up there is the unmistakable dullness of grief in his brooding eyes. 'My mother is dead. Reta is dead, Alice.'

For the second time that afternoon Alice's hand cups her mouth. There is a box of tissues on the desk and she reaches for it now, although she is dry-eyed. 'What happened, Kosey?' she whispers, drawing one from the box.

Kosey Okello sighs sadly. His fingers stroke the desktop. 'Oh Alice, she was ill for some time, kept it to herself, you know. It was cancer. She was a nurse. She knew what to expect. She only told us towards the very end. I think Subira and me, we knew by then anyway. My mother said she didn't want any kind of fuss.'

'I'm so sorry. I will never forget how kind she was to me, Kosey, all those years ago, how kind you all were.' Alice's hands are busy shredding the tissue as she talks. Kosey nods.

'She wasn't very kind to me,' I remark, still leaning back against the wall. Alice responds by diving into the box and plucking out another tissue.

'My mother didn't forget you either, Alice. We found this while we were going through her things.' Kosey pulls a sealed envelope from his pocket and lays it in the centre of the table. The name 'ALICE' is written in capitals in black ink on the front of it. My host stares down, her eyes tracing the lettering, an expression very like wonder etched on her face. Long after Kosey has left she is still looking at it. But she doesn't open it until she is back in her flat, business over for the night. She is in bed. I am sitting cross-legged in one corner. Bear-as-Was is stretched out on the drawn coverlet at the bed end. The headless budgie has made a nest for itself in the overhead lampshade. And the monkey has finally settled under the duvet, leaving a few hairs, like shiny snippets of copper wire, on the white pillow. Alice's side light is on, the open letter in her trembling hands. We are all waiting. The monkey's head peeps out from under the duvet. The dog rolls into a sitting position. The budgie cranes its neck-stump over the edge of the frosted-glass shade. And I lean forwards. We all want to know what Reta has to say for herself. Perhaps it is an apology for how she treated us.

'Dear Alice,

I am writing this at the same table where we sat and had tea together all those years ago. You have been with me so much recently. I sit in the spare room and remember the first night you slept there, how scared you were. I stand in the kitchen and I hear you laughing with Kosey. I look at the portrait of Kesia and it is your eyes I see. You are haunting me, Alice. I am sorry your marriage with Carl was not a happy one. Kosey is sure you are still living in Paris, that you run a restaurant there. I expect your father would be very proud of you if he knew. Does he know, Alice? Does he know where you are? Have you been to see him?

What bothers me, Alice, as I near the end of my life, is not the words I have spoken, but the words I have not spoken. When I lost my husband, when I lost Kesia, I felt so angry with myself. I left so many things unsaid and then it was too late. It is not too late for you, Alice. Go home and see your father.

With love always,

Reta.'

Alice sleeps clutching the letter tightly in her hands. We ghosts nod at one another. Already I can feel growing in my host, the determination to return to England and visit her father. It seems that, despite being dead, Reta Okello still has the power to turn our existence upside down. Seven months later we leave Paris, arriving by train at London's Waterloo Station, on the first leg of our journey to see Ralph Safford. The others are overcome with excitement. They

331

tumble pell mell down the escalator in a rush of yellow and green feathers, rust and ruby fur, and into the muggy tunnels of the London Underground. I slink behind, filled with the most terrible sense of foreboding. Not that I expected an intelligent considered response to our changing circumstances from a motley crew of fairground apparitions. But such an undignified arrival, with the monkey 'hallooing' hysterically, the dog dashing about barking and snorting, and the budgie pin-balling off the tiled ceiling and walls, well . . . it shows such a lack of breeding. I have nagged Alice incessantly about this insane plot of hers.

'Was it wise to dispose of the restaurant?' I asked. 'Especially when it was doing so well.' And, 'Are you quite certain we will be welcomed back into the Safford family, after an absence that seems, even to me, a trifle prolonged?'

But, after receiving Reta's letter, Alice was intractable.

It doesn't take her very long to track down Harry. We go to an internet café in London. My host sits down before a screen, starts busily tapping on a keyboard, and before the dog has time to pace the length of the room, finds what she is looking for. Then she speaks to someone on the shiny silver phone she keeps in her bag, and jots down a number in her diary. Finally she calls Harry and after a stilted conversation a meeting is arranged for Saturday at 3pm at his home in Kent.

'He wasn't pleased to hear from me,' mutters Alice.

We are making our way back to the hotel, our motley retinue barrelling alongside. 'Ghosts from the past, Alice, do not always have the warmest of receptions when they show up,' I explain tactfully. My host shoots me a sideways glance. I beam back angelically.

Harry – 2006

It is the weekend. Carmen is dressmaking in the dining room. The fabric she has chosen, a slippery azure-blue silk, is draped over the dining-room table, as if the sky has collapsed on it. I glimpsed it through the open door half an hour earlier, making my way, coffee in hand, into my study. I am online reading *Which* reports on washing-machines, listening to the comforting 'grit-grit' of her sewing scissors as they slice around a pattern. It is mid-afternoon, and a feeling of euphoria is radiating outwards from the pit of my satisfied stomach. The lunch, traditional roast beef, puffs of crisp golden Yorkshire puddings, a selection of perfectly cooked vegetables, followed by apple pie, thick clotted cream and cinnamon custard, was excellent. Fifteen-year-old Edgar woofed it down, and sped off to the rec with friends to play footy. Tiffany, thirteen and going on twenty, stayed over at a friend's last night and has not yet returned home.

Dimly I am aware first of a drowsy warmth enfolding me, then a thin ringing noise piercing the silence. This gathers in volume until the blare of it is deafening, needles of pain stabbing my eardrum, making me dizzy. The screen before me blurs and I close my eyes, grateful that I am sitting down. I know something is about to occur. I am not a fanciful man, and yet I know this with absolute surety. The jangle of the ring tone jars on me like an electric shock. My eyes spring open, my hand shoots out automatically towards the ivory telephone, and then halts mid-air.

I think it is on the fifth ring that Carmen calls to me, but it may be the sixth.

'Are you going to get that, Harry, or shall I?' Her voice is slightly muffled, and I imagine her speaking through a mouthful of pins.

Almost simultaneously I reply. 'I've got it.' And I have. I am clasping the receiver and holding it to my tingling ear. The thrumming stills to a sweet silence. I do not break this with my usual cheery, 'Harry Safford here'. Whoever is at the other end is reluctant to speak too. For a moment, perhaps no more than a few seconds, we are both speechless. Then, there is the lisp of a gulped breath.

'Hello, Harry?' That's all she says. 'Hello, Harry?' That's all it takes. My heart pounds, the tang of coffee in my mouth sucks all the moisture from it. The blood pummels my ears, makes them burn.

'Hello, Alice,' comes my reply. I picture her voice bouncing like a ball along shady time tunnels. I reach her, at the very end of the last tunnel, standing in a blast of brilliant sunshine. She is in the flat on The Peak of course. Where else? Her body rigid, her eyes trained on the barred windows, stripes of light and shadow falling across her face. From the other end of the line there comes a trembling exhalation, a cross between a sigh and a few beats of laughter loosely strung together. But if she is surprised that I know instantly who it is at the other end of the line, she never says so.

'I'm in London, Harry. I want to see you.' Another shuddering intake of breath. 'I want to see all of you.'

Staring down at the keyboard I spot a minuscule insect cresting the summit of the Home key. I wince, stroke the key with a fingertip, and crush it. It is so tiny that it barely leaves a smear. We falter on, Alice and I, slowly approaching that inescapable point where our two lifelines will converge. I am ashamed to say that if I could plot an abrupt change of direction, I would, in a heartbeat. I do not want to see Alice. I do not want this ghost from the past stalking me in the present, dragging unwelcome baggage from the island behind her. Neither, I feel positive, will Nicola, or for that matter Jillian. I skip around my missing sister's increasingly direct questions about our father. How do I tell this Rip Van Winkle that her adored father is dead, that whatever plans she has entertained of an emotional reunion this side of the grave are impossible.

Neatly, and, as our conversation tumbles on, not so neatly, I side-step my role of messenger. We siblings will tell her together, I decide grimly. The meeting is arranged for the following Saturday. I ring off.

'Everything alright?' sings out Carmen.

'Oh yes, absolutely fine,' I return brightly. What is the point in breaking with the Safford family's lifetime tradition now?

The subsequent calls, first to Nicola, and lastly, because I cannot face it, much, much later on to Jillian, have echoes of that earlier, discarnate communication with my long-lost sister. We progress halt-ingly. Alice is back. Not for prodigal Alice do we wait with open arms, ready to kill the fatted calf, to celebrate her return with joy unbounded. Not for her will we cry 'our sister was dead, but now she is alive! Alice was lost, but now she is found. Hallelujah!' At first, the news renders both Nicola and then Jillian incapable of speech. Gradually, suspicions, dark and a long while brooding, help them regain their composure. Soon they are able to form coherent sentences. What on earth does Alice want after all these years? There's no money left, if that's what she's after. And if it's not the money, it must be something else, that none of us has thought of. Besides, what good can possibly come of this repatriation? Finally, grudgingly, both Nicola and Jillian come to the same conclusion I have, we are *destined* to see Alice. We might as well get the pantomime over with.

The allotted day, that might have been set for world destruction, considering the growing dismay I experience as it approaches, dawns fair. The time scheduled for Alice's advent is 3pm. Both Nicola and Jillian arrive shortly after half past two. We three take up poses in the sitting room, like actors positioning themselves on stage just before curtain up. It is my guess too that each of us is suffering the equivalent of first night nerves. Nicola and Jillian each occupy one of the two armchairs. I sit uneasily between them, in a dining chair that I carried in earlier for the purpose. The sofa we leave conspicu-ously empty. If any of us sits there, we might rub shoulders with our revenant sister. We might even have to concede that she is real, flesh and blood, merely human.

The clock on the mantelpiece ticks loudly, as clocks will when you give them your undivided attention. Upstairs, Edgar's football thumps periodically on his bedroom floor and, in consequence, on the sitting room ceiling. Grey leaf-shadows, thrown by a young golden ash rooted in our front lawn, flutter on the cream walls. Striations of moss-green grass, gritty grey tarmac, rosy brickwork, tiled roofs, and bluebell skies, ribbon the windowpanes.

'What time did you say she'd be here?' asks Nicola, her tone deliberately careless. As ever, her clothes, a full midi skirt in oyster-grey, French navy blouse, brown leather ankle boots, finished off with silk twill scarf, look impeccable.

'3pm. She said she'd be here at 3pm,' I reply, a finger easing my shirt collar. It feels uncomfortably tight, pinching my neck. I would like to take off my tie, polyester, a harlequin design that I'm rather fond of. But somehow it seems essential that I be properly dressed for Alice's manifestation. This thought arrives with an astute partner. There is no prescribed style, formal or otherwise, for a tryst with a sister who has been missing for thirty years.

At the sound of a car Nicola turns expectantly to the window. I notice, not for the first time, that her hands look very red and sore. Eczema? Hadn't Mother said that Father had terrible eczema once? Yes, that's right, when we were young, that it ended his career in photography prematurely. I ponder on whether perhaps it is a hereditary condition. She sees me scrutinising her hands, and slips them self-consciously into her bell sleeves. Jillian gives an enormous sigh and makes much of looking at her watch, an unnecessary gesture with the clock directly in front of her.

'It's . . . it's a quarter to three,' she says. She has a frog in her throat. She clears it and tries again. 'It's a quarter to three,' she repeats too loudly.

'Mm,' I affirm, with an upward lift of my chin.

Jillian plucks at her neck absently. It looks slack, not quite a turkey's but on its way. We are all getting older I'm afraid. And yet, the Alice

I envision leaping out at us from the past is a teenager, hooking her dark hair behind her ears, her voice high, her eyes clear and large. Above us the football thumps. I gaze up and shake my head, grinning indulgently.

'Boys eh?' I comment with a breathy laugh.

'Hmm . . . not having a son I wouldn't know,' manages Nicola with a brief smile.

'Actually Amos is very good,' Jillian says sanctimoniously.

'Lucky you,' I rejoin with a disbelieving smile, thinking that young Amos is anything but. I am sweating under my suit jacket and would dearly like to strip it off. Jillian, I observe, is underdressed for the occasion, slouching in some sort of sloppy, cotton-jersey affair, yellow and blue dots, a bit like pyjamas. Really, she might have made a small effort. I feel irritated as my eyes run over my eldest sister with distaste. Her hair looks greasy and untidy. In yet another reincarnation it is bluish black. Far from making her look younger, the stark funereal shade against her putty complexion puts years on. No make-up. Trainers. It is as if she intends our mythical sibling to see how unimportant this meeting is to her.

We all jump when Carmen pops her head round the door. She has changed into her best taffeta dress reserved for special occasions. The fitted bodice and full skirt, patterned in blue and green polka dots, looks well on her slender frame. Her nut-brown frizzy hair is caught up in a yellow velvet bow, and she has applied lipstick. I detect a waft of her subtle perfume too, and think ruefully that she has gone to more trouble for Alice, her sister-in-law, than her real sister has.

'No signs of Alice, the guest of honour, yet?' she inquires. Our heads all rise in unison at that, hearing the name spoken out loud.

'Not yet,' I say jovially. Jillian scowls thunderously. Nicola gives a pained sigh.

Carmen hovers for a moment clutching the side of the sitting-room door. 'Right-oh. I'll get on with preparing tea, then,' she announces gaily. She disappears and is back an instant later. 'You know, I've never met Alice. She was long gone by the time we got together, isn't that right, Harry?' My wife's voice climbs to a high-pitched trill when she is excited, as she is now. I give a fleeting smile and nod. Carmen's hazel eyes sparkle in anticipation. She searches our expressionless faces for an answering effervescence. Finding none she gives a small shrug. 'I expect you'll have lots to talk about,' she declares, her head nodding as if persuading us.

I am not so sure. My stomach rumbles noisily. I smile apologetically at my wife and at my sisters. Carmen takes this as her cue to hurry off to the kitchen. Once she has gone Jillian volunteers the time again, and again, some five minutes later. Talk is desultory. Schools. Holidays. Mother. Of Alice, the reason for this gathering, nothing is said. At quarter past three the front doorbell rings. We all leap up like jack-in-the-boxes, as if someone has simultaneously jabbed pins in our posteriors. We pile out of the sitting room and into the hall. It turns out to be one of Tiffany's friends from the Close, Sonia, a skeletal girl with delicate features, a nose-stud and a white streak in her shoulder-length dark hair.

'Is Tiffany in?' she demands in a bored monotone, as she casts mint-green eyes over us in mild surprise, Nicola to my right, Jillian to my left. Behind us, Carmen cranes forward interestedly. Even Edgar, clutching his football, stoops and peers down from the top of the stairs, his eyes concealed in a mop of tousled brown hair.

'Tiffany's gone swimming,' I furnish absently, stepping forwards and dodging Sonia, determined to discover where Alice is hiding.

'Oh okay,' mutters Sonia, viewing us all with puzzlement, as if doubting she has called at the correct address.

A young girl pedals past on a pink bike ringing her bicycle bell enthusiastically. Across the road Nancy Harben gives a neighbourly wave as she wrestles her green recycling bin back up her drive. A Siamese cat eyes us lethargically from her warm roost on a sunbathed doorstep. But of Alice there is neither sight nor sound. I am about to scuttle back inside and close the door on Sonia, when I hear the hum of an approaching car. We all do. We strain our ears to pick up every nuance of this vehicle's engine, as impressed as if it is a Tardis transporting Alice into the present.

'This is her now,' I tell my sisters on an amazed rising inflexion. Our eyes root on the entrance road to the cul-de-sac. Tiffany, made curious by my heraldic announcement, pirouettes in her marmalade miniskirt. She executes the move with praiseworthy alacrity considering her clumpy black boots, and follows our gaze. As the Tesco's delivery van rounds the bend, our shared sigh ascends and swells like a dense cumulus. Once again we take up our opening positions in the sitting room, still awaiting curtain-up. By half past three however the cracks are definitely beginning to appear.

'Where *is* she?' snaps Nicola, fiddling irritably with the fringe of her scarf. She throws herself about in her chair as if she is on a roller-coaster ride at the fair.

'I'm sure she'll be along shortly,' I soothe. I am on my feet and standing at one of the windows, spider's-leg fingers lacing and unlacing busily. Uncomfortably, I survey the short stretch of road, visible from my sitting room.

'For Christ's sake, this is typical of her!' cries Jillian, out of her chair and pacing before the mantelpiece.

Considering we have not seen Alice for thirty years, my feeling is that none of us can say with any real confidence what our sister's typical modus operandi is.

'Are you sure she said three o'clock?' checks Nicola, hair mussed after her ride, feet tapping a military tattoo on the carpet.

'Yes,' I say uncertainly. In fact, suddenly I am not sure of anything. I rub the ball of my palms over my temples. A wave of tiredness sluices over me. I did not sleep well the previous night, and made several forays into the kitchen to sustain me. The result, acid indigestion, only served to prolong my wakefulness.

'Perhaps you should have put her off, Harry,' Jillian ventures critically.

Suddenly I feel ridiculous, sitting starch-stiff in a work suit on a warm Saturday afternoon in September, waiting for my vaporous sister.

'Good Lord, Jillian, what do you expect?' I fire, rounding on her. The grey shadow leaves quiver on the wall in a sudden breath of wind. Jillian raises her eyes to heaven, a gesture that further inflames my temper and sends it crackling into life. 'What would you have done then, eh? Told her to piss off for another thirty years?' I growl.

Jillian folds her arms, hands tucked protectively into her armpits. 'That might not have been a bad idea,' she admonishes quietly, her head wagging.

I march over to my chair and throw myself into it. It is reproduction Regency, and it creaks in protest. I remind myself that I am large and it is small, and must be treated more respectfully if I don't want it to buckle under me at a climactic moment. I determine to corral my emotion into speech alone, and sit forward charily. 'Brilliant, just brilliant, Jillian!' I hiss. 'Banish Alice. Tell her never to contact us again. That would solve everything, wouldn't it?'

'You never know till you try,' counters Jillian, with a stubborn thrust of her bottom lip. Somewhere far off an ice-cream van jingles irreverently.

'This isn't getting us anywhere,' Nicola breaks in. 'Harry's right. If he tried to put Alice off, she'd only have come back again at a later date. We need to deal with this now.'

The football thumps several times above us, followed by Carmen's voice distantly berating our son. His truculent reply is just discernible too.

'Well, maybe I don't want to see her. Isn't that my right?' Jillian is shouting. Her cheeks glow red, and her slate-blue eyes contract into pinpricks behind their lenses. 'She walked out on us without a moment's thought, didn't she?' She flounces towards the door blinking back tears. 'Haven't I got the right to walk out on Alice?' she yells flinging the door wide. And there, with the comic timing of a slick farce, is Alice!

'Look who I found wandering around the Close, all lost and forlorn,' Carmen twitters in a motherly tone. She beams like a shepherdess who has found her missing lamb and ushers Alice forwards. Our sometime sister steps timidly into the room. She is nearly invisible, camouflaged by the enormous bouquet of flowers she carries. The arrangement of tropical orange, red and sulphur-yellow flowers is so unnecessarily extravagant that it adds to the growing atmosphere of burlesque. And there is wine as well, and chocolates. Alice has all eventualities covered. Nicola and I are upstanding for our sister. Jillian, a few feet from the door, is riveted to the spot as if carved from stone.

'Alice. How . . . nice. How . . . nice to . . . to see you,' I stutter, crossing to where the bouquet sways. She pushes the gifts towards me, Alice, trying to purchase approval. Taking them, I feel a stab of remorse, remorse for the lost years that will never be recovered. 'For us? . . . how . . . nice, Alice. Wine and chocolates too. Aren't we spoilt?' A truism if ever I uttered one. Carmen dashes forwards and takes the presents from me.

'She was wandering about the Close looking abandoned. So fortunate I spied her from the hall window. I said to myself, I'll bet that's sister Alice, looking for us. Anyway, I'll go and put these in water and get the tea.'

In the moments that follow, while we surreptitiously study Alice, I speedily amend the mental picture I have formed of her over the years. Alice had taken on in my mind the proportions of some vengeful virago, malice bristling in every fibre of her being, bent on destruction. But the middle-aged woman who stands before us is petite, unexceptional, ordinary even. Her hair, though still tucked behind her ears, is cut into a bob, faded to a mousy brown. Her clothes are classic cuts in neutral shades. Her features are small and neat, the lines that have formed around her eyes, her mouth, that crease her brow, are not the grooves of a tempestuous nature, but the tracery of stoicism and quiet fortitude. I gesture Alice to the settee. Nicola and I retake our chairs. Briefly I lock eyes with Jillian, while she battles with the urge to flee this confrontation. At length, defeated, she too sits. And the clock ticks on.

'I'm . . . sorry . . . sorry I'm late,' opens Alice breathlessly, perched on the edge of the settee, as if frightened she might sully the covers. 'I got . . . lost.'

This last has me wrestling down the urge to guffaw with helpless laughter. Just a bit, comes my unspoken slightly hysterical rejoinder.

I ponder the probability of double meanings presenting themselves for every sentence spoken on this momentous afternoon, and hope I can keep a straight face.

'Well . . . never mind. You're . . . you're here now,' I console out loud.

What follows is like wading through wallpaper paste. Just what do you say to a sister you haven't seen for thirty years, a sister who you thought might very well be dead, buried, a sister whose grave you have imagined on some lonely windswept cliff top more than once? What do you say to a sister who has come back to life, and not just any life but yours? So, how have you been keeping, Alice? It's incredible, thirty years and you haven't aged a bit. Tell us Alice, we'd love to know, your vanishing trick, how exactly does it work?

'So . . . where . . . have you been living, Alice?' Nicola voices courageously. However, her eyes are averted, fixed on the outspread fingers of her hands laid on the armrests of her chair. She looks fascinated, as if seeing them for the first time. Jillian is sitting very still, containing herself. Probably for the best, I muse wryly.

'I've been living in France. Paris actually,' Alice says.

'Oh really?' responds Nicola as if she doesn't quite believe her.

'Yes. It's a beautiful city. The Eiffel Tower lit at night. The Seine. Wonderful art galleries too.' For a few minutes she describes Paris as if she is a travel agent selling a holiday.

As I listen, I imagine Alice buying her bread at a patisserie, Alice at the Louvre drinking in the enigmatic beauty of the Mona Lisa, Alice at the Moulin Rouge, staring wide-eyed at a froth of colourful petticoats, listening to the yips of the dancers with unconcealed delight. Alice looking up at a silvery moon, wondering . . . wondering if her father, across the English Channel, is stargazing too. I have visualised hundreds of Alices over the years. Alice on a sheep farm in Wales, her adoring sheepdog, a Bear double, prancing by her side. Alice in the North, pinched with cold, trudging down a snowy pavement leaving a trail of drab-grey footprints in her wake. Alice in Ireland, perched on a slab of rock on the Giant's Causeway, waiting for her fisherman husband to chug home. In my mind I have journeyed to locations the world over, and seen Alice in every imaginable setting and costume. And yet, the expression in her limpid eyes as she looks back at me is unchanged, one of all-pervading sadness.

'What did you do there . . . in France . . . in Paris?' Jillian asks as Alice's tour of the city comes to an end.

'I worked . . . um . . . in a restaurant.' Alice circles her shoulders waiting for our reaction.

'Sounds excellent,' I say, genuinely impressed.

'You were cooking?' asks Nicola in surprise, probably recalling Alice's poor appetite.

'Waiting tables?' Jillian speaks over her sister.

Alice, one hand on her knee, starts pleating the hem of her midnight-blue skirt.

'Well, both really. Cooking and waiting tables. Actually more chopping vegetables than cooking. I sort of worked my way up.'

'Ah?' Nicola sits forward interestedly.

'Up where?' Jillian says deadpan.

Alice talks of her mentor, Pierre Ramirez, the restaurant owner, how he trained her on the job and promoted her when he felt she was ready. I look into her anxious face and remember. Alice, I remember when I was sick, had a fever. I must have been very young, five, or perhaps six. Not much dialogue to the footage, just you dressed in a white apron. You wore a matching white scarf with a red cross painted on it, knotted at the back of your neck, under your hair. I lay in a rattan cot, far too small for me, limbs sticking out rebelliously, you tidying them back in, undeterred in your ministering.

'I am Nurse Alice,' you piped up authoritatively. 'I am going to make you better, Harry.' And you smoothed my hot forehead with a tiny cool hand, your dreamy brown eyes fixing mine. You mixed medicine on a trolley. You were a stork, one bare foot stroking the calf of the leg you stood on, concentrating on your apothecary's duties. In a small yellow bowl you stirred orange juice and sugar and jam painstakingly with a metal spoon. I heard it scrape and chink against the china. Then you held it to my lips while I sipped it. It was sticky and sweet and I can still taste it on my tongue now.

'So in the end you were the manager?' rejoins Jillian incredulously, as Alice finishes explaining how she worked her way up in the restaurant.

'Well done,' Nicola comments, her eyebrows raised, her hands miming applause.

'It wasn't quick. It took ages, years. I left for a bit and went back again.' Alice's tone is one of apology. 'There was so much to learn. I made so many mistakes.'

'Mm.' Jillian shoots me a meaningful look.

'Still, not bad going,' Nicola remarks with a trace of envy.

Alice has stopped pleating her skirt, and now fiddles with the hair behind her ears. 'I became close friends with the owner.' She coughs and clears her throat. 'When he died he left it to me.'

'What?' Nicola's ears prick up. 'The restaurant? The entire restaurant?'

'Mm, yes.' Alice nibbles on a nail.

'What about his own family?' I ask, picturing a tribe of irate Parisians shaking their fists at Alice.

'He didn't have any. Over the years we became close friends,' Alice tells us defensively, as if responding in court to prosecuting counsel.

'What kind of close friends?' Jillian says and there is a slanderous undercurrent in her voice.

'Oh not in that way. He was like . . . like . . . well a bit like a father to me,' Alice falters. 'Losing him was awful,' she adds tremulously under her breath. None of us is inclined to break the silence that follows this statement. It is Nicola who finally tackles it.

'Well, well, he must have thought a great deal of you, Alice.' Her tone implies that this is nothing short of miraculous. Alice hangs her head. Another long hiatus follows. Then Alice questions each of us in turn about how we have filled in the missing years, leaving Jillian to last. I outline my job selling life-insurance, talk about Carmen, the children. Nicola mentions she is divorced, has moved fairly recently to East Grinstead, and that her daughter Zandra is hoping to attend

344

art college. We sound a bit like one of those trailers for American TV programmes. Previously on the Saffords . . . Only our previously does not flow in quite the same way. We jounce and bump along like an old cart on a rutted track.

Alice turns to Jillian.

'What about you, Jillian?' she inquires diffidently.

Jillian shrugs. 'I'm married. Happily,' she adds emphatically. 'We're living in Hastings. We have a son, Amos, and he's—' She breaks off to say what is really on her mind. 'You could at least have rung to let our parents know you were safe. All you would have had to do was pick up the phone.'

Alice's head swings up and she flinches, as if someone has spooked her.

'I did write. I sent the letters to the flat on The Peak. Three of them.' We all exchange looks of disbelief at this. 'Well, perhaps they never arrived. I rang Uncle Albert as well,' she offers lamely. She takes in our accusatory stares. 'I did,' she adds softly. She rubs the side of her forehead, her fingertip massaging it with a circular motion, and wets her lips. 'I . . . I . . . it never seemed . . . it was just the wrong—' She limps to a painful stop. A television can be heard upstairs, excited dialogue followed by canned laughter.

'So . . . are you married?' asks Nicola.

And while Alice talks of a man called Carl and a marriage that I know will have been doomed, I am back on the first boat we owned, *White Jade*. We are anchored in a peaceful bay. Mother is reading the paper in the stern, sipping a glass of wine. Father is fishing close by. And we, Alice, sister and brother, are splashing in the cold, clear sea. We are watching the honeycomb light waver and fracture over our pale white bodies, making them elastic and fluid. Our vision is hazy with salt smart, the edges of our island life sanded smooth. We are owls blinking slowly at each other in tacit understanding. This idle space should be filled with our game, we agree. As the boat lifts and strains at its anchor mooring, we slide in turn behind the wooden stepladder. We grasp the sides of a framed square, our makeshift television screen. The sea slaps against

345

the curved hull, and sloshes back into us. But we refuse to be thwarted.

We parrot advertising jingles, act out adverts, snatches of our favourite programmes. You giggle, sea spray dribbling from the corners of your mouth and I desperately try to keep a straight face, choking on a mouthful of salty water as I deliver a sloppy line.

'It didn't work out, the marriage,' Alice finishes wanly in the 'now', where there is no room for game-playing.

'Do you have any children?' Jillian asks.

And when Alice says no, inexplicably Jillian erupts in staccato questions. 'Why not? Didn't you want any? Too much responsibility? Too expensive?' Alice fidgets, coils a strand of hair tightly around a finger, uncoils it, starts again with the next finger. She mumbles about the time not being right, her career in the restaurant, other pressing commitments.

Do you recall how we played 'Kick the Can' on the long, hot summer evenings, Alice? How the can would be placed with precision between the two rows of garages, over the rusty manhole-cover, the golden evening rays bouncing off it in jags of champagne light. I would squeeze behind the hedge and garage walls, my heart thudding madly, my face crimson and slick with sweat, gagging back hiccups of laughter. Brushstrokes of filigree cloud would tarnish as they slipped away into the night. The wind would sigh with contentment. Taking a deep breath, charged with adrenalin, at last I would dare to peep round the edge of the wall. For a second our eyes would meet, then I would break cover. We two would streak towards the can as if our lives depended on reaching it first, me to kick it, you to keep it upright at all costs. You nearly always outpaced me, with my big belly hampering me. Then your foot would slam down on the tin lid.

'One, two, three, Harry,' you would yell in exultation, 'you're out!' I would grind to a stop, my shoulders slumped in defeat. Then seconds later I would recover, and hands in pockets, swagger off, your victory cry echoing in my ears. 'One, two, three, Harry, you're out!'

And it was okay because it was my sister who'd beaten me, it was Alice. No shame in that. Pride, that's what I felt as I joined the others, swinging my legs on the low wall of defeat, under the rippling green fingers that fringed the palms.

'How is Father?' Alice breaks into my reminiscing.

Eyes slide guiltily away from her. The stillness expands. There is no means of softening this news. You cannot say, well, Alice, you must be brave, Father is a little dead right now. Alice traces our conspiratorial exchanges, one to another. She ages in a second, her expression settling into stark lines of terror. Nicola coughs and fingers the pendant at her neck. It is a Chinese character fashioned in gold, Fu, symbolising good luck. It has an ironic glint to it. I close and reopen my eyes. I will tell her I decide, but Jillian is already talking.

'I'm sorry, Alice, but he's dead,' she tells her baldly. Alice's head is on one side, her brow scrunched, as if she is trying to decipher the meaning of Jillian's words. Her hands saw at the air, seeking something tangible in it. 'Actually, Alice, now I come—'

'Jillian!' Nicola interrupts on a warning note.

'What?' Jillian speaks so sharply that her teeth clash. 'I'm just telling her the truth. Father's dead. It's a shame that Alice is too late. I'm sorry for it.' But you can tell she is not. Her voice has just the hint of jubilation in it. 'Surely she must have considered the possibility this might happen?' she continues. 'You've been out of our lives for thirty years, Alice, not a long weekend,' she debates reasonably. Alice nods dumbly and with a great effort draws herself up. Then I am up too, explaining that it was a heart-attack, quick, painless. Nicola interjects that she was there, with him, that he didn't suffer. I feel I should hold this chimerical Alice, wrap my arms around her trembling shoulders. I take a step closer but I am embarrassed. She feels like a stranger, not my sister. She is whey-faced and for a moment I think she might faint. An old-fashioned word that conjures up ladies in Empire dresses, backs of hands touching their flushed brows, comes to mind. Swoon. Alice swoons.

'Nooo!' It is like a sigh, like air leaking out of a slow puncture in a lilo. I hurry to prop her up, Nicola rushing to assist me. Awkwardly, one side apiece, we hold up this sibling wraith.

'Honestly, what did she expect!' mutters Jillian, contemptuous of the attention Alice is garnering. Nicola casts her a withering look.

Jillian shrugs, wearing her lack of repentance ostentatiously. 'It's not my fault, the way this has worked out,' she offers in her defence.

'When?' Alice asks, her lips barely moving, her voice no more than a thread.

'He died about three years ago, Alice,' fills in Nicola. We lower Alice back into her seat and retake our own.

'I'm too late,' she says, but not to us, to herself.

'Well, you could go and see his grave instead,' Jillian says trenchantly. I shall be generous, and say that Jillian did not deliver this with cruel intent. But all the same Alice shrinks back on the settee. Where, I think, is Carmen with the tea and that fruitcake I saw her baking yesterday?

'I looked after him. So you needn't worry. I didn't desert him. I looked after them both,' Jillian bugles into the sudden quiet.

'But Mother's alive?' Alice says, only just managing to keep despair at bay.

'Oh yes,' I rejoin. 'She's still alive and kicking.' The chord of jollity I strike is inappropriately redolent of Santa Claus, after he's washed down his mince pies with one too many sherries. Rapidly, I adjust my pitch to one of sympathy, explaining about the care home we found, how pleasant it is, how well Mother has settled in.

'I'd like to visit,' says Alice, the way in a fairy story you might say, I wish it with all my heart. 'If it's alright with you,' she adds as an apprehensive afterthought.

Jillian pouts, but, before she can offer up her views on the request, Nicola is speaking.

'I don't see why not. I'm sure she'd love to see you and—' She breaks off, nettled to see the start of a ladder on her stockings. She picks at it and frowns, then begins afresh. 'Mother comes and goes, Alice. You mustn't be surprised. Let's just hope it's one of her lucid moments, eh?'

'It must have been nice to devote all your time to your career,' is Jillian's next barbed observation. 'I'd like to have had a career, Alice. But circumstances prevented it.'

Before Alice has time to respond, Nicola jumps in to say how felicitous our discovery of Greenwood Lodge was. She describes the attractive country setting and how well Mother has settled into the routine. But Alice's blank eyes show that she is not listening. While she is talking Carmen brings in the tea, together with her magnificent cake. After depositing the tray she scampers away, leaving us to catch up she says. For the next quarter of an hour, thankfully, we are all diverted, pouring, sipping and eating, especially me. And there are paste sandwiches too, with lashings of butter, just the way I like them, piled up on a plate, a sprig of parsley on the top. Carmen has made plenty for everyone so I quell my rising panic, though oddly my siblings seem reluctant to tuck in.

As we sit, the Safford children at their tea, I feel the hand of time whisking us back through the years, until we are there, ranged about the dining-room table in the flat on The Peak. Father is carving, and bloody juices coat the gleaming silver knife and dribble down the sharp blade. Mother is clasping her wine glass. The sunlight catching on the crystal planes creates a jewelled tessellation bewitching us all. Alice is chirpy, eager to please. Nicola's calculating eyes flit about, as she adds, divides, multiplies and subtracts the sum of all our misery, turning it to her advantage. Jillian sees her father's striking blue eyes soften as they sweep over her little sister. She glares at Alice. Her own eyes, flint-cold, narrow in hatred. And I concentrate every molecule I have on the food in front of me, on shovelling forkful after forkful into my mouth. Chew, chew and swallow, chew and swallow, barely time to breathe. But back then I had faith, unshakeable faith, that there would come a day eventually when the hole would be plugged.

The fuzzy television voice filtering down from upstairs is suddenly choked. An eerie hush descends. I feel a cold draught from somewhere slither under my collar. My mouth stops working on my bolus of cake crumbs. We all stare aghast as the teapot, the milk jug, the sugar bowl, the cake stand, and the plate of sandwiches, Royal Albert China all, a gift from Carmen's parents, start to vibrate. What I notice first are the ripples on the lily-white milk pond. This is followed by the rapid tinkle of the lid quaking in the teapot's grip. The sugar bowl adjacent to it, repeatedly nudges its hot belly. The cake stand judders. The plate starts to slide on the glass-topped coffee table, just millimetres, but its laboured progress, nevertheless, can be clearly tracked. The empty plastic tray with its design of orange and yellow marigolds, leaning against the side of the coffee table where I set it, topples over onto the carpet.

I am on my feet, wheeling round, my eyes raking the room. 'Stay calm everyone, I'm sure it's nothing.'

'God Almighty, what's happening?' Nicola exclaims, rising from her chair.

'Harry, do you think it's an earthquake?' This last is Jillian, also standing now, clutching her cup of tea in one hand, head raised, scanning the ceiling worriedly. Only Alice does not move, I notice. Her expression is one of tragic resignation.

'No, no, surely not an earthquake. Not here,' I mumble.

If we were sitting on the runway at Heathrow airport as a jumbo jet roared past, its wingtip only feet away, the phenomenon would have had a simple scientific explanation. But we are not at Heathrow airport, we are at tea in the sitting room of No. 14 Victoria Close.

The large flat-screen television mounted on the wall to one side of the fireplace suddenly swings out on its supporting arms and bursts into life. A whirlpool of coloured pixels drains into a central black unblinking eye, accompanied by a painfully discordant din. Scraps of words, cries, exclamations, moans, a burst of Chinese opera, growls, wailing, chattering, announcements, the British National Anthem, the chirruping of a bird, a terrified scream, the clatter of Cantonese, gunshots, an explosion, a whimper, all slur into each other. The overhead Savoy pendant lamp starts swinging gently, then blinks on. Light glows through the misted glass shade, and almost immediately starts to flicker and crackle. As if in answer, the CD player's two speakers boom into life, thundering out music.

Nicola's hands are clasped, resting protectively over her hunched head. Jillian is pointing at Alice. 'She's doing this. Can't you see, Alice is doing this.'

Alice holds her arms out and shakes her head as if to prove she has nothing hidden up her sleeves. 'No. No. It's not me.'

'*I Am The Walrus*,' I mouth, 'The Beatles.' I recall, amid the furore, that I had listened to the album the previous night. 'I must have left it switched on.' Then all our heads snap up. The ceiling appears to be trembling. A small cloud of plaster dust puffs out from the light fitting.

'Christ!' gasps Nicola just as the curtains, sprays of lilac on a magnolia background, free somehow of their tiebacks, draw together. Then as we watch, grotesquely mesmerised, they swish open, and yet again they close, an encore in a puppet theatre.

Slowly Alice rises to her feet, her eyes darting about the room. 'Stop it! Stop it now!' She twists her body and wriggles her shoulders as if wrenching herself out of someone's grip. We all duck as the overhead lightbulb explodes, the blackened splinters of glass pinging against the interior of its shade. In reply, the television gives a blinding flash, then dies. With a final agonised groan, The Walrus sinks in an ocean of white noise, before being swallowed completely. A whine from somewhere rapidly descends several scales to a deep guttural roar, as the curtains inch back letting in blocks of afternoon sunlight.

'Oh my God!' exclaims Jillian in a hushed tone. Glancing around I see the armchair she was sitting in leaning over tipsily, beyond the point of return, then thwacking heavily on its side. Jillian jumps, letting go the teacup she is holding. Warm liquid cascades all down the front of the strange blue and yellow sweatshirt she is wearing. The cup and saucer smash into pieces on the glass top of the coffee table. Jillian screams. She fixes Alice one last time, before she flees, sobbing. We hear her trainers squeaking as she runs across the hallway's wooden floor. The front door slams.

'I didn't do it,' mumbles Alice, first to Nicola and then to me. A car engine is gunned, fires, and tyres squeal in the drive as it speeds off.

Carmen appears looking stunned, the jaunty yellow ribbon trailing across her face, hair awry. Eyes bulging, she surveys the devastation in our lounge. 'What's . . . what's happened?' she stammers, eyes lifted to the brown wisp of smoke snaking out from the exploded ceiling light.

'It was an accident. We'll soon put it to rights,' I assure her, trying to arrange my face into a relaxed smile and failing miserably. My brow has been pinched into a deep frown for so long now that it aches.

'Don't worry, Carmen. It's only one cup and you can always get replacements,' Nicola consoles her sister-in-law, dropping to her knees. She starts to scoop up fragments of Royal Albert china from the table and the carpet. In the background, Alice is still protesting her innocence. Carmen takes in the spilt tea soaking into the carpet pile and without a word dashes off. I am tracing with a forefinger the hairline crack I have spotted on the coffee table, when she reappears with a basin of soapy water and a sponge. She kneels and scrubs frantically at the honey tea-puddle on the cream Axminster. Alice leans over Carmen stammering how sorry she is, that she will pay for any damage.

'Do let me help you clear up?' she begs my wife's bobbing head.

'Good heavens no, you're a guest!' Carmen tells her, rocking back on her heels, closing with finality on an unmistakably manic note. She waves her away with a flapping hand. I am using a napkin to mop up the splashes of tea on the tabletop. Nicola rises and places the broken china carefully on the mantelpiece. Then she turns to examine a trail of drops that have plopped like fat pebbles between coffee table and the overturned armchair. She swivels and stares at Alice. Our sister has drifted apart from us, her skin leached to a whitewash. A sense of purpose settles on Nicola's face as she looks at Alice hovering by the open door.

'I'll give you the address and number of Mother's care home,' she says, finding her bag by her armchair. She fumbles in it and produces pen and paper. She scribbles something down. 'And the church, I've written down the address of the church where Father . . . where you can visit Father.' She hesitates for a moment. 'I'll give you my mobile too. And I'll speak to Mrs Bowker, the manager at Greenwood Lodge, tell her you're coming.' She scrawls her mobile number down too. I peer over her shoulder as she does this. She looks up and locks eyes with Alice. 'Alright Alice?'

'Yes, that's fine, Nicola,' Alice mumbles awkwardly. There is a pause of a few seconds.

'Anything else, Alice?' My voice is more abrupt than I intend it to be.

'No, no . . . no nothing else,' Alice falters, one hand circling the wrist of the other, rubbing it as if to ease a pain. Another pause. Carmen looks up. Her cheeks are very pink, and there is a blot of tea together with a dusting of cream carpet fibres on the silk skirt of her dress.

'Then perhaps you should—' I begin but Alice interrupts.

'I'd better get going, Harry. Thank you so much for the lovely tea, Carmen.'

Carmen leaps up, sponge in hand. 'Do come and visit us again,' she says, but she makes no move towards her guest.

'Mm . . . that would be lovely,' says Alice quietly, then sighs desolately.

In tandem, rather I think in the style of a Laurel and Hardy silent movie, Nicola and I cross to Alice. Inexplicably, the clock on the mantelpiece begins to chime. It is 5:15pm. We march Alice to the front door. Nicola hands over the slip of paper. Alice nods. She looks like a famous actress who has just inadvertently revealed a shameful and unforgivable secret about herself on national television.

'Goodbye Alice,' we mutter, speaking in unison. We do not make another date. For the last time I stare into Alice's melancholic eyes. She gives a slight lift of her head, turns and walks sedately to her car. She reaches it just as the thirteenth chime rings out. As the reverberations fade, I see Alice as before, the termagant whose powers of destruction are apocalyptic. I close my front door on her before the engine even starts up.

'Harry, what happened in there? You saw it. Heard it. So did Jillian. We all did.' Nicola stands in the hallway, eyes wide with fear, her dry red hands fluttering about her, sketching abstract shapes in the air. She lowers her voice to a fierce whisper. 'There is something . . . something about Alice. It's Alice. Harry there . . . is

353

something . . . something . . . ' she winds down like a clockwork toy and grinds to a halt with a gasp.

'I know, Nicola, I know,' is my rejoinder. Then I shake my head and put a finger to my lips, and Nicola nods in tacit understanding.

Now they're all gone, I'm feeling a wee bit peckish, hazarding a guess at the exact amount of paste sandwiches left over, and whether I'll be able to cram them all in. I expect I'll find an empty corner.

Ghost – 2006

We hare down country lanes in the hire car, the dog complaining that he feels sick, the monkey sticking its deflated head out of the window and squealing dementedly as the wind rushes at its puckered, effulgent features. The budgie, a scintillating flash of butter yellow and bright green over our heads, supplies us with an air escort. Craning my ghostly neck around the raving monkey, I glance up, wince at the brilliant sun, then gaze into the blue mantle of sky that encompasses it. It is marbled with shifting translucent pearly wisps as transient as sea foam.

We park by a sheltered wooden gate and bundle out before a church built of mottled stones, in browns and greys and beiges, with a slate roof. It has high, arched, stained-glass windows, and a steeple that sits like a witch's hat over a bell-tower, a metal cross perched right at its pinnacle. And there is a clock on the side of the tower, with golden hands that glide slowly round its blue face. When we arrive people are filtering into the church. We steal past the great wooden doors, and down a verdant slope to a graveyard. Behind us we hear muttered prayers and muffled singing. We pass a huge tree, a wooden seat encircling its trunk. We walk through a sea of gravestones daubed in milky-green, mustard-yellow, rust-brown and ivory-white lichens. Some stand sentry, dominoes, bolt upright, marking the life-spans of unflagging spirits, others lean wearily towards the earth, worn down by wind and weather, and still more are cracked and crumbling, the names inscribed on them long since rubbed away.

But we pass on, to a distant stretch of paler green, set aside for those still smarting from the wound of death, their names scalded into marble and stone with fresh tears. We walk slowly down one row and up another. Right at the end of this we find a black marble tombstone with gold lettering upon it. There is an urn squatting on it, with large red and white plastic roses poked into its metal grid.

Alice reads:

In Memory

of

RALPH SAFFORD

1927 to 2003

Loving husband to Myrtle

Devoted father of Jillian, Nicola and Harry

Alice stands back and rereads the epitaph. For once, the dog, the monkey and the budgie seem subdued. A blackbird, alighting on a tree close by, bursts into song. As the last notes melt away, it cocks its gleaming head, its yellow eyes swivelling curiously at us. Leaves rustle in the breeze. Beyond the boundary of the churchyard, I follow a mass of a dark cloud slipping silently over a field of waving golden grasses.

'My name is not there,' says Alice, her voice small and flat.

She is holding a dainty spray of daisies tied with white ribbon. She loosens the ribbon, picks the plastic roses from the urn one by one, casts them aside, and replaces them with the fragile flowers. I linger respectfully a few yards down the path, to give my host some privacy.

Alice hunches down by the side of the grave, her fingers raking the clipped turf. I am not sure how long she sits there, perfectly still, her face a blank page. But when at last she stands, her cottonwool legs very nearly crumbling under her, the service in the church is over and the people have gone to their homes.

Greenwood Lodge, when we find it some time later, is an ugly Victorian villa set back from the road, with bits added onto it, like the Wendy houses children play in. The main building has a gabled roof and bow windows, and is painted a pale green. We are greeted by Mrs Bowker, a big, dark-skinned woman, who reminds me of Reta Okello. She has a mass of black, springy hair, anchored down with several shiny steel grips, and a way of laughing through her speech.

'Welcome, welcome. You must be Alice,' says Mrs Bowker, shaking Alice's hand vigorously. 'Your sister Nicola rang me and said you were coming.' She draws us into a rabbits' warren of corridors and shady rooms.

'It is so lovely for Myrtle to have a visitor,' she says, leading us through to the rear of the building, then into the 'dayroom', where she explains the home's residents are resting after lunch.

Alice is having a hard time taking anything in – not the shabby wallpaper, or the drab furniture, or the rumpled old faces that line the walls, faces from which confused eyes are horribly magnified behind spectacles thick as the bottoms of glass bottles. Nor is she really aware of the faint odour of urine, mingled with stewed vege-tables, and stale bodies. The drone of the vast television does not register either. Alice starts to search the faces for her mother's, until Mrs Bowker, who has stopped to speak to a few residents, glances back and sees what she is doing.

'Oh no, dear, Myrtle is in the garden, sitting on the bench by the monkey-puzzle tree. She likes her own space I think, dear. Doesn't want to mix too much with the rabble.'

Mrs Bowker pushes open some French windows, and we are soon all tearing down the garden path, the headless budgie bringing up the rear with a flourish of its bright plumage. Then we stride over a bumpy lawn of velvet moss, dandelions and molehills. Finally we thread our way through a few shrubs, and there, in a small clearing overlooked by a towering monkeypuzzle tree, is Myrtle Safford. Our first sight of her seems to wind Alice entirely. The dog too halts in his tracks, his planar head turning this way and that, as if he cannot believe the evidence of his own spectral eyes. Much as I might expect, the gremlin starts pointing rudely, shaking with laughter. And the budgie crashes into the monkeypuzzle tree, pricks itself on the spiky foliage, slumps to the ground, and immediately starts to thrash about as if in its death throes, hardly likely considering.

I am more composed, though believe me it is easy to see why Alice is so shocked. Gone is the fine lady we used to see sweeping down the corridors of the flat on The Peak. She is slumped on a wooden bench as if she had no spine to prop her up. Her face is bloated and her eyes puffy. She has not just double chins but treble ones. And the mane of rich dark hair has moulted, so that now her scalp is patterned with bubblegum-pink diamonds and crescents. The thick snake of a plait, that once upon a time she wound round and round her head and pinned into place, has shrivelled to a worm. Her slack skin is creased. She has dark red shadows in the hollows of her face. Now she wears glasses, the large rectangular lenses set in thick dark frames. And her eyes, which once flashed with pride, contempt and haughtiness, have grown small and dingy as the British pennies Alice has in her purse. Her hands, anchoring a brown and blue wool rug over her lap, are freckled with age-spots. She is still wearing a fine dress though, a black and white kaftan. But the hem looks scuffed with dirt, and sequins are trailing from a loose thread at the collar. A single diamante earring droops disconsolately from one of her earlobes. Strangest of all, squashy, fat, luminous-orange trainers hug her feet, together with thick aquamarine-coloured socks, printed with small red strawberries.

'How are you, Mrs Safford?' Mrs Bowker greets her. For the present Alice is struck dumb. 'I've brought a visitor. I understand you haven't seen her for a bit so this will be a real treat. See. It's Alice!' she says. She stands back to reveal my host, as if unveiling a long-anticipated work of art.

Slowly Myrtle looks up, eyelids contracting in the sunshine. Her movements are jerky, her head teetering so much on her neck that she looks the way she did sometimes in the evenings in the flat on the Peak. The sunlight, falling through the spiky branches of the monkeypuzzle tree, makes serrated patterns of light and shadow on the grass. Mrs Bowker waits a few seconds, while Mrs Safford's dull eyes flick over her daughter, taking her in.

Now she looks past Alice at Mrs Bowker. 'I want you to bring the tray out here, Ah Lee, with the bottle of whisky, the tub of ice, and tumblers. Do you understand?' she slurs grandly.

'Oh yes, Mrs Safford, right away,' Mrs Bowker tells Myrtle Safford brightly, winking at Alice. Then to us she says, lowering her voice to a whisper, 'I'll leave the two of you to get acquainted again. If you need anything, just shout,' she calls back over her shoulder.

Alice sits down on the empty wooden bench opposite her mother. I shoo the beasties away, determined that here my host will have the privacy denied her in the churchyard. They cooperate, albeit reluctantly, vanishing into a coppery-leafed bush. Alice clears her throat. She combs back her hair with her quivering fingers. She inches forwards on her seat, and tilts her head this way and that, in a vain attempt to get her mother's attention.

'Mother, it's me. Alice,' she says at last. Unconsciously, one of her hands finds the wooden arm of the bench, and runs forwards and back along it, as if she is stroking it. 'I've been away, Mother, remember. For a long time. For a very long time. Well . . . thirty years, Mother. I . . . I've come home now. I can come and see you, if . . . if you like? Would you like that?' She is hesitant at first. 'I've been living in France. I sent you letters, three of them. But perhaps you didn't receive them. Anyway that's where I was, in Paris. I was married for a time. I wrote and told you. Did you get my letters? Oh, it doesn't matter. I would have loved you to have come to my wedding. I thought of you, pictured you there. We . . . we lived in a big airy flat with views over the city. I think you would have liked him, Carl. I did. Well, I loved him of course . . . at first. It didn't . . . didn't work out though. But I was happy for while. For a while I was . . . I was happy.' She speaks as if she is trying to convince herself. There is a burst of birdsong, but I cannot see the bird anywhere. Beyond the monkeypuzzle tree is a tall fence. Not much can be seen over it – a line of treetops, the roof of a building that may well be a barn, and still further away, on the rise of the next field, a handful of cows ambling about. Distantly I hear them lowing.

'My guests will be here soon,' Myrtle says, the light bouncing off her lenses as she glances about her. 'I must get ready. Where's Ah Lee? I think I'll wear the purple dress tonight. Do run along now, I'm far too busy to chat.' Her tone is dismissive. She closes her eyes.

Alice hesitates, fighting the impulse to obey and leave. Then she stops the stroking motion of her hand, balls her fist and raps the armrest firmly. She takes a huge breath as if she is about to dive into a deep pool. 'I've been to see Harry and Nicola, and even Jillian. You know, Mother, given time, I think we just might patch things up.' Alice's voice is brittle. 'They're doing very well, aren't they? They have families of their own now. Just think. Husbands and wives . . . and . . . and children. They have children. Funny isn't it? I . . . oh, I haven't got any children myself. Carl and I, well . . . we didn't have any in the end.' There is a catch in her voice. She lays the flat of her hand at the base of her throat and presses.

'Beth dear, I think I'm going to have to let that amah go. She hasn't brought the whisky yet. Whatever will my guests think.' Mrs Safford's eyes are still closed. She flaps a hand at a drowsy bee bumbling past. Alice stares down at the grass, and watches the progress of a trail of ants bent on shouldering a biscuit crumb.

Keeping her hand in place as if the gesture will steady her voice, she speaks. 'You'll never guess what, Mother. I can talk French.' She looks up into her mother's face, still searching for a sign of recognition. 'I wasn't very good at it when I was at the Island School. I only got a B pass in my O level. Do you remember? But now I can talk French. Isn't that strange?' Alice waits a beat. Myrtle opens her eyes, and licks her lips with a lazy swipe of her tongue, in a way that reminds Alice of a lizard catching flies. Alice gives a soft whinny of laughter. 'I expect you'd like to know what I've been doing all these years. I put it in my letters. I so hoped you'd reply. But most likely they got lost in the post. It happens all the time. I ran a restaurant. Well, not at first. To begin with I just helped out in the kitchens. But in time Pierre promoted me. Oh, that's Pierre Ramirez. He owned the restaurant. He was my boss. He was very kind to me. You know he reminded me a bit of . . . of . . . well, anyway he was good to me. I watched the handover of Hong Kong on the television. I thought of you both there while the rain came down and everyone got soaked.'

The bird delivers another explosion of song, even more frenzied this time, as if its life depended on being noticed. 'He willed the restaurant to me, Mother. I put it all in a letter. But it must never have arrived. You'd have got in touch if it had, sent me a reply. Of course you would.' Her voice drops until it is barely audible. 'It was so sad when . . . when . . . Pierre died. I was with him. I held his hand. I thought if I held his hand he wouldn't go, but he slipped away just the same.' Now her tone lifts perceptibly. 'I was the owner, Mother, can you imagine? Your daughter running a restaurant?' I had staff, paid their wages.' Alice nods emphatically, like a child who knows they won't be believed. 'Mm . . . really, I was. If you'd seen me at work you would have been so surprised.'

Then suddenly she shakes her head as if trying to wake herself. 'Imagine me being good at languages, and running a restaurant. Can you believe it, Mother?' Her delivery is speeding up, getting faster and faster as if she hasn't time to stop and breathe. 'I went to see a play in London. I did, Mother. I had some free time and I thought that I'd like to see a play. It was called *Moon for the Misbegotten*. It's a wonderful title for a play, isn't it, Mother? "M" is such a generous consonant, don't you think? So warm and round. Like marshmallows, and mattresses. Murderers too, I suppose. I hadn't thought of that. And well, "Misbegotten", that word, starting as it does with "mis", that's significant I think. Because life is about missing all sort of things, isn't it? Then the "begotten" part, to me that sounds like the words are tripping and falling down a flight of stairs, that they just can't stop themselves.'

Myrtle looks over Alice's shoulder. 'Ralph could never deal with the staff. Too kind by half. You have to be firm with these people. He should have got rid of Amanda too and he knew it. She became a liability, a threat to all of us. In the end I had to do it for him. I had to rescue him. The little bitch would have been our ruin if I hadn't stepped in. So I sorted it out once and for all. Would you like to know what I did? Is that why you're here, Beth?' The spread fingers of each hand rest on the arms of her glasses, adjusting their position.

'What . . . what did . . . you do, Mother?' Alice asks. There is a quaver in her voice, as though she is frightened to hear the answer. 'What did you do . . . do to Amanda?'

She lowers her hands into her lap. Her eyes glint behind their lenses and her mouth breaks into a secretive smile. 'I took care of it. I told her at the Boxing Day party. Outside the amahs' quarters. I said, "Would you like me to tell Phillip that you're screwing my husband? Or perhaps I should go and tell your children, tell young Oliver and pretty little Jemima that their mummy's opening her legs, not for their daddy but for Uncle Ralph." Oh that made her angry, spitting like the common alley cat she was. "I expect you'd like me to say making love. Is that what you think you're doing, Amanda? Oh no, darling, love's got nothing to do with it. Don't fool your-self. You're Ralph's whore, no more than that. I'm Myrtle Safford. I'm his wife. He knows his duty. He won't leave me. You are never to go near him again, Amanda. Do you hear me?"' Now her hands clench tightly in her lap as her voice rasps out. '"If you do, I'll find out, and I'll destroy your family. I'll smash it apart, until your chil-dren can't look you in the face."' She gives a rough, mirthless snort. 'She knew she couldn't stay away from my Ralph, knew she couldn't help herself.' Again she laughs, her flaccid mouth closing on the soft snigger. 'She knew what she had to do. She didn't waste any time. She got on with it. Poor Amanda, flying through the air like a trapeze artist, only no one caught her. She was no match for me and she knew it.'

No sound comes from Alice, but the tears brimming in her eyes spill over and slide down her pale cheeks.

'So you see, I kept the family safe. And Amanda wasn't the only one who tried to take my husband away.' Alice looks confused, scared. 'My own daughter. My own flesh. I took care of that too. Burnt those letters she sent. One, two, three . . . whoosh. So pretty. I dealt with her.' Alice's hands move to cover her ears, then change course and, almost violently, wipe away her tears. 'Of course Ralph's dead now, so I don't have to worry about her any more.'

Alice shakes her head slowly from side to side. Then she is still, speaking quietly. 'I . . . I was . . . so sad to hear about Daddy, about him – I'm sorry he didn't get my letters. But he knew,' she says with dignity, 'he knew how much I loved him. Even if he didn't see the letters. I went to his grave, this morning. My name isn't there, Mother. My name, it isn't with the others. There's Jillian and Nicola and Harry . . . but not me. Alice isn't there. I'm not there, Mother. As if . . . as if I never was.' She stops and sucks in her mouth. There is a moth in her stomach. I sense it, a giant moth. Its wings are coated with sticky black gum. It twists and buckles inside her. Its head is not furry and soft. It is as rough as the texture of shark's skin. She feels it nosing about, grating at her, feels the juices it writhes in turning to a burning acid. 'I was . . . was—' With the flat of one hand she strikes her mouth, as if trying to clear it of an obstruction. She sucks in a breath and her small chest rises with the effort of it. 'I tried, Reta, but . . . but I was just . . . just—' This time the air is sobbed in. 'I'm . . . sorry, that's all!' she finishes, sinks back on her bench, and folds. A long moment passes.

The bird is silent now. On an impulse, Alice drops to her knees before her mother.

'Look at me!' Her hands reach out and lightly touch the folds of Myrtle Safford's dress. Her mother's response is almost leisurely. She inclines her head, the gesture imperious, and gazes down at her daughter. Just for a second the lenses of her glasses flash, blinding Alice, then their eyes meet. 'It's me, Mother. It's Alice!' Alice does not speak, she beseeches.

Mrs Safford leans forward in her seat. The movement sends her earring swinging. The sun snags on it, and light splinters and ricochets upwards. She puts her head to one side and frowns, as if she is trying hard to remember something, someone. For a few seconds she studies Alice's features, the way you might search a map for a familiar landmark. Then she edges even closer. Her eyelids relax. Her face is empty. Alice can feel her mother's breath against her skin, can detect a trace of sourness in it.

'Who . . . who are you?' Myrtle Safford asks her daughter. 'I don't know who you are.'

Alice lifts herself up then, hypnotically climbing to her feet, her look glazed, seeing nothing at all. And that's when I catch it. It is just a flicker, deep down in Myrtle Safford's eyes, but it is unmistakable, the cold glimmer of recognition. Almost imperceptibly, the corners of her mouth twitch upwards, as if . . . as if she is acting, the way she did sometimes in the flat on The Peak, as if she knows the audience has been entirely taken in, as if she is enjoying her very own private joke.

Minutes later we leave, our entourage creeping out of the bushes and racing after us. But to my consternation Alice follows signs not to London but to Brighton and the coast. There is a harrowing stiffness in her posture. And I have sinister misgivings when she parks her car close to the seafront and climbs out. The day shrugs off its warmth as the five of us head down to the beach.

Alice crunches over the pebbles, looking neither to right nor left. The dog trots behind, nose to the ground in a heaven of sea scents. The monkey bounces off the stones like a ginger beachball, gurgling joyously on each bumpy impact. The headless budgie soars alongside the gulls, causing quite a stir. And I skitter after Alice, trying hard not to lose my airy footing on the uneven surface. At last we stand before a monstrous thing, like the skeleton of some great sea serpent that has washed up on the shore, and perished there.

'The old West Pier,' Alice mutters. 'There was a fire. It's all burnt out.'

Day-trippers still freckle the beaches – strolling adults, children at play, paddling and shouting, young lovers sharing a last kiss. The merry-go-round is winding down, the music fading away. The buzz of traffic is diminishing. A couple of dogs bark and rush into the breaking waves. They lollop out, spinning their coats, showers of droplets distilling the waning light. A kite, a dash of red and yellow, tail dipping, sails high above us. A man bends to retrieve bats and a ball. A solitary voice cries out excitedly. Boats bob and dip in the blue arms of a capricious sea. Gulls loop and dive and screech, owning each kingdom in turn – the mounds of pebbles, the reaches of the wooden windbreaks, viridescent with lanky tresses of seaweed, the wide scope of changeable sky, the rough blanket of the sea. They spy, they swoop, puncturing the blue-green drum with their hooked yellow beaks, emerging with some wriggling silver titbit, and streaking away to gobble it down in solitude, unhampered. But Alice is oblivious to all this, choosing rather to stand before the bones of the beast.

Suddenly I sense the sun has withdrawn its beneficence, and the sky has transformed itself into a scumble of mutinous grey. The pebbles that looked so bright in the golden sunlight, varnished with the surf, are all over salt dust, drab and monotonous. The sea breath grows frosty and murky. Seaweed ribbons sprawl like beached, lifeless snakes. The people have gone. The merry-go-round is still, its jaunty tune suffocated. The seagulls huddle together on the frame of the beast. The cold curls about me, reclaiming its own. I seek comfort in the solid beat of Alice's heart, slinking down into the elastic passages that wind through her body. I feel the beat of that munificent organ reverberating through her. I am held in thrall by the swell of her life-giving lungs. On I journey, pumped through oak-solid arteries that thin presently to a web of veins, and still further, coursing through her tiny capillaries, slim as gossamer threads, delicate as coral tips. Alice sits, hugging her knees. Bear-as-Was is by her side, smouldering eyes trained on her face, while the monkey whirs about my host's head, humming tunelessly.

I know there is ice settling in the marrow of my host's bones, that her skin is stamped with cold, that her red cotton dress is no protection against the fast approaching night. I stand guard, ghostly arms akimbo, while that doltish bird, deserting its new-found feathered friends, circles over us. Its puny body seems to have bloated strangely, like a waterlogged corpse. It has swapped its bright plumage for a leathery bilious-yellow skin, encrusted with scurf. Suddenly it lumbers down, and while it hovers before Alice's milk-white face, the mess of clotted blood at its neck oozing like a sluggish stream, I detect the unmistakable stench of death hanging on the air. The monkey's droning builds and builds until Alice's head throbs with it. Her hands reach up to cup her ears, desperately trying to block out the dissonant whining.

Now the winged creature crashes to the pebbles, and with a sequence of clumsy belly-flops makes its way down to the sea's edge. The dog, coat ablaze, the monkey riding him like an impish jockey, races to the shoreline. They dart into the creaming waves, then rush back to us, barking and chattering invitingly. I scowl at all three in turn, saving my grimmest face for the dog.

'In life you hated the sea,' I spit at him. But the dog only nips at Alice's dress, tugging at it, while the monkey on his back performs some hideous parody of a belly-dance, rippling its glittering body and reeling Alice in.

Alice stands. No matter how hard I try to push her up the beach towards safety, she eludes me. She walks as if in a trance, over the pebbles to meet the furling tide. She bends, the sea catching at the heels of her sandals, lapping greedily at the soft brown suede. She stares enraptured at the mashing foam and at the rolling crystal gyres of the incoming waves. I try to pull us back from the deep, try to skim over the smooth flat stones, drawing Alice with me. But I seem to have no stability, no point of gravity. I skid about as if I am a novice on a skating rink. The wind, now picking up, pierces us with sharp needles of rain. Alice wants to sink into the pebbles, huddle under their mass, have the weight of all those stones quilt her in, like clods of earth. Blackness descends, unstoppable, cloying. Alice slips off her sandals and steals towards the bones of the beast. I have no choice but to follow. Then I hear them, my ancestors, and know they are coming for me.

'Lin Shui! Lin Shui!' they implore, 'let us lead you to the other side of night.'

When I glance back at the deserted beach, I think I see a child, a golden-haired child clad in black rags, crouching behind a windbreak. Then I turn and Alice is wading into the icy water. The dog paddles at her side. The turgid bird, a few yards ahead, arrows down into the now cinereous depths. The monkey floats on its back, blowing black bubbles and winking roguishly. Alice's red dress spreads out and flowers about her. My host is a red hibiscus blossom and the sea lusts after her. She barely feels the gelid sludge pushing into the soles of her feet, the pressure of it sucking us down. Deeper and deeper she goes. Trails of icy brine net her numb limbs, dragging her down. Over us climbs the oppressive bars of the beast. It blocks out the moon. We slip silently between its slippery, charred beams.

The sea drinks Alice down into a tenebrous vortex. I wind myself around the slimy bones of the relic, catching at Alice as she falls. I burrow into the fray of seaweed and barnacle, into the spirals of lucid shells, and snag on the spiky black pins of sea urchins. In an instant the water is veined with moonlight. The tiny fish come then and nibble on us, their silvery mass moving like one organism. They are curious of me. They are curious of the others, the dark entities weaving through them, the shadows that are neither fish, flesh nor fowl. They are curious of Alice dying among them.

Further and further we descend, until silt fingers rear up from the seabed to take her. I know, as I huddle down in the cavernous, cold depths, that this is the puissance of death, its touch sweetly savage. Alice's heart grows sluggish and prepares to beat its last. But I am not ready yet, not yet. Nor is my host. I seize hold of Alice by the jellyfish trails of her hair. I fill my spectral hands with it, and grip hard. I fix on the sea's skin stirring above us, and I heave, with all the living energy I can summon. Alice's body shifts. Again I heave. And again. The fingers disintegrate into muddy clouds, grudgingly relinquishing their mermaid prize. We rise, my host and I, through the icy currents, up and up, until in a splash of rage I wrench Alice from the fist of the sea, and cast her back on the pebble-strewn shore. She chokes and splutters. Her body spasms. The sodden sea breath pours out of her, and the element of air, of life, gushes in.

As our bedraggled little band makes its shivering way back up the beach, I meld with Alice.

'*Bù dào huáng hé xïn bù sǐ*,' We have not come to the Yellow River yet, to the place of despair,' I tell her gravely.

And Alice must have been listening to me, because the following day she books us on a flight back to Hong Kong. We are going home.

Ghost – 2006

The flight is unremarkable. The arrival . . . anything but! We do not touch down on the tongue of Kai Tak airport that used to lick out into the sea, but at Chep Lap Kok airport on Lantau island. The Fasten Seatbelt sign snaps off. As Alice gathers together her hand luggage, there is a frisson of excitement pulsing between us. We are on the move, and much, much more important, we are home. We elbow into the throng making its way towards the open cabin door. Alice pauses at the top of the portable steps, and takes a deep breath of sweltering mid-afternoon air. I feel it instantly, a geyser of life force jetting up from the tips of her toes, energising every cell. For me, arriving on the island has the opposite effect. It is as if Alice's oxygen, that vital gas that once buoyed me up, has metamorphosed into a deadly, boiling lava. I feel it dousing my spirit, petrifying me until . . . until what? Until I am no more than a stony imprint in time! From this moment on, however gradual, I know I am wilting, and Alice is growing steadily stronger.

But this is only the first sign that Hong Kong may not be the oasis I was expecting. My negative reflections end abruptly when something catches my eye. It is the maniacal monkey, scrunched up tightly, twinkling in the unforgiving sun like a globe of rusty metal-filings. Then, startling us all, it launches itself, in the fashion of a kamikaze pilot, down the steps.

The *bump, bump, bump* of its staccato progress is accompanied by a exhilarated *Yaaaah*! This explosive tremolo turns out to be its final aria. As it bounces off the last step and onto the tarmac, there is a sudden Boom!, accompanied by a shower of auburn sparks. We rush down to investigate but incredibly all that remains of the demented anthropoid is a tiny pile of dirt. Closer inspection reveals this to be nothing more than soot, soon dispersed by a gust of fuel-tainted air. It seems the monkey has detonated like a simian grenade. A quick look back confirms that the dog at least appears unscathed. Although, having witnessed the alarming spectacle, I note he is picking his ghostly canine way down the steps with the utmost care. And that is when another coruscation draws my attention. Flattened against each of the aircraft cabin windows in turn are an iridescent green torso and two variegated grey wings. Clearly the budgie, restored to its former petite proportions, cannot find its way out. But Alice is hurrying on, and I do not intend to be left behind.

'Sorry, but it's every ghost for itself from here on,' I call up from the dusty tarmac to the headless budgie. 'Besides, this island never was your home. If you stay put I'm sure they'll fly you back to Britain.' I shrug my regret to show I am not completely lacking in emotion. The dog snatches one cringing glance at a 'plane window curtained with a spray of budgie feathers. Then, with a yelp, he races after us, in his panic very nearly knocking Alice over. As we go through Immigration, a Chinese officer glances at the stamp in Alice's passport that reads 'Hong Kong Citizen'. On the strength of that he waves through the three of us. From here we take an express train to the Hong Kong Island terminus. And all the while our eyes grow round as dollar coins, for the country we remember has become a mighty dragon whose life-blood never stops flowing.

As far back as I can remember it was busy, but now it is frenetic, the pace of life at a sprint. We have never seen so many people, all rushing somewhere, glancing down at their watches, clasping mobile phones to their ears, grasping suitcases and briefcases and bags fit to burst with bright things from markets – vegetables, fruits and flowers, bottles, parcels and packages. Truly, I had forgotten how noisy the sound of Cantonese and Mandarin can be, as people shout and gossip, and negotiate and bargain, and give directions, and argue, and make up.

There are trains and trams and buses and cars and lorries and motorbikes and bicycles, all jostling one another, winding along roads, through the tunnels and over the bridges. Victoria harbour has become a vast moving collage of cargo ships, junks, ferries, sampans, pleasure-cruisers and police patrol boats. Girdled about us is the sea, the jade-green bangle of the sea, offering up the three of us to cerulean skies and a fiery sun. It is hard to believe the sleepy little island of Hong Kong I first came to with father all those years ago ever occupied this same spot. We are carried along like a cork bobbing on water until we find ourselves walking, as if in a dream, by the waterfront. We stare up open-mouthed at the crowd of spangled giants, skyscrapers, sleek and silver, defying gravity with nonchalant ease.

We find a hotel that looks out over the harbour, across to the Ocean Terminal and Kowloon. And the very next day we start to search for somewhere to live. I imagine us finding a fine house on The Peak, but what we finally end up with is a Pokfulam flat no bigger than a broom cupboard. Alice is philosophical.

'It has a view and we can watch the sun set. That's what counts,' she insists.

But another shock lies in store. Alice decorates, she furnishes the flat, and we settle in. She starts to have Mandarin lessons and, as the year turns the corner, to think about finding employment, for the money from the restaurant, she says, will not last indefinitely. Day by day her vitality grows, as mine wanes. Spring arrives and the temperatures start to soar. Since our arrival the dog has whined incessantly about the heat, until I am quite out of patience with him. So it comes as no surprise when he takes up his familiar refrain on a fine day at the start of June.

'I am *soooo* hot!' he grumbles, standing in the minuscule sitting room, inches from the whirring fan. 'I can't stand it. It's simply diabolical. I'm being cooked alive.'

I am lolling on the settee, my now customary exhaustion leaving me a semi-invalid. Alice is in the kitchen, washing up and whistling cheerily.

'Oh do give it a rest,' I drawl fractiously at the dog. 'Why must you always complain? You seemed to have no problem with the hot climate when you were alive.' In a weak gesture of protest I waft the air with a pearly hand.

'But you don't understand,' grizzles the dog through his now some-what dull, dish-brown muzzle, 'I am *soooo* hot I think I may be melting.'

'Don't be such a hypochondriac,' I mutter contemptuously, shifting my phantom limbs into a more comfortable position. Experience has taught me that these lesser apparitions are prone to exaggeration. I try to grab a moment's respite to reinvigorate myself, but when I look up the dog is nowhere to be seen. With a supreme effort I levi-tate off the settee and seek out poor roasting Bear-as-Was. There is no sign of him. On the floor however, below the fan, is a sticky brown mess and, from it, a trail of acrid smoke spiralling towards the ceiling. Acrid smoke tainted with a distinct whiff of old dog!

'Bear! Bear-as-Was, is this some kind of practical joke?' I demand, poking a cloudy finger cautiously in the burnt-almond gunge. There is no reply. All is quiet. Seconds later, Alice bustles in, tweeting like a spring bird, cloth in hand. She pauses over the glistening puddle on the wooden floor. Two lines pinch together above the bridge of her nose, as if she has a vague recollection of something. Then she gives a dismissive shrug and without a moment's hesitation she wipes up Bear-as-Was, trots back into the kitchen, and washes him away down the plughole.

Ghost – 2007

I am struggling to keep pace with Alice now and she knows it. I hobble after her like an elderly relative, longing for nothing so much as peace. Together we watch the sun set from the small veranda of the Pokfulam flat. It is like standing beneath a waterfall of mutating lights – gold and red and copper, tumbling into purple and blue and green, only to drown minutes later in cauldron-black. Alice, I know, is thinking about tomorrow. I am thinking too. I am thinking that I no longer want to say, 'Not yet. I am not ready yet.'

One sultry night I hunch at the end of Alice's bed, studying my host as she sleeps. The cicadas chirrup, as they did through the long nights we spent together in the flat on The Peak. Alice's breathing is easy, effortless. There is a bloom upon her cheeks. Her eyes flicker under their closed lids, and I wonder if she is dreaming of the future, a future she must face alone? Sensing me watching her, tuning in to my monologue of thoughts, as I have to hers for a lifetime now, she stirs and sits up. As she does so, she is made silver-white in a spill of moonlight, like . . . like a ghost. Her hair is mussed up. She yawns widely, pushes back her sheet and hugs her knees. She is wearing a baggy cotton pyjama top that swamps her. For a long moment we face each other. Unconsciously I realise I am mirroring her, lost in my army jacket, clutching my own misty knees. From far off comes the sound of a motorbike buzzing like a wasp, approaching then receding. A car engine turns over, the coughing slurring until it finally grinds to a stop. A door slams.

'Alice,' I start, 'Alice it's—'

'Don't,' Alice ambushes me. 'Don't say it.' Her voice is hushed but pertinacious.

Another long moment drags by. It is strange, I muse, looking at my host, how well I have learnt her – the changing light in her eyes, the line of her nose, the curve of her mouth, the lift of her brow, the way her little finger crooks when she is uneasy, as it does now. I follow the rise and fall of her chest, and I can feel it too, the rushing in of the air, the release of it.

'Alice,' I try again, 'it's time.'

'No!' says Alice. 'No! You're wrong. It's not, not yet. Stay with me a while longer?' she implores. Her eyes are liquid. Her hands tremble slightly, only very slightly, and her heart beats wildly. 'How will I manage without you?' she mumbles, as if to herself. 'I can't manage without you. I just can't. If you leave, I'll be adrift. I'll be alone.'

'Alice, I am so very tired,' I tell her. 'So weary of this world. Let me go Alice, please.'

Alice nibbles a fingernail, then rakes back her hair and forces out a smile.

'It'll change. You see if it doesn't.' She reaches her hands entreatingly towards me. In return, all I can offer is a barely visible ripple of my gossamer fingers. Slowly, Alice's hands drop. She looks away to the window, to the first pale tendrils of the approaching dawn. 'How will I cope . . . how, without you by my side?' she murmurs to herself.

I manage just the trace of my broken-toothed smile. 'Oh Alice, you will do very well. It wasn't me, you know, dragged along by the rushing river.' The curtain blows in a breath of wind, and the moonlight shivers like a little sea stirred. 'I was always on the bank, out of the current, running to keep up. You're the one who endured, not me.' Alice's fingers interlace, and there is challenge in her unblinking eyes. 'I fished you out a couple of times when it looked as if you might go under,' I allow in a ghostly undertone, wearing this new-found modesty like an ill-fitting garment. 'That's all.'

Now Alice fixes on an expanse of white wall. When she turns

back to me her face is resolved. 'I want to come with you,' she says. But her eyes are hooded, hiding the truth.

I shake my head. I do not speak, I simply share the weight of ploughing on, here, in this element of air, how painful it is for me now. By the second I become more drenched in the desire to eschew this half-life.

'Ah Alice, let me go?' My susurration falls away, a silken sigh.

Alice presses her lips tightly together for answer, and her face seems to close down. I feel the way I imagine an old dog feels, kept hanging on, not for its delight but for the comfort of its owner. I never considered when I latched on to Alice that I would need her blessing to sever the tie. I was so busy hanging onto life, not for one moment did I entertain the possibility that I might have a surfeit of it. It is as if I am fastened to her by a thread. Only a thread, but it serves as well as an unbreakable chain. Only Alice can release me, set me free and let me rise up to where the clouds are hemmed with gold, where the ink-black sea is infinite, spinning with chatoyant, timeless stars. Life has become a drudge, not a joy, and all the while I am kept under close surveillance by my hawk-host.

On the 1st of July we watch the ceremony marking the tenth anniversary of the historic handover of Hong Kong to the Chinese at the Convention and Exhibition Centre. Throughout the weekend there are colourful parades and swirling dragon dances. The sky cascades with fireworks. We note the conspicuous absence of the bad British fairy from the feast, excluded from the proceedings by Beijing. We see also the pro-democracy protests that follow, where tens of thousands march in Causeway Bay and Wanchai. The people are demanding better pay and more justice. They explain they want the right to vote in their own chosen leaders, a promise not yet delivered. And they describe the new flag of Hong Kong, the representation of the white Bauhinia blakeana flower, standing out against a red background.

'This is *our* flag,' they say, and their eyes shine with patriotism.

The images crowd in upon me now, a cluster of smoky islands, scattered like amethysts in a spinach-green sea. Boat people, clambering with the agility of spiders over the rigging of giant junks as they nose out of Aberdeen harbour, brown-patched sails, plumped-up pillows in the wind. Stooks of rickety shacks thatching the hillsides. The pomp and ceremony of the British – crisp, snowy linen, white helmets, gold tassels, gleaming swords, and men keeling over under a scorching noon-day sun.

A kaleidoscope of exotic produce – golden mangoes, bunches of prickly russet lychees, the mottled honey-gold skin of pomelos, the Lincoln green frills of bok choi restrained by their elegant, veined white stalks, clusters of tiny buttercup-yellow blossoms frothing among the Chartreuse fingers of choi sum. Warrens of cloth alleys, packed tight with bolts of every imaginable fabric, mesmerising the eye with whorls of colour, seducing the flesh with their seductive voile kisses. Bench stalls buffeted by wind and weather, through to emporia several storeys high, crowded with painted porcelain, and carvings, from musk-scented cedars to the dark glossy limbs of blackest ebony, cool jade in frosty white, through celadon, and darkening to that most highly prized emerald green.

Birds clucking and cooing, pecking frantically at the wicker mesh of their basket-cages. The sweet, pervasive taint of garnet-red raw meat, banded with thick yellow fat, emanating from carcasses dangling from huge blue-grey hooks; stone floors blotched liver-brown, drains running red with blood. Steam, rising like genies from bowls of tangled noodles, at makeshift restaurants on street corners. A swaying, apricot-coloured paper lantern suspended from a bamboo cane, its leaping flame casting mysterious shadows, as you seek for the pearl of the moon among a fold of crushed velvet night. Young Chinese men, muscles taut, clambering up towers of glazed buns. Tiny girls dressed in shimmering silks and satins, their faces works of art, their hair braided and looped, adorned with shiny diadems, perched up high like miniature goddesses on festival floats. Ears blasted with the cacophony of bursting firecrackers. Lacy pink blossoms of peach trees, standing quivering in bud, rows of shy princesses ready for the Chinese New Year.

Walls of fire, leaping and licking down the blackened flanks of

charred hillsides. Typhoons pounding the island to its very foundations, their screams reverberating at its core. Shoulders of mud sliding
down precipitous slopes, loosened by torrential rains, gobbling up
whole buildings. Opalescent, milky bodies, stealthily wrapping themselves about the island's high peaks. Wizened brown faces split in
wide, gold-toothed grins. New-minted babies' faces, topped with
sheaves of crisp black hair, breaking into gummy toothless chuckles.
I swell with love for my dramatic, invincible, resilient home. It has
been tossed and turned by history, shaken by the rigours of nature,
and has emerged thriving, vibrant, and ever more magical. All this I
turn over, knowing that soon I must leave.

One evening bonfires are lit all over the island. It is the fifteenth
day of the seventh moon, the lunar month in the Chinese calendar;
the ghost month. Red, yellow and blue flames, flay the encroaching
gloom, appeasing the restless spirits of the dead. It is the festival of
Yue Lan when Hungry Ghosts roam the island. Death – sudden,
violent, premature – has cheated them of life's bounty, and of the
funeral rites that would have secured their peace. And so, once a
year, when the gates of the dark kingdom are flung wide, the restless spirits surge back, bent on filling their bottomless bellies with
all life dared to withhold. Paper offerings – model homes, cars and
money – blaze. Plates are piled high with food for the dead. The air
is laced with the heavy scent of incense, and prayers are muttered
fearfully by old and young alike.

How can I tell Alice, as she watches the celebrations enraptured,
that the air is thick with ghosts, with snatching shadow hands, and
greedy, covetous eyes? How can I explain the drag of them, the
craving I have to slough off my host, and dance my fury with demons
on the world's edge? How can I make her understand I want to stalk
the island's shores, where the sea's husky chords lure men to watery
graves? Silently I watch my ancestors weave wildly among the living,
brushing warm flesh with their last glacial, stagnant breaths.

While Alice sleeps, her head pillowed on her hands, I stand on
the small veranda. The hot night air throbs with phantoms, swooping
and diving, twirling, scuffling and thrusting, brawling, grabbing,

clawing and wailing at the living. They reach towards me with their scrolling glassy fingers.

'Come. Join us, Lin Shui. Slip away and leave the living to their clumsy workings,' they murmur, their siren song dipped in honeydew.

Again and again they call, catching at my army jacket, tempting my febrile spirit until it jerks and tugs to be away. All that binds me is a thread; no more than that, a single thread fastening me to Alice. But it is enough. Soon they are gone, leaving me behind.

Ghost – 2007

'Let's walk today,' persuades Alice. 'The weather is splendid. It will reju-
venate us.' She dismisses my empty laugh, and strides off, pulling at
my leash, so that I have no choice but to follow. For once she does
not choose to stroll about the Peak. Instead we take a taxi to Aberdeen
harbour, also known as Heung Gong Tsai or Little Hong Kong.

These days the waterfront is crowded out by towering apartment
blocks. And yet the land almost seems to extend gawky limbs into
the sea, so chequered is it with houseboats and sampans, a floating
village. There are banks of Chinese junks, their hulls protected with
black tyre circlets. Makeshift tarpaulins in glaring greens and blues,
draped over wooden frames, provide relief from the growing heat of
the rising sun. The air is pungent with the scent of salt and refuse
and fuel, alive with the shouts and cries of the boat people, with the
noise of chugging engines, and slapping, splashing water, and the
ceaseless murmur of traffic.

Where once there had only been the Sea Palace and the Tai Pak,
gently swaying on their moorings, now the former is gone and the
latter rubs shoulders with the mighty Jumbo restaurant, and many
other smaller businesses. Against a background sponged with the
shifting hues of the sea comes the panorama of browns, the gradient
of charred crusts to mellow biscuits, claimed by the fleets of wooden
vessels. Day and night, boat-dogs, yellow, cream, brown and black,
dash up and down patrolling these floating homes, or lie semi-coma-
tose panting in a patch of shade, lulled by their rolling waterbeds.

Everywhere foaming sprites burst from the ruche of sea, sluicing the sides of the boats as they snake through the busy channels. They are shaped from nothing more solid than salt water and air, rise up and are dashed to bits, only to be instantly reborn in dazzling white froth. And overlaying this are the slashes of red signs, from where Chinese characters stand out in gleaming gold relief, drawing in customers. Washing flaps from poles and rigging. The smells of cooking and washing rise as one on the warm air currents. This Little Hong Kong was my home, where I lived and worked and slept and dreamed. 'Was', not 'is'. It is Alice's home now, not mine.

For a while longer we wander about drinking in all manner of sights and sounds, a glut for the senses. Alice is about to hail a taxi when we glimpse the child, an urchin, dressed in skimpy black rags, skin shining like varnished cedar, wispy hair a shade of the purest gold, on fire with the sun's touch. A distant memory lifts and stretches, before clouding over. Then he is streaking past us, his bare feet slapping on the paving stones, glancing back over his shoulder. Dark eyes flash arrestingly, his thin mouth splits in a wide, mischievous grin, white teeth aglitter.

'Follow me if you dare,' he seems to say.

And we find ourselves shouldering our way through the crowded streets, hungry for another glimpse of the entrancing child. We turn a corner, and there he is again, just yards ahead of us, small brown hands beckoning us on, a stream of laughter bubbling from his lips, setting the tiny Adam's apple, no bigger than a cherry stone, bobbing up and down. The silvery sound seems to transcend all others. He does not speak and yet we both hear it.

'Catch me if you can! Catch me if you can! Catch me if you can!' The chant fills the air. Then off, off he races, and we speed after him. Even now I feel it, every brief sight of him infusing me with a sparkling zest. There he is across the street, his head wagging cheekily, his hair tinsel-gold, the lustre of those magnetic eyes urging us forward. And there he is peeping out from behind a market stall. Follow him as he dodges a chain of nursery children trustingly reaching up to grip the giant hands of their carers. He's turning into a deserted alley, puffs of dust rising in his wake. And now he's darting up the path that skirts the necropolis, the city of the dead, the Chinese Permanent Cemetery. He's winking at us, an elfin creature, speeding round the solemn, ashen monuments in giggling, giddy hoops, arms outspread. We stumble after him, echoing his laughter, my face bleached lace, Alice's, rosy-cheeked with her exertions.

Some of the graves have mounted upon them touched-up photographs of their dead occupants. Dabs of florescent pink daub the gaunt cheeks; clothes, so drab in life, grown toxically brilliant in death. And I see, as we rush past, desperately seeking our elusive pixie, that their tallow faces are ridged with broad smiles, that their glossy eyes are full of promise. Into the sudden stillness comes a soughing threnody, as their stiff lips shape my name.

'Lin Shui! Lin Shui! Lin Shui!'

The susurrus murmurs, like thousands of grass snakes, slithering at our heels. As we track our fairy child, Alice is panting, fighting for breath. Her chest hurts as if it would burst. Her heart batters at her ribcage A wave of nausea starts to engulf her. But I – oh, I am new made, moving with the ease of the sunlight playing over us. Then the grass becomes scrub, and the scrub a rutted path, climbing steeply, and I know where it leads. It leads up the mountain, up to The Peak. It is Alice who drags her feet now, head circling to gaze back the way we came, and it is my spirit that forges ahead, carried like goosedown on the hazy air. The ragged child is always just beyond us, as the sun throbs down, leaching the blue in its kiln to a blazing albescence.

Then we are upon it, and it is as ordinary as meeting with an old friend, clasping them to you and feeling the years peel away. It is, of course, the place where I died – almost died – where a shred of me clung tenaciously to life, worrying at it ever since. Alice, coming up behind me, gulping frantically for breath, suddenly senses it. She jars to a stop and recoils.

'So far and no more,' the child flutes into the torrent of light. I spin and so does Alice, and he is there; not on the path, but hunched in the branches of a tall tree, that reaches up to us from the olive tangle below. And I know him now. It is the child who crouched with me beneath the mantle of the morgue, the child I glimpsed on Brighton beach. It is the angel of death. Not a bleach-boned skeleton in a hooded cape, grimacing and clutching a glinting scythe, but a small boy with hair of spun gold, glazed cedar skin and eyes as deep as infinity. But to Alice he is an alien. She bristles at the sight of him, knowing he has come to claim his own.

'That's where my body snagged; there, below the child. It's only an ancient wound in the bark now, but then there was a sturdy branch. For a time I sat beside my corpse, watching my blood spill into the wide greenness far below. Then I broke it, the branch, so she fell and was hidden, burying my shame from . . . from . . . from them.'

I glance up and see the air is teeming with the wavering wings of myriad gilded butterflies, where once there were only swarms of bloated carrion flies. All this I communicate to Alice in the excited tones of a child showing a parent the very spot where they enacted a scene to make all proud. The urchin chuckles. He seems to rise until the tips of his bare feet balance on his branch. His crown of gold hair is brushed from above by a bracelet of green leaves. Then he is circling his arms outwards, opening them to me in invitation.

And I want so much to go that the pang of longing seems all there is of me. But still I am shackled to Alice, standing desolate at my side. I guide her tenderly to an overhang of rock a few feet above the path. And there we sit, my host and I, above us the branches of a small fir tree affording some shade. The soft breeze ruffles the fists of dark green pine needles above our heads. Alice sighs, and such a sigh that had I a heart I know it would have broken in two. I merge with Alice, and the voice, clear and calm in her head, is mine.

'My father was a teller of stories, Alice. When we returned from a night's fishing, the sun rising, and me squinting at it with tired eyes, the salt drying on my skin, I would draw my quilt onto the deck of *Heavenly Sea*. I would let my body sink into it, the sun a balm to my exhausted muscles. Then Father would produce his small clay pipe and pack it with strands of tobacco. And when it was lit and drawing well, he would sit cross-legged at my side, and in his deep, melodious voice he would tell his tales.

'My favourite was of the Chinese daughter of a rich warlord. Her father bought her a small white bird in a beautiful gilded cage. She watched the bird flit about all day and it enchanted her. In the evenings she would knot a tiny silk thread about the little bird's stalk leg. Then she would walk in her cool green garden, captivated to see it hop and flutter before she jerked it back to her.

'As the days passed the bird fell into an impenetrable despondency. It hunched into itself on its golden perch, its black-bead eyes jaded as they raked its prison. And the girl knew that if she did not set it free, one day it would pass away, and she would find it stiff and cold lying at the bottom of its cage. So one evening, when she went for her walk, she paused on a wooden bridge that arced over a narrow babbling silver stream. She bent to the bird, hopping miserably at her feet, and with the tiny silver scissors she kept tied at her waist, she snipped the thread. For a moment the bird hesitated, its head cocked, eyes held by the severed cord. Then suddenly it stretched its wings, lifted into the air and vanished into the dark canopy of trees. Although the girl pined for a time, that time passed. And eventually, despite thinking fondly of the little bird, she missed it hardly at all.'

I slide out of Alice and am there by her side. Her expression is bleak. She interlocks her crooked little fingers in her lap, then tries in vain to pull them apart.

'It was the story I loved best. What I imagined as I drifted off to sleep, with the deck of *Heavenly Sea* rocking very gently under me, and Little Hong Kong stirring and wakening around me, was how it felt, that first moment, as the bird rose up, flying free.'

I can hear, as well as feel, Alice's painful breaths shuddering in and out. The child crouched in the tree is quiet now, as if he too is waiting for the moment of release. The cicadas trill. In the undergrowth below us, insects burrow. The fallen leaves rustle. The grasses swish. An Asian Koel takes flight, the light possessing its jewel-red eye, the stroke of its blue-black wings finding their rhythm. A few more long beats. Alice inhales the fragrant pine-sap. Shadows dance on the pale canvas of her skin. I sense her little fingers growing fluid, see them fork apart. Alice turns to me. In our locked eyes two spheres meet.

I slip into her, feeling the heat of her one last time. She hugs herself, though she knows you cannot hold onto something as insubstantial as air.

Her breathing grows shallow. The beat we have shared quickens as if readying itself for separation. I draw myself from Alice and her arms slacken.

'Who will catch me now when . . . when I fall?' she mumbles brokenly.

She does not blink. She makes no sound. Her eyes fill. They are rimmed with mercurial light. They brighten and rupture, and the silver tears course down her cheeks. She buckles, bringing up her knees, trying to find purchase for her feet on the craggy rock face. Then, with the slowness of a flower opening, her face lifts to me. She sniffs. The collar of her dress is sodden with spent tears. But now her eyes blaze with something else.

'It has been extraordinary sharing my life with you!' The smile begins in Alice and ends in me, as everything always has.

Keeping her eyes fixed on mine, she nods her assent. The thread snaps and I hesitate. But the butterflies are closing in and the boy has become a golden eagle, outstretched wings seared with fire. I have been a long time 'undead'. Gripping onto water, that's what it is like, holding onto life when its substance has fled. It is hard work and I want so much to play, to let it all go. Then I am riding the eagle of death. I am there, clasping onto him as he ascends, higher and higher, out of time, my ghost liberated, sailing into the setting sun. I have one last fleeting impression of Alice. See, she is there on the path far below, the splash of her red dress moving upwards towards The Peak. The last thing I notice is a detail, nothing more, but I mark it. It is the carriage of her shoulders. Surely they are straighter, more open. If I didn't know better, I would say that a weight has been lifted from Alice.

Ghost

I am dead, fully dead. Resting in peace. No half-life now, no turning back. What's done is done. For surely you understand the dead, the 'fully dead', cannot return to life. I expect, being alive, you would like me to tell you what it's like to be without a fleshy husk, to know the vessel that contained you has long since been eaten away by worms and returned to the primordial dust from whence it came. I should imagine you want to know where your spirit is when it no longer roams the earth. How, you ask, does it go with the dead? We have our tomorrows, you say, but what do they have to compensate?

Where I am, the most I can do is assure you that there is no hunger or thirst, no pain or sorrow, no disease or injustice, and no yearning. But what of pleasure, you want to know? Is this death of yours an endless round of pleasure? My answer to that is human pleasure, much like pain, has a shelf-life. Oh, I am above such temporal treats now. My sybaritic death style must sustain me for . . . well . . . for an eternity. Whereas you poor mortals know nothing you have will last. You scurry about endlessly trying to satisfy your desires, ironically counting yourselves lucky to be alive. It is not my intention to make you jealous, but the truth is that I am basking in empyreal radiance.

Naturally you would like to know how Alice has got on without me. I do visit from time to time. Oh yes, of course I do. We all do. Even the dead can be curious occasionally, although I must explain that when I drop in, it is not the way it used to be. Ellipses between our worlds occur every once in a while, and when they do I drift by and there is Alice. But, as I say, it has all changed. She is no longer conscious of me. Even if I had a voice she would be deaf to it.

But I have encountered her several times – in a market filling her basket with Chinese pears, buying a spangled Garoupa fish, choosing a bunch of yellow chrysanthemums, chattering in Mandarin to the stallholders. Oh yes, Alice seems to have mastered the language. Her pronunciation is a little idiosyncratic but on she goes, blissfully unaware of her solecisms. So sweet! She works part-time in a Sichuan restaurant, gives lessons in French conversation, and is taking classes in Chinese painting. She writes to Nicola at least once a month and every now and then she'll telephone her for a chat. I eavesdropped on the last call. It seems Alice's siblings are surprised that she's made her home in the new Hong Kong. Oh yes, Alice is very industrious these days. Once, roaming about the island, I found her sitting on the prow of a small boat, kicking at the sea spray with her bare feet and scattering salty diamonds over the swell. One might almost have said she looked happy, if that isn't too strong a word.

The last time I saw her was in her flat. It was late in the evening, and she was curled up on the plump cushions of her rattan settee reading a book. Suddenly the ceiling light started to flicker. Alice's head snapped up, and when the light snuffed out completely she got herself in the most dreadful panic. It wasn't me though. Poor Alice was quite overcome with emotion as she hunted in a kitchen drawer for a new bulb. I wanted to tell her that long gone are the days when I am the cause and I have an effect. But of course my lips are sealed now. Overall, Alice seems surprisingly contented, and I am genuinely pleased about that. She deserves to come at last to a peaceful plateau, after what has been, for the most part, a fairly treacherous climb. Besides, didn't I say I am at rest, so why would I begrudge my one-time host the same calm shallows?

I am not being mendacious when I say this. It is perfectly true: almost all of the year I am as tranquil as a slumbering infant, halcyon, serene . . . that is until the seventh month in the lunar calendar, the ghost month, the festival of Yue Lan. I'm not greedy. I don't hog the entire month the way some of my ghostly colleagues do. Three days is quite sufficient for my needs, the three days that precede the fifteenth, the feast of Yue Lan. At that appointed time I leave Yinjian, the world of darkness. I burst out of its gates, and inside me – oh there is such a hunger, such an emptiness eating away at me, that I will do anything to fill it.

As I roar to the earth, skim over the South China Sea, corkscrew in tight hoops above the island, I see that I have company to share the sport: three Hungry Ghosts also bent on filling the chasm hewn out of them by death. There is a galloping mastiff, a massive beast, his eyes, scorching grape coals, his rat-tailed fur red as Mars, snapping voracious jaws at the clouds, his bloodstained muzzle flecked with acid-yellow foam. There is monkey with a mighty pendulum-like gait, skin withered as a dried sour plum, but agile as a cobra when it's time to strike. It has grown, this monkey, to the proportions of a great ape. Its pleated flesh is bald and scabby, but for a few stray patches of fur, oxblood, tipped with bronze. Its rotten yellow teeth are bared, while its sticky fingers, finished with razor-sharp claws, excoriate the skies. And there is a bird too, huge as a vulture, but headless, gore dripping from its ragged neck. Sparse, bilious-green feathers spike its torso, huge glaucous wings lash into a cyclone the air it tears through. And all the while, its fish-hook claws seek for fleshy purchase.

We hell-raisers rampage about the island, consuming everything in our paths. So light your bonfires, let your infernos compete with the stars. Hurry to put upon the crackling pyres your offerings – your model houses and cars and boats, your furniture, your clothes, your televisions and radios, your computers and your mobile phones – all fashioned out of crisp paper, stiff card and matchstick wood. Gold and geranium-red, silver and leaf-green, kingfisher-blue with copper trim, a shower of living colours to feed our flames. Throw on your wads of money, packs of 'hell notes', and see us guzzle them up with our fiery, blistering tongues. Burn your incense and your

387

joss sticks. Do not stint. Take handfuls of them, and shake them at the heavens till the trails of smoke grow thick as fog, blinding our smarting, rapacious eyes. Shut up your doors, close your windows tight, hold close and closer still your babies, with their juicy papaya plumpness, soft and yielding to our primed fangs. Keep your children safe indoors, under your watchful eyes.

And whatever you do, stay away from the sea and its restless, pounding, bloodthirsty surf. Or, believe me, we will have you. Never doubt it! We will gorge ourselves on the foolish ones, the ones who scoff, the ones who swim out of their depth, who wander the beaches at night, who brave their rickety, fragile boats. We will drag them down to the sludgy tar on the ocean bed, feast on their distended meat, devour their waterlogged hearts and season their marrow with sea salt before sucking them dry.

Oh, I almost forgot. On the last night of Yue Lan make sure you lay a place at the table for the absent ones. Starve yourself and pile *our* plates high. Serve us tender slices of chicken, chunks of spicy pork, slithers of succulent beef, shreds of crispy duck, bowls of fluffy white rice and glistening noodles. Heap cakes and sweetmeats upon the altar, build towers of luscious fruits, labour without rest to slake our epicurean appetites. Hope upon hope that you manage to reform us this time. That, cleansed, our spirits will be released to the pure lands. That we will not come back in a twelvemonth to gorge ourselves on your riches, to feed on your families, to pick you to the bone. Pray that we will not curse you, and bring the fury of the damned down upon your brittle human heads.

No one takes the festival of Yue Lan more seriously than Alice, when the Hungry Ghosts roam the earth. She takes armloads of paper offerings to her Chinese friends, and feeds them to the starving fires. For three full days she shuts herself up in her Pokfulam flat, closes the windows and locks the doors, refusing to answer the ring of the doorbell or the hammer of a closed fist, no matter who the caller claims to be. Meticulously she lays four places at her table and, while she fasts, in each sets down plates filled with tempting delicacies. She burns incense and chants prayers to appease the restless spirits. She takes immense care. It is almost as if someone or something has warned her of the dangers.

All children have nightmares. The fisherman's daughter I used to be was no exception. There were times when she would waken with a cry and sit up gasping for air. Her almond eyes would be round with terror, her brow dewed with sweat, her lips trembling. When her father came to her and asked her what was wrong, her reply was always the same. 'The ghosts, the Hungry Ghosts had come for me, Father. The sky had grown dark with them. They blotted out my sun. They tried to take my breath from me, to thrust their icy fingers into my body and draw it out. I was so afraid.'

'Was your mother among them?' her father would ask his daughter with a gentle smile, smoothing back the hair from her dampened forehead.

'I don't know. I think so, Father,' she would answer, trying hard to remember.

'Then you have nothing to fear.' When Lin looked searchingly into her father's dark eyes he would nod reassuringly and add, 'Some Hungry Ghosts can be guardian angels, my daughter. They will hold hell at bay for all eternity to keep you safe.'